Perfect Roger

By Lindsay C. Ross

For Anne.

Any resemblance to anyone I know or have come across in life is purely coincidental. All characters in this story are fictional.

For more information and books by Lindsay Ross visit:
www.lindsayross.co.uk

CONTENTS

3

Part 1. 1960 - 1980

1. *Han Sen*

Being seven years of age, Han Sen was completely terrified of having his head shaved. The thought of the razor scraping across his scalp made his stomach pitch and his legs go rubbery.

Wearing a yellow robe and being away from home for a whole year? I'll get used to those, I will, he said to himself, over and over again.

The first week of his conscription into the monastery did go some way to calm his nerves. Despite the tenseness of his first scalping, he quite liked the coolness around his head, and around the rest of his body thanks to his silk robe.

His eyes would start to glaze over in some of the morning classes, but the afternoons were much better; spent by a cooling waterfall, or in a forest clearing with the sun dappling through the trees. The monks would read discourses from the Enlightened One and invite the bouzes to air their views. Han Sen liked that. A listener rather than a speaker, he learnt more about the Buddha's Four Noble Truths, and about the Cambodia of 1967.

He developed more of an understanding as to why people gave material possessions away, why Phnom Penh taxi drivers tipped their passengers, and why accidentally crushing a beetle underfoot was equivalent to the manslaughter of a deceased relative simply enjoying their afterlife.

To his intense relief, the older monks in their flowing orange robes were not the child molesters some of the older boys in the village had led him to believe. Would he mock the younger boys like that in a few years? On consideration, he probably wouldn't.

In the fourth week, one of the older monks, Hem Suvorn, selected Han Sen to accompany him on an annual five day trip to the high ground north of the Tonle San River. All they took with them was a walking stick and a blanket each.

On reaching the highest point of the sweltering wooded hillside in Virachay, Hem Suvorn showed Han Sen the surrounding landscape, pointing with his old walking stick. 'To the North West is Laos. It used to be called Vientiane. Some say it is even more beautiful than Cambodia, an earthly paradise with the Mekong River at its heart.' Han Sen was astonished, he had never been as high-up before, let alone seen another country. 'To the East is Vietnam. It is a divided country. The North is communist, whilst the South try to fight them off with the help of the Americans.'

'What is a communist?' Han Sen asked, looking up at the older monk.

'Well, the Vietnamese used to be Buddhists just like us, but some of them lost the vision of Nirvana and decided that they would follow the path of striving to work for its own sake, and to increase and multiply. Then the government in the North decided that they would make everyone equal. That's what Communism is. Everybody works the same, earns the same, has the same.'

'That's not such a bad thing is it, Hem Suvorn?'

'No, when everybody is in agreement. The problem with Vietnam is that the people of the South want to live like they do in America. So now the Americans see North Vietnam as a threat to the rest of the world and want to help the South in its fight to remain independent. That is why there are bombs over Cambodia,' Hem Suvorn finished with a sad expression.

'They shouldn't be bombing our country. We never hurt anybody.' Han Sen said, indignation sounding in his voice.

'You are right, and we probably never will.'

'Can't someone tell the Americans?'

'Well, Prince Sihanouk is telling the Americans. The problem is that the North Vietnamese soldiers come into Cambodia to launch attacks against the South. That's why the Americans drop bombs on Cambodia, to try to stop them.'

'Prince Sihanouk should tell the North Vietnamese then,' Han Sen persisted.

Hem Suvorn smiled ironically. 'What you suggest is a very logical step. But the North Vietnamese are a very aggressive nation. They would probably turn on Cambodia if Prince Sihanouk appeared too demanding. No, I think Cambodia has to remain neutral as it always has done. We must pray that things we can't control will resolve themselves.'

Han Sen thought for a while, then said, 'But if we're neutral and we have always been neutral, outside people shouldn't harm us, shouldn't be killing our people. It is wrong.'

'The Americans think they are doing right. They apologise to Cambodia but at the same time ask for our assistance. They see Communism as a threat to world peace, not just here in North Vietnam and in Cambodia.'

'Is Communism really that bad? Is it worth going to war, and innocent people losing their lives?' Han Sen asked.

'Nothing is worth that, Han Sen. Problems always come when people lose sight of the teachings of the Enlightened One, and they look for other ways to achieve what they want in life. There are Communists in Cambodia too, you know.'

'Well they should go and live in North Vietnam then,' Han Sen said.

'Look, young man, you are very intelligent. Your mind is logical and you are patriotic, as we all should be. But there are some things that it is my duty to teach you while you are a bouze. Always remember your aim is Nirvana - complete freedom from greed, anger, ignorance and intolerance. You will remain strong forever if you remember those words.'

Hem Suvorn continued the geography lesson, showing Han Sen the sweeping vista of Cambodia from their mountaintop viewpoint. 'From the Chuor Phnom Dangkrek mountains in the North on the Thailand border, down through the Temples of Angkor and Tonle Sap Lake, to Phnom Penh and Kampot in the very South, this is our country Han Sen. It will remain our country if we all remember the words of the Enlightened One.'

'I will, Hem Suvorn, I will,' Han Sen replied solemnly.

They both came down the mountain smiling, with a spring in their step. Han Sen because he had never been down such steep slopes and struggled to stop himself from going head over heels. Hem Suvorn because he had enjoyed their discussion and the young boy's curiosity.

On their way back, they stayed longer at the same villages they had trekked through on the way to the mountain. All the villagers were curious to know what their climb was like, how the weather had been at the top, what views they had seen and how lucky they were to be able to experience such earthly delights.

The discussion would then invariably move on to the subject of food. What do you like and how much do you want? Would you like something to drink also? And so it went on until the orange clad monk and the yellow-clad bouze were quite full, and ready to offer prayers for the village and its inhabitants. The immediate surroundings would go suddenly very quiet, the elders of the village would appear together with the local holy man and strings of prayer-flags quickly erected. Rhododendrons and begonias in large buckets magically appeared and smoke producing baubles strewn around as if a festival were about to commence. Hem Suvorn led the prayers while Han Sen looked on, listening intently.

'May all beings be filled with joy and peace.
May all beings everywhere,
the strong and the weak,
the great and the small,
the mean and the powerful,
the short and the long,
the subtle and the gross:
may all beings everywhere,
seen and unseen,
dwelling far off or nearby,
being or waiting to become:
May all be filled with lasting joy.

Let no one deceive another,
let no one anywhere despise another,
let no one out of anger or resentment
wish suffering on anyone at all.
Just as a mother with her own life
protects her child, her only child, from harm,
so within yourself let grow
a boundless love for all creatures.

Let your love flow outward through the universe,
to its height, its depth, its broad extent,
a limitless love, without hatred or enmity.
Then as you stand or walk,
sit or lie down,

as long as you are awake,

strive for this with a one-pointed mind;

your life will bring heaven to earth.'

The holy man chimed his finger cymbals repeatedly to show the villager's appreciation of this fine prayer and blessing. The male villagers smiled in gratitude, the females all wiped their eyes; the thoughts of the monk were pure and beautiful, and they all loved him with a powerful intensity.

Hem Suvorn and Han Sen picked up their blanket rolls, threw them over their shoulders, bade farewell to the villagers and were off again. A gang of several small children and mangy dogs accompanied them some of the way until eventually, the monk and the young bouze were on their own, trudging along the dusty track towards home.

Han Sen's father worked at the Ta Veng Electrical Works. This project had begun life in 1953 and was a typically Cambodian affair, constructed over a very long period. The driving force behind the enterprise was a Scotsman called James Henderson. He had settled in the Ban Lung area to make his fortune out of mining sapphires; initially hand-panning the surrounding rivers and streams, achieving modest success. He married a local girl and converted to the Buddhist faith, endearing himself to the natives in so doing. He soon realised that if they were going to get anywhere with mining sapphires, the process would have to be automated and enlarged to an industrial scale.

Electrical power was always going to be a requirement for the project he was envisaging, so he negotiated a knock-down price with a broker in the USA for four ship generators and a switchboard using his own family money. He then paid for ocean shipping and five individual trucks to make the delivery from the port of Sihanoukville in the South of Cambodia to Ta Veng in the very north. Henderson travelled with the truck convoy for the five day journey.

Cambodia did not have a road system in 1953. More like a series of cart tracks that veered haphazardly from town to town. One of the trucks fell into a ravine, the driver having inched too close to the edge of the two hundred foot drop as they were negotiating a mountainside pass. The driver, miraculously unhurt, having leapt clear of the truck as it teetered on the edge, immediately proceeded to make a small cairn type monument as if in homage to the departed truck and its fourteen- ton load. The electrical works was constructed using only three generators.

Henderson had already constructed the majority of the structure that would house the power plant alongside the river, close to the site of the intended sapphire processing plant. The equipment was slid off the backs of the trucks and onto their respective plinths by means of two locally hired bull elephants, their skilled handlers, the strongest and bravest male villagers available and rollers made up from hardwood tree trunks. The work required to install the generators, make all of the service connections and complete the building work took seven years. The final touch was the mounting of a small brass plaque by the main entrance door with the inscription:

The Ta Veng Electrical Works,

Erected 1960 to provide power for Ta Veng and surrounding

areas.

Diesel generators from the Liberty Ship Robert Louis Stevenson,

built in California USA 1943, to feed the victims of war.

This energy is the sum of free will and love.

By the time the Electrical Works was complete, James Henderson had lost his appetite for building the sapphire processing plant and was content to continue hand-panning for sapphires, running the electrical works almost as a hobby and enjoying the simple Buddhist lifestyle he had so eagerly embraced. Ambition became a thing of the past. Who cared about squandering the family money when life had become so immeasurably rich? Han Sen's father, Preap, who had experience with fixing small agricultural machines and was by nature mechanically minded, soon became the unofficial Chief Engineer of the electrical works.

Although Preap Sen received no money for his work, it was his passion. The engine hall was kept in immaculate condition. The red floor tiles were mopped daily, the shiny green machinery and highly polished brass gauges all lovingly tended.

One end of the empty concrete plinth built for the doomed generator had been made into a flower bed that was normally festooned with perfectly tended chrysanthemums. At the other end was a small temple where Buddha sat in majestic contemplation, surrounded by shaped shrubs, dwarf trees and painstakingly formed brass candle holders rising around him in an upward spiral. Visitors were required to remove their footwear and leave them on a rug by the entrance door. Busily escorted by Han Sen's father, always with a rag in hand, ready to rub off thumbprints or mop up leaks however slight, they would walk around the plant-room in reverential, hushed tones, marvelling at the eerie excellence of their surroundings. Henderson and Han Sen's father agreed, this was a temple in its own right – a temple to the Enlightened One, and to engineering.

The electrical works was where Han Sen spent most of his formative years. From the age of three, when his compatriots and his brothers and sisters would be playing in the village or around the family home, he would be either in the electrical works plant-room under the close supervision of his father, or in the small compound at the rear of the building where the fuel and lubricating oil were stored. His young vocabulary became a curious mixture of Khmer and technical pigeon English.

'We could make and repair a lot of this stuff ourselves,' Henderson said to Preap Sen one day, referring to spares and general repairs to the machinery and ancillary equipment. 'What we need is a workshop with a lathe, a welder, a milling machine and some test gear.'

'I have an Uncle in Taiwan who deals in machinery, perhaps he could help us,' Preap Sen replied.

'Get me his number, I'll call him,' Henderson said.

Six months later a truck arrived loaded with machinery direct from Taiwan. Although second-hand, the machines allowed them to do basic machining and repairs, saving the enterprise money on spares and having to send broken items away. The young Han Sen was in his element, his father teaching him the art of machining metal into intricate, precise shapes and how to design and weld metal structures to be put to all sorts of uses; trolleys, skids, brackets, gates, anything useful.

As he grew into his teens, Han Sen worried about his private vision of the future and would discuss this with Hem Suvorn, 'My father works at the electrical works all day for the benefit of the village, my mother works in the fields all day for the benefit of the village, then comes home and cooks for us. I think I want to do more with my life. Is that wrong, Hem Suvorn?'

'No. There is nothing wrong with wanting to achieve an ambition Han Sen, just as long as you remember the words of Buddha and you live in joy. Remember:'

'On life's journey faith is nourishment,

virtuous deeds are a shelter,

wisdom is the light by day

and right-mindedness is the protection by night.

If a man lives a pure life nothing can destroy him;

if he has conquered greed

nothing can limit his freedom.'

The old monk cleared his throat and continued with another sutra;

'Live in Joy, in love,

even among those who hate.

Live in joy, in health,

even among the afflicted.

Live in joy, in peace,

even among the troubled.

Look within. Be still.

Free from fear and attachment,

know the sweet joy of living in the way.

There is no fire like greed,

No crime like hatred,

No sorrow like separation,

No sickness like hunger of heart,

And no joy like the joy of freedom.

Health, contentment and trust

Are your greatest possessions,

and freedom your greatest joy.

Look within. Be still.

Free from fear and attachment,

know the sweet joy of living in the way.'

He looked down at the boy in front of him, 'Remember, the Dali Llama taught us:

'As human beings we all want to be happy and free from misery.

We have learned that the key to happiness is inner peace.

The greatest obstacles to inner peace are disturbing emotions

such as anger and attachment, fear and suspicion, while love and

compassion and a sense of universal responsibility are the

sources of peace and happiness.'

Han Sen sat with his eyes closed, hands together in prayer. He was, he supposed, at the point of a perfect inner peace. He would never forget these moments with the older monk and would continue to search for them throughout his life. This was the way. This was Nirvana.

The monk and his apprentice returned to the village along the riverside track, shafts of late morning sunlight slicing through the dense overhead foliage. 'What is this ambition you speak of, Han Sen?' the monk said.

'I love being in the workshop, sketching and making things in steel or aluminium or whatever we have. That is what I would like to do when I finish my education, and I'm not sure I can do it in Cambodia. I think I need to travel to achieve my ambition. Maybe America, maybe Europe, maybe China or Japan, I don't know.'

'I can see you have given this quite a lot of thought, my boy.'

'I just want to make sure I make the right choice.'

'May the teachings of the Enlightened One help you along your path.'

'You have helped me find my destiny, Hem Suvorn. You and my father, my mother, my family, Sen Henderson, Mrs. Tetratha at the schoolhouse and my father's uncle in Taiwan. Everyone I know has helped me,' Han Sen said.

'Don't forget Ta Veng on your worldly travels. You make sure you come back and see us.'

'Of course,' Han Sen replied. He couldn't imagine life without the wise old monk.

In 1973, the political tensions across the country began to boil over. The North–South Vietnam conflict had worsened. American planes were dropping bombs ten to twenty miles inside Cambodia in an attempt to flush out the North Vietnamese.

The Communist Party of Kampuchea (CPK) had been formed by several young left-wing intellectuals, concerned at the level of corruption within the Sihanouk administration. The Prince loftily denounced these upstarts, jokily terming them the Khmer Rouge. As the strength of their dissent grew, so the administration began to rely more and more on heavy-handed repression to quell it.

These high level political and military manoeuvrings had little effect on daily life in Ta Veng. Han Sen was politely still attending Mrs. Tetratha's classes in the village, knowing that he had outgrown their usefulness. He would spend much time considering his limited educational options, often discussing them with his father, who he knew would often vote for the quiet life in favour of conflict.

They were sitting in the fuel compound one day. Han Sen was trying to convince his father that further education was the way forward. 'Maths and science are important to us father. We all struggle with just simple maths in the workshop. Calculating cutting angles and tolerances is more or less impossible without more advanced mathematics. We all love Mrs. Tetratha but she can't teach us these things, she doesn't know them,' Han Sen said, conviction in his voice.

'I cannot argue with you, my son. We try our best, the same as we have always done through the eyes of the Enlightened One.' His father stared into his small cup of chai, rolling the leaves around inside the almost-empty cup in contemplation.

'The school year ends in a few weeks. I would like the opportunity to go to the Sam Lok School in Ban Lung. I know that they teach eleven to fifteen year olds. If it means living in Ban Lung during the week then I will do it. We know some people there and the temple is also there,' the boy pleaded.

'Ban Lung is forty miles away, Han Sen, you are only thirteen. We are still responsible for you, your mother would be worried sick, and your brothers and sisters. Me too,' his father replied.

'I would be the same father, but I will show you with the strength of my application to study, that missing each other for a while will be worth it in the long run. You will see, I promise.'

'You really are the strangest child, Han Sen. I do not understand where all this determination comes from. We have had these discussions before and I am beginning to think that to argue further would be foolish. I will talk with Mama and Rep Chebon in Ban Lung to see if we can make some arrangements. I, for one, cannot stand in your way any longer.' His father shook his head as a sign of his reluctant acquiescence, but was immediately engulfed by his son's flailing arms and his grinning face. They hugged each other and laughed deeply for a few minutes. The decision had been made; this very determined boy would be the first in the family, indeed probably in the whole village, to attend a senior-grade school.

2. *Communists*

Han Sen remembered the Chebon family. His father would often call in to see his old friend Rep Chebon on his visits to Ban Lung on his old motorcycle to buy spares for the generators. In particular, Han Sen remembered their four daughters, two of whom were older than him and strikingly beautiful. The thought of living away from home was bad enough, but the thought of living with two older girls made him very nervous. In his family he was used to having moral support from his five brothers if ever there were any girl–boy issues with his younger sisters, which there quite frequently were.

'Mama, Han Sen smells of diesel again, tell him to go to the river and wash!' He had crept in one night, straight from the electrical works. His oldest and generally sweetest-smelling sister, Lao, called out from her bed at the far end of the children's sleeping room. She regularly combed the jungle for resins, tree bark and herbs to make incense which would burn in small pots dotted around the house. Han Sen knew she used the scents on herself too.

'But Mama, Lao smells of Uod and Aloe. Yuk!' he countered, too exhausted to contemplate going all the way to the river for a wash at the behest of his sister. He knew he would lose the argument once his mother got involved, he hoped fervently she was asleep.

'Han Sen,' his mother's voice rang out from behind his parent's partition. 'Go and get a wash. Smelly child!'

'Oh, Mama, I don't want to, I'm tired,' Han Sen pleaded.

'The place smells like the electrical works, go and get a wash!'

He reluctantly put his shorts and shirt on again, and headed off in the bright moonlight towards the forest path that ran alongside the Tonle San River. On the outskirts of the village, he passed a small cabin which was used by the village elders as a meeting place. He could see candles burning and hear people talking. Han Sen, ever curious, put his ear against the lower timbers of the cabin. He heard one voice, it sounded excited, like it was breaking good news.

'Just in the last few days, the CIA have put Lon Nol officially in charge again. Sihanouk was in Paris, probably gorging himself on fine food and whores. This time it was a military coup, they have allied Cambodia with the US, abolished the monarchy and renamed the country the Khmer Republic.'

There were rumblings of discontent from within the cabin. Han Sen guessed there were four or five persons present. Another voice arose above the general hubbub of conversations, a voice that even to Han Sen's young ears, immediately stood out as carrying authority.

'Comrades, this is good news. The Americans have put the fat general in charge again for their own ends. The political climate within America will not allow them to get further involved in the business of Kampuchea. We now have a legitimate struggle against the forces of greed and corruption that threaten our country. I will talk with Sihanouk; he will want to keep his snout in the trough. He will support us, you'll see.'

Another voice joined in the conversation, 'If we are to overthrow Lon Nol, we need the Vietnamese. They have offered us their support; twenty-five thousand troops and as many Chinese weapons as we need.'

The authoritative voice came in again, 'They will be under our control. I do not care how many Vietnamese troops are available to us. We will be in control. We cannot trust them, look at the way they use Kampuchea without asking anyone. They are pigs, as bad as the Americans. Once we have overthrown the fat general we send them back to where they came from with a very strong message: they are never to enter Kampuchea again.'

Han Sen was staggered. These were not village elders discussing whether or not to build another cabin or extend a track. This was war. Who were these people in our village talking about using twenty-five thousand Vietnamese troops to overthrow the government? He had overheard conversations between his father and Henderson that there was unrest across the country, but in Ta Veng? He continued on down to the river, immersed himself in the cold, moonlit water for ten seconds, and headed back to the family home, his mind racing with intrigue.

In the morning he told James Henderson about the conversation he had overheard.

The big Scotsman shook his head sadly and said in his Caledonian Khmer, 'Aye, the Communist Party of Kampuchea, Iang Sery and Saleth Sar. We need to keep an eye on that lot, they're a bigger bunch of nutters than Lon Nol's lot, or Nixon come to that. Lon Nol kills and exiles thousands of Vietnamese, the Khmer Rouge kill anyone they can get their hands on, nailing old ladies to their huts and setting them alight, ripping babies limb from limb. Then they say they want to turn us all into communists, communal living, food production, eating, education, you name it. I tell you if they were to come down Sauchiehall Street in Glasgow on a Saturday night breathing their politics, they'd get murdered and rightly so, I'd buy whoever did it a beer. The trouble is Han Sen, at the moment people are prepared to listen to them and support them. You mark my words; it'll all end in tears.'

Han Sen wished he had not mentioned it to Henderson. He knew there was a lot more to this communism than met the eye. The tone of the voices he had overheard were sinister and frightening. Did the Khmer Rouge really do those dreadful things?

Life with the Chebons was certainly different to life at home in Ta Veng. The only similarity was the family home, one room that was used as a communal living area during the day that split into curtained-off bedrooms during the night; the parents on one side and the children on the other. Han Sen was put into a further curtained-off area on the children's side.

Although all still strikingly beautiful and intelligent in Han Sen's eyes, he was surprised to discover that the girls never actually stopped talking. They would ramble on, seemingly for hours about trivial things; who did this, or who said what and to whom, or when to wear what clothes what smelled nice and what did not. His older sister Lao used to discuss such matters some of the time with her younger sisters back at home, but never to this extent. One evening, he was sitting on the step outside the cabin half-listening to the girl's conversation when Rao, the second from oldest, unexpectedly asked him, 'Han Sen, do you have a girlfriend back home?'

He could see that the girl was making an effort by bringing him into the conversation. Slightly embarrassed, he answered, 'No I don't.'

'Do you like girls?'

'Yes of course. I have three sisters, I have to like girls.'

This made them laugh. Rao continued, 'Our father always says if we had brothers we would be different. Just think Raya, we could fight each other and exploit the girls if we were boys,' she playfully punched her older sister on the shoulder and pinched all of her younger sisters in turn. She smiled at Han Sen, 'Only joking. Have you been a bouze?'

'Yes, six years ago, when I was seven,' Han Sen replied.

'What was it like?'

'Well you learn all about the Enlightened One and what he taught us, and you live with the monks in a monastery and you go to beautiful places and discuss things and meditate and when you walk into villages, you get lots of food and drink and people love you. It was great.'

'But you don't want to become a monk when you finish school do you?'

'No. I would like to, but I really want to be an engineer.'

'An engineer? Why?'

It was a good question. He had expected; what do they do? 'Well I like designing and making things and getting them to work.'

'What sort of things?'

Han Sen struggled in his mind to think of something interesting; he sensed that wall-brackets would not be the answer that would set their imagination on fire.

'My father works in an electrical works and I use the machinery in the workshop to make things from metal and repair parts that break on the power plants. My father and his friend taught me.'

'Wow, you're clever.'

'No I'm not, there is too much I don't know,' he smiled back at Rao.

His modesty had silenced the girl temporarily. She looked down at her toes.

Her older sister entered the conversation, 'If you can do all of that, why do you come here to school and stay with us?'

Another good question he thought, maybe they were not so daft after all. 'Well, because we can only go so far with what we know. We would be able to do much more if we had, say, maths to work things out, or could speak better English and talk with other engineers in different countries. Geography helps too, knowing where the countries are.' He became aware that he was gabbling in front of the girls and stopped himself.

The youngest girl Lai, who up to now had been lying on her stomach, supporting both cheeks on her elbows with flat hands, listening avidly to the older one's conversation suddenly stood up, smoothed down her dress, calmly walked over to Han Sen, tapped him lightly on the shoulder and said, 'You're it!' She then sprinted away giggling, glancing over her shoulder in anticipation. The older girls, shocked by the impetuousness of their youngest sister, looked at Han Sen, unsure of what his reaction would be.

Laughing in surprise, he got up slowly to give the young girl a head start, then sprinted off in headlong pursuit of the surprisingly fast three year old. Her older sisters shrieked with delight, rushing to get up and prepare themselves, knowing that Lia would soon be emerging from the gloom of the evening looking for potential tagging victims. The youngest of the four sisters had unwittingly broken down any barriers between Han Sen and her family.

*

Sam Lok School in Ban Lung had two classrooms and three elderly teachers, the most elderly being the headmaster who had interviewed Han Sen and taught mathematics. His name was Dr Chepra and his teaching style was simplistic - he would tell the pupils once how to do something, then they were on their own. No questions allowed, no help given. If a pupil got something wrong, he would administer a casual caning with a thin bamboo switch. The switch was kept hanging on the wall by the blackboard as a grim reminder of the pain that would ensue if they were to lose concentration and miss something. To a degree this worked well; Han Sen being keen to learn, had no difficulty and made steady progress. However, there was a high dropout rate, and at the end of the term the class size had dwindled from forty pupils to just twenty. This suited Han Sen as he was able to concentrate better with fewer distractions.

As well as Dr Chepra, with his unique style of mathematics tutorage, there was Mr. Ik who taught English and geography and Mr. Hsu who taught the sciences. Both of them were very reasonable teachers, with no resemblance to Dr Chepra. Their classes were full all year round.

Outside of school. Han Sen would help the family with tending their crops and animals and keeping the home in order. Even Mrs. Chebon received some assistance with cooking meals. Rep Chebon would smile bemusedly and scratch his head when faced with the image of Han Sen sweeping the dust from the cabin floor or helping the girls carry the clothes down to the river for washing.

Rao Chebon was only thirteen, a year older then Han Sen. Like her sisters, she had already physically developed and the boy was surprised to find himself sometimes completely powerless in the presence of this raven-haired beauty. She would be the first to greet Han Sen when he woke up in the morning and when he returned from school. When they went to bed at night, she would be the last to whisper goodnight. In the evening and at weekends when the family visited the Elephant Temple, Rao would always be by his side. He was deeply flattered by the girl's attention and worried that their attachment would not go unnoticed.

Raya, the eldest of the four sisters, had to say something. It was her duty as the eldest child. 'Rao, the Enlightened One teaches us that attachment is an obstacle to inner peace,' Raya commented one day while the two of them were at the river washing clothes.

'What are you driving at Raya?' Rao answered.

'You are in love with Han Sen, we can all see that,' the older girl asserted.

'You seem sure of your words,' the younger girl said. 'Probably surer than I am.'

'Surely you know whether you are in love or not?'

'Raya, I admit to being attracted to the boy as we all are. We all love him as a brother - even you.' the younger girl said as she rinsed on of Han Sen's shirts carefully.

'You are with him continually, you cannot stop yourself.'

'If that means I am in love, then so be it.'

'Rao, I know that one of the principle teachings of the Enlightened One, is that covetousness is on a par with ignorance and greed. You probably think I am showing resentment, I am not. I am speaking as an older sister and with love. I merely think you both need to be careful. The boy is twelve, you are thirteen. Just think of the consequences of your actions; father would not be happy if he were to find out that you two had started a relationship.' Raya wiped her hands on her dress and hugged her younger sister.

The younger girl took heed of Raya's advice if only for the sake of family peace. Han Sen noticed the girl's cooler attitude and, despite his own infatuation, was slightly relieved.

Ban Lung was a strategic point in the movement of Vietnamese troops between Vietnam and Cambodia, with the North Vietnamese initially supporting the CPK in their struggle to overthrow the Lon Nol government. The Americans continued to bomb Cambodia in an attempt to flush out the elusive communist headquarters, the only effect being that hundreds of innocent Cambodians lost their lives and the Vietnamese communists moved further into Cambodia to continue going about their business. As the fighting dragged on, the CPK, the chrysalis of the Khmer Rouge, attracted more support from Cambodians who detested Lon Nol because of his association with the Americans, and saw Prince Sihanouk as their rightful leader.

Although Han Sen had a unique insight into the political situation in his country due to his previously overheard conversation in Ta Veng, he was still confused about the war going on all around them.

There were people like James Henderson who had a passionate loathing of communism and communists, whereas others seemed to support the idea of a communist way of life.

'Rep Chebon quite likes the idea of living as a communist,' Han Sen responded to one of Henderson's many disparaging remarks about the turmoil in Cambodia.

'Oh he does, does he? He's obviously no idea of what it'll be like.'

'He thinks we'll be better off and that it doesn't sound that bad.'

Henderson gave Han Sen a withering look. 'Well, I'll tell you something, Han Sen, my boy; it would be the worst possible thing for this country.' He settled into a comfortable position on the steps of his cabin, stoked his pipe with some of his special tobacco, getting it going with some effort, and began talking. 'My father owned a shipyard on the River Clyde in Glasgow. They used to build ships for ship-owners all over the world. If you wanted a high quality ship delivered on time and to the price quoted, you'd go to Henderson & Co. They were the best. Sure, my father and his partners made money at it. Sure, you could possibly call them greedy, but I'll tell you something, they worked damn hard for it. My father would think nothing of working an eighty or ninety hour week. He was passionate about building ships and passionate about not letting his customers down. He employed 1,500 local people to build his ships and when the yard was in its early days, they were grateful for the work. Good honest toil for a fair wage, nothing wrong with that, you'd say.'

Han Sen nodded in agreement. 'What's a wage?'

Henderson laughed, 'The UK is not like Cambodia, son, over there you work for somebody who pays you money, a wage or wages. Sometimes weekly, sometimes monthly, understand?'

'Yes I think so. Your father would build a ship for someone and that person would pay your father money, then your father would pay wages to the people who built the ship. Did your father get a wage too?'

Henderson smiled, 'Yes of course, son, but it wasn't called a wage, it would be called a profit. He would build the ship for less than his customer would pay and he would keep the difference. When I say keep, he obviously paid all his workers first because without workers he wouldn't be able to build the ship in the first place. You could say that they were the most important people in the whole process. Then he would have to pay his suppliers for engines and other bits and pieces, the rent for the shipyard, any money he'd borrowed would have to be repaid and finally tax to the government. Then, if there was anything left over he would take a wage for himself as well as making sure that he had some money in reserve for replacing old machinery or developing new ship designs.'

'Wow, it all sounds very exciting, I'd love to go on a ship on the ocean,' Han Sen said, aware he'd never seen either.

'Yes, my father loved ships, it's what drove him on through all the hard times,' Henderson said, puffing ruminatively on his pipe.

'There were hard times?'

'Yes. The trouble started with the unions.

'Unions?'

'A body of folk all working in the same industry, who get together and protect themselves against the bosses if they think they're treating them unfairly. The union wanted its members to earn more money and work less hours. Then the communists got involved with the unions, pushing them to go further and further with walkouts, strikes, demonstrations, even propaganda about my father. They accused him of exploiting hard-working folks, doing everything out of greed.'

The Scotsman's pipe had gone out. He ignored it, and carried on.

'Well, the mistake my father made was to stand up to the unions. He sacked some of the troublemakers, they called them shop-stewards in those days or union conveners. So the union called for a walk out. Three weeks it lasted. That and the constant disruption they caused with meetings, conferences, demonstrations, and all in company time too.'

He tapped the pipe on the side of the step, clearing out the ash, re-stoked it and sucked it into life with the help of his old Zippo lighter. 'One of the ships going through the yard at the time was delayed. This caused his customer to lose a contract. That was bad enough but the next ship was delayed as a knock-on effect. The customer cancelled his agreement with Hendersons, losing them two ships a year over ten years, which was the bulk of their forward order book. The customer transferred the order to the Far East and got them built at a quarter of the price. And the communist unions still wanted more wages! They were nothing but trouble. They wanted my father and the other bosses and the managers to earn the same as the workers. To ride a bike to work, eat the same food in the same canteen and live in the same small house. It would never work in a month of Sundays, son. If there's no incentive to go out and work, there's corruption, it's as simple as that. The union leader lived in a bigger house than my father, how ironic was that? Who was paying his wages? Of course it was the workers, the very people he was supposed to be supporting.' Henderson's pipe had gone out.

'They say the Khmer Rouge will win,' Han Sen said. He didn't like the sound of communism so much now.

'Aye well laddy, in that case, we're all doomed,' he said, making the last word reverberate. He got up with a spring in his step, ruffling Han Sen's hair. 'I'll just away and get ma' bagpipes, that'll cheer us up.'

Han Sen sighed. On one side, the wordly-wise and experienced Henderson, and on the other, the majority of Cambodians, including his family, all willing the Khmer Rouge to win their war against the government forces. His bad feelings would not go away.

3. *The Khmer Rouge*

Han Sen was fifteen and in his final year at the Sam Lok school in Ban Lung when early in 1975, Saloth Sar, otherwise known as Pol Pot, the leader of the Khmer Rouge left Ta Veng for the capital, Phnom Penh. The war between the Khmer Rouge and Lon Nol's Khmer Republic forces was about to reach its conclusion.

On 1ˢᵗ April, Lon Nol fled the country as Khmer Rouge forces closed in on Phnom Penh. On 12ᵗʰ April, the USA closed its embassy in the capitol and flew its staff home. The replacement premier, Long Boret, offered to surrender to the Khmer Rouge on condition that there would be no reprisals against those who had been loyal to the Republican Government. The Khmer Rouge refused and the Government unconditionally surrendered on 17ᵗʰ April.

As the first Khmer Rouge troops arrived in the capitol, they were greeted by crowds of Cambodians waving makeshift white flags, the new national colour as decreed by the regime.

The first Han Sen heard of the Khmer Rouge victory was in class the next day. All of the school had been asked to assemble in the courtyard to listen to a speech from the headmaster. Dr Chepra was in a strange mood, one that his pupils had never seen before. His speech was grim yet floridly articulate.

'The forces of the Communist Party of Kampuchea, otherwise known as the Khmer Rouge, are finally in power in our capitol city. I don't know for certain, but this may be the last few days of our school here. We have heard many rumours about the new regime. They want us to live in the countryside, not in the towns and cities. And they want you children to work in the fields to produce food for your fellow countrymen.'

Most of the children knew something of the policies of the Khmer Rouge but hearing it from the authoritative voice of Dr Chepra made it a harsh reality.

'As well as working and eating communally, they also intend to close temples and liberate all Buddhist monks.'

Han Sen immediately thought of Hem Suvorn. He stared at the headmaster, he imagined his friend without his robe and without his faith. He needed to get back to Ta Veng.

'Money will be abolished. There will be no more markets.' As far as most of the children were concerned, these items were unimportant, they knew or cared little about money. Dr Chepra continued, 'All of the ethnic minority Vietnamese will be expelled, I think this may also include other minority groups - Chams, Thai, Chinese and possibly Laos.' This hit home harder, the North east region of the country was an ethnic patchwork and a high proportion of the children had origins in surrounding countries. The children looked at one another nervously, how many would have to go?

'Please don't be alarmed, I am merely telling you the facts as I see them. It is likely that the situation will not be as bad as I am stating. At least you will know something of what to expect when they are fully in charge.'

Dr Chepra continued looking into the distance and holding his bottom lip rigidly in place between sentences. 'Children of Sam Lok school. This has been the last few days of us being together. My fellow teachers and I have tried instilling in all of you, the essential importance of learning and to understand the sciences and languages. Do not just accept things as they are. Find out. Discover. Learn. Please try and remember this as you go through life. Always talk of the Sam Lok school with pride and reverence.'

He stopped abruptly and looked down at his shoes. The air in the schoolyard was still and silent, all of the children's gazes were fixed on him. Eventually, he looked up and continued, ignoring the tears streaming down each cheek. 'We hope by our efforts that this education has given you an opportunity in life, and that you will remember it and cherish it. Now is the time to be at home with your family. The Enlightened One will always be with you in your path through life. You are free to go. Goodbye and good luck.'

Han Sen watched as Mr. Ik and Mr. Hsu helped the emotionally overcome Dr Chepra back to the school office. Despite his severe style of teaching, the school had been the old man's life. The children glanced nervously at one another.

The first squad of black-clad Khmer Rouge to enter Ban Lung arrived later that week. Grim faced and unsmiling, they immediately began evicting the bewildered inhabitants from their homes. Families were given ten minutes notice to prepare for what they were told would be a three day journey. Stragglers and those who refused to obey were beaten with rifle butts, some told to kneel and simply executed on the spot with a single shot to the head. No one was exempted. The local hospital was emptied, doctors forced at gunpoint to cease operations and leave, the patients staggering out into the street or left to die on the operating table. The main route out of Ban Lung was clogged with the exodus of evacuees. Stocks of food and water accumulated for them were inadequate. Many succumbed to heat and exhaustion, with infants the old and the sick the first to die. Their relatives forced to leave the bodies at the roadside.

Han Sen, although terrified himself, could only assist the horror-struck Chebon family with their enforced departure as much as he could. He struggled along the road at the rear of the family group carrying as many household effects as possible, trying to keep the girls positive despite their wide–eyed fear.

He was torn between assisting the Chebons and getting back to his own family in Ta Veng.

Rep Chebon was typically pragmatic. 'You go, Han Sen, you go. We'll be all right.'

It was obvious to Han Sen that they would struggle without another pair of arms and the girls' spirits would sink without a source of positivity in the group. 'No, I am not going to leave you like this. Maybe when we reach our destination I will be able to find my way to Ta Veng, or wherever they take our family to.'

Rep Chebon leaned close to Han Sen and, talking in hushed tones, said, 'You know we are originally from Laos. The Khmer Rouge may not want us around. I don't want you to get caught up in all of this.'

Han Sen smiled at the older man, 'I am already caught up in all of this – don't worry, we'll stick together until we are settled. Besides the Laos are good people, they have been in Cambodia for hundreds of years, the Khmer Rouge would not dare to touch them.' He remembered the main man in the cabin that night in Ta Veng, and the hatred of Vietnam in his voice. 'If you were Vietnamese, then I would be worried,' he added.

'You are a brave man, Han Sen, and intelligent. I will never be able to repay you.'

The boy thought about this and replied, 'You have already repaid me by allowing me to stay with you while I attended Sam Lok School.'

'You are our family my boy. Let the thoughts of the Enlightened One shine on us and help protect us!'

Han Sen again dropped to the back of the family group to harangue the girls and chivvy up their otherwise quickly sagging morale. There was a spring in his step that the older girls picked up on.

'What were you two talking about then?' Rao asked as she struggled along the roadside with Raya, supervising their younger sisters in front of them. They were all carrying clothes in holdalls and various quantities of household goods. 'Here take these,' she said, passing her collection of pots and pans to Han Sen.

'I was just saying I'll be staying with your family for a while longer, if that's OK?'

Despite being scared about the uncertainty of their futures, all of the girls smiled at the boy and Rao lightly touched his shoulder, 'I should not say this, but I am so pleased to hear that.'

The surviving inhabitants of Ban Lung arrived at their pre-designated Khmer Rouge destination; a small village set in a jungle clearing with a riverfront area. Han Sen recognised the village, he had stopped there with his father one day en-route from Ban Lung to Ta Veng. He seemed to remember a motorcycle problem of one sort or another.

The large throng of bemused evacuees was split up into four groups of roughly one 100 families each. They were then set to work building shelters, then to clear further into the jungle to give themselves room to build communal living areas and land for the cultivation of rice.

The Khmer Rouge in charge immediately ordered that all the belongings be put in a collective pile. They were now the property of the state the startled people were told. Each person was issued with a spoon and a plate. This was to be the sum of their entire earthly possessions from now on.

Han Sen looked on as the selection and ethnic classification of people began to unfold in the village centre. The original villagers who had been under Khmer Rouge indoctrination for some time were classed as 'base' people. They supervised the 'new' people from the towns and cities. The 'new' people, including the Chebons and Han Sen were then to be split into further categories: 'Deportees,' the ethnic groups considered by the regime to be unnecessary. Han Sen's prediction to Rep Chebon of Laos being able to stay was unfounded - Laos, Chams, Vietnamese and Chinese amongst others, were all to be deported. The second main category was a 'candidate,' this was anyone with a relative from an ethnic background who could be considered at some time in the future to be on a par with the third and highest main category, that of 'full rights' people. These were identified as Khmers, or at least second-generation Cambodians. It was rumoured amongst the new arrivals that only full rights people would ever understand or sympathise with Pol Pot.

Han Sen stood with the Chebons in the long queue waiting to be given a classification by the unsmiling Khmer Rouge committee, sitting at a low table in the very centre of the village. He was furtively mulling over in his mind how to respond to the questions he knew were going to be asked. It was obvious that he was not a family member; he was much taller and fairer skinned than any of the Chebons.

'I am your son in law,' he whispered to Rep Chebon. 'I'm Loatian too, don't forget.'

The older man whispered back, 'You'd better say you're married to Raya. You don't have to do this, Han Sen. It could cost you your life.'

'I know. I need to stay with you, you're all I've got here,' the boy replied, looking on at the fearsome, heavily-armed Khmer Rouge cadres gathered around the committee table.

When it was their turn, the family group including Han Sen went to the table and were quickly asked by the dour, elderly man in charge; 'What is your family name?'

'Chebon,' Rep Chebon replied.

'Original nationality?'

'Laotian.' Then he said quickly, pointing at Han Sen. 'Apart from him. He's my son in law and he's Khmer.'

Han Sen was about to deny it when he realised he could be putting the older man and his family in even more jeopardy by doing so. He quickly stopped himself.

'OK, you will all be deported. He stays as a candidate,' the miserable man declared. He looked up at Han Sen, 'Your name, age and occupation?'

'Han Sen, I am seventeen and I am an engineer.' Two truths out of three isn't bad, he thought to himself.

'An engineer, eh? We'll have to keep an eye on you then. We just want people to do a good day's work. Pretty titles don't get noticed around here, you know.' The cadres in the background sniggered and looked the boy up and down.

'We would like to stay together please,' Rep Chebon stated politely.

'Very well,' the old man said as he struck through Han Sens details on the list. 'He gets deported too, serves him right for marrying a Lao.' The cadres all laughed. The old man continued, sensing an audience. 'If you don't know this saying already, you soon will. 'To preserve you is no gain, to destroy you is no loss,''

The cadres jeered and whistled in mock salutation to the old man. Creeps, thought Han Sen. If ever there is a day of reckoning, he'll get his all right, looking at the old man with a hatred that took him by surprise, he'd never discovered this emotion in himself before.

Thus Han Sen and the Chebons were put to work. Lai, the youngest of the Chebon girls, was assigned to a 'weak strength' work group, tending small gardens, turning over manure and feeding and clearing out the chickens. At sunrise when the rest of the family were reporting for work in the fields, she was given two hours of 'education' in a newly built classroom. This was indoctrination by the Khmer Rouge, determined to bring up children to recognise the goodness of their communist principles and to respect the Angkar, the organisation that allegedly provided everything for the people.

The rest of the family worked from sunrise to sunset. There was no rest time, only *veay samrok*, literally; attack time. They only wore black, expressions of individuality were not allowed. The centrally issued food consisted of a thin soup made of trokuon, a nutritious but not very tasty plant. Starvation was a way of life, they were hungry all the time. Fishing or foraging in the jungle was forbidden. Angkar will provide.

The first to die in the Chebon family was their mother. What started off as a mild illness, termed a disease of the consciousness or laziness by the Khmer Rouge, turned into pneumonia. With only a weak herbal medicine to provide any respite from the terrible fever, she died a lonely death within ten days of its onset. Of course the family were distraught but there was no time to grieve, the local commander was demanding his rice production quotas be met and everybody had to carry on working.

Han Sen became the unofficial mother of the family from this point onwards, providing moral support and listening to the girls problems and trying to find ways around them. Lai gave them all a powerful insight into the Khmer Rouge doctrines from her experiences in the morning classes.

'It's funny,' she said quietly as they all settled down to sleep in the communal dormitory one night. 'We are in school but Angkar does not allow books or anything printed on paper.'

'Shhh, Lai, someone will hear,' Raya whispered to her.

'OK, I'll be quiet. No one is allowed to travel without Angkar permission, no one is allowed to own anything. Buddhism is banned and only Cambodian people will be allowed to live here. What's going to happen to us?'

As father Rep was asleep, Han Sen felt the weight of responsibility for the little girl who had first broken the barriers between him and the family not so long ago. 'I don't know what we can do, Lai, the country has turned upside down. Most people thought the Khmer Rouge were our saviours, come to save us from the repressive Sihanouk, but actually they are monsters. They are treating people worse than animals. Why are we growing all of this rice? They say rice was the cornerstone of the Khmer Empire yet the Khmer Empire more or less finished in the 13th Century. They seem to be living in the past.'

'We could escape to another country,' the little girl said quietly, lying on her mattress looking up at Han Sen, her four sisters crowding around the cot.

'Thailand, we could go there, they have beaches in Thailand!' Rous, the second youngest, entered the conversation excitedly.

'Sshhh!' Han Sen whispered quickly, 'If they hear us they'll…well I don't know what they'll do, but don't let anyone hear you say things like that.'

'Oh please, Han Sen, we can't go on like this,' Rous continued in a quiet yet forceful whisper. 'We're all completely exhausted. We're always hungry. All we do is plant rice all day. We must try and escape.'

'Rous, the borders are sealed. The Khmer Rouge has laid mines and booby traps that kill people trying to escape Cambodia. We would have to travel through the forest at night,' Han Sen countered. He was thinking that the thought of travelling hundreds of miles through the forest and open country at night would stop the girl from pleading further. He was wrong.

'Great! When do we go?'

Just as Rous' final syllable ended, a loud male voice broke through the dark of the night in the dormitory, 'Han Sen! Han Sen! Wake up – we want you to do something for us. Come on, hurry!'

As the girls dived for cover under Lai's cot and Rep Chebon awoke, startled, Han Sen put on his long black shirt and made his way over to the main doorway where the voice had emanated from. He stepped outside, recognizing the old man from their first days in the village.

'Han Sen, you're an engineer right? Good with your hands, make things out of metal?'

'Well yes.'

'Good. A colleague elsewhere in the country needs someone like you, I'm going to send you there. Pack some things, you're going now.'

'But my family,' Han Sen said, immediately suspicious of the old man's demand. 'I can't just leave them here.'

'Course you can, they'll be here when you get back. Shouldn't take you long – a month or two.' The old man turned to go.

'Where in the country?'

'Phnom Penh. Now go and get your stuff, there's a lorry waiting to go at the top of the village.' The old man continued walking back to the administration building.

With the feeling of hatred crossing his mind again, he walked back to the family group of cots, the father and four girls all looked at him expectantly. 'They want me to go to Phnom Penh to do something for them.'

'You're going?' Rep Chebon asked.

'I don't see I've got much choice. He did say it would only be for a month or two.'

Rao looked at Han Sen as if she were about to say something, then cast her head down and her body shook with convulsions, tears streaming down her face silently. Her three sisters formed a ring around her, holding her tightly as she sobbed, they all looked on at Han Sen with alarm.

The bare-chested Rep Chebon put a hand on his shoulder softly, 'Take care, my boy,' he whispered in his ear. 'Come back soon. We all love you.' The older man too had tears in his eyes. One by one Han Sen hugged the girls, leaving Rao till last, holding her slightly longer and wiping some of the tears away from her moistened cheeks before finally leaving. He didn't take anything, none of them had possessions anymore, it all belonged to the state didn't it?

The military truck took almost twelve hours to reach Phnom Penh. The tubby, black-uniformed driver was silent and brooding for most of the journey apart from when they stopped for something to eat at a military station. Han Sen was prepared to sit in the cab and eat nothing, when the soldier unexpectedly beckoned him inside to the canteen area, asking him what he would like to eat and drink. Han Sen was wary as the display of food was enticing to the point of nausea, considering he had eaten only thin soup and occasional rice for five months. There was fried pork and beef, baked fish, plain rice, fried rice, stir fried vegetables, bean sprouts, noodles, freshly baked bread chapattis and as much tea as they wanted. Han Sen stared at the contents of the display, wide eyed and open mouthed. The glum caterer behind the counter asked him to make a choice, Han Sen pointed to the soldier's freshly prepared tray, saying wordlessly to her: another one of them please.

The fat soldier slouched at the long wooden table, carelessly slopping food into his mouth. Han Sen joined him with his small tray crammed with impossibly beautiful smelling food, not quite believing this was happening to him. He delicately tried a sliced carrot and was overwhelmed by the flavour and the feeling of guilt in not being able to share this with his beloved Chebon family, or indeed his own family back in Ta Veng. So overwhelmed that he had to have another, and another, and another, then the rest of the vegetables, then the meat, then the fish, then the noodles, then the rice. He wolfed the lot down and drank a complete pot of tai before the soldier was halfway through his meal. The soldier stared and then began laughing as he watched the performance of this very thin boy. He laughed to the point of crying. 'I'm sorry, boy,' he said, wiping both eyes with the back of his hands, 'I forgot, they don't feed you camp people. Watching you eat was like feeding time at the zoo!'

He offered Han Sen the rest of his meal as a mark of respect.

Han Sen thanked him but declined, 'Later,' he said. 'We can eat later?'

'Yes, yes, we can eat later,' the soldier chuckled as they returned to the cab of the truck.

It was dusk over Phnom Penh by the time they pulled into the entrance of a small chapel in the southern part of the eerily deserted capitol city.

4. S-21

Although parts of Cambodia had been under its influence since the late 1960s and unofficial control since the early 1970s, the Khmer Rouge regime was still in its infancy. This infancy gave cause to a certain paranoia, some would call it insecurity among the leadership, that counter-revolutionaries were a threat to be taken seriously.

Commands from the leadership regarding the complete restructuring of Cambodian society seemed unambiguous, yet as these words filtered down to a local level, misinterpretation by the local cadres was rife, and made life for the inhabitants of Cambodia risky. Strictness and brutality went hand in hand. People were rounded up and executed for the smallest of infringements; speaking a foreign language, wearing glasses, crying for dead loved ones, even scavenging for food.

The Khmer Rouge actively hunted down former leaders of the Lon Nol government. Lon Nol himself and his deputy, Long Boret, were executed within the first few days of their governments surrender. These executions seeming to set a national precedence within the Khmer Rouge organisation that said anyone associated with the old way of life, or could be in any way un-pure of thought, was considered a threat. Former bureaucrats, even former businessmen were targeted and killed, sometimes along with their whole families; the thinking being that family members were probably tarnished by association.

Keeping a sane head amidst the bloodbath had its perils too, even to committed members of the Khmer Rouge. Some were executed for failing to find enough counter-revolutionaries to murder. The term `purge` legitimised the act of murder in the eyes of the leadership and became synonymous with death on various scales encompassing single killings to ethnic cleansing and, ultimately, genocide.

The drivers behind the purging activities were the Santebal, the Special Branch of the CPK. The officer in charge was Kaing Khek Iev, also known as Deuch to his friends and his enemies. The old man back at the camp who caused Han Sen to discover hatred within himself was a Khmer Rouge regional commander who knew Iev. They were both originally from Kompong Thom. This was also where the Khmer Rouge leader Pol Pot originated from. To complete this high level cabal of senior Khmer Rouge figures from the Kompong Thom region, Iev's senior lieutenant in the Santebal was Mam Nay, a gangly, acne-scarred former biology teacher. It was Mam Nay who Han Sen reported to the next morning.

'So, you're an engineer, right?' The man did not look up from his desk in the dimly lit crypt of the former chapel.

'Yes, sir,' Han Sen responded. 'At least training to be...'

'You are a communist. Been on any courses have you?' The man asked abruptly, still looking at the document on his desk.

'Yes, sir,' Han Sen lied. This was becoming a habit he thought to himself.

'Know what it's about, why we're doing this?'

'Yes, sir; for the betterment of Cambodia and its people.' Lies were becoming second nature to him now. Perhaps that was the problem, all of the Khmer Rouge were liars.

The man looked up suddenly and snarled, 'Know what pain is, do you? Ever had a bone broken, or a toenail pulled out, or a white hot needle stuck up your arse?'

'Er no, sir,' Han Sen was alarmed. Who was this man?

'Because that's what we do here. We torture people to make them confess to crimes against the Kampuchean people. Once they've confessed, we send them away. They don't ever come back. They remain silent forever.' A glimmer of a smile crossed his shadowed face. 'That means we can do whatever we like with them here, there are no limits. You can let your imagination run wild, really wild.'

Han Sen felt the true meaning of terror that morning. He wanted to cry. This man was a monster, truly a monster. He had seen local nobodies corrupted by power but he was guessing this man was a senior member of the Angkar. How had Cambodia allowed these types of people to take charge?

'Come, I'll show you what we want you to do.'

Han Sen followed the man from his office to the other end of the crypt, past a series of recently built cubicles. He could sense and smell people all around him; there was a continual low murmuring in the background and an acrid smell of human waste. They entered a large, brightly lit room through a vaulted doorway with two bare light bulbs in the ceiling, and several more that were not switched on. Several hooks protruded from the ceiling and a short man in the corner was cleaning a heavy steel link chain with a rag.

'This is our interrogation chamber. We get invaluable information from our enemies in here.' He laughed. 'For some reason, people become very co-operative when they arrive in this room.

Especially when they meet this man. He seems to have that kind of effect on people, don't you, Nath?'

'Sir?'

The man turned around slowly and stared at Han Sen rapaciously, his crossed-eyes looking Han Sen up and down, visibly savouring the boy's presence.

'Stop that, Nath, he's one of us. This is Han Sen, he's going to be working with you. He's an engineer. We brought him along to make things for you.'

The man's attitude changed suddenly into a smiling effusiveness. He offered a hand that the wary Han Sen had little other option but to shake. 'Pleased to meet you, Han Sen. Sorry about that, how are you today?'

Han Sen was shaking, his breathing laboured. They wanted him to make things? It didn't bear thinking about. He somehow knew these people would not be asking him to make brackets for hanging flower baskets.

'I'll leave you two to get on then,' the older man called out as he disappeared through the door back into the crypt. 'Get him a room, Nath, and show him where to eat.'

'Come on then,' the man called Nath said, all smiles again. 'I'll show you the best part of the job. If we're lucky we might just be able to get some breakfast.'

They went back up the worn, stone staircase that he had come down earlier with the overweight lorry driver, out of the building and along the deserted street into a large, three-storey building next door. On entering the building, Han Sen's mouth opened wide in amazement; it was the grandest inside of a building he had ever seen. The hallway contained two huge chandeliers, twinkling in the morning sunlight. They hung above a curved wooden staircase winding its way gracefully up to the first floor. Beautifully formed pieces of furniture were scattered around liberally. To Han Sen, they almost seemed to be alive, their curved legs emulating the human form. Heavily embossed velvet wallpaper hung from floor to ceiling, absorbing and deadening the sound of their voices. Despite such grandness, there was a fine layer of dust everywhere.

'It's the old Belgian embassy. Not bad, eh?' The short man said as they entered the large, equally impressive dining room. 'We even managed to keep the cook,' he said as they stood in the open doors leading onto a balcony overlooking a garden that would have been fabulously manicured, but was now starting to look overgrown.

'Here, help yourself,' he said opening the lids on several tureens, each containing a variety of cooked meats, fish, rice, noodles and fresh bread. Fresh orange juice and a coffee pot sat on the table behind the tureens. 'We have to time it right in the morning; the old man eats around eight, if we get here about now, we get what's left over, which is normally pretty good. My mother always used to say, you can't go to work on an empty stomach.'

Han Sen wasn't hungry, and so helped himself to some orange juice.

When the short man had finished eating, he gestured Han Sen to follow him again. 'Come on, I'll show you downstairs.' They went out onto the terrace and down some small steps to an open door leading to the basement of the house. 'This is the old servant quarters, you can have any of these rooms,' he said as they walked along the corridor flanked on both sides with closed doors. 'And this is what you can use for a workshop.' They entered a large, well lit room with a bench in the centre and worktops around the periphery below high windows. Several hand-tools were scattered on the bench and some steel bars and plates stood in a pile in the corner.

'I'm not quite sure what they want me to do,' Han Sen said, looking around bewildered.

'Well, let me try and put you in the picture. I was talking to the old man a few weeks ago, and I just happened to mention we could do with someone who could make some things for us. You can't buy the sort of thing I'm looking for. Not that you can buy anything in Cambodia any more,' he added with a tinge of irony.

'What sort of things?' Han Sen asked, not sure he really wanted to hear the answer.

'Oh, all sorts. Fire-grates, hooks, clamps, a mobile water feature, they'd all make the job easier. We're expanding see? Soon it won't be just me, there'll be a whole team of us doing this job, so we'll need more of everything. The boss thinks big you know.'

'A fire-grate? What do you do with one of them?' Han Sen asked. Again he wasn't sure that he really wanted to know the answer.

'For hotwork, you know like heating up needles. That's another thing we need by the way,' he added as an aside. 'Yes when you heat them up to white hot and put them into somebody, they soon go cold you know. If we all have a little fire grate we could reheat them quickly instead of rushing back to the kitchen fireplace all the time, that's a right pain in the arse. Get it?' He nudged Han Sen with his elbow, then started laughing, almost uncontrollably. Han Sen could feel the orange juice rising in his stomach.

'And the water feature, that's to put it out, is it?' Han Sen asked, sensing his own naivety.

'No don't be daft, it's for when they go to bed at night, I've been reading about the Indo-China wars. Those Chinese were clever bastards, you know; they used to leave a tap dripping overnight in the cell area, used to drive the prisoners nuts. I want one of them, well, probably several. The boss reckons we'll be moving in under six months the rate we're going. Let's face it, we're not short of empty buildings around here, are we?' He laughed again.

Han Sen asked him where the toilet was. He was surprised to see he had a choice of toilet bowls to be sick in. Was this some other horrible Khmer Rouge practice or was it some form of outrageous Belgian vanity?

'How's your electrics?' Nath said as Han Sen shakily emerged from the toilet.

'I don't know too much about wires and cables,' Han Sen replied truthfully.

'Oh that's all right, we'll get by. I know a little bit from my days in the electrical works.'

'Electrical works?' Stop asking questions he said to himself. His Dad always said his curiosity would get him into trouble one day.

'Yes I did my apprenticeship at the Kompong Thom Electrical Works.'

'Oh,' Han Sen replied, praying this was a sufficiently polite response. Hopefully, just enough to discourage another flow of dialogue from this maniac. It wasn't.

'We had twenty megawatts in those days, four steam turbines and two diesels. We used to strip each turbine once a year. That was really exciting.' The short man's one good eye gazed into the distance, happy memories obviously rekindled.

Han Sen managed to stop himself asking any further questions. Instead, he wondered to himself why someone trained as an engineer ended up torturing people. Was he about to go through a similar process? He could see that he was going to have to be strong-willed to resist getting pulled into any sort of relationship with this man. Yet at the same time he needed to show enough enthusiasm to make sure he wasn't going to be discovered as someone who didn't believe in the cause.

The diminutive, cross-eyed torturer was right. The prison did move. Twice. By the end of 1976 there were so many people feared by the regime that the final location of S-21, the official Khmer Rouge name, was a three-storey school building in the southern outskirts of Phnom Penh, housing up to 1500 people at a time.

Han Sen had set the workshop up in the basement of the former Belgian Embassy in such a way as to make it highly disadvantageous for his boss to even think about moving it. In this way, Han Sen was at least able to keep a distance between him and the increasingly horrific things that were going on at the prison. All Han Sen had to do was deliver the instruments with which the torturers were able to extract the information they required. His frame of mind was simple and fixed rigidly; he was not doing this for anyone's benefit apart from his own and his family and friends. He was determined to stay alive, to get back to the Chebons and to his own family in Ta Veng. He also knew that the alternative was probably far worse.

Amateurish attempts at extracting information by the Khmer Rouge often involved the killing of whole families one by one until the victim either confessed or dreamed-up something plausible to tell their inquisitor. At least what they did in S-21 was a one-on-one experience that afforded some dignity to the whole sorry process. Han Sen justified his actions by knowing that most of the inmates were in fact Khmer Rouge. He knew obviously that a lot of innocent people got swept up in the post-Sihanouk euphoria, but to sign up to full CPK membership and carry out some of the bloodthirsty things that the Khmer Rouge were carrying out all over the country was wrong. For this reason, he was able to consider what he was doing as revenge on behalf of the women, children and all the decent- thinking people of Cambodia.

He often asked Buddha for guidance that he was doing the right thing. Not that he had much of a choice, other than to continue and hope that someone, somewhere, would step in and put an end to all of this suffering.

Ignoring the moral and ethical side of what he was doing, this was a formative time for the young Han Sen in an engineering sense. He had set up the workshop with no expense spared, Mam Nay giving him free rein to bring in machinery as he wished. With the services of the overweight lorry driver and his large truck, they looted the very best of the machinery available in the evacuated city and set it to work in the basement of the embassy. He was able to build practically anything they wanted, even learning basic electrical circuits from the short torturer.

The development process was the difficult part. Nath would come and see him most nights. 'Han Sen, we need this bone breaker modifying a bit. I can't get enough pressure, could you put a longer handle on it? I had to use a sledgehammer this afternoon, and the mess is a nightmare to clear up.'

'I'll put a bigger handle on it by tomorrow.' Han Sen took the implement. He could never look the short man in the face. He feared being sick over him.

'You really should come over and have some fun, you don't know what you're missing,' the short man said, smiling. He was elbowing Han Sen, who stood at the workbench taking the fearful contraption apart.

'I'm squeamish, remember?' Han Sen said. He was referring to the one and only time he had been in the same room when Nath was at work. He had walked into the room inadvertently to find him brushing a live power cord across the soles of the victim's bare feet. The victim was suspended with wires from the ceiling by hooks screwed into his rib-cage. Han Sen rushed from the room and was violently sick. The man's screams would live in his memory forever.

'Squeamish, yet you make all these things for us?'

'I'm only an engineer; everyone has a right to a life as far as I'm concerned,' Han Sen replied, safe in the knowledge that Nath would not want to lose his source of specialist hardware by telling Mam Nay about his 'soft' leanings.

'Yes, unless they've been telling the CIA about what we're doing, then it's definitely...' and he made a cutting noise, running his index finger across his throat from one side to the other.

Han Sen thought to himself, the sooner the CIA or somebody, stepped in and did something about the Khmer Rouge, the better. He thought long and often about escaping from the desperate situation he found himself in. But in a country where travel without permission was banned, and life on the street so cheap in the eyes of the Khmer Rouge, he always kept returning to the fact that he was better off biding his time and waiting for something to happen. The Khmer Rouge couldn't last forever, he kept telling himself.

As the prison expanded, Nath became more demanding. He not only wanted more quantity of what he called his standard items, he wanted more elaborate devices to impart the most horrendous cruelty on the wretched inmates. It seemed to Han Sen that he dreamt up a lot of his ideas overnight, breakfasts were the worst time for his crazy ideas.

'If only we could have a table-top machine that we could strap people to, you can do a lot more with them in that position. It would be faster and more efficient for me and my team.' He would make detailed sketches of what he wanted in a small notebook that he would show to Han Sen excitedly. 'Look, like this, see? It would be great if we could have something like this.'

The sketch showed a flat-topped table with clamps for the neck, arms and legs. The top of the table was effectively two sliding carriages that expanded apart via a gearwheel on the side of the fixed part of the table. His dreadful imagination didn't stop there, though.

'This machine could be the basis of something really clever. Look, if you put a rail on one side or even both, you could have a carriage that slides up and down the whole length of the table. You could attach anything to the carriage, anything at all.' He smiled expectantly at Han Sen.

'Oh I see, like a light to see what you are doing. Or a fan so you don't get too hot,' he answered, thinking if this machine was for any purpose other than torture, he could get quite excited about it, view it as a challenge.

'No, you idiot, a blowtorch or a circular saw or a drill or, I don't know, a heating element to brand people with, the list is endless. That's what I'm saying, this machine would give us a lot of flexibility.' The crazed persecutor looked at Han Sen with an imploring passion in his eyes.

I'm sure your inmates would be pleased about that too, Han Sen thought sadly. 'Yes I see,' he said eventually looking at the sketch.

'When can you make a start on it?' Nath asked, serious now.

'I'll draw up a list of materials and let you know what I need.' Han Sen responded, as always, pleased that Nath was preparing to go.

'The lorry driver will take you to wherever you need to go. You know where all the places are by now, don't you?'

'Yes, although there may be some things we won't be able to get, but we'll see,' Han Sen said.

'Good lad, see you tomorrow,' the short man replied, obviously pleased that his protégé was showing some enthusiasm for his little project.

So it was three weeks later, despite repeated, deploring requests from Nath for sneak previews, all denied by Han Sen, when the prototype was finally unveiled and christened the Multi-Stretch by the diminutive torturer. He was beside himself, walking around the machine, touching and caressing the impressive looking steelwork, full of ideas for improvements and refinements already.

'Ah, Han Sen, this is fantastic. One day we'll motorise the hand wheel, probably by push button. Or even by remote control from another room. I wouldn't be able to hear the screams any more, do wonders for my tinnitus.'

Han Sen looked on. Yes he was pleased with the machine. As always though, he was dreading the in-field development that always happened whenever he built something new. Nath was the ultimate tester, never sparing Han Sen any of the gory details, always looking for improvements.

'They love the Multi-Stretch.' Nath announced at breakfast one morning.

Han Sen assumed he meant his senior commanders. 'Who do?'

'My inmates of course. Not a complaint yet.' He laughed. 'I want you to make me another one. But this time make it so it can be anchored to the floor. It does move around a bit when you get to the interesting part.'

Han Sen was beginning to struggle with what was right, and what was wrong. He was pleased with the product and the way it worked, yet totally horrified and ashamed at the use it was being put to.

Life shouldn't be like this. He promised himself that in the future it wouldn't be.

5. *The Realisation*

'Mam Nay says we need to get rid of people quicker and easier,' Nath said to a wary Han Sen at breakfast one morning. 'Look, I've got some ideas.' He opened up his notebook.

Han Sen knew immediately that his time had come to an end at the madness that was S-21. He suspected that the subject of wholesale slaughter was going to be broached by the short man sooner or later. He had rehearsed in his mind many times how he would make his escape, it seemed that now would be the time

He decided in those few seconds that he would be leaving that day and take his chances against the Khmer Rouge desperados. He was guilty of enough already, the thought of wholesale slaughter was something he couldn't bear to even think about. If he made his distaste too obvious, he would literally be under the threat of his own creation. There were no more choices.

He grimaced suddenly at the short man, holding his stomach with both hands. 'Aagh, my stomach's been bad all morning. Excuse me, I've got to go.' He rushed out of the room, leaving the surprised Nath at the breakfast table. His notebook open at a page showing a sketch of a building with a large chimney. Matchstick men formed a queue and arrows showed their direction into the building. Only in, Han Sen noted. The chimney had a plume of smoke wafting upwards.

Han Sen hoped he looked sufficiently pale-faced and troubled on his return from the toilet. He had no need to worry.

'Here,' Nath said, offering Han Sen a small glass of herbal medicine. 'Take this, it'll settle your stomach. I've got some water for you to wash it down with. I know the medicine doesn't taste very nice.'

'OK, thanks. I'll take it in a minute. It's like cramps, they come and go.' Han Sen gasped quietly for effect.

'Yes I know. It's the worst, stomach pain,' Nath said, concern showing on his face. 'It must have been something you ate. You need to be more careful. My wife washes everything we eat. You can't be too hygienic these days.'

Han Sen looked at him warily. 'Sorry, I'm going to have to go to bed. Can we talk about your plans later, or tomorrow?'

'Han Sen! Tch tch!' The older man admonished him gently. 'I need you better. You get off to bed, I'll come visit later to see if you need anything.' He got up from the table and helped the convincingly stricken youngster down the stairs to his bedroom, laid him on the bed, tucked him in, ruffled his hair and turned to go. 'Oh, nearly forgot your medicine! I'll be back in a tic.'

Han Sen managed to smile weakly as Nath put the herbal medicine and the glass of water gently by the side of his bed and with another ruffle of the hair was gone. Away to his work, Han Sen thought grimly. He got up and tipped the medicine down the sink, his mind racing as to how he was going to get out of Phnom Penh, back to the Chebons, then onto Ta Veng.

He packed the only personal possessions he owned; a spare shirt and trousers, into a small tool-holdall and checked the workshop for anything that might prove useful. He put in a torch, matches, a large screwdriver and a new, one-inch wood chisel that the fat lorry driver had mysteriously presented to him for carrying out some repairs to his truck.

Han Sen had no sooner zipped the holdall shut when the fat lorry driver himself appeared at the doorway. 'Hi Han Sen, there's not too many bodies for me to get rid of today. Is there anything I can do to help?' he asked politely.

Han Sen thought quickly. 'Well, actually,' he said, pointing towards the second part-built Multi-Stretch machine. 'You could take a look at this for me.'

The lorry driver sauntered over to the bare steel construction, curiousity on his face. Meanwhile Han Sen had picked up a short length of steel channel section from the pile in the corner. Just as the lorry driver bent down to examine the steel structure, Han Sen's carefully aimed blow hit him hard across the back of the head. The man collapsed to the floor and, worryingly for Han Sen, continued to groan. Sorry old buddy, Han Sen thought to himself, I can't leave you like this, and hit the fat lorry driver again in the same place with the length of steel. The groaning stopped this time.

Han Sen stared at the large bulk of the lorry driver prone and lifeless on the floor. Worry that he'd killed him filled his mind, to be quickly replaced with thoughts of escape. He hoped the feeling of guilt would be a price worth paying. He went through the lorry driver's pockets and found the truck key. He then calmly walked out of the building, leapt up into the truck cab, throwing his holdall onto the passenger seat, started the engine and drove off in the direction of the river. He knew where he was going as long as he kept the river in sight.

He retraced the journey that he and the overweight lorry driver had made three years earlier from the north-east of the country. Luckily the truck was full of fuel. He stopped after a few miles and changed into the black shirt and trousers so he at least looked like one of them. The lorry driver had left a baseball cap and a machine pistol on the front shelf of the truck cab. Han Sen put the cap on, pulling it down over his eyes and examined the pistol. It was worn, he wondered how many people it had threatened or killed or both. It appeared to be in good working order with a full clip of ammunition. He tucked it into the door pocket making sure the safety catch was on, re-started the truck engine and continued his journey.

As he left the near-deserted city and entered the countryside, he was saddened at how such beauty was slowly being destroyed by this crackpot regime. The countryside was virtually all now used for rice production. The paddy fields glistened in the morning sunlight, peppered with people tending the rice plants. Among them, ever watchful, black-clad Khmer Rouge militia. The towns he passed through were still mostly deserted. The only people allowed in being senior CPK party members and trusted military leaders. Han Sen drove for ten hours without stopping, wondering how he was going to get into the village where he hoped the Chebons would be. What was he going to say or do if they were there? Should he take the risk? He chided himself for the thought; the Chebons were his family, he owed it to them to do whatever he could. But in this country run by the Khmer Rouge, what could he do? Take them to another village with communal eating and starvation rations where they were just as likely to die as where they were at present?

As he neared the village, a plan evolved in his mind. Instead of leaving the truck in the jungle and entering the village surreptitiously as he initially thought, he decided to brazen it out. He would drive the truck into the centre of the village, demand to see the local commander and request that he take the Chebon family away for questioning. They were suspected of, well it didn't matter really, in fact it would probably be better for them if he said nothing. After all, he looked like Khmer Rouge, he had just spent over a year working for a senior member in the capitol city. The worst thing that could happen was that the commander would either remember him from his previous time in the village, or want to make a phone call to verify his request. It was nine in the evening and he had the lorry driver's machine pistol, two good reasons for going straight in there now, he thought.

The village was the same as he remembered it. He parked the truck outside the administration building, checking the pistol in the waistband of his black trousers and pulling his cap down tight over his eyes. He cut the engine and walked into the building. The old man sat at a desk in the corner of the room studying a document. The same feeling of undiluted hatred arose in his stomach.

The old man looked up. 'Yes? What do you want?'.

'You have a family here with the name Chebon?' Han Sen asked authoritatively.

'And what if we do?'

'I have to take them away for questioning. I am here as a representative of Mam Nay at Tuol Slong prison.'

'Do you have any paperwork?'

'No. Mam Nay says he will ring you in the morning to clarify the situation.' He knew the old man would be flattered to have such a senior figure contact him directly.

'Guard!' A bespectacled black clad youth appeared from outside. 'This man is here to collect a family called Chebon.'

The youth consulted a battered black exercise book on an adjacent desk. 'Yes, they are in the smaller cabin, follow me.' He walked briskly towards the door.

Han Sen followed the youth into the night. They walked towards the riverfront past the large sheltered communal dining area and on to the smaller of the two huts in the village. They had all lived in the larger hut before. Was this a bad omen?

'Chebon!' The youth called when they reached the open entrance. 'Someone to see you!' As they waited, Han Sen relived the horrors of working from sunrise to sunset on an empty stomach.

The figure approaching them was small and emaciated. Han Sen barely recognised Raya. He pulled his cap down lower over his eyes hoping she would not recognise him and inadvertently give the game away.

'Get the rest of your family,' the guard said. 'You're all to go with this man.'

'I'll see you on the way out,' Han Sen said to the guard. He hoped he would leave them.

'OK.' The guard turned and began walking back to the administration building.

Han Sen took his cap off. 'Raya,' he said in a low voice.

'Han Sen!' She looked at him with surprise, then suspicion. 'You're not one of them now are you?'

47

'Ssh, no I'm not,' he whispered quietly. 'I'm here to take you away.'

'Where?' The bewildered girl asked.

'I don't know yet, probably Ta Veng.' He wondered again whether they would all be still alive.

'There's only Rao and I left Han Sen,' Raya said, tears starting to flow. 'They worked Papa to death. There was no rice from the last harvest, the commander sent it all to Phnom Penh. He told us we had to meet our quota. Rous and Lai both died from the same disease as Mama, there was no medicine. It's so good to see you.' She reached up and flung her thin arms around him and he could feel every bone in her undernourished body. Tears seeped into his clothing and her body quivered as she sobbed.

'Come on, Raya,' he said after a short while. 'We need to get out of here.' He followed the girl into the hut past the hundreds of sleeping people, and stopped at the cot where Rao was dozing. He could tell she too was emaciated and gaunt, just like her sister.

'Han Sen!' she cried, propping herself up on an elbow.

'Sshh, he's come to take us away.' Raya whispered urgently to her younger sister. 'We have to move! Don't say anything, people will hear.'

'Han Sen!' the younger girl repeated in astonishment. She bit her lip but her tears had started as well.

Both girls immediately busied themselves collecting what few belongings they had. They followed Han Sen out of the dormitory and up towards the parked truck.

As they got nearer, the old man appeared at the door of the administration building, the light from the office highlighting his profile. 'You're Han Sen, aren't you? The engineer who went away to Phnom Penh? I thought I recognised you. You're not taking them anywhere.'

Han Sen thought quickly, 'Both of you, get over by the truck, this side,' he whispered to the girls, gesticulating towards the passenger door. He approached the building purposefully. The youth and an additional older Khmer Rouge guard had appeared, 'Yes commander, I am Han Sen, I am under strict orders from Mam Nay to take this family back to Tuol Sleng straight away. If you choose not to comply, I fear you will have some difficult questions to answer from our Chief of Security.'

'But they're your family,' the old man shouted, pointing at Han Sen feverishly. 'You are not going to walk out of here with them! Guards, arrest this man!'

By now Han Sen was within five yards of the old man. He had hoped to get him inside, instead, realising that both guards were armed and about to draw weapons, he lunged at the commander. Grabbing his arm and wrenching it up behind his back, at the same time withdrawing the pistol from the waistband of his trousers, he held the gun to the old man's temple.

'Make a move and the old man's dead,' he said to the two guards, who both looked at him, the younger one terrified, the older reaching for his weapon with a look of cool savagery in his eyes. Han Sen realised in a split second that this one didn't care either way if the old man lived or died. He released the safety catch, took the pistol aim from the old man's head and shot the older guard clean through the forehead. The guard fell forward, his head lying within two yards of where Han Sen was standing.

The younger guard was shaking with his hands in the air. 'Don't shoot, don't shoot!'

'Throw your gun over to the girls,' Han Sen called to him. The youth complied. Raya hurriedly picked the gun up, and pointed it with both hands at the young guard who had his arms in the air again. He wrenched the old man's arm further up his back and pulled him into the office and back over to his desk where he sat him down, still with his arm in a vicelike hold.

Han Sen spoke quietly into the old man's ear, 'I remember your phrase; to preserve you is no gain, to destroy you is no loss. Well you destroyed three good people from my family and probably hundreds if not thousands of others here from starvation and lack of medicine, so I am going to destroy you. I apologise before the eyes of the Enlightened One but I have no other option.' For the second time that evening, he put the pistol to the old man's temple and held it there momentarily. Han Sen felt that the old man was expecting death, maybe even welcoming it. He certainly offered no protest. Han Sen squeezed the trigger and the old man's blood flooded onto his shoulder and left arm as the bullet exited the side of his head. The dead man slumped forward onto the document he had been reading, blood forming quickly into a pool, heading towards the edge of the desk and spilling onto the floor.

He walked quickly out of the door gesticulating towards the youth, 'You're coming with us. Get in the truck.' He opened up the passenger door of the truck, pushed the eager youth in followed by the terrified girls and slammed the door shut. He then ran around to the other side of the truck, leapt into the driver's seat and they were off in a crash of gears and spinning of wheels.

*

Han Sen started to shake as he steered the truck away from the village, the enormity of what he'd just done catching up with him. His only thought had been to get the girls away from the village, the older guard had posed a threat, somebody needed to put an end to the old man's cruelty and Han Sen had been in the perfect position to do it. 'What's your name?' he asked the youth sitting next to him.

'Chea Suoy,' he answered nervously.

'How old are you, Chea?'

'Seventeen,' the youth replied.

That meant he was probably fourteen or fifteen, Han Sen thought to himself. 'These are my sisters Raya and Rao. I lived here for a year before the Khmer Rouge asked me to go to Phnom Penh. You hated the old man too, right?' Han Sen asked, anticipating the youth's reply.

'Yes. He was a monster. You did the right thing, I congratulate you. Why did you not kill me too?' the youth asked, his voice tense.

'Because you do not have hate in your eyes, and you are young enough to learn from life. I am sorry for killing the older guard; it was a split second decision. The Enlightened One will be the final judge.'

'He was almost as cruel as the old man,' the youth replied. 'You did the right thing.'

'He was a mother's son,' Han Sen said. 'Probably a husband too. Someone will miss him.'

Raya spoke for the first time. 'Han Sen, do not chastise yourself for what you have done. You did what you saw fit to do, to preserve all of our lives. You will have an inner peace again; what you feel now is remorse. It is only natural.'

'I just hope the Khmer Rouge do not take reprisals against the other villagers,' Han Sen said.

'The Vietnamese are coming,' the youth said. 'The Khmer Rouge do not have long. They have done so much wrong to our country, and to our people, that when the Vietnamese arrive, the people of Cambodia will turn against the Khmer Rouge.'

'The Khmer Rouge will fight. They hate the Vietnamese,' Han Sen replied. There was a silence. 'We need to ditch this truck somewhere.'

By his reckoning they were only about forty miles from Ta Veng. To stay in the truck would become increasingly risky. He had stolen the truck from a senior commander, injured and maybe killed its driver, killed a regional commander and one of his guards. There would undoubtedly be people looking for him. Besides, if the youth was right and the Vietnamese were coming, to pretend to be Khmer Rouge would also be risky. It would be best to return to being peasants and trek through the jungle on foot. They ditched the truck in a remote part of the jungle and set fire to it, then set off in a north easterly direction for Ta Veng.

What they found in Ta Veng shocked Han Sen. Largely deserted, most of the buildings in the centre of the village were either completely missing or smashed to pieces. Further away from the centre, the damage was not so great and his family home was still standing; it looked, not surprisingly, like it had been unoccupied for a long while.

They went to the electrical works. The building structure was still standing, the machinery still there, but smashed. Someone had attacked all of the breakable parts on the once beautiful machines with a sledgehammer, rendering them useless. The plinth for the missing generator, the former shrine and centrepiece of the building was starkly bare, Buddha and his immaculate surroundings long gone. Even the brass plaque had been attacked, hanging sadly by one screw, a large dent twisting the words. Han Sen looked on grimly, wondering whether he would ever find his family.

The two girls and two boys sat down by the riverside in the shadow of the electrical works to try and decide what to do. Han Sen, saddened by the destruction, yet anxious for his loved ones, was mooted. 'So, it is likely that the whole village will be living and working in a commune somewhere around here. All we have to do is find it, but what then?'

'We have guns, Han Sen,' Preap Suoy said eagerly. 'We can go there and demand their release.'

'I am not going to kill again; I am ashamed enough already.' He thought of his mother and father and James Henderson and Hem Suvorn, what would they think if they knew he had killed? What would they have done in his position? What would they do now? He threw the fat lorry driver's pistol into the river, the youth did the same with his.

'I say we should head for the Vietnamese border,' Raya said. 'I am like you, Han Sen, but I fear going back into captivity. Yes, we need to find your family and friends but at what cost to you and us? God forgive me for saying this, you are our dear friend, but we are still alive. Would they want us to put ourselves back into the hands of the Khmer Rouge just to be with them. It may make us feel better but what will it do for them?'

Han Sen looked at the girl. Sometimes her words could be brutal, yet always honest and brave.

Rao looked at her older sister, emotion flickering across her gaunt face. 'Raya, whatever we decide, let us never part.' She carefully put both arms around the older girl and buried her head in her shoulder.

Raya held her sister who was now quietly sobbing and looked at both boys with a determined expression. 'Let us hope that we come across somebody who knows something. Come, we should go.'

It was at that moment that a hoarse voice called out from within the electrical works, 'Han Sen, Han Sen, don't go!'

An emaciated, dirt-stained, heavily-bearded old man emerged blinking through the remains of the eastern wall, wearing a pair of tattered shorts around his pathetically narrow waist. Han Sen looked on at Hem Suvorn in disbelief.

'My old friend,' Han Sen said, walking over to the old man. 'Where have you been?' They hugged one another, tears running down the old man's weathered cheeks.

'Oh Han Sen, you don't want to know,' he laughed. 'First we had the Khmer Rouge, now they've disappeared and the Vietnamese have taken over. I'm not sure which is worse. I'm staying out of the way until someone tells me for sure what's going on.'

Han Sen was surprised. 'The Khmer Rouge have disappeared already? Why is the village still empty? The house where my family live, it's empty,' he said, a stark realisation dawning on him. 'Where is everybody?'

'I don't know, there was a lot of killing, many mass graves. Those people, they were all mad. They outlawed religion completely. They killed their own.'

'Where was the commune?' Han Sen asked.

'On the riverbank about four miles north.' The monk pointed with his painfully thin arm.

'I must go there,' Han Sen said, looking around him restlessly. The three youngsters were preparing to support him.

'There's nothing there now, Han Sen,' the monk said softly. 'I was there yesterday. There's nothing left. The administration building has been burnt out, no paperwork left, nothing.' The monk hesitated. He knew what Han Sen would say next.

'But, if there's nobody there, that means everybody has either gone somewhere else, or they are dead. Where else would they have gone?'

The monk looked at Han Sen. He did not need to say anything.

Han Sen sat down. Raya and Rao both crouched down touching his shoulder. He was unable to speak to them, the girls had been through so much, Hem Suvorn too. All of them. 'Do you have family, Chea?' he asked the youth.

'I do,' he replied. 'But I am not sure whether they are still alive. I heard about a year ago that they were OK. I should really go back to the Western region soon.'

'Yes, of course.' Han Sen had the sudden thought that the youth's parents could have been victim of one of his instruments of torture, or his sister or his brother. Or maybe they were one of the S-21 death-squad targets. Or both, who would ever know? It would take decades for the authorities to uncover mass graves and identify victims, if it ever happened at all. For his family's sake, he hoped it would happen one day.

'I do know that Henderson was one of the first to die,' the old monk said, breaking Han Sen's reverie. 'He refused to do anything they told him. Called them commie geeks. He stayed at the electrical works until the end. He had all three generators running flat out when they shot him. Then they smashed the place up. I'm sorry. It was as much your father's place as it was Henderson's.'

'He was a great man, Hem Suvorn, he taught me so much.' He shivered and looked at the ground. Despite the comfort from the girls and meeting his old friend again, he felt very alone.

The old monk looked at Han Sen. 'The last time I saw Henderson, do you know what he said to me? Tell that Han Sen when you see him next, to get across to Taiwan, to go and work for his Dad's Uncle on the machine tools, he'll make his fortune out there. That's what he said.'

Han Sen realised then that he couldn't stay in Cambodia. Not after all of this. 'Sounds a good idea. I'm not sure about the fortune, but Taiwan sounds good. Anywhere other than Cambodia, I guess. You could come too, Hem Suvorn.'

'No, no,' the monk replied. 'My place is here. I will rebuild the monastery brick by brick if I have to. I'm too old to think about anything else.'

Raya looked at her sister and then at Han Sen, 'Our mother was part Chinese. Rao and I both speak Mandarin. We could come with you, help with the communication.' She looked back at her sister who nodded without looking up.

They stayed in Ta Veng that night, eating fish caught by Chea and roasted on a fire behind the electrical works, followed by fruit and nuts foraged by the girls from the jungle. It was the first proper meal they had eaten in days. For Hem Suvorn, months..

The following morning, they had a concerted look around the village and surrounding area for any signs of the Sen Family, there were none. Loss was all around them.

They hid as they heard vehicles approaching. A convoy of military trucks entered the village. They stopped and Vietnamese soldiers spilled out, stretching their legs and setting up makeshift food preparation facilities. The group of Cambodian survivors negotiated with a suspicious Vietnamese officer to hitch a ride south on one of the supply trucks if they could help unload at the other end. The officer, on hearing their story, begrudgingly agreed, telling them they would be leaving in thirty minutes. He also found a truck heading west for Chea to travel in with the same arrangement.

'Goodbye, Hem Suvorn. Don't forget what Chea taught you about the fishing,' Han Sen said, smiling at the old monk.

'As long as I just rescue the fish from drowning, I'll be OK, won't I?' He laughed. 'You be sure to come back and see us one day, my boy!'

'Of course! You will have the monastery rebuilt and full of bouzes again in no time, you'll see,' Han Sen said.

The old monk closed his eyes and put both hands together. The four youngsters huddled close to him amidst the throng of military activity. 'A very short prayer from the Buddha for the journey, for my friends.'

'Thousands of candles can be lit from a single candle,
and the life of the candle will not be shortened,
happiness never decreases by being shared.'

He opened his eyes and smiled at all of them in turn. 'May the Enlightened One always travel with you.' He kissed each of the two girls and Chea, He hugged Han Sen. 'You take care of these girls, young man.'

'Yes, yes,' Han Sen replied. 'As soon as I get to civilisation, I'll send you a new robe!'

He was the last one to climb onto the back of the lorry full of fed and watered Vietnamese soldiers. As the truck lurched away from the village, heading south for Sihanouksville, they waved until the old monk disappeared from view.

6. MS Bamboula

To the casual observer, the Motor Ship Mamboula looked as if it wasn't even worth scrapping, more rust seeming to cover its surface area than painted steel. Built originally in 1942 the ship now spent its twilight years running general cargo between ports on the South China Sea. Sometimes it would venture as far as the East Coast of India, and Japan or Korea to the west. The ship's crew would protest to the owners in Limassol if they were given a passage of more than three days, the engine prone to breaking down at every opportunity. The sorry looking ship sat alongside in the river port of Sihanouksville, her creaking derricks slowly offloading cargo in nets onto the bustling quayside. The ship's diesel generator belched clouds of acrid black smoke out of the funnel every time a load was lifted.

Han Sen and the two girls arrived at the port in the back of the military truck and assisted the driver and his colleague to unload the cargo of ammunition boxes. They looked around for a way of finding out where the ship was going next. Raya took charge, haranguing one of the stevedores. She returned with the news that it would depart the following day for Hong Kong, then Shanghai, then Kaohsiung. From his limited geographical knowledge from Sam Lok School and even more limited knowledge of distances, ship speeds and offloading times, Han Sen could see the journey would be at least a week, probably more. The next task was to find out if they could work their passage. Raya volunteered again suggesting that both girls go together to find and discuss this with the ship's captain, hoping he would take pity on two young girls who had lost their families amid the wreckage of Cambodia and were looking to get to Kaohsiung to find their sole remaining relatives.

They watched as a small white van pulled up adjacent to the ship's gangway. From the lettering on the side of the van, they could see it was the ship's agent. A dapper-looking Khmer gentleman got out of the van with a briefcase in hand and headed for the gangway. Han Sen intercepted him, 'Excuse me, sir, we are trying to get to Kaohsiung. Do you think we would be able to work our passage on this ship?'

The man looked at Han Sen, and at the two very thin girls standing behind him. 'All three of you?'

'Yes, sir, I am an engineer and the girls here are excellent cooks.'

'You could ask the skipper, his name is Constanides,' the man said, looking at his watch.

'How do we get to see him, though?' Han Sen gestured towards the guard at the bottom of the gangway. 'Could you introduce us?'

'Yes, very well. Come with me,' the man said. 'Hurry, I haven't got all day.'

'New ship's crew,' he called out abruptly to the guard as he led them hurriedly past and up the ship's gangway. They walked along the main deck and stepped through a doorway into the accommodation of the ship.

The combined smells of diesel fuel, engine oil and fried food hung in the air. They went up two dark, narrow staircases finally arriving at the Captain's cabin behind the navigation bridge. The agent knocked on the door. 'Captain!'

A deep voice came from within the cabin, 'Yes, what is it?'

'I have some people here to see you, they want to go to Kaohsiung. One engineer and two cooks.' He looked at Han Sen, then at his watch again.

A large, swarthy man with black hair bryl-creamed back, and a white shirt with epaulettes opened the door. He looked at the agent, then at Han Sen and the two girls. 'One engineer and two cooks, eh?' he said in a heavily accented Greek accent. 'Which is which here?'

'I am the engineer, sir. My two sisters are excellent cooks. We need to get to Kaohsiung, the Khmer Rouge murdered our families. We have an uncle in Taiwan who we are desperate to see. We will work as hard as you want us to, sir.' Han Sen hoped he didn't sound like he was pleading too much.

'Could you strip and rebuild a diesel engine, boy?'

'Yes sir. I've spent most of my life working in the Ta Veng Electrical Works. We had Kelvin diesels, sir. I noticed your generator is smoking badly under load. If you have the tools and the spares, I'll put it right for you,' Han Sen said eagerly.

'OK, excuse me, please,' he said. 'Chief!' he shouted along the passageway.

A short, white-haired man in oil-stained, once-white overalls emerged from a cabin and ambled slowly along the alleyway towards them. 'Yes Captain?' Another heavy Greek accent.

'This boy says he is an engineer and is good with diesel engines, he says he could fix your generator, do we have spares and tools?'

'We have most of what we need,' the Chief replied. 'Apart from the time, that is. We need to keep the main engine running.'

'OK, good. You three report back tomorrow morning at eight sharp. We sail for Hong Kong on the afternoon tide, so we'll see what you can do in the morning, then we'll make a decision. You'll share one cabin, and we'll feed you, and that's all. OK?'

Han Sen smiled at the large Greek Captain. 'Thank you, sir. We won't let you down.'

The impatient agent accompanied them off the ship, shook hands with Han Sen and the girls, wished them good luck and departed. They slept that night on a bed of pallets and tarpaulins in a dockside warehouse, their only company being the rats scurrying around them while they slept.

The following morning they reported to the guard at just before eight and were ushered onboard. The girls were shown to the ships galley where they were set-to-work assisting the Chinese cook and serving the crew's breakfast. Han Sen was shown down to the cramped and dirty engine room by the old Chief Engineer. He showed him the generator in question. It was one out of three that was still running, the remaining two in a semi stripped down state, obviously cannibalised to keep one running. Han Sen immediately started assessing what tools and spares he would need to strip the machine, the old Chief showing him their on-board stocks. By lunchtime he had made his assessment and reported back to the Chief. The Captain put his head around the Chief's cabin door as the two sat at a table poring over Han Sen's list.

'Well, can he do it?' the Captain asked.

'We need a gasket set but he thinks he can make most of them. Yes, it is obvious he knows what he's doing,' the Chief said with slow deliberation. 'I think we can use him.'

'Good, come on then. I'll show you your cabin and you can make a start.'

The ship sailed on schedule that afternoon, with Han Sen and the two girls having settled into what was the owner's suite. In comparison to the bare steel everywhere else inside the ship, the wood veneer panels, recessed lights and padded seats would have been considered modestly luxurious in 1942. Now it was just plain shabby.

Bobby, the dapper, effeminate Greek steward, fussed around, obviously happy to have guests on board. 'Mr. Sen, you sleep in here, feet this end, head that end. In rough weather, sandwich yourself in with a chair like this.' He demonstrated by placing a chair backwards hard-up against the seat front. 'Here's some clean sheets and a spare pillow. OK?'

Han Sen nodded, smiling. 'Thanks.' No one had ever given him sheets before, let alone clean ones.

'Now, you two girls, you'll be sharing the bed. Here's some clean sheets for you. I've put some towels and some soap in the toilet. I've given you some kitchen whites so you can wash your clothes and hang them up to dry in the toilet. If you play your cards right, you could probably wash Mr. Sen's clothes too now he's got a boiler suit,' he said winking. 'We'll go into town in Hong Kong and buy some clothes for you, the prices are pretty good, I've already organised a whip round among the crew, don't worry about money.'

The girls, not being able to understand English, recognised kindness immediately, giggled and thanked the old Steward in Khmer many times over.

Han Sen started work in the engine room that afternoon and from that point on only emerged for meal-breaks and late at night to sleep. By the morning of the third day, he had got one of the two stripped-down generators running with parts he had found in the store, parts the ship's crew didn't know they had.

The old Chief was delighted. 'They don't make engineers like that anymore,' he said to Captain Constanides that night over dinner. 'The boy is a genius. I was hanging on to some old broken engine parts down there thinking I might be able to repair them one day. He's got the welding set going and welded them all up. That's how he got Number Two generator going. For someone so young, he's got so much knowledge and determination. It's amazing.'

'The girls are making a difference too,' the Captain said quietly so as not to be overheard by the steward or the cook. 'You can't help noticing the cleanliness of the kitchen and the quality of the food over the last day or so.'

'What I wouldn't give to have someone like him on the payroll,' the Chief ruminated, staring down into his empty tea cup.

'Well you know the company's attitude to spending money as well as I do,' the Captain replied. 'Don't worry, I'll make sure they all get kitted out in Hong Kong, I'll be able to hide a couple of hundred dollars against ships expenses.'

'Good. Bobby is organising a whip-round amongst the crew. The money will help them when they get to Taiwan,' the Chief said, pleased Han Sen wasn't slave labour any more.

The ship docked in Hong Kong the following morning. After measuring Han Sen for trousers, shirts and shoes, Bobby and the two girls went into town armed with various currencies from the crew collection, and 200 Hong Kong dollars courtesy of the Captain. The ship's ledger entry showing the payment as just another gift to one of the countless port officials in the region whose avarice generally outshone their usefulness. Han Sen stayed in the engine room, keeping an eye on the repaired generator, at the same time starting on servicing the smoking set. The girls returned in time for lunchtime duties, laden with bags and brimming over with excitement about the shops in downtown Hong Kong. Han Sen was summoned from the engine room to the crew's mess and looked on in amazement as the girls showed the collection of T-shirts, jeans and trainers to the assembled crew.

'Boy these girls are shrewd,' Bobby was telling the Captain. 'We walked out of one shop because they didn't offer us a discount. We were just about to walk out of this one as well when they had a sudden change of heart and gave us another 5%. I felt sorry for the sales assistant, she was almost in tears at the end. These girls have got negotiation skills that Atilla would have been proud of.'

'I'm sure they'll be able to get a job and somewhere to live in Kaohsiung pretty much straight away,' the Captain replied, smiling at the girl's happiness and gratitude. 'I don't think they're used to having stuff given to them.'

'They are both still painfully thin. Those Khmer Rouge bastards all need shooting for doing that to their own people,' the Steward looked on, anger in his eyes.

'Yes, but at least they're still alive. Make sure you feed them up whilst you can,' the Captain said, turning to go. 'I've got to go and see how this cargo's doing.'

'Aye-aye, Captain,' Bobby said, winking at the girls.

Raya and Rao leaned on the ship's rail as the ship slipped its mooring that night and cut a careful path through the teeming waterway of Hong Kong Harbour. The bright downtown lights and the homely looking skyscrapers of Kowloon Island formed a spectacular foreground to the natural amphitheatre of the Sha Tin Mountains. They watched with awe as the aquatic melee went on around them. Precariously laden houseboats, ferries and traditional wooden sailing junks all jostled for space, seemingly oblivious to any danger that the much larger ship presented. As the ship got further out into the harbour, the girls awe heightened as a jet airliner came into land at Kai Tak Airport, cutting directly across the ships bow's in a maelstrom of power, noise and flashing lights. The ship eventually reached the open calm of the South China Sea and set an east-north-east heading for Shanghai. The atmosphere on board the ship calmed slowly after the euphoria of Hong Kong.

It was early morning of their fifth day on board the MS Mamboula when the ship anchored off the great mass of greyness that was Shanghai and the all-enveloping People's Republic of China beyond it. Han Sen had completed all of his repair tasks in the engine room; the ship now had two operational power plants and the Chief had a list of parts drawn up for repairing the third generator and restocking the parts store.

In the tradition of the Ta Veng Electrical Works, Han Sen continued to assist the Chief and made himself busy fixing small leaks, cleaning, polishing and painting. By the time they had dropped their cargo at Shanghai, made the short crossing to the Island of Taiwan and berthed at Kaohsiung, the engine room clearly showed the results of Han Sen's near obsessive work ethic. What was previously a grimy, oily, dark and dangerous mess was now sparkling, bright and functional.

'My, oh my,' the Chief said to Han Sen as they looked down onto the glistening vista from the engine room mezzanine. 'I don't believe what you've done in the short time you've been on board. Don't you ever stop working?'

'Yes of course - to eat and sleep,' the boy smiled.

The old man shook his head, and motioned that they should go up top. 'Come on. Those girls of yours will be getting impatient.'

Following formal bows, handshakes, a kiss from each of the girls in turn for all of the ship's crew and two kisses for the slightly embarrassed Captain, the three young Cambodians walked down the gangway and stood on the Kaohsiung dockside looking up at the assembled crew on the main deck of the MS Mamboula.

'Thanks again,' Han Sen called out.

'Good luck and come and see us next time we're in port,' the Chief replied. 'You can come and fix the last generator!'

'I'll do it,' Han Sen said, waving.

The old Chief grinned, gave them a double thumbs-up and a final wave.

The two girls and Han Sen turned and headed for the port exit. They were on their own in Taiwan.

Acting on Bobby's advice, the first place they headed for was the Seaman's Mission, just a short distance down the road from the main port entrance. Han Sen quickly found Sen Industrial Inc in the telephone directory and noted their name, address and phone number. Having never met his Dad's uncle, he was reluctant to call him with no warning. Instead, he asked the old man behind the counter for directions. In reply, he drew diagrams, gave them bus numbers with an idea of frequency and a taxi telephone number just in case. The three thanked him, bade him a pleasant day and set off to walk to the industrial area on the other side of town where Sen Industrial Inc. was located.

The journey was an interesting, if slightly daunting, insight into the city of Kaohsiung and the country of Taiwan. It was the biggest and busiest city any of them had been in. The main route to the industrial area from the docks was in a north east direction along Jhongshan Road. The route took them through the poorest area of the city where children and dogs played in the streets among untidy, high density tenement-style buildings. The street then broke into a semi-commercial area with low rise offices and larger shops. Then came the glitzy high-rise hotels and department stores. All three looked up in awe at how far the buildings reached towards the sky.

As they walked past the towering Grand Hi-Lai Hotel on Chenggong 1st Road, they stopped to watch porters unload luggage from large, expensive cars.

'One day, when I have my own business,' Han Sen said to the girls, 'I will direct my customers to stay at that hotel. They will be so happy with what I produce for them, I will visit them after work and they will offer to buy me dinner. But I will insist on buying my own dinner.'

'You want to start your own business?' Raya asked.

'Yes,' he replied. 'Look around you. There are opportunities here. This is what it must feel like to be in America.'

'But what about your Uncle, I thought you wanted to work for him?' Raya asked, level-headed as always.

'Yes, yes I do. We need jobs and if he can offer us something then we'll take it,' he said to re-assure the girl. 'It will be a stepping stone for us, and I look forward to meeting my father's uncle. If my father was anything to go by, he will be a good man.'

'I have a feeling that he would let his customers buy his dinner,' Raya smiled at him.

'But you don't know him, how can you say that?'

'It is sometimes a sign of grace to accept gifts offered in good faith.'

'OK, OK, I am sure you are right, oh wise one,' Han Sen said. There was never any point in arguing with Raya, she was always right.

It took them three hours to reach the small industrial estate. Sen Industrial Inc. was a large, glass-fronted showroom crammed with all types of machinery and engineering tools. They stood outside looking at the building and its contents. After a two-week journey, they had finally reached their destination. The next few minutes would decide if they would be welcome in Taiwan or not.

They entered the building.

An old bespectacled man with a goatee beard was behind the counter holding an animated discussion with a smartly dressed customer. The conversation was in Mandarin, and Raya translated for Han Sen. 'The man behind the counter is unhappy with a payment this man is requesting, they will retire to a back office to discuss the matter further.' The man behind the counter ushered the suited man into an office, and called out to the waiting group. 'He's asking if we need help,' Raya said to Han Sen. 'Try your Khmer on him, I think it's Mr. Sen.'

Han Sen walked slowly to the counter, the man showing signs of impatience. 'Excuse us, sir, we are looking for Mr. Sen.'

The man replied in Khmer, 'I am Mr. Sen.'

'Sir, we are from Cambodia. I am Han Sen - your nephew's son. This is Raya and Rao Chebon, they are close family friends. I do not wish to interrupt your business, perhaps we should come back later.'

'You? You are the son of Preap from Ta Veng?' The small man was obviously astonished. 'Unbelievable,' he said making for the office. 'Hold on for a second.' He put his head around the office door and spoke in a flurry of Mandarin. Moments later, the suited man was shown through the exit door, filling his briefcase with papers as he went, smiling and apologising at the same time. 'So, Han Sen, let me look at you,' Mr. Sen said taking hold of Han Sen's shoulders, looking up into his face.

The closeness brought instant recognition and Han Sen saw his father's eyes in the man.

Mr Sen spoke softly. 'What brings you here, my boy?'

The phone rang. A car pulled up outside. 'Sir, I have news from Cambodia. It may be better if we come back later.'

'Hold it there.' Mr. Sen went into another frenzy of activity. 'Ranjiv!' he shouted at the top of his voice, then answered the phone and barked some fast and furious Mandarin into the mouthpiece. As he put the phone down, a tall Asian man in overalls came out of the back of the showroom wiping his hands with a rag. More fast Mandarin ensued and the freshly arrived customers were being dealt with by Ranjiv. Mr Sen flicked a bolt on the main door and flipped the door sign to read 'Closed'.

'Come,' he ushered the group into the side office, showing them to a conference table. 'Please, have a seat. Ranjiv will deal with the showroom and make us some tea when he's finished. Emic! Come and meet your great nephew.' A smart bespectacled man probably only a few years older than Han Sen emerged from a back office, 'Han Sen, this is Emic my youngest son, he looks after the books for the business.' The two shook hands, Emic bowed and smiled at the two girls. 'Now then, Han Sen, you need to introduce me to our two young friends here,' he said, smiling at the two girls. 'Then tell me all about what's been happening in the old country.'

Part 2. 1962 -1982

7. Roger

'Uncle Robert and Auntie Gillian are coming over on Sunday,' Margaret Collins announced to Roger. Her seven year-old son was sitting at the kitchen table, single-mindedly playing with a Lego garage and an army of small plastic characters. 'They'll be bringing your cousins Pip and Amy with them, that'll be nice, won't it?'

'Great,' Roger said. 'Can we play surgeons?'

'Surgeons, what's that darling?'

'Oh nothing, just like doctors really.' Roger had started piling the little plastic characters up on a make-believe funeral-pyre.

'They're only young, darling. They won't want to play any rough games. You could play snakes and ladders with them. We'll probably have a game of rounders in the afternoon.'

'Hmmm, as long as Uncle Robert lets me win,' Roger said, wondering whether the best place for his plastic figures mass funeral should be on the forecourt of his Lego garage, the petrol pumps being so handy.

'I'm sure he will, darling. He did before, didn't he?' she replied.

'Yes, but Pip was cheating. I'd have won easily if she hadn't tried to get me out,' Roger said. Finally deciding that mass funerals were all too bothersome, he walked across the kitchen and tipped all the Lego men into the kitchen bin.

'Roger! These toys cost money, you know. You don't put them in the bin just because you're fed up with them!' She opened the bin and began picking the Lego men out one by one. 'Pip still has flashbacks from last year's game of rounders. I want you to promise me you won't hit anyone this time.'

'But she would have got me out!'

'That's the very idea of playing sports and games – some people win and some people lose. It wouldn't be much fun otherwise, would it?'

'Is there anything to eat?' Roger moped. The word 'sports' summoned up the many tellings-off he'd received over the years. It wasn't his fault - people wanted him to win, *he* wanted to win. He just went that extra step to make sure his competitors didn't have any chance of beating him. From destroying all of the books he read as a child – so no other child could read the same book – to smashing all the painting equipment in the nursery so his would be the best painting. Then there was the clubbing of his cousin with the rounders bat just in case she got him out again. Pre-emptive strikes had always been Roger's philosophy on competing. Fairness was not a concept he had been able to come to terms with just yet.

Uncle Bob and Auntie Gill arrived on the Sunday as arranged, with their two slightly nervous-looking daughters. The men disappeared into the garage to discuss old motorcycles and beer whilst the women stayed in the lounge with the children, eventually disappearing into the kitchen to prepare lunch, leaving their offspring ostensibly playing snakes and ladders. They heard the first screams from one of the girls five minutes later, the crying six year-old running into the kitchen.

'Mummy,' Pip sobbed, clutching her throat. 'Roger strangled me with his rubber snake.'

Whilst the mother placated her little girl, Margaret chastised her son. 'Up to your room! Right now! Why do you have to be so horrible all the time?'

'But Mum,' Roger replied, a look of hurt injustice crossing his face. 'She was cheating again.'

'Roger, how many times do I have to tell you? It's a game. Now get to your room.' She looked at her sister. 'Sorry Gill. Can I get you a drink, Pip? Don't worry, Roger will calm down later.'

The game of rounders never took place, the thought of Roger with a bat in hand was somehow too vivid in their collective memories. Margaret's recollection of the conversation regarding her son's intended game of 'surgeons' was bought back into sharp focus later in the afternoon when Amy sidled up to her and said, 'Auntie Margaret, we wondered whether you had anything we could use as an anaesthetic. Roger said something about Chloroform.'

'Chloroform? Oh my God,' she cried, leaping up from the sun lounger and racing into the house. 'Roger, no!'

Neither of the two girls had seen the large carving knife that Roger had stolen from the kitchen earlier in the week and naturally assumed that Roger was play-acting when he suggested an operation on the older of the two girls. Luckily for Amy, Roger's keenness to plunge the ten inch blade into her lower abdomen was delayed by the two girls' insistence that some anaesthetic be administered. Roger's mother almost breaking the door down and the ensuing stampede of agitated parents into Roger's bedroom to find Amy strapped crudely to Roger's bed, was sufficient to call an abrupt halt to Roger's diabolical intentions.

'Depression?' David Collins said to the family doctor on hearing Roger's diagnosis for the first time. 'He seems OK to me.'

'It's a 1969 way of saying your son suffers from a severe form of anxiety,' the doctor replied. 'Nothing to worry about, the medication is very good these days, hardly any side effects.'

'Surely there is something we can do other than give him drugs?'

'Well yes, I can think of a few suggestions, not specifically medical but you could try spending more one-on-one time with the boy. Take an interest in what he does. Encourage him to try different things, so that he has a varied set of interests; this would make him into a more rounded person and able to deal with the knocks he'll get in life, make him more resilient, if you know what I mean. Channel his aggression, feed it into something positive, make sure he doesn't have time to sit around thinking about things. Maybe even a pet of some sort. A relationship with an animal could be therapeutic for him, maybe show him the value of friendship and camaraderie.'

The conversation with the doctor served as a wake-up call to David. Ever since starting his re-insurance business; Liechtenstein Re three years back, he was always conscious that he spent too much time working.

'The doctor reckons I need to spend more one on one time with Roger,' he said to Margaret over dinner that night as they discussed the Doctor's diagnosis. 'I've always spent as much of the weekend with Roger as I possibly can.'

'A few hours on Sundays?' Margaret said

'Darling!' He looked at her with genuine surprise. 'I am running a two million pound business – it *does* take a lot of my time. All of this doesn't grow on trees you know,' he said, gesturing around at their large, modern kitchen. 'And we need time together, don't we?' He got up and went around the table to massage her shoulders. 'Besides, the more effort I put into the business now, the earlier I'll be able to let Roger take over and we can slope off somewhere over the horizon – no?'

'Hmm,' she groaned, enjoying his touch. 'Try and get home earlier darling, and spend some quality time with him. It will help him get through this, whatever it is - depression.'

'I don't understand it, he has everything he wants. And more! Why is he depressed?'

'He hasn't changed since he was a baby. He's always had a nasty, vengeful streak. It's like he isn't our child sometimes.'

'You're right, the doctor's right,' David said, collecting up the dinner plates. 'I will spend more time with him. From now on I'm going to start delegating, whether Edgar likes it or not.'

After much debate, it was decided that they would get a dog, a Doberman. It would be called Herman in recognition of its German ancestry. There though, any parallels with its fellow national's qualities of superior intelligence and ruthless efficiency, ended. The animal, in common with the breed as they later discovered, was blessed with very limited brainpower. Training the beast was a haphazard process involving bribery and cajoling with titbits of food and kind words. Harsh words made him lie down and cower, a paw over each ear, all hurt.

As a pup, it had a voracious appetite for furniture, constantly attempting to ingest anything and everything in the house. Chairs, sideboard, kitchen cabinets - all suffered appalling damage at the gnawing teeth of Herman. Harsh words were frequent at this stage of his upbringing. Even Roger, not averse to destroying the odd household item himself in his frequent fits of temper, would join in the castigation process. Both parents took this as a good sign as long as the castigation stopped at verbal admonishments. Roger being Roger though, would want to broaden the scope of the process and would dream up horrible punishments for the animal including elaborate execution ceremonies.

As time went on, the relationship between boy and dog grew into something approaching mutual respect and understanding. The dog became sufficiently streetwise to stay out of Roger's way when he was in a foul mood, and Roger began to appreciate just how far he could push Herman before the animal would wish to vent serious retribution.

The dog displayed similar personality traits to those of Roger amongst its own kind. When he was with the family he was placid, irrepressibly affectionate and curious. Put him in the company of other dogs though, and carnage would invariably ensue. The local park became his killing ground. Smaller dogs would, without prior notice, immediately want to relieve their bowels on seeing, hearing or scenting Herman's intimidating persona. David took control of the situation by only ever publicly releasing the dog in tightly controlled circumstances.

All in all, following his weaning-off of the furniture diet, and controlling his appetite for cold-blooded savagery in doggie company,

David and Margaret both agreed that Herman was a good thing, and that Roger's social skills had improved since he came into their lives.

*

The year six class had been tasked with clearing up the garden area of the school. Roger was loitering behind the potting shed, studiously avoiding anything that looked like physical work. Roland Jenks, the largest boy in the class, was being told off by the teacher, Miss Ramsey, for ripping up the plants instead of the weeds.

'But Miss, I didn't know. They looked just like weeds,' Jenks said, upset at being told off.

'Jenks you're worse than useless at weeding,' Miss Ramsey said. 'Let one of the girls do it. Go and find Collins – he can give you a hand to move some of these bags of compost.'

Jenks dutifully handed the hoe over to one of the girls and went off in search of Roger. 'Oi, Collins,' Jenks said on discovering Roger shirking behind the potting shed. 'Miss Ramsey says you've got to help me shift the compost bags.'

'Well, tell her to go and shift them herself, fatso,' Roger said, sneering.

'I'm going to tell her you said that,' Jenks countered, turning to go.

'Boo-hoo, I'm scared. Tell her that she's an ugly old bag too,' Roger scoffed.

Jenks stopped in his tracks and turned around. Roger had unknowingly touched on a sensitive spot - Jenks loved Miss Ramsey with a passion. 'What did you say?' he asked, knowing full well.

'Are you deaf as well as Welsh, fat boy?' Roger asked casually, unaware of the red mist descending on the powerfully built Jenks.

'You little shit,' Jenks shouted as he charged towards the wide-eyed Roger, flattening him on impact with a mixture of weight and velocity. With Roger pinned to the ground on his back, the larger boy straddled his chest and started punching him as hard as he could. 'You don't care about anyone, do you?' Jenks screamed. 'I hate you, I hate you!'

Miss Ramsey heard the commotion behind the potting shed and came running over to separate the two boys. 'Jenks stop! Get off him this minute! What do you think you're doing, boy?'

Jenks slowly got to his feet, looking down at the bleeding Roger with disdain.

'Well, answer me, what on earth is going on?' Miss Ramsey demanded to know.

'Nothing, Miss, I just lost my temper.' Jenks said, examining his hurting hands.

'He's a fat troublemaker,' Roger said through tears of pain.

Jenks made to rush Roger again but Miss Ramsey caught him and held on voraciously. 'Collins that's enough! Get yourself cleaned up and go see matron. Jenks, you come with me,' she said, noticing curious faces appearing at the side of the potting shed. 'The rest of the class get on with what you are doing, I won't be long.'

Once they were back in the deserted classroom, Miss Ramsey sat the distraught Jenks down at his desk, took a chair from the opposite row and sat adjacent to him.

'I know you, Jenks. That was not you out there, was it?'

'No, Miss,' he said, sniffling. 'I've never hit anybody before.'

'It was something Roger did or said, am I right?'

He was shaking so much, he could barely get the words out. 'Yes, Miss.'

'I'm not going to ask you what he said or did, because we all know what he can be like. What I am going to ask you may sound a bit daft,' the teacher hesitated. 'But I want you to try and help Roger. I know this sounds crazy, but he needs someone to look up to. A role model, if you like. You've just given him a beating, I'm of the opinion that someone was going to do it sooner or later, it just so happens it was you. Can you take him under your wing a bit from now on? Let him see that you don't hold a grudge and that tolerance is the best strategy. Can you do that for me Roland?'

The boy looked at the teacher, the woman he loved unconditionally. 'Yes, Miss, I'll try.'

'Good boy. Now stay there, I'll go and find Collins and we'll see if we can patch it up between you.'

Five minutes later, Miss Ramsey came back to the classroom with a bruised but cleaned up Roger. She got Roger to sit down next to Jenks and stood in front of both of them.

'Right you two. You've had a fight. Now if either of you have ever watched boxing on the telly, what do the two fighters do after they've finished fighting? While they're still in the ring, that is. Do either of you know?'

Both boys remained silent.

'I'll tell you what they do then. They embrace each other. Or shake hands, or give each other some sort of sign that says, it's all over now, we can be friends again, and by the way, I'm sorry if I hurt you but it had to be done. That's what they do at the end of a fight.

Now I don't know what caused the two of you to fight each other but if I know anything at all about the people in this class, I would guess that you Roger said something to Roland that made him very angry. Is that correct, Roger?'

'Yes, Miss'

'Thank you for being honest. Now whatever it was you said to Roland, do you think you really needed to say those words? Did saying them make you feel any better or make you feel happy?'

'No, Miss.'

'So the point I'm making is that both of you are a lot less happy than before you said those words. They didn't serve any real purpose at all. Think about that every time you open your mouth to speak in future. Ask yourself, is what I'm about to say going to make me, or the person I'm saying the words to, unhappy? If the answer is yes, what do you do, Roger?'

'Don't say the words, Miss.'

'Very good. What I am going to ask you to do is look out for each other. Roger, you're one of the cleverer ones in class, I want you to help Roland when he's got a problem. Roland, you're big and strong, you help Roger if any of the older kids cause him any problems. OK?'

'Yes, Miss,' they answered in unison.

'From now on, you'll be sitting next to one another in class. I want you to shake hands, because that's what men normally do to show that they respect one another. Boys?' She gestured for them to shake hands, which they did, somewhat haltingly. 'Thank you both, and don't forget what I said, you're to help one another out. Back to the rest of the class now.'

So it was with Miss Ramsey's somewhat unconventional assistance, the two were thrown together. Roger, with Jenks as an ally, became a more malleable pupil and got noticeably easier going. Jenks with Roger as an ally became much more assertive and confident. Theirs would never be a friendship; more a relationship based on a grudging respect. Neither of them would forget the events in the garden that afternoon, and Miss Ramsey's words.

Although Roger had been ejected from the Cubs at an early age, some of the boys at school, including Jenks, were still in the Scouts and sometimes talked about their days at the local sailing base. Somehow it appealed to him.

'Dad, can we go sailing?' Roger asked one day.

'Sailing?' David asked, surprised.

'Yes – you know the Scouts go to the sailing base every month,' Roger said enthusiastically.

'Did you want to join the Scouts again?' David asked, even more surprised.

'Well not really, but if it means I can go sailing, then yes, I suppose I'll have to,' Roger said.

'You'll have to behave yourself, son,' David said to him, looking him in the eye to make sure he understood. 'No more temper tantrums; they won't take kindly to you sinking any of their boats. We may also have to do a bit of grovelling to get you back into the Scout Group; they don't forget, you know.' Then he muttered, 'I hope the boy you set about doesn't go there, I'm thinking more about his parents, they were the ones that pressed the assault charges.'

'No, he left a few weeks after he joined, according to Jenks. I promise I'll behave, Dad,' he shrugged, rolling his eyes to the heavens. 'Because I really want to do this. Scout's Honour.'

Sailing became almost an obsession with Roger, if he missed a session for any reason, he would be irritable and grumpy. When he was sailing it was as if he was born to it, the movements needed to jibe and go about and all the other techniques required for manoeuvring the small wooden Coypu dinghies around the lake seemed to come naturally to him.

David took them to the London Boat Show in 1974. Roger was so excited looking around the big boats that David soon got wrapped up in his enthusiasm and ended up agreeing to look at a second-hand sailboat. David and Margaret had never seen Roger so excited as the day they drove to Southampton to take the boat for a trial sail. He thought the boat was the best thing he'd ever seen. This huge glass-fibre structure was magic. It had an engine, a galley, a really comfortable bed to sleep on but best of all, it had a huge mainsail. The Solent was too windy for them to put it all out that day. It was Roger's ambition from then on that the mainsail would be hoisted at the very earliest opportunity, and the spinnaker put out too. He craved the feeling of speed through the water, just like he had in his Coypu.

8. *Tania and Snowy*

The one and only time that David bribed his son was when he bought the boat they had trialled in the Solent that summer. Roger's part of the deal was that he would go to the local grammar school; keep a positive attitude and work hard in order to leave with some decent qualifications.

The forty-something foot glass-fibre boat was duly handed over in the South Coast marina and christened Tania - not for any reason other than the fact that David liked the name and Roger couldn't think of anything he liked better. His love affair with the boat lasted exactly one vomit-sodden trip around the Isle of Wight. The boat, and particularly the sea, turning in Roger's mind from the best thing in the world to the most awful two things ever created. Tania was sold the following season.

Roger's resolve to change his attitude towards school did not last long either. The appalling anti-social behaviour that he displayed so effortlessly at nursery, infant and junior school continued at a slower, more relaxed pace at senior level. His previously insane competitiveness had been tempered somewhat by his sailing experiences. His love of being on the water in the small dinghies somehow just about overcame his instinct to destroy his fellow sailing enthusiast's boats, even when they did manage to beat him. His early attempt to disable competitor boats was stamped on hard by the sailing instructors.

Jenks kept Roger out of serious trouble at school most of the time, but problems would arise when the big Welsh lad wasn't around. The lesser troublemakers of the school would inveigle themselves with Roger in the hope of him doing something particularly dreadful that they would be party to but wouldn't necessarily get the blame for. They would lead him into situations with potentially perilous consequences, purely for the sake of it. One of the leading proponents of this form of troublemaking by proxy was an old adversary of Jenks' called Billy Cooper. He was the un-named leader of a group of under-achievers in the class immediately below Roger's. The bottom class.

'Hey Collins, Hilary Saunders fancies you,' Cooper said to Roger one lunchtime as they were queuing for sausage and chips in the canteen. 'She told me.'

'Yes, yes, of course she does, Cooper. What about Pat Barry then? Dumped her, has he?' Roger asked sceptically. Pat Barry was the acknowledged hardest of the hard. Rumoured to be a champion boxer in his native Ireland before his family came to leafy Surrey, everyone took great care in treating Mr. Barry and his lady of the day - currently Hilary Saunders - with the utmost respect.

'Yes, of course he has. Don't fancy soiled goods then?' Cooper asked.

'She's all right, I suppose, not exactly Raquel Welch but she'll do.' Inwardly, Roger was turning to jelly. Of course she'd do, she was beautiful, far too beautiful for him, but maybe…

He followed Hilary and her friends after school that night, furtively lingering out of sight until all of her friends had gone their separate ways. Then he made his approach. 'Are you doing anything later?' he asked her quietly on the street corner.

'What do you mean? Why are you asking me?' The girl responded, obviously unaware of any Cupid's bow, potential or otherwise, poised in the early evening glow of summer.

'Well, you know, I thought we could go somewhere and, you know, do something, or something,' Roger stammered.

'Are you mad? I don't know you. I don't even know who you are or where you come from. Now just bugger off,' she turned to go.

'Wait,' Roger put his hand on her shoulder.

The girl screamed, 'Get off me, you freak!'

It was at this very moment that Pat Barry and two other compatriots emerged from a side-road. All three looked over in astonishment and immediately started running towards the inadvertently mismatched couple. On sight of the infamous Barry and friends, Roger's first thought was that Cooper was going to die a slow and painful death. His second thought was one of pure self-preservation.

He said to the girl hurriedly, 'Look, I'm sorry. Bloody Cooper told me you fancied me. I'm going to kill him. Tell Pat I brought your pencil case or something, can you? I'll give you a tenner.' He glanced over the girl's shoulder, the three boys were almost on them.

'You alright, Hil?' asked Pat Barry, the leather soles of his brogue shoes slamming into the pavement as he came to a halt. He was glaring at Roger, his heavy eyes saying *I'd really like to hurt you.*

'Yes, Pat, I'm fine. This boy found my pencil case. Lucky, wasn't it?' The girl said calmly, smiling up at her Gaelic beau.

'What was he touching you for then?' asked the hackled-up Irishman.

'Oh he's naturally tactile, he can't help it,' said the girl. She was laughing gaily now. Life was such a breeze.

'He's what?' asked Pat Barry still looking at Roger, the bloodlust in his eyes unabating.

'Tactile. You know, it's a kind of syndrome, you've only got to look at him – you can tell he's a bit simple,' the girl expounded, really getting into her stride now. Roger was slightly hurt but nonetheless still madly in love.

The Irish boy turned to Roger. 'Well, I tell you something, Collins, if I find out you's been trying to chat me' bird up, I'm personally going to cut your balls off. Then I'm going to make you eat them. Got that?' As if seeking confirmation, the emerald-isle pugilist proffered Roger a distinctly unfriendly double-slap on the cheek as a final flourish. He and his colleagues turned, with final glares all round, and walked back the way they had come from. 'I'll see you later, Hils,' Barry called over his shoulder.

'Yes, bye Pat,' the girl called out demurely, and to Roger she said quietly yet incisively, 'Tomorrow then. Two fivers, in an envelope, in my desk. See you.'

Roger's first instinct was to rush around to Cooper's house and show him a thing or two about life, like how heads can get accidentally on purpose flushed down toilets. But having seen at first hand the operational skills of the delightful Hilary, decided that revenge could take on a much more elegant dimension, given some thought and planning, and not least of all, an element of surprise.

He walked home deep in thought. Didn't Jenks tell him once that Cooper kept rabbits?

So it was that the next morning, in the lower tutor group classroom, Billy Cooper opened up his regulation top-opening desk, to find Snowy, his four and a half year old, lop-eared doe rabbit neatly and clinically dissected from neck to tail, with his outer flesh pinned, textbook style to the inside bottom surface of the desk. The unfortunate animal's entrails parked tidily in a heap on its right hand side. Cooper immediately ran out of the classroom screaming, at the same time trying vainly with both hands to halt the flow of vomit that was projecting itself involuntarily from the very depths of his stomach. Several of the girls in the class fainted, despite being told in no uncertain manner by the class tutor to stay away and not to look, they just couldn't resist a peak. Some of the less squeamish class members painted vivid descriptions to their erstwhile classmates, causing some of them to also faint. Matron had her busiest day since ward rotas in World War 2.

There was an inquest, and Roger did get found out, having been spotted with a writhing sack late at night by a nosy neighbour who informed the police. He was shamed by the headmaster in front of the whole school for his pains. David and Margaret offered to replace the rabbit but their offer was declined, the Cooper family being in official mourning for their beloved and irreplaceable Snowy. The tragic animal became folklore in the school from that point onwards.

Roger's final school years were an academic disaster. He felt, and this was probably the view of most of his teachers, that he was there simply to make the numbers up and because attending school was compulsory. His relationship with Cooper developed into a blood feud, with mutual death threats being a regular occurrence, Jenks being the one who managed to forcefully keep them apart from one another. Hilary did dump Pat Barry eventually and whenever she passed Roger in the corridor there was a knowing look that passed between the two of them, sometimes even a smile which never failed to set Roger's juices flowing, so much so that he would often have to go and sit down and cross his legs and wait for the bulge in his trousers to recede.

His lack of effort at schoolwork caused problems at home. David still made it clear that he wanted Roger to take over the business one day, and the more he pushed Roger to work harder, the worse Roger would perform. This downward spiral did nothing for the relationship between the two of them and Margaret was often the go between, ferrying between the two brooding males of the family with ultimatums and suggestions that invariably fell on deaf ears. Roger's only interest was sailing, and even that was limited now to a visit to the sailing base once a month or even less.

He left senior school in 1977 with one pass at CSE in Biology. This prompted the mother-of-all showdowns between Roger and his father.

'What do you mean, you couldn't be bothered? Did you have something else more important to do? Your whole five years at the grammar school have been a total waste!'

'All you ever think about is what you want to do, your bloody Scouts and your business and your motorbikes and your church. You don't care about me. What does it matter to you that I haven't got any qualifications? All you want me to do well at school for is so I can take over your precious business. Well you can go and fuck yourself, because I'm not interested in it.'

'Don't you dare use language like that in front of your mother!' David retorted, red faced, 'Can we not talk about this adult to adult, please?'

'Yes we could, but it would be the same thing all over again, wouldn't it? What are you going to do with your life, Roger? And when are you going to take over the business, Roger? I'm sick of it. I'm leaving this dump, just as soon as I can.' With that he walked out of the kitchen and up the stairs to his bedroom.

Margaret cried as David held her. 'Where oh where did we go wrong, David?' she sobbed. 'The things we've done for that boy, we went through hell in the early years, and it hasn't got any better.'

'He'll come around, my love, he'll come around, they all do eventually, so people tell me,' David said, ever the optimist.

For the first few weeks after leaving school, he rose late, skulking around the house, getting extremely bored, taking his frustration out on his mother, and disappearing for long spells to avoid contact with his father.

It was David who broke the silence by strolling into Roger's bedroom one evening.

'Rodge, do you want a job?'

'Not really, depends what it is, I suppose.'

'Look, I know it's not much but you did seem quite interested in biology and nature; Jim over at Badgers Farm is looking for help at the moment. Money would be all right and the hours not too long. Fancy it?'

'No, you get covered in shit there, don't you remember?' They had spent a bit of time there when Roger was young. No comment was made at the time but the turkey sheds had obviously made a lasting impression.

'Did you have something else in mind then?' David asked, expecting the worst.

'Well, yes actually,' Roger said, waiting for the surprised questioning onslaught.

'Yes?' David asked breathlessly.

'Could I work for Lichtenstein Re for a while?' Roger looked his father in the eye.

David was shocked. 'Well, yes, of course you can, son. Did you have in mind what you wanted to do?'

'No, there must be something I could do there though, isn't there?' Roger asked, hopefully.

'Yes, yes of course, we'll find you something. What about the train every day?'

The thought of sharing a carriage with his dad every morning and every evening made him feel sick. 'I was thinking, you know, your flat? Could I live there during the week?'

The company had a small flat in the Barbican for visitors on business trips to London. David was appalled. 'No, Roger, I'm sorry but that flat is in almost constant use, and besides, you're only sixteen, you couldn't possibly look after yourself living on your own. The Barbican is full of older people, it's no place for a youngster. In fact I don't think the flat management company would let you live there on your own.'

'Well there's a surprise, I'll never be able to do anything on my own then, will I?' Roger said resignedly, turning over on his bed, going back to the magazine he'd been reading.

'Look, son, there's nothing that would please me more than you coming into the business. You know that I want you to take the business over eventually. What I'd rather you do is go out and get some life experience and come back into the business when you're ready. I'll give you all the training you need then.'

'Can't you just sell it and give me the money instead?' Roger asked, still facing the wall.

'Son, that's just plain daft, you've got to do something with your life.' David said.

'According to you - yes. I'm happy doing what I'm doing now, thanks,' Roger said with an air of finality.

'You keep on about us treating you like an adult, and look at you. You've got some serious growing up to do.' David looked at his son for a while, then left the room shaking his head.

After almost a year of getting on everybody's nerves, Roger eventually got a summer job instructing at the sailing base and helping to maintain the boats. He was a gawky seventeen year old, still with no real friends and still not sure what direction he should be going in. Somehow his passion for the water and the Coypu dinghies overcame everything and he lost himself in his work through the summer of 1979.

Charlie, the head instructor, was an ex yacht-skipper, originally from Melbourne, Australia. He had fallen out of a Bosun's Chair whilst making a mast repair on one of the boats he'd worked on. The fall sent him crashing 15 metres onto the deck of the boat, fracturing his spine in the process; he now pushed himself around in his wheelchair, his eyes still full of passion for the sailing life. Often during the day and sometimes at the pub after work, Charlie would mesmerise Roger by telling him stories about life at sea. The conversation would nearly always be about the boats he'd sailed on, the characters he'd sailed with and the experiences in various foreign parts during his life as a skipper. He laughed long and hard on hearing about Roger's horrible time on his dad's boat.

'You didn't give it enough time, mate. You've got to give your sea legs time to mature,' Charlie said, beaming at him. 'Even seasoned sailors are still chundering after the first week, they always have to watch what they eat before going on watch.'

'Well, I doubt if anyone would employ someone like me with one CSE in biology,' Roger said disconsolately.

'You are joking, mate? I know people who would give you a job tomorrow! These racing boat types are always after fit young blokes like you who know how to put a boat about in a wind, get the best from her, you know? Come on, I've seen you out there - you know exactly what you're doing. Tell you what, if you fancy it, I could get you a job on a yacht in the Caribbean before this place closes next month for the winter? I dare you to tell me you don't fancy it!' Charlie sat back, bronzed arms crossed, looking at Roger with that familiar beaming smile.

Roger looked at Charlie as if he had just been electrified. His mind was racing with thoughts about bigger boats, sunny climes and, girls.

'Sailing? In the Caribbean? Who with?' was his Mum's spontaneous reaction to Roger's announcement that sailing was to be his chosen profession, at least for the next few months.

'Look, Mum, rich people and corporations own the boats; they need crew to race them. I know how to make the boats go fast. It's about the only thing I really know how to do well. I can earn money at it and it's what I want to do. Don't worry, I'll be all right.'

'I'm deeply envious son,' David smiled proudly, 'this will be really good for you. Do you need any money?'

The last question stopped Roger from making his usual withering reply. 'Well, actually Dad, the air-fare would be a great help. I've got some money saved but it won't cover that. 600 quid should be enough.'

And with that he was off to Nassau for his very first Race Week. Roger's first full time career had begun.

9. Curtis McGraw

Roger sat in the aircraft wondering just what lay in store for him in Nassau. He thought back to Charlie finding out from one of his old sailing chums that a race-boat owner was looking for experienced crew. Charlie then called this owner, a Mr. Curtis McGraw Junior, originally from Van Cleave, Mississippi, now a successful fruit wholesaler on the island. He had described to the American businessman in glowing detail, the finer points of Roger's racing skills in small boats.

'Hear what you're saying Charlie. This boy, you say he's been on just the one big sailboat? What you trying to sell me here, son; a green gilled rookie?' Roger, standing next to Charlie in the workshop at the sailing base, hearing the staccato Southern drawl through the telephone earpiece, imagined a fat man in a white suit, matching Stetson and a large Havana cigar, chewed at the end.

'Mr. McGraw, I promise you, this boy is something special. I can vouch for the fact that he can make a boat go as fast as you'll ever see it.'

'Well, Charlie, if he gets out here and he's got his head over the rail instead of playing with them sails, making m' boat go fast, he'll be on the next plane home. Trust me on that one, boy!'

'Shall we make the arrangements then Mr. McGraw?' Charlie grinned at Roger.

'Make that Curt, can you? Go ahead, Charlie, put all the expenses on my account.'

Charlie fisted the air low down several times, eyes gleaming, phone still at his left ear.

The American drawl continued, 'Call my London office number, they'll make all the arrangements for the kid. He needs to be here by Friday, first race Sunday. This is all on your head, son. If it don't work out, your name will be mud in the industry, I can guarantee you.'

'Thanks Mr. McGraw, I wouldn't have called you if I wasn't sure.'

'We'll see the kid on Friday. You take care. Baah now.'

'Bye Mr. McGraw, I mean Curt.' He put the phone back on the cradle. Charlie grabbed hold of Roger and hugged him. Roger, unused to physical contact, briefly considered whether he'd been too hasty. Nonetheless he hugged Charlie back to show his gratitude.

Sitting in the Boeing 747 en route to the Caribbean, sipping his pre-dinner drink and watching the in-flight movie, he thought for the first time in his life just how lucky he was. Gratitude was not a concept that had been a regular visitor in Roger's mind and now, he vowed that one day he would visit Charlie and somehow show just how much he appreciated being given this opportunity. He was astonished at how powerfully he felt about not letting Charlie down and making the McGraw boat a racing success.

The full blast of the Caribbean early summer temperature and humidity hit him immediately on stepping out of the aeroplane. The lush vegetation on the hillsides in the distance and the scudding, cloudy-bright sky told him he'd arrived somewhere a million miles away from Surrey, and for a moment he suddenly felt very daunted and a little homesick.

Having claimed his solitary suitcase and cleared immigration and customs, Roger emerged blinking into the sharp daylight of the arrivals hall. Among the crowd waiting for the travellers to emerge, he spotted a middle-aged, peak-capped chauffeur holding aloft a sign with the words, R. Collins – McGraw Strutt scribbled untidily on the front face. Roger signalled to him, whereby the chauffeur broke into a huge grin and started bursting through the throng of waiting drivers and families.

'Mr. Collins – welcome to Nassau, sir,' he announced, bowing deeply. 'Let me take that trolley, you must be tired. I am going to take you to see Mr. McGraw, then onto your apartment. We'll probably go to the boat in the morning – too late today, you'll need to rest. Did you have a good flight?' And so it went on until they pulled up outside the swankiest downtown office building Roger had seen since his arrival. The driver introduced him to Mr. McGraw's PA, and said formally, 'Roger; I shall be outside in the motor. See you when you're done.' And was gone.

The PA showed Roger into Mr. McGraw's spectacularly large office.

'Hello Roger! I've heard all about you. Curtis McGraw, call me Curt,' he said, shaking Roger's hand vigorously, at the same time gesturing Roger to the leather Chesterfield over by the fireplace. 'Charlie tells me you know how to handle a boat. I'm trusting Charlie on this one; you must be good.' It was a statement rather than a question and Roger was momentarily unsure of what to say.

'Yes, Mr. McGraw, Curt. Charlie and me would race each other on the lake quite a bit. I've won a few competitions, too.'

'What sort of boat, son?' McGraw asked, settling down into his leather chair with a cigar, the only artefact that Roger had imagined correctly.

'A Coypu sir, seventeen feet overall, wooden hull, they do twenty knots in a Force Five,' Roger said confidently.

'Hah - sounds scary! And what about this larger boat? Your, er, short-lived seagoing experience? What was that?' McGraw asked, enjoying himself.

'My Dad's Westerly forty-nine footer, lovely boat,' Roger lied. 'He's still got it but he doesn't use it, too busy with other things.'

'I know the problem – reckon you're up to Ocean sailing?'

Roger felt comfortable with McGraw's direct and disarming questions. 'If I can make the boat go as well as I can with the Coypus, sir, then we'll be onto something,' he replied.

'Hey, that's the spirit, son. I'm a great believer in giving people an opportunity to prove themselves. Our boat's bigger than your old man's. It's a sixty foot racer, ketch rigged with a spinnaker. When that spinnaker's up, she's good for twenty five knots downwind. All depending on who's in charge though, son, if you know what I mean,' he said winking. 'We'll go down to the boat tomorrow and take her out around the bay, maybe around the island, see what you think. Get a good night's sleep.'

The driver drove Roger to his apartment on Ocean Drive, wished him a pleasant night's sleep and arranged to pick him up at nine the following morning. Roger couldn't believe how friendly everybody was. This really was a tropical paradise. He called his mum, excitedly telling her all about the take-off and landing, the island, his chauffeur, Mr. McGraw and his own apartment.

On the end of the line his mother was spellbound. 'Roger, you are so lucky – how will you ever repay Charlie for all of this?'

'The best way for me to repay Charlie is to make Mr. McGraw's boat really go – that's what he wants me to do and that's what I'll do,' Roger replied.

'Will you be all right with the sea?' she asked. 'You've got your tablets, haven't you?

'Yes, Mum, don't worry, I'll be fine,' he replied.

Roger was up at five; he couldn't wait to get down to the boat. As he looked out from his balcony over the harbour towards the milky blue sea, he noticed a long, lazy swell coming in from the Atlantic. Probably not the best sailing conditions, but boy, was it beautiful.

Emess One was breathtakingly beautiful. Even sitting alongside the jetty he could tell this was a seriously fast sailboat, worlds apart from the pot-bellied cruising boats Roger had seen in the Solent. The vivid morning sunlight glinted on the brilliant white gel-coat and the polished alloy deck fittings. The sleek, shallow hull seemed to be perched on top of the jade blue water rather than in it.

Roger looked up, shielding his eyes from the sun's glare, seeing the black aerodynamically shaped mast, the spars and the rigging wires towering high above the dock. The first shot of adrenalin started to flow as he surveyed the scene on the dock that morning. He looked for similarities to the Coypu sail rig but there was only one; that being the mainsail, attached to the mast and the boom, but on a scale of about one to a thousand. The foresail and the spinnaker were completely new to him; he would have to watch how that whole process was handled on board.

Curtis McGraw raised his head above the washboard recess and beckoned Roger on board. 'Morning, son. Welcome to *Emmess One*. Come on board, we've got some goodies for you.'

Roger climbed carefully onto the sparse white deck and made his way along the boat and into the cavernous cockpit area. They were surrounded by double handed winches and coils of various coloured ropes, the whole area dominated by the massive black, intimidating boom. Glimpsing down into what on normal boats would be a saloon, he saw it was completely bare, no seats, no deck-head or cabin floor lining, just bare fibre-glass. No comfort here, he thought to himself. Comfort on a boat was weight, and weight slowed you down. This was a lot more like the Coypu than he had anticipated, he thought, smiling at the ridiculous comparison.

'This is all yours, son,' Curtis McGraw said, laying out a tray containing all the accoutrements required for being a crew member on a racing sailboat. 'Two sets of quick drying shorts and sail tops, all with our logo. We like to keep it modest.' He chuckled, the McGraw Strutt logos emblazoned on practically all of the material area. 'Ray-Ban sunglasses with stogies to keep them on your head, deck shoes, sun block and a complete set of foul weather gear stashed below in the wet locker. How's that?' he asked, beaming.

'Wow, all for me?'

'I'm expecting great things from you, Roger,' the brash American replied. 'It's important to look the part, especially when you're the winning team!'

He guessed this was Curtis McGraw Junior's way of motivating people. He liked the bullish American, and so far did not feel intimidated. No matter how tough it became with his new boss, he was still being driven by Charlie.

They left the dock in the afternoon, Roger having been introduced to the crew of eleven and given a complete rundown as to how the boat was run and what each individual piece of equipment was for. It was intended that Roger would sail as the tactician, reporting to the skipper of the boat and the owner. He started off on the helm, guiding the boat around the bay with the large six-foot diameter, leather-clad steering wheel. The thousand to one comparison to the Coypu he'd noticed earlier on the dock was equally applicable to the excitement he was feeling at driving this huge boat.

As they cleared the harbour, the engine was switched off and both sails were rigged in earnest to make the most of the stiffening breeze. Roger's sailing instincts began to take over and as Curt called out headings, so he trimmed the boat to give them maximum speed for the conditions, all the time watching the binnacle mounted compass heading. He could feel the power in the boat generated by the two massive sails, they were running into the wind and tacking to give them the best advantage. They rounded the Southern end of the island and headed downwind. The spinnaker was raised and the boat reached twenty-three knots, with Roger calling out instructions to the crew and Curt at the helm.

'You did good, boy, I'm impressed.' Curt said to him as they stepped off the boat onto the dock. 'We'll show those suckers tomorrow,' he said gesturing towards the growing group of racing boats at the far end of the harbour. 'On Monday, when we're all done racing for a while, I'll show you my other boats; you're not going to be short of things to do round here, Roger, my boy.'

*Emess O*ne easily won the race the next day. Roger really didn't have to try that hard, although of course he did because this was a good opportunity to prove himself. He kept the crew on their toes right the way to the finish, continually making them trim the sails to get the absolute maximum from the boat. They all came back to the dock exhausted but exhilarated and Roger was the talk of the marina. This boy was destined for great things.

Roger settled easily into this boating, sailing and racing apprenticeship in the idyllic surroundings of Nassau. Although there was a serious social scene amongst the yachting communities around the various harbours, he kept himself to himself, preferring to go back to his apartment at night, cook his own meals and read or watch TV. Being Roger, he still saw no reason to have friends, indeed he thought it was probably better he didn't fraternise with the crew too much. If he was seen to be too friendly, it would be harder to shout and scream at people and get them motivated to win the races. What he wanted was a Jenks figure, someone to keep him out of trouble and on the straight and narrow.

Throughout the first few weeks, the skipper taught Roger a lot about boat handling, navigation and general maintenance and for the first time in his life Roger unwittingly became an avid student. The skipper only had to show him once how to do things and trust became a key part of their relationship.

Of Curt's other boats; a fat, lazy cruising sailboat; an even fatter, lazier motor boat; and an extremely fast looking powerboat with enough engine in the aft third of the boat to make the back end look as if it had been partially scuttled, Roger noticed that the powerboat didn't get used much. There was the occasional weekly excursion, usually on a weekday afternoon that was always driven by an outsider and not a regular member of the McGraw-Strutt boat crews. It became apparent one afternoon from the loud Hispanic oaths coming from the powerboat that one of the engines was not starting. The flustered, overweight Spaniard, charged with driving the boat that afternoon, came over to Roger and the skipper.

'Hey boys, the number three engine, it no work,' he said, sweating profusely. 'You got to help me, I got to go out in it,'

'C'mon Rodge, let's go and have a look, it can't be that serious,' the skipper said. They lifted the engine hatch and inspected the engine, but nothing was obviously wrong.

'Roger, can you try to start it from the cockpit? We should at least be able to see what's happening.'

Roger clambered forward into the driving seat, and on a thumbs-up signal from the skipper pressed the start button. There was a loud clicking noise instead of the usual whine from the starter motor.

'OK – that's it! It's the starter solenoid. All we need is a big screwdriver to short the terminals out and we can get you going,' the skipper said to the waiting driver.

'How do I get back then? I don't know a starter motor from the Holy Mother,' the driver asked, shrugging his shoulders.

'You could take Roger with you just in case. We'll get a new solenoid and fit it tomorrow.'

'OK, *hombre*, let's go.' The impatient Spaniard motioned to Roger to let the lines go.

The skipper showed Roger how to short the terminals across with a large screw-driver. They then started the engine and closed the large hatch. He jumped onto the dock. 'We'll see you later Rodge, make sure you hang on!' He said, watching Roger strap himself into the deeply padded navigator's seat.

The Spaniard was obviously used to handling this boat. He slammed it into reverse gear and withdrew slowly away from the dock, at the same time starting the number two engine. Once clear, he engaged forward drive and gunned the big un-silenced petrol engines. The surface-drive propellers cut viciously into the clear harbour water and the acceleration pinned Roger back into his seat.

The boat tore across the top of the waves. The speed log was registering 72 knots, the fastest Roger had ever been on land or water, and the Spaniard's greasy long black hair was flapping against the high-backed race seat. He glanced behind and was staggered to see the twin rooster tails made by the semi-submerged propellers, twenty to thirty feet in the air. Roger didn't say anything; he didn't trust himself to open his mouth, even when it was closed, his cheeks were billowing out of control. He assumed the Spaniard was in training for some kind of race, although he did look a bit casual in his Hawaiian shirt and Chinos. Didn't powerboats like this normally have a throttle-man and a navigator?

They slowed down after thirty minutes running at seventy knots. They were approaching an old fishing boat and the Spaniard opened up radio contact with the boat, speaking in rapid Spanish. They powered alongside the rusting trawler, coming to a stop with the engines still running. The Spaniard pressed and held a button down on the console to open up a large hatch on the fore-deck, the trawler crew started throwing small sealed packages the size of shoe boxes through the open hatch and into the small cargo hold. Each package making a muffled thump as it landed in the foam-lined hold.

Once the hatch was full of packages, the Spaniard gave the thumbs-up to the crew, spoke harshly in Spanish into the radio again, manoeuvred clear of the vessel and gunned the throttle until they were back up to 70 knots, heading in the same direction as before.

'Dried fish - for the tourists in the Keys,' the Spaniard shouted sombrely at Roger. 'We make good money during season. We have to be fast though.'

Roger felt sure he was about to say something else, when they were both startled by another noise competing with the harsh throb of the boat engines; it was the unmistakable sound of a helicopter. They both looked around to see the small glass fronted Bell chopper with two uniformed figures in the cockpit looking down at them. The machine was only fifty feet above and probably the same distance behind them, it was as if they wanted to land on the boat, they felt that close.

The Spaniard uttered several untranslatable oaths and started up the third engine, the speed of the boat increasing steadily up to eighty knots. There were now three rooster tails, each rising thirty foot in the air. The pilot of the Bell had his windscreen wipers on. Roger could see a land mass in the distance over to port and lots of small islands linked by a causeway; he guessed it to be the Florida Keys.

'Stop the boat, you are under arrest,' came the instruction from the helicopter over an extremely powerful loudspeaker. It was now level with them and fifty feet above the water on the boat's starboard side. The marking on the white and red helicopter clearly stated US Coast-Guard. The co-pilot held the radio/megaphone handset and barked out further instructions. 'There is a heavily armed coast guard cutter one mile away. If you don't stop, we will instruct him to use his cannon and blow you scumbags out of the water. Stop the boat.'

Roger was not quite sure what the Spaniard was going to do next, did he have another engine? Were the dried fish in reality deadly weapons useful for blasting coastguard helicopters out of the air? Could the boat submerge, Polaris-like and head towards the sanctuary of the South Pole? Surprisingly, as far as Roger was concerned, the Spaniard casually pulled all three throttles back until the boat came off the plane and halted fairly abruptly, the waves lapping dangerously close to the engine-heavy aft deck of the boat, the heavier payload probably not helping. He then sat back in the race seat, took out a large Havana cigar, struck a match, lit the cigar and put his feet up on the dash, as if to say; it's a fair cop, I had it coming. He smiled at Roger.

'Sorry, *gringo*, I've only got one,' he said, gesticulating with the cigar. 'They're beautiful. My mother, she always say to me, Bonites, she say, when everything's against you, you may as well let them have what they want, because sooner or later they going to get it anyway.

Hah, what the hell.' He switched all three engines off and sank deeper into the seat under a cloud of cigar smoke. 'I'm too old for all of this anyway,' he sighed.

As the late afternoon sun cut across the bow of the boat. Roger sat back too, pleased that the pounding through the waves had stopped. He couldn't help smiling to himself, bemused by the whole bizarre situation.

All this trouble for a few dried fish?

10. Troublesome Fish

A crestfallen Bonites with Roger alongside watched the Coastguard cutter steam towards them from being a pinprick on the horizon, to being the biggest white and red steel object Roger had ever been that close to. The ship towered over the wallowing powerboat. Instructions to the waiting deckhands were being called out over the tannoy system in a broad American accent. The two of them secured the powerboat to the cutter and scrambled up a boarding ladder to the main deck of the ship. Two crew members from the ship immediately boarded the boat and began searching the cockpit area, the engine bay and finally the forward area, one of them emerging from the open hatch talking furiously into a walkie-talkie. The other signalled for the deck crane jib to be lowered, and began preparing the boat for lifting, the tannoy voice echoing his request.

They stood on the main deck of the ship watching *Emmess Four* being craned onto the aft deck. Water ran away in torrents as the sleek hull hung suspended in mid-air, its shiny propellers flailing. Bonites complained bitterly under his breath. 'Hah! They lied. One mile away! We could have made it to Key West easily, the horizon is at least three miles away at that level.' He gestured in hopelessness at the sea all around them.

'What do you think they're going to do with us?' Roger asked, genuinely excited by the whole process.

'They gonna take us to Miami and caution us. Then they gonna put us on a plane back to Nassau. Then they gonna either eat all the fish, or they gonna sell all the fish. That's what they gonna do.' Bonites sighed resignedly, to him this was obviously just a small setback.

'Welcome aboard boys, and thanks for waiting for us. I'm the skipper of the Mary J Constantine, how you all doing today?' The skipper was clad in a bomber jacket and aviator sunglasses, and spoke with a relaxed Southern drawl. As he didn't get an answer from the bemused pair, he continued in the same vein. 'Well I can see you're both a little shocked to be guests of the US Coastguard on such a beautiful day, so I'll just explain the situation. Our eye in the sky monitored your rendezvous with the fishing boat earlier on. Now normally, we're OK with that 'cause we know about the Creedy Fish that you boys like to sell to the tourists while it's still fresh. Now, we been hearing rumours recently that there's some people in Colombia who are after exporting some of their prime narcotic produce to the

USA by sea, so we thought we'd do a few checks. Now we know that the fishing boat had been in Punto Estrella just this last week, so as you were the ones bringing the cargo into US waters, we thought we'd do a little look-see, a quick stop and search, eh, *hombre?*' He smiled at Bonites who for the whole duration of the captain's explanation was looking into the distance with a hurt expression on his hugely moustached face.

Again, not getting a response, he continued, 'Now, what do you think we just found in your cargo hold?'

Bonites looked up for the first time. 'Fish, we know it's fish.'

'If I told you that we estimate the value of your cargo at roughly seventeen million dollars by the time it hits the street, would you still say it's fish?'

Bonites looked up again, this time he looked out to sea and uttered several further expletives in his mother tongue.

'No, boys,' said the skipper, continuing when Bonites' tirade had receded. 'It's not fish. It's grade A, pure cocaine, and you're both under arrest. Bosun take these men to the brig and keep them in separate cells until we reach Miami. If you're hungry boys – see the bosun, he'll feed you all you want. Have a nice day now.' He strode off in the direction of the wheelhouse.

It was only then that Roger began to understand just how serious their position was, not that he was worried about the Spaniard, but he'd heard about drug traffickers before, and the sort of prison sentences they attracted. Ten years? Fifteen? Maybe more. Oh, shit. All this, just because a bloody engine wouldn't start! How unfair was that?

The Bosun, a USCG uniformed version of Captain Hook, with a pointy face and a constantly surprised expression, accompanied them down three deck levels and into the forward part of the ship. By the time they reached the six-cell complex that formed the brig, Roger was feeling distinctly queasy. The ship was side-on to the Atlantic swell and rocking fiercely from side to side. They were each shown into one of the American style cells, with steel bars forming the entire front face.

Bonites immediately entered some form of higher state, rocking backwards and forwards on the cell bench, eyes closed and uttering oaths in his mother tongue. Roger picked out snippets like 'Cocksucker,' and 'Gonzales,' and something about his erstwhile employer *'follar buro.'* Roger couldn't help laughing. Even with his elementary understanding of Spanish, he knew that this meant having marital relations with donkeys. It was obvious Bonites was not a happy helmsman.

Eventually, to Roger's relief, he felt the ship's engine revs increase and it turned around, away from the swell. He guessed it was heading on a North Westerly course for Miami. Captain Hook re-appeared asking if they wanted any food or drink.

'No thank you, you baboon-headed motherfucker,' Gonzalez responded, rounding it all up with a hearty clearing of the throat and a messy expectoration of phlegm into the alleyway between the cell blocks, narrowly missing the Bosun. Unintentionally.

'Do you mind not doing that on this ship, dago-brains?' the Bosun expounded, obviously shocked by the Spaniards behaviour. 'This is the US Coastguard, you know, we can get you locked up for less than that.' He laughed in outrage as he realised what he'd said. Then moving closer to Bonites, he said quietly, 'You do that one more time *gringo*, and me an' the boys'll take you up on deck for a good old-fashioned keel haulin'. Got that, shit-face?'

Bonites cursed some more under his breath, 'Your father was a polecat and your mother showed her tits to strangers...'

Roger could see that he really wasn't in the mood for giving up, although he did at least hold fire on any further phlegmy projectiles.

Curtis McGraw's boating activities were centred around a legitimate boat charter business. He ran this as an interesting sideline to his successful fruit exporting activities. The racing sailboat was his passion, the other boats were a bit of fun for him. The fact that he could keep his boat interests more or less self-financed by chartering the two luxury boats to wealthy American tourists, and the powerboat to Bonites' employer, Gonzales the Spanish fast-fish merchant, made it all the more attractive. He could write any losses off against his tax return every year and everyone was happy, the IRS included.

He was not best pleased when the US Coast Guard rang his charter booking secretary to inform her that his powerboat had been impounded and that the charter party, a Mr. Bonites Pasquale and a Mr. Roger Collins were under arrest for the suspected importation into the USA of a Class A narcotic.

On overhearing his young booking secretary struggling to comprehend what the official on the other end was telling her, McGraw stormed over and literally ripped the phone out of her hand. It only took him a few moments to comprehend the ramifications of the situation. 'But that's my boat and that's my race chief you've got over there,' he spluttered. 'We have a whole season of racing ahead of us, you can't do this to me!'

'Sir, are you or are you not, the registered owner of a Cigarette powerboat called *Emmess Four* registered in Nassau?' the official calmly inquired.

'Well yes, sure I am. I charter the boat out to customers. Listen, I don't give a damn about the boat, just give me back my boy!'

'Sir, as I told your young lady, the boat is currently impounded on the Coast Guard cutter en-route for Miami. The crew are under arrest and will be in the Southern Miami Police Headquarters until further notice. We have notified the Nassau police who will be coming over to see you with some colleagues from Miami. I would ask that you give the police your fullest co-operation.'

'Fullest co-operation? My race chief! He's from England! He's only been in the country for one month! He wasn't crew, the goddamn Hispanic kidnapped him! My boy was an unwilling accessory to the crime!' The ebullient Mississippian was in a red-faced, slamming his hand on the table and kicking furniture type rage.

'As I said, sir, we will be interviewing all parties and ask that you give our colleagues, when they arrive, your fullest co-operation. Good day, sir.'

McGraw slammed the phone down and glared at the receptionist. 'Get that boat skipper up here right away, before the police get here!'

The skipper arrived shortly and was totally shocked to hear the news. 'Roger? Under arrest? Oh my God, he was only on the boat in case the engine stopped and they had to restart it. The starter solenoid had blown, the Spaniard insisted he had to go and that was the only way he could have gone with all three engines.'

'Well the police are coming here any minute now. Listen to me, the Spaniard talked him into going. We did not volunteer to send him. Got that?'

'Yes, Curt. Those damned Hispanics, they always told us it was dried fish; always has to be eaten within a few hours of the drying process to get the best flavour. It was drugs all along?' The skipper couldn't get the words out quickly enough.

'Those greasy slime-balls. Gonzalez is gonna swing for this,' McGraw responded acidly.

'Where do we stand with the police though?' the skipper asked, a worried expression on his face.

'We're OK, we absolutely rule out any illegal activities in our terms and conditions of charter,' McGraw responded. 'The feds can string up the lot of them as far as I'm concerned, but we need to get Roger out of the frame.'

As he finished saying this, his PA announced the arrival of the local police in the lobby downstairs.

McGraw and his skipper were taken to the Police Headquarters in downtown Nassau in separate cars, and led away to separate interview rooms. Two hours later they were both released on bail. As the two men walked along the sidewalk heading for the cab rank, a trail of dense cigar smoke in their wake, McGraw ranted: 'It's besmirchation, that's what it is. I'm on trial by association and Roger'll face the same prejudice. Those damn Hispanics, using my boat to import that filth. I can't even have the satisfaction of mincing Gonzalez's jewels, they've already arrested him! He sells fish for Christsakes. I can't believe he's a Mr. Big in all of this. I reckon we're dealing with one of the *Bolas Grandes* in the Columbian mafia. Seventeen million dollars' worth, in my boat. Those assholes! Someone's gonna pay for this.' The cigar butt that landed in the gutter was heavily chewed.

On their return to the office, McGraw was straight on the phone to USCG Miami. 'What do you mean you're not able to tell me? That's my boy and my boat you've got there. I want that boy, he's as innocent as you are in all of this. You understand?'

The young girl on duty had obviously been trained in how to deal with irate members of the public and answered in a calm, reasoned tone. 'Sir, the two members of the charter party have been arrested by Dade County police officers, they are currently being questioned. I suggest you ring the Police HQ tomorrow, they may be able to give you a clearer picture of the situation by then. I can let you have the number if you like?'

McGraw knew that he wouldn't sleep that night, so he decided to get on the next plane to Miami, check into a hotel and try to get to see Roger in person.

He arrived at the Upper East Side Police HQ on Biscayne Boulevard at eight that evening. The burly, morose desk sergeant was not helpful. 'You can't see him, they're still being questioned. Try again in the morning.'

'But he's my boy, I've got to see him.'

'He ain't going nowhere. Leave your number. If there's any development we'll let you know.' The sergeant closed the desk log book, the conversation was over.

'I'm at the Biscayne Bay Marriot, thanks for everything.' McGraw slapped a business card on the desk, turned and disconsolately walked out of the gloomy police building.

He returned the following morning. This time the desk officer was a woman and somewhat more polite than her predecessor. She came back after checking with the investigation team. 'Sir, as you know, your young man is under arrest for smuggling narcotics. He is still being questioned and my colleagues feel that bail will not be offered in this case.' The desk sergeant looked up at McGraw with a smile tinged with regret.

'Ma'am, my boy is completely innocent in all of this. He was only on board the boat in case the engine stopped. He's my race chief, he's no drug smuggler, he's from England!'

'Sir, are you the owner of the boat?' She asked, as if an idea had suddenly occurred to her.

'Yes ma'am, I am,' McGraw responded. Eager.

'Well sir, you would very likely not be allowed to see the boy anyway, that would in most cases be a violation of your bail conditions,' the desk sergeant said in an empathising tone that threw McGraw off track.

'Yes, well, you have a point there, ma'am. All I want to do is get my boy out of this mess.' McGraw took a chance in appealing to her motherly instincts.

'I fully understand Mr. McGraw. All I can suggest is that you go back home and wait for the local police to contact you. Our team will inform the police department in Nassau immediately something transpires from the questioning today. I'm sorry, sir, that's all for now. Have a nice day.' She smiled brightly, he swooned slightly. She ended the conversation with a firm finality, yet at the same time made McGraw feel like he'd scored a first date.

All McGraw could manage to say through his rose-tinted vision was, 'Yes, ma'am. Thank you, ma'am.' He beamed in wonderment at her uniformed magnificence. 'Here's my lawyer's card for the boy. Bye ma'am, I'll wait to hear. You take care.' He felt himself saluting her.

Roger called his mum. His dad answered.

'Hi Dad, it's me, Roger.'

'Son! Great to hear from you! Where are you today and how are you?'

'Well, I'm OK, but I'm in a bit of a situation here. You know Mr. McGraw has several boats? Well I was out on one of them and the coastguard stopped us and it turns out that the boat was loaded with drugs and I'm in Miami under arrest for smuggling. The guy I was with does the trip all the time, they bring dried fish into the Keys for the tourists, he was as shocked as I was. He's under arrest too.'

'You're under arrest for smuggling drugs?'

'I was only on the boat because one of the engines wouldn't start. Bonites, the guy I was with, couldn't make the trip on his own. I was with him just in case he needed a hand to get the engine going again.'

'This man, McGraw, this is his business? This is what he does?'

'No he exports fruit to the US, the boats are just a sideline.'

'Do you have his telephone number? I need to speak to this guy. I'll get Brabazons to deal with this one and get you out of there.'

'Dad, it's OK. Mr. McGraw will do everything he can. I was only ringing to say I was OK and that you might not hear from me for the next few days. Honestly Dad, I'm OK, and I'll be getting out of here just as soon as Mr. McGraw gets here.' In his mind, Roger was imagining the futility of home-counties solicitors attempting to influence the combined force of the US Coastguard, the Miami Police Department and the local DA's office. He'd already been well informed by the detectives interviewing him that they thought the death penalty was too soft a sentence for smuggling drugs into the US.

'When did all this happen then, son?'

'Earlier today, it's nearly midnight now.'

'Your mum and I will be on the next flight out,' his dad said with conviction.

'Dad, no! Please. I'm OK. I'll ring when I'm out.'

'Roger, how do you think we're going to sleep or carry on our normal lives knowing that you're locked up all those miles away? As parents we've got to come.'

'Look, all I'm saying is that I'd rather you didn't, at least not just yet. If things start to look bad, I'll let you know. Look I've got to go, they're calling me over,' he lied. 'Bye Dad, love to Mum.'

'Yes, bye son. We both love you very much, don't forget that. If you need -' Roger put the phone down before his Dad finished speaking.

Despite the protestations of McGraw's lawyer, Roger was formally charged the next day with being an accessory to the crime of importing narcotics into the USA. He would be held at the Miami

Federal Detention Centre pending the trial date, the detectives told him this would probably be two to three months away.

Miami FDC was an imposing twenty-four storey building on the corner of NE 4th Street and North Miami Avenue. Roger was transferred on his own in the back of a police cruiser. He had no idea what happened to Bonites, he didn't want to know either. He was probably blabbing about everything and everyone he knew in order to reduce his sentence. The police would not be content with merely taking Bonites out of circulation; they would almost certainly be trying to get to the Mr. Big in all of this.

His parents arrived at visiting time that evening. As soon as she spotted him sitting at the small table awaiting his visitors, his mother broke down.

'Roger, Roger, Roger,' she cried, rushing towards him, arms outstretched. She engulfed her son in an embrace.

Roger was surprised to be close to tears himself and felt himself surrendering to his mother's all-enveloping hug, pleased to take in the familiar scents of clean hair and perfume. He could feel his mother's body shaking with her tears. She didn't let go until she had them under control and stepped back, wiping her eyes with a handkerchief and blinking. Roger stepped towards his father who offered a rather less emotional handshake. Roger basked in the moment, enjoying the attention and high drama.

'You're so handsome with your sun tan and your sun-bleached hair, my darling,' his mother said, lips trembling, breathing unsteady. 'I can't believe they've put you in a prison!'

'This isn't a prison mum, this is a detention centre,' Roger said calmly. 'I'm only here until the trial – they reckon two to three months' time.'

'Two to three months?' his mother shrieked. 'They can hold you in here for that long?'

'Mum, if they find me guilty, they could send me to prison for ten years, maybe more,' Roger said.

'Ten years!' His mother sobbed in anguish and despair. His father comforted her. 'You're our only son and we know you haven't done anything wrong,' she managed to stammer through her tears. 'I'll die if they put you away for that long.' She broke down again, inconsolable. 'David, we must do something.'

A campaign of public awareness was launched by Liechtenstein Re's London based PR firm with the intention of making the US public aware of Roger's innocence. Curtis McGraw also provided ammunition for the campaign in his fight to clear his and Roger's name.

Meanwhile, in the FDC, Roger was reasonably happy. He had his own small cell with a soft bed, TV and reasonably normal people as inmates. He did get quite a bit of attention as his fellow prisoners grew to recognise the campaign that was going on in the media to bring about his release but Roger was sufficiently streetwise not to antagonise those who taunted him. Most of it, he reckoned, was pure jealousy: Where's my campaign? I'm innocent too.

Roger would always remember the trial as one of the worst days of his life. He was unlucky to get one of the most right-wing, attention seeking judges on the circuit. His key witnesses were McGraw and the Skipper.

The cross examination by the prosecution was loaded, one simple question came to the fore: did you or did you not, assist with the importation of illegal narcotics into the USA?

There was only one answer, no matter how it was put. The answer was yes. The jury found him guilty despite all protestations of innocence made by defence witnesses and lawyers. The court was adjourned for one week.

On re-sitting, the judge summed up the proceedings. 'Ladies and gentlemen of the jury, we realise that Mr Roger Collins is not a player in any of the Columbian drug cartels. We know that he does not benefit directly from the proceeds of this crime. He is only twenty years of age, therefore vulnerable and impressionable with many years of learning ahead of him, including from this. As a non US national, he is probably unaware of the scale of problems caused by Class A drugs in this country. 'However, this is a serious crime and a custodial sentence is the only option if we are serious about eradicating this scourge, this threat against our society.

The judge then leaned across the bench and focused on Roger. 'Roger J Collins, I hereby sentence you to 12 years imprisonment in a Federal Penitentary. This is commuted to seven and a half years, taking into account the circumstances. Repatriation to a UK prison will be possible, depending on whether or not an extradition request will be forthcoming from the UK authorities.'

Roger was taken away to the South Miami Federal Correction Institute where he was to serve his sentence. He had the distinct feeling that life from this point onward was not going to get any easier.

He wanted his Mum.

11. The British Inmate

Roger was escorted off the prison truck by two silent, brooding guards and marched to a large reception area where he was shown into a small, windowless interview room. After a fifteen minute wait, a uniformed, middle-aged woman with horn-rimmed glasses and a severe expression entered the room. She sat opposite him and opened a folder containing two pieces of paper. She asked him a series of mundane questions in a disinterested way, writing the answers down on the uppermost sheet.

When the form was complete, she addressed Roger, looking at him for the first time, 'OK, young man, this is the South Miami Federal Correction Institute. Life in here is as tough as you want it to be. If you thought you were in any way tough outside, then forget it. In here there will always, and I do mean always, be someone who is a lot tougher than you. In your particular case, you are young and you are British, both of these facts tell me that you will be especially vulnerable to some of our more, let's say, seasoned campaigners.

'My general advice to everybody is to keep out of trouble, but being males, hardly anybody listens. There are three golden rules in here; one, don't ask the warders or other inmates for any favours; two, don't do favours for others, anyone asks you, make your excuses but don't do it; three, if you see trouble developing, walk away. Do not intervene. If you follow those simple guidelines you'll complete your sentence and walk away from here in one piece. Any questions?'

'Yes, when do I go back to the UK?' Roger asked, an edge of deliberate naivety in his tone.

'Excuse me?' replied the woman, bemused.

'Well, I'm not staying here. My lawyer said I'm going to be serving my sentence in a UK jail, he's applied for extradition, it's going through right now,' Roger responded. 'Black and white isn't it?'

'That is a matter between you and your lawyer. We are purely responsible for ensuring you carry out the sentence that the judge handed down to you,' the woman said coldly.

'But you've made a mistake, I should be going back to the UK right away,' Roger said, showcasing his British indignation.

'No, it's you who are mistaken. It is really very simple. You committed a crime in US territory, therefore you serve the sentence here until we are instructed otherwise. Besides, extradition requests take months, sometimes years, it's all in the hands of the politicians.'

She picked up her folder and stood up, hands on hips, her body language making it obvious she was done.

'This is outrageous,' Roger said, warming to the theme, 'I demand to see my lawyer.'

'You can demand all you want, hon, the only person you'll be seeing today is your cellmate and some of the warders,' the woman said as she rapped on the door. 'OK we're ready, you can take him away.' One of the burly warders appeared at the door to take Roger to his cell.

'Cellmate? You mean I will be sharing my time in here with one of your psychopaths, like in Alcatraz?' He knew he was pushing his luck by this stage. The burly guard gripped his arm. Roger looked at the guard as if the man had just defecated on his sitting-room Wilton.

'I say, no need for that, old boy. Desist, there's a good fellow,' Roger said, sounding as annoyingly British as he could. The guard gave a low grunt, squeezed his arm with both hands and frogmarched him out of the office. Roger shouting out behind him to the woman, 'What is your name and rank? I will be quoting this conversation to my lawyer.'

'Roger,' she said, clearly exasperated. 'Trust me, with that attitude, you will be dead. Soon. 'You can quote me on that one, please do.'

Roger was led to his cell, still complaining to the burly guard, 'I'll see her, the bitch. She needs taking down a step or two. Women, eh? Bit of power and they think they've got you eating out of their hands.'

They reached Roger's cell in E Wing after walking for what seemed like forever down the wing building containing literally hundreds of cells. The burly guard spoke for the first time as Roger sat down on the bed. He leaned close to Roger's face and said, 'Listen, son, I don't know what you're in here for but she was right, if you carry on acting like that, you're going to be dead-meat within a month. Now wise up and just keep your mouth shut. There's some seriously dangerous people in here would take severe offence at some of that shit.'

'Look, I was caught with $17m worth of cocaine on my boat. I think you'll be witnessing a spot of hero worshipping around here pretty soon. Who is Big Daddy round these parts anyway?' Roger replied, with all the Englishness he could muster.

The guard laughed. 'You crazy? This ain't no comedy show. You going out of E Wing in a box, you carry on like that, you hear me?' He turned and stomped out of the cell, 'Big Daddy, huh!' he said as he slammed the heavy door shut and turned the key, flipping shut the spy-hole in the door. Roger was on his own at last, or was he? He glanced up at the top bunk, there appeared to be an extremely large body at rest under a blanket. He swallowed. Mum, he thought to himself, where are you?

David Collins was experiencing similar difficulties with authoritative US females to those of Roger, except he was 38,000 feet in the air above the North Atlantic in coach class on an American Airlines Boeing 747. He'd asked his PA to make a booking at the last minute with British Airways, but American was the only sensible option time-wise to get him to Miami on the same day that Roger was sentenced. Every time he travelled coach or economy or any of the other politically correct terms for second class, he regretted it. He especially regretted it on American airlines, they tended to put the surliest, the most reluctant to please - and yes - old, stewardesses on cabin service. He thought to himself that perhaps the US airline personnel departments targeted retired Prison Service employees as possessing the right blend of no-nonsense discipline and good-old down to earth bad-manners. This would ensure that their customers wouldn't risk their wrath by frivolously requesting second helpings, or red wine instead of white, or sparkling mineral water instead of still. A good way of maximising profits, if you don't mind losing customers.

David sighed as he stretched his legs to try and relieve his aching back in the cramped seat.

The trouble with David was that he couldn't bring himself to make the booking for first class or even business class. Such was his evangelical fervour in controlling company expenditure that all of his employees were banned from claiming anything other than economy tickets anywhere, anytime. This was a good way of his leading by example, even if it was uncomfortable, sometimes painful.

On arrival at Miami International, having negotiated his way through US immigration, David took a yellow cab to the prison. Today was a Thursday and visiting time was on Sunday between two and eight PM. Due to the circumstances of Roger's fresh arrival and the fact that David had flown all the way from England, the warder on reception reluctantly agreed to let him see his son.

'Only for half an hour, mind. It's more than my jobs worth for him to disrupt the pattern on the floor upstairs,' the guard said sorrowfully. David thanked him profusely, wondering whether a tip would be appropriate. Deciding it would probably be seen as a bribe rather than a gesture of thanks, he chose not to.

*

Roger looked nervous. 'Hi Dad,' he said, looking at the floor. 'They don't like visitors outside of visiting hours on Sunday.'

'Yes I know, I got the message from the warder on reception, thought I might have to bribe him to get to see you,' David laughed. 'How's things?'

'Could be better. When are they going to get me out of here?' Roger said.

'I was on the phone to Brabazons this morning. The application for extradition is with the Home Office today. They seem to think it will take a month or two, apparently the Foreign Secretary has to look at the papers and sign the document. It's surprising really, how high level it all is, something to do with maintaining Anglo-American relationships.' David smiled hopefully at his forlorn son, 'We'll have you home in no time Rodge, you'll see.'

'Yes but only so I can serve my sentence in a UK Prison, they'll put me in Wormwood Scrubs, you see if they don't,' Roger said, referring to Her Majesty's West London prison made infamous by some of its high-profile inmates.

'At least we'll be able to see you regularly,' David said, regretting it immediately.

'What, when I'm sharing a cell with Reggie Kray, or Jack the Hat Mcvitie? Yes, you'll be able to see me regularly all right, tending flowers on my gravestone,' Roger said with bitterness in his voice.

'Look Rodge, I know this is none of your fault and I know prison isn't a very nice experience for anyone to go through, but you've just got to be strong and get on with things sometimes. You're young, you're intelligent and you know how to look after yourself. You'll come through the other side of all this and you'll laugh about it one day,' David said, doing his best to sound optimistic.

Roger looked at his father, a mixture of anger and incredulity crossed his face, David prepared himself for the worst, 'I've got to go back upstairs in a minute to face a twenty-two stone, black psychopath who I'm going to be sharing a cell with for the next however long it'll be. While you get back on a nice comfy aeroplane and swan off back to your luxury lifestyle. You call that having a memorable experience?' he said in disgust.

David thought of responding with an apology for not bringing a machine gun whereby they could both make a desperate bid for

104

freedom, but thought better of it. 'What's your cell like, then?' he asked, knowing their conversation was over.

'Six foot by six foot, bars at the front, bucket in the corner, oh and a large black murderer on the top bunk. It's a real experience.' Roger stood up, looking around for a way out. 'Guard! Take me back to my cell,' he demanded. He turned round to his father, 'Thanks for coming, Dad, see you real soon.' He walked towards the door.

David stood up, calling out, 'Rodge! Let me know if you need anything. We can post anything you want.'

'Money. I'll probably have to pay people to stay alive.' Roger opened the door and the guard on the other side led him away.

David sat back down again, head angled low, looking at the floor in despair. It had been a long day. He somehow knew this would be the result. He decided he would stay over in Miami and fly back after the weekend. He gritted his teeth. He would make visiting time on Sunday, whether Roger liked it or not.

Quentin McDonald Davis III was from the small community of Troy in Orange County, Florida. He was a large-boned, country boy who loved his Mum, his Dad not so much, but at least he held a grudging respect for the man who had raised him. Not given to intellectual pursuits, Quentin was encouraged by his parents to go to Miami in 1978, ostensibly to work with his wealthy cousin who had a thriving downtown bookmakers business on the Lower East Side. As it turned out, his cousin was a drug dealer who worked part time for a bookmaker to turn the bucks and give the impression to outsiders, and to his family, that he was a respectable businessman.

Quentin was not one for dabbling in the white powdery substances that his cousin dealt in. He took umbrage against him in a big way, this umbrage ultimately turning into physical violence whereby his cousin accidentally ended up dead and Quentin ended up in prison serving an eight year sentence for manslaughter.

He was dozing on the top bunk when Roger was first brought into the cell. He was just about to pop the blanket and size up this arrogant sounding British dude, when the guard took Roger away to see an unexpected visitor. The large Negro was sitting at the bare table when Roger returned.

'Call me Quentin. What's your name?' he asked, looking menacingly at Roger.

Roger swallowed, 'Roger. Roger Collins.'

'You from England?' Quentin asked with feign surprise.

'Yes Surrey, England.'

'What you here for?'

'Well, I was a passenger on a small boat and they found some drugs in it.'

'*Some* drugs?'

'Yes well, quite a lot actually. I didn't know anything about it, they told me it was dried fish.'

'They?'

'Yes, some Spanish people who borrowed the boat.'

'Fish, huh?' The large Negro started laughing. 'Spanish people. With fish. Where?' he asked, looking at Roger gleefully.

'In Nassau,' Roger responded, uncertain now.

'Hahh! And I thought I'd heard everything,' Quentin said, slamming the table with one of his large, shovel-shaped hands. 'You got caught with some Spanish people, with a boat full of fish off of Nassau? Don't tell me, a small fast boat, right? En route to Miami, right? Did it stop by an old trawler to load up?'

Roger nodded.

Quentin suddenly stood up, the table in front of him falling away as his huge stomach brushed past it, his face was glaring in anger. He grabbed the startled Roger around the back of the neck with one large hand, encircled his other free hand around Rogers throat and lifted the boy into the air so Roger's terrified face was on a level with his, his feet dangling against the big man's knees.

'I'm in here for killin' a drug dealer, boy. I don't take kindly to low-lives like you poisoning the country's youth. Now if we gonna get on at all, you got to just reassure me that you ain't never, ever going to do anything like that ever again, you hear me?'

Roger nodded eagerly, breathlessly.

'You don't mention nuthin' to nobody regarding drugs, y'hear? The large black man's nose was almost touching Roger's, his eyes large and glaring.

Roger nodded again, choking.

The negro suddenly took both hands away, letting Roger drop to the floor.

'Sorry 'bout that Roger. Hi I'm Quentin,' he said, offering a hand to Roger, part handshake, mostly to help him up from the floor.

'Thanks,' Roger said, coming to a standing position. 'You could say I know where I stand with you now.'

'You're damn right, brother,' Quentin chuckled. 'One day I'll tell you the story of why I'm in here and then you'll understand.'

'I look forward to hearing that.'

'One day, Rodge, one day,' Quentin resumed his position at the table, having put it upright again. He looked at Roger and saw he wasn't carrying anything, 'Got any food, newspapers, magazines, books even?'

'No sorry, this is my first time. I didn't realise,' Roger said.

'That's OK, my folks are coming at the weekend, they'll bring me something, won't be any titties though. Some British pussy would have been nice, Rodge,' he said as an aside, leering disgustedly.

'Yes, I know what you mean. Sorry.' Roger shrugged his shoulders.

'You're not a faggot are you, Roger?' Quentin asked him casually.

'A faggot?' Roger said, unsure. 'What do you mean?'

Quentin sighed. 'A brown-hatter, a shirtlifter, someone who dresses on the other side, a godamn fairy, for christsake!'

'No, not at all, no. I've got a girlfriend at home, she misses me, I'll show you her letters when they come. She likes to write,' Roger said hurriedly. 'She may even send some photos over.'

'Hmm, I look forward to that very much. Perhaps you'd like to tell me all about her later on.' Quentin said, flickering his eyebrows and pursing his lips.

'Yes, OK,' Roger said, looking at the fragile looking top bunk.

Quentin must have been thinking the same thought, 'You can have the top bunk,' he said, smiling. Roger smiled back at him nervously.

Roger was more relaxed when his father came to see him again on Sunday. 'Dad, I thought you'd have gone home by now, thanks for staying on.'

'You OK, son? You seem a lot happier today,' his father remarked.

'Yes well, I'm learning the ropes, it's not as bad as I thought,' Roger said breezily.

'Excellent. I bought you some goodies.' His father emptied the contents of a very thoroughly searched bag out onto the table. 'I bought you some chocolate, some chewing gum, a weekend newspaper, a couple of books, a couple of magazines, some toiletries and that's about it.'

'Oh, thanks Dad,' Roger said with genuine gratitude. 'This is really good of you. My cellmate was kind of expecting me to bring some stuff when I first came here. I said I'd remember the next time.' He laughed.

'What's he like, your cellmate?' his father asked.

'Oh he's big and black and he's a murderer, just as I suspected,' Roger said, leafing through one of the magazines on the table.

'He *is* a murderer? Oh no, Roger, can't they move you?' David said, alarmed.

'No, he didn't mean it and he really is anti-drugs, he's looking out for me. He's called Quentin, there's nothing to worry about. Honestly, he's a big honey monster, most of the time,' Roger said nodding his head and smiling. 'I'd even introduce him to mum, he's that nice.' He added as a confidence booster for both his parents, he knew his father would report all of this back to his mother.

'Well, you just let me know if things start getting out of hand,' his father said. 'I'll go see the governor if I have to.'

They chatted lightly for the rest of the hour, as if the previous visit had not occurred. As he left the prison, having hugged Roger and told him to take care, even kissed him, David thought this was probably about the most enjoyable exchange they'd had since before the boy's adolescence. He was glad he had stayed, and looked forward to relaying all of the good news to Margaret.

On arriving home, David exerted as much influence as he could on the Foreign Office to get the extradition application moving along. He obviously didn't like the idea of his son being in prison, but a USA prison just seemed that much harsher than one in the UK.

David would ring the stiff, miserable civil servant called Appleby at the Foreign Office in Whitehall weekly. After the first three weeks, the progress seemed to stagnate. Every time David called, Appleby would be defensive and annoyingly evasive.

'I'm sorry but the cousins just don't want to play ball on this one. They're stonewalling us. You can understand their attitude; their legal system is as keen as ours to set precedents. Your young man was an accessory to an extraordinary large crime, a crime that the voting public in the US want to see people being punished for. They won't want their trophies being sent off overseas to complete namby-pamby, meaningless jail sentences in open prisons with short parole periods. If they committed the crime in the US, the lynch mob mentality takes over, they want them publicly strung up in full view to deter others from coming to their country and doing the same thing. It's High Noon in Miami, I'm afraid to say.'

'Wait a minute, whose side are you on? This is our 20 year-old son we're talking about. He's innocent, he was only on the boat in case the engine broke down. You know that, the court knew it and the judge knew it,' David argued.

'Look, Mr Collins, I'm afraid to say it, but he is guilty, guilty of being an accessory to the worst kind of crime. People don't mind a spot of embezzlement or honest robbery; you know, robbing from the rich to give to the poor, that sort of thing. They get applauded for their cheek and bravado. This is cocaine, Mr. Collins, this stuff ruins people's lives. People die either through taking it or dabbling in the stuff; even the mafia had a moral dilemma about whether or not to get involved in it. You mention the crime has anything to do with drugs and that person has immediately got blood on their hands. It's primea-facea.'

'So where do we go from here, Mr. Appleby?' David responded calmly.

'I'll try my contact in the US Justice Department one more time, I'll telephone you when I have some information. Goodbye, Mr. Collins.'

12. Hilary and her Uncle

The letter bore a Miami postmark. Posted on August 16th, it had taken three weeks to arrive. The handwriting was not very neat, obviously male. Someone who didn't write regularly. Hilary was curious as she stood in the hallway that Saturday morning, envelope in hand. Who could this be from?

Roger! She involuntarily held her hand up to her mouth as she read the letter.

She read the letter twice before she could take it all in. Even then, she still couldn't understand why he had written to her, of all people. She remembered the incident with Pat Barry and Roger at school. It sounded from the tone of his letter as if he wanted a relationship – funnily enough just like the first time they met. Well, it wasn't every day a convicted felon writes to you from the USA. Perhaps it would have been more glamorous if he'd been on death row - no that was cruel. He had mentioned he would be taking over his Dad's insurance firm when he got out of jail which could, she supposed, make him a ready-made millionaire. She wasn't by nature a gold digger, but a girl had to think about these things, didn't she?

Anyway, a relationship with a jailbird, especially a jailbird in a foreign country, sounded ideal from a point of view of preserving the one thing in her life she was determined to hang onto until marriage - her maidenhood. She decided to write back to him and enclose a photograph of herself as he had requested. One of her favourites actually – she looked dead sexy with an off the shoulder top and, for her, heavy make-up. Yes, she decided. That would knock him for six in his little prison cell. She remembered that he was not attractive in the conventional sense of the word, but his longish blond hair and his little boy lost looks had a certain *'je ne se qua'* she thought as she put the letter back into its envelope for safekeeping.

Uncle Vern was Hilary's Dad's brother. The brothers had the same eyes and both possessed an entrepreneurial spirit. Her Dad owned his own garage, while her Uncle, having joined the army straight from school, had completed thirty-one years before retiring. He now lived in Hong Kong and ran his own import-export business - something he had dreamed about for all of his army days. Her Dad always said his brother was involved in some 'shady' goings on. Implying in not as many words that he was an arms dealer, his military background and no doubt a string of high ranking international contacts from his army days making it a natural progression from soldiering.

Hilary had recently been given a highly-privileged insight into her Uncle's business activities. She would remember the experience for the rest of her life, including the day he made her an offer she could not refuse.

In July, Vern had been in the UK for a family wedding. Hilary and her Uncle had the first dance of the evening reception together and spent much of the evening chatting at the table, interspersed with dancing and conversing with other long-lost relatives. For some reason they had seemed drawn to one another that night.

'So Miss Saunders, an HNC in business studies, eh? Leaves your Dad and me amateur business people feeling very proud, if slightly humbled, I must say,' he said, beaming.

Hilary blushed. 'I enjoyed studying. I tried law but found it a bit stiff. Thought business must be more interesting and I was right. It is,' she said brightly.

'Many congratulations, sweetheart. What are you going to do now?' he asked.

She laughed. 'It's a bit embarrassing actually. I've got firms falling over themselves to offer me a job, I don't quite know what I want to do yet.'

'Oh come on, modesty doesn't become you, Hilary. You must have some idea. Bright young 22 year-old?'

'Well, I do know I want to run my own business, but not straight away; I need to get some experience first. My Dad says he'll help me get started, you know, with premises and the like when I'm ready.'

'Have you had a holiday yet this year?'

'No. I only finished exams in June. I was going to book somewhere in Spain with some friends, catch the end of the season, but I don't know if I can be bothered really. Sun, sea and sand is all very well for a few days,' she giggled. 'After that it's just boring.'

'If I were to ask you to come back to Hong Kong with me to experience business life first-hand for a while, what would you say?'

She looked at him, momentarily shocked. 'Oh Uncle Vern, I'd love to but I wouldn't be able to afford it, I'm still a penniless student.'

'Well, look at it like this, you've spent the last four years, probably longer, studying. Now you've got what you want, you deserve a treat. This treat is on your Uncle Vern. I'll put you up in a five star hotel in Kowloon overlooking the bay. You can spend as much or as little time in the business as you want. Obviously I'd value your input as I'm fairlynew to it all. I'm afraid the Army taught me a lot about life but not much about how to run a business. We get by but there are some very big opportunities out there. What do you think?'

'It sounds fantastic, a dream come true. I know from Dad that you run a business, what is it that you do exactly?'

'We buy and sell. Manufacturers in the region need raw materials, so we import a range of bulk plastics; polyurethane, polyamides in powder or pellet form. That's the boring bit. The most profitable for us is the export side. In some cases the same manufacturers sell through us to our contacts in Europe and the US, anything made of plastic; household goods and a lot of toys in one form or another.'

'My Dad thinks you're involved in arms dealing,' she laughed.

'Yes, well, I can't say that the opportunities haven't come up, and still do actually. I tell everyone I'm involved in plastics and let them draw their own conclusions. Some people think I sell plastic explosives, because of my military background. You're one of the few people who know what I really do, so keep it to yourself,' he said, tapping the side of his nose, smiling. 'Let's keep the intrigue going for a while longer.'

'I really need to talk to Mum and Dad. It sounds great Uncle Vern, thank you for inviting me.' She kissed him on the cheek.

'I must warn you, Hils,' he said, looking around to make sure no one was within earshot, then leaning towards her conspiratorially. 'Some of the toys we deal in are, how shall I say, of an adult nature. They're sex toys,' he said, mouthing the middle word. Hilary had never seen her Uncle Vern embarrassed or shy about anything before. 'Now you can see why I don't like broadcasting the business thing, you wouldn't believe the profit margins or the size of the market though. Massive!' he said, as if in recompense for causing Hilary alarm.

'Wow,' Hilary said slowly, intrigue showing on her features.

'Are you coming then?' he asked.

'Of course.' She said, deadpan. 'When can we book the tickets?'

Her month stay in Hong Kong turned out to be an inspiration for Hilary. The busy pace of life in the colony suited her. She worked twelve hour days during the week and Saturday mornings in her Uncle's office, analysing and improving stock control and invoicing systems for his busy office staff. Lunchtimes would invariably be spent at the noodle bar on the industrial estate, her Uncle cracking jokes and conversing in Mandarin with the locals about horse racing and rugby. Hilary was astonished by how much he had been accepted as part of the community.

At night they would dine in one of the many excellent restaurants in town, or if the day had been particularly fraught, at one of the restaurants in the hotel, after which she would go directly up to her room, kick her shoes off and relax for a while before going to bed, exhausted.

It was Hilary's last night in Hong Kong and she was at her Uncle's large, high rise apartment on Kowloon Island, his housekeeper clearing away their dishes.

'So, Miss Saunders, what do you think of what you've seen?'

She took in the spectacular night-time view of Hong Kong Harbour and said, 'I see wonderful things all around me. I love it here, it's pure fantasy. The Hong Kong Chinese are so hard working and industrious and cheerful, they're always smiling. It's infectious and I love it.'

'I fell in love with the place the first time I came here too,' he said, sipping tea noisily from his small cup, Chinese style. 'It was in 1953, just after the Korean conflict. Our regiment waited here for nearly three weeks for a troopship to take us back home. We had the time of our lives. I vowed then I would come back here one day, and here I am,' he laughed.

'And here I am too,' she replied, 'I spoke to Mum earlier, I think she thinks I'm on drugs or something, I'm so high at the moment.'

'It doesn't have to stop here Hils,' he said, looking at her across the table.

'I've got to go home, Uncle. I can't stay here, much as I'd like to,' she said.

'I don't mean that Hilary, of course you've got to go home. I mean our business relationship. You want to set up your own thing in the UK, I want to develop a market there. It would make perfect sense if you were to sell what we produce here. I could help fund you initially, give you extended credit for the goods or take payment when you sell them, whichever. We're family, we're close, we can do that sort of thing. No?'

'Oh Uncle Vern, you've been so good to me. This place, here, Hong Kong, the Far East, it's all so unbelievably fantastic. And now you offer me this.' She could feel tears coming. 'It's all too much. I need time to think about it, I'm sorry.'

'Hils, Hils I'm sorry too,' he came around the table. 'Look, my love,' he said holding both of her shoulders. 'Forget what I said. Take it out of your mind, OK? Let's just concentrate on getting you home safely for the moment. Absolutely no pressure, understand? Don't worry about your daft old Uncle. Come on, sweetheart, wipe your tears, here.' He offered her a clean serviette.

She sat at the table with her head in the serviette for a few moments, then, regaining her composure, she said shakily, 'It's not you. You're the sweetest man I know. It's just the situation I'm in, with all of these fantastic opportunities in front of me.' She looked at the view over the bay. 'I hope you understand,' she looked at him. 'I'm not being silly, am I?'

'My dear, I think I'd probably feel the same way. I'm flattered you think the way you do. We've got something special here Hilary and this is not Vernon Saunders, the cold blooded businessman speaking, this is your old Uncle Vern who loves you dearly. Think about it Hils and let me know your decision when you're ready. Now then, are you ready for some more tea?'

On arriving home, she discussed her Uncle's business proposition with her parents. Following further discussions between her Dad and Uncle, it was decided that there was no reason why Hilary should not become the UK agent for Vernon's Hong Kong based business. Her parents would act as advisors in the early days. Having appointed a solicitor and bought an off the shelf company, she wrote to Uncle Vern outlining what she and her parents had all agreed were reasonable terms for their future business relationship.

Her Uncle was on the phone the day he received the letter, 'Great news, Hils, and I like your terms. There are a couple of little things I'd like to add before we all sign on the dotted line, ready to make a note?'

'Yes, go ahead,' Hilary replied, she looked at her watch. It was two pm. She wondered idly whether he was in the office or his apartment; it would be ten o'clock in the evening, Hong Kong time.

'Well I can increase the credit terms you are proposing from 60 days to 120 days. I've spoken to my bank about this and they are willing to accept the fact that your business is an extension of mine. This means that you are effectively my European warehouse, the stock you hold is effectively mine until it's sold or on 120 days credit. Does that sound OK to you?'

'Yes of course, I take it there's a downside to this?' Hilary said, she knew her Uncle well enough by now.

'Aha, that's my girl, sharp as mustard,' he said, laughing. 'Yes there is. I want the word exclusive taken out, or at least I want our agreement limited to the marital aids product range. Remember I said I have some contacts in the UK who buy our industrial products? I don't want you thinking you have a completely exclusive agreement, are you with me?'

'Yes of course, that's fine with me. If you make the changes and fax it over, I'll get it drawn up for signing.'

'OK m'dear, I'll be over in two weeks' time; we can iron out any outstanding details and sign it then. I'll bring some samples with me so that everyone can, ahem, study them and find out how they work and all. I've got a new catalogue on order too. Have you thought of a name for your business yet?'

'Yes. My initials. H.P. Sauce,' she replied quickly.

'Of course, Phillipa. That's brilliant.' he chuckled. 'I'll get the printers to do a UK version mock-up for your approval.'

'Make sure it's got a full stop after the H and the P though, I don't want a plagiarism case against us from the real sauce people, and no Limited at the end either.' Her business training was kicking in.

'OK, will-do, see you in a fortnight then, my lovely.'

'Bye Uncle, take care and thanks.'

The terms and conditions of trading were agreed during Uncle Vern's first visit and they all signed the contract document. Hilary's dad signed a lease on a small industrial unit with storage and office facilities. Hilary and her Uncle Vern went on a whistle stop tour of the UK, visiting his 'industrial' contacts to explain the proposed new set-up. At the same time appointing dealers and stockists of H.P. Sauce products. These were potential customers that Hilary had drawn up as part of a marketing strategy.

Her Uncle had become her business associate from the Far-East. The first shipment would arrive in the UK in approximately five to six weeks. The groundwork was complete. Hilary's dream had come true.

Part 3. 1980 - 1990

13. Han Choy

Great Uncle Sen listened intently as Han Sen told him the story of how he and the two girls had come to arrive in Kaohsiung. It was some time before the old man could bring himself to speak. The silence was not uncomfortable; all four of them were lost in their own thoughts.

Their host eventually spoke, 'We have suffered deep losses at the hands of those monsters. You have lost your parents and brothers and sisters and close friends. I have been deprived of a beloved nephew and his family. I have written to my brother in Kampong but he has not replied, I do not know if he is alive or not. I fear the worst.' He stood up and bowed deeply to each of the three. 'Han Sen, Raya and Rao, let us be strong together and remember the teachings of the Enlightened One. We shall go to the temple now and we will light candles in honour and remembrance of our families. We shall never forget them. We can also rejoice that you are here and with us now – no more harm will come to you.'

The visit to the temple was an act of cleansing, of washing away the grief, the hatred and some of the inner turmoil. Han Sen and the girls were becalmed by the serenity and peacefulness surrounding the Buddha. The light from their candles symbolised the aura of the person the candle represented. The people they had lost would always be with them in their journey through life. The lost and the living would never be alone with Buddha as their guide.

Han Sen had told the old man everything apart from the killing of the Khmer Rouge guard and the commander of the camp near Ban Lung. This was something that only he and the girls would ever know about. The acts would never be justified in his mind, but as he looked at the two girls quietly crying in the light of the five candles, he knew he would do it again for them. They didn't know it, but they both gave him inner strength against the doubt and the recrimination in his own mind. He prayed for inner strength to be able to cope with his own demons should they ever have to part ways. He also prayed that day would never come.

'What is mine is yours, my son and daughters,' Mr. Sen said as they strolled through the immaculate gardens surrounding the temple. 'I am an old man, my time on earth is limited. If you decide you want it, we will be stronger as one, we will work together to honour and re-build our families. You three shall come and stay with me for as long as you wish; we will be honoured and privileged to have you as guests.'

'Great Uncle, we thank for your kindness. We will repay you with hard work and gratitude.' Han Sen was once again feeling comfortable in surroundings that inspired and humbled. The girls nodded in agreement.

'As you wish, there is no need. My business fulfils the needs of my customers and of my family. I do not chase the course of global expansion or domination any longer. I was full of ambition when I first came to Taiwan. But craving and ambition are the ways of the unenlightened.' The old man looked around him at the perfectly manicured bonsai trees and the burgeoning gladioli. 'Now life is split between The Enlightened One and our family, these are the important things in my life.'

'You will forgive me if I show signs of weakness then,' Han Sen said.

'Weakness, my son?' the old man said, puzzled.

'Yes, I want to start a business. I know nothing else other than I have a skill that others will benefit from. I can make a living for all of us.'

The old man chuckled. 'Congratulations, my boy. You sound like me in my early days. It is not a weakness, it is an admirable thing that you show ambition and a dedication to something that you are good at. You and I have a lot in common, unlike my sons who seem to have most of their mother's traits; a likeness of numbers and their manipulation, and they are both happy in their accountancy careers. But I could not think of anything more boring. Tell me, will it be some form of engineering?'

Han Sen told him about his early experience in the workshop at the electrical works in Ta Veng with his father and Henderson.

'Henderson!' the old man exclaimed. 'I remember that Scottish rascal your Dad worked with. Of course - we shipped all the machinery for his workshop. I didn't think he was ever going to pay me, but he did in the end,' the old man chuckled. 'So you cut your teeth on machinery that we supplied. Well, well.'

Han Sen then described his work at Phnom Penh under the Khmer Rouge, including the Multi-Stretch machine and the plans for mass-murder.

'They wanted you to build their tools of genocide?'

'Yes that is why all three of us are here now.'

'I can't believe they wanted to go that far.'

'I was able to justify in my own mind what I was doing because most of the people in the prison were Khmer Rouge. While they were in the prison at least they weren't out on the streets killing more innocent people. That and the fact I didn't have a lot of choice. When I saw their plans for ovens, I knew I had to get out.'

'Dreadful, dreadful,' the old man tutted. 'I see from the news that they have been pretty much overrun now. The Vietnamese have carried out their own purges. The country sounds like it's a mess but at least it's mostly rid of the Khmer Rouge.'

'I will miss our home country. The countryside, the people, the monks especially. But I don't know if I could ever go back.'

'Taiwan has been good to me. It will be good for you too, you'll see.' The old man put one arm around Han Sen and the other around the two girls. 'Come, we shall all go home now. I will introduce you to your new family.'

Mr. and Mrs. Sen lived in a relatively spacious four-bedroom apartment. Their son Emic still lived at home, and their other son Raj had just left home to live in Taipei. In contrast to Mr. Sen's sometimes chaotic business style, life in the Sen Household was tranquil, every room containing a minimalist shrine with Buddha, a plant, an ornament and two candles. Mrs. Sen was a rotund, jolly person who ruled the household with un-bendable forthrightness. There were no arguments in the Sen household, everyone did as Mrs. Sen bade them.

The girls found work in the catering trade. During the day they prepared traditional Taiwanese xiaochi, the Kaohsiung 'little eat' specialities of fish balls and milkfish. Then they would work the night markets seven nights a week, selling their cooked food to the locals and tourists. Han Sen started working at his Great Uncle's business, initially in the repair workshop with Ranjiv. He enrolled at a local college two nights a week to learn Taiwanese and improve his English. Within the first few months he was able to communicate effectively in both languages and started playing a bigger role in the business. The languages enabled him to study the range of machines offered by Sen Industrial and get involved with customers, discussing the relative merits of one machine over another. This enabled him to see how the businesses of their customers worked, what they did and how they did it and so customers began to rely on his expertise and uncommon graciousness. Han Sen was in his element, and without knowing it, was becoming a major asset to the firm.

Great Uncle Sen decided to semi-retire in early 1981 at the age of seventy-two; he was ready to devote himself fully to the temple he had helped build up over the years. Several discussions took place between the rest of his family and Han Sen about what would happen to the business.

'It seems no one is interested in taking over the reins of Sen Industrial,' the old man said with some sadness.

Han Sen detected some mischief too, the old man wasn't stupid; he knew how much his business was worth, he just didn't want to sell it. He decided to reply in the same tone, 'Oh Sen-San, it must be so sad to see something you've built up over the years go to make someone else's profit.'

'Han Sen, you know that is not the reason I have regrets. Money is not important to me. Nothing would give me more pleasure than seeing one of your great cousins or you take it over. My sons seem intent on a life of counting numbers and you want your own business, what am I supposed to do?'

Han Sen had been thinking about the old man's predicament and decided now was a good time to make his suggestion. 'Great Uncle Sen, you really would rather one of us took over, than sell the business, even though the money raised would allow you to completely finish your temple, and probably buy another one?'

This made the old man red faced. 'How many times? I am not interested in money; the temple will finish itself. Besides,' he added wistfully, 'we'll get bored if we finish it too quickly. Forty years is just about right. You cannot rush these things, my boy.'

Han Sen continued, 'If you are happy for me to take over Sen Industrial, I would of course be deeply honoured but I would want to make changes.'

A glimmer of a smile appeared on the old man's face. 'Changes? In what way?'

'We sell the remaining stock of machine tools, not replace them, and we turn Sen Industrial into a manufacturing company. Same building, same staff, but we will make things, we won't just buy and sell them anymore.'

'Make things? What sort of things?' the old man asked, wide-eyed.

'I've been looking into what our customers make, particularly the companies who make plastic goods. It seems the rest of the world has an insatiable appetite for plastic goods. I am thinking, initially at least, of household goods, but they would be extremely durable, clever designs, unique. Sen Industrial would be a manufacturer of high-quality, innovative household goods. The householders of the US, Germany, Britain will be falling over themselves to get their hands on our products!'

'But some of our customers are old friends Han Sen, we would be competing against them. Mind you, they always made sure they got the best deal out of me,' the old man stroked his goatee beard, thinking aloud.

'The whole world is our marketplace Great Uncle, there is more than enough for everybody. Your customers make their products, ours will be in a different league. Look, I'll show you.' Han Sen went to his room and brought back a catalogue of household products from one of Sen Industrial's biggest customers and his notebook. He showed the old man how every product in the catalogue could be made from just two plastic moulding machines, one large, one small, both working around the clock. Then he showed him his notebook full of designs, mirrored against the catalogue but with subtle improvements in quality and price.

'My boy you've been busy,' the old man looked on in wonderment. 'When have you found time to do all of this?'

'Sometimes at night when sleep does not come easily. I enjoy it,' he shrugged.

'And you don't think it's stealing? The designs from our customers, that is?'

'Yes, it probably is, but show me a patent on any of it. Once we're established as manufacturers, we can start to think of special designs, but to get us off the ground let's copy and improve.'

'You are wise way beyond your years, Han Sen. How can I fail to see the wisdom in what you are suggesting?'

'You mean, you think it's a good idea?'

'No, I think it's a crazy idea,' the old man said straight-faced. 'But at the same time it sounds great to me. Let's do it,' he jumped up, broke into a fit of the giggles and hugged the delighted Han Sen, 'It's great to be crazy once in a while. When do we start?'

Great Uncle Sen decided to put off his retirement and watched agog at the commitment of his young great-nephew in establishing this major change of direction for the business. Han Sen, too, was constantly surprised by the sheer vitality of the old man and the way in which, even at his age, he was still curious to learn new things and put forward sound advice and practical solutions. Together they made a formidable team.

They bought two second-hand plastic moulding machines and a variety of moulds, enabling them to produce items more or less straight away. Then they introduced themselves to several of Kaohsiung's import-export agencies, offering them a range of high-quality household goods at very competitive prices and quick delivery times.

Han Sen used the larger of the two machines for producing 'big' items such as buckets, bowls and crockery drainer racks, and the smaller one for producing pan scourer handles, cutlery drainers and fly swatters amongst a myriad of other things. The machines were set up behind a partition at the back of the showroom, so that the front window space could still display what was left of their stock of machine tools. Customers would visit and struggle to be overheard against the din made by the two machines, invariably leaving with a bargain as Mr. Sen was impatient to release capital to fund their manufacturing. Sales reps would call only to be told that Sen Industrial would no longer be buying machines to re-sell, and would leave annoyed and slightly confused.

They turned down their first order.

Sunshine Trading Inc wanted 100,000 black plastic buckets with a heavy wire handle and wooden hand grip within one month. Han Sen quickly calculated that at an average production time of ninety seconds a bucket, this order would take them four months working around the clock, assuming no down time. He tried to persuade the customer to take part orders, but they refused. This was an order for one container load of plastic buckets, take it or leave it. He looked amongst his competitors for an opportunity to buy the 75,000 plastic buckets he couldn't manufacture in time, reckoning that if they took the order they would just about break even.

Great Uncle Sen was not happy. 'No, Han Sen. This is not good business.'

'But Uncle, we have an order. Our first order: we have to fulfil it.' Han Sen was desperate to keep his customer happy.

'If we can't make money on it, then we don't do it,' the old man was adamant.

Han Sen was exasperated. 'But this is our first customer.'

'No buts. We are not running around sweating, wasting time and energy and not making any money. We make more from interest if we keep our money in the bank. This Sunshine company will be making plenty on the deal, they will be selling our buckets for probably double what they are paying us, you can be sure. I am sorry Han Sen, I have learnt from my mistakes and I wish to give you that benefit. We make forty percent profit or nothing at all. That way we are able to pay our staff reasonable wages, our suppliers on time and most importantly, we will make the company bigger and better. You need to phone them up and politely decline the order.'

Han Sen gritted his teeth and made the call. The Sunshine episode taught him two harsh business lessons: one, that in the household goods industry, volume was king, and two, in business in general, if you do not make a decent profit, there's not much point in doing the deal. He vowed never to have this type of difficult conversation with his Great Uncle Sen again.

Sen Industrial survived its early years as a manufacturer by keeping the machines running around the clock producing items that would go into storage to satisfy bulk orders. This was a strategic gamble on their part. They knew if the product quality was high enough and the price was right, repeat orders would keep coming in. Their other strategy was to develop close working relationships with sub-contractors so they could diversify their product range. In this way they were able to start producing well-engineered, innovative peelers, graters, can openers and other essential household items. The level of repeat orders gradually rose and they were able to invest in more machinery and skilled staff. By the end of their second year of trading, the converted showroom was bursting at the seams with machines and people. The ambitious young engineer and the wise old businessman had struck a rich vein of success. The old man was set to retire, happy in the knowledge that his great nephew was successfully running his business, albeit in a much changed format. They discussed expansion frequently.

'I think we need 40,000 square feet. 30,000 production, 10,000 design and administration,' Han Sen said to the old man after they had been to the temple one day. Mrs. Sen and the two girls were preparing dinner.

'Maybe on a bigger plot so you can expand in the future without moving,' the old man said, looking up from his newspaper. 'There are some new units on the Cheuygong 2nd Road that Mr. Tsai from the temple has built. They look about the right size, but there is no shortage of industrial space anywhere around here.'

'No, I'd noticed that,' Han Sen agreed. 'I also want to change the name.'

'Change the name? Why?' The old man looked taken aback.

'Not because of the name Sen obviously, I just think that the word industrial puts people off, that's all. I would rather something a little more, ephemeral, something that suggests happiness. That's what we're doing, we're making people happy by the quality and ingenuity of our products.'

Great Uncle Sen gave his nephew a sideways look and returned to his newspaper, 'I suppose you're right, what's in a name?'

'I guess I'm looking to the future, too,' Han Sen said. 'I don't want to be making household goods for the rest of my life.'

'You don't?' The old man looked at him.

'No, of course not. Eventually, I want to produce something clever, something with more of a human interface, maybe with some electronics. I don't know, I can make anything if I put my mind to it.'

'Specialise my boy, specialise. Stick with what you're good at, if you want my advice.'

'Yes, I will Uncle,' he said. 'I will.'

Han Sen, now conversant in Taiwanese and some Mandarin was able to understand Mrs. Sen when she issued orders around the house and no longer had excuses for not carrying them out. The girls had their own stall on the night markets and worked almost as many hours as Han Sen. The three of them talked between themselves about getting an apartment of their own but they all agreed that there was not much point, especially as Mr and Mrs. Sen enjoyed the comings and goings of the household and would miss them.

Since coming to Taiwan, both the girls had filled out physically. They were no longer the gaunt, under-nourished survivors of the killing-fields. They had matured into confident, bubbly and vivacious young women. And they were not short of admirers, especially the younger Rao who was classically beautiful with a perfect complexion and an easy smile. Raya, also a beauty, had a quiet authority about her that could be mistaken for aloofness or coldness. She was naturally protective towards Rao, something that would sometimes cause Rao to shout angrily, and feel frustrated that she was still under the control of her elder sibling.

Yet, through all of this, neither of them started relationships with the many eligible men available to them. Instead, they preferred to live a simple life where the small things mattered; the quality and presentation of the food they made for their customers; the cultivated perfection of the shrines and the gardens at home and at the temple; and the serenity of the household.

The one unspoken thing between them that both girls shared in an extraordinary and a typically uncomplicated way, was their love for Han Sen. They had many long, quiet discussions in the bed they shared in the Sen household, eventually reaching the conclusion that they had no wish for anyone other than Han Sen in their lives, and that the only way of ever satisfying and expressing the love they felt for him was for all three of them to share it.

On the night they reached this decision, Raya gently pushed her sister towards the edge of the bed. 'You go, sister. Be back by morning.' Rao quietly slipped out of the bed and was gone.

Raya held a silent vigil alone with Buddha that night, praying she had done the right thing. Rao returned in the early hours and they slept closely until morning.

The following night in bed, Rao cried, her silent sobs gently shaking the bed. Raya reached over and held onto her, 'We can both love him, Rao, can't we?'

'Yes we can, sister,' the younger girl replied shaking, her back still to the older girl.

Raya kissed her and softly departed.

14. Heavenly Dildos

The sun was setting over the Straits of Taiwan, shimmering across the craggy sea and reflecting on the container ships waiting patiently at anchor for a berth in the container port to become free. Han Sen viewed the scene from the large window in the master office of the new empty factory.

The massive, sprawling port complex of Kaohsiung was a source of some inspiration to Han Sen. Every time he watched one of the leviathan container ships leave the port destined for Europe or the USA, he would think of the future, and how one day, those same ships would be carrying his products.

Great Uncle Sen and his property developing friend, Mr. Tsai were downstairs in the glass-fronted lobby. Han Sen finished looking around the various offices upstairs and leaned thoughtfully on the handrail overlooking the splendidly finished marble floor below.

His Great Uncle must have made an offer, as he could hear Mr. Tsai complaining. 'But San Sen, I could not possibly accept. The price is below my build cost. You must be able to see that this is a quality building, lovingly erected with care and pride.'

'Of course, my friend, that much is obvious and I apologise if I have underestimated the value of your great creation here. We are but simple engineers looking for new premises to carry out our humble trade. Now if I were to say to you we would be willing to reciprocate and offer you our existing building for a similarly attractive price, I'm sure that would make the transaction somewhat more appealing to you?' The old man eyed his friend expectantly.

'You want me to buy the Sen Industrial building?' Mr. Tsai seemed surprised.

'Why yes, you're a developer, aren't you? It's a prime site - ripe for development. It could become the cornerstone of your portfolio. Once we are installed in your beautiful edifice here, you will be proud that you created the very backbone of Sen Industrial. My great nephew will be manufacturing products for customers all over the world. They will come to Kaohsiung and we will tell them - our Mr. Tsai built this fine building. Global corporations, international hotel chains, they will all be beating a path to your door to beg you to build their buildings. It will be the best move you ever make,' the old man finished in a flourish of fluttering palms and a beaming smile.

Mr. Tsai still looked unconvinced, but unable to resist the flattery bestowed on him by his old friend, eventually took the bait. 'OK, so how much do you want for your old building?'

With that, Mr. Tsai was whisked outside by the old man and amid a range of quick-fire Taiwanese and repeated gestures of avowed sincerity or helplessness or both, it appeared to Han Sen, watching the negotiations from inside, that the deal had been done. He went down the two flights of wide stairs, through the ground-floor lobby and onto the massive expanse of the production floor. He had never felt so excited or so nervous before. He felt the weight of expectation on him from Great Uncle Sen, from the forty or so employees they now had, but mostly from himself. He knew they would be successful; they had been before. There was so much to do and never enough time to do it. He must delegate and manage effectively if the company was to grow. He looked forward to walking through the production area when the machinery was installed. Having machinery around him was a calming influence and gave him confidence. He knew where he stood with machines, they either worked or they didn't - it was a different story with people. He glanced across at the starkly empty room to the side of the building that he had earmarked as a staff canteen. A small shrine would be good here, he thought to himself, just to let his workers know where his inspiration came from. Perhaps Buddha would be able to enlighten them during break-times.

He sat on the bottom step of the marble staircase in the entrance lobby and wrote out a list of things he needed to do the following day in his desk diary which he was in the habit of carrying around with him. There were a few meetings already pencilled in, but if they were to move premises, the meetings would need to be cancelled and rearranged for another time.

His Great Uncle and Mr. Tsai came back into the lobby with smiles and bonhomie all round.

'Han Sen, my boy, we've got ourselves a new factory,' his Great Uncle exclaimed. 'Mr. Tsai and I have reached an agreement on the purchase of this factory and a two year extendable option on one more next door for the same price. In return, we pay the offered price less an amount for our old building.'

'Not just one factory then, Uncle,' Han Sen was astonished. 'You've bought two?'

'My son, with your talent we will have outgrown these two factories within five years, you mark my words. You've already said you don't want to stop at household goods, well you won't have to now,' the old man was delighted with himself. Han Sen thought he may do his famous two footed jig, but he refrained. Instead, he hugged Mr. Tsai. 'Thank you old friend, when can we move in?'

'As soon as you wish,' Mr. Tsai said with an indulgent smile playing on his lips. 'When can I move the bulldozers in?'

'You *are* going to knock down the old Sen Industrial building then.' Great Uncle Sen said.

'Yes my friend, I have to get some of my money back you know,' Mr. Tsai said smiling broadly.

'It has been part of my life for so long now,' the old man said sadly. 'What will you build in its place?'

'I have plans for a 72 storey luxury hotel with a shopping mall covering the lower floors. Your land will be just perfect.' Mr. Tsai grinned broadly.

'You old rascal,' Great Uncle Sen said, eyebrows raised. 'You wanted my old place all along. Hah! I envy your style of negotiating. I see these units will be your loss leaders in this case. Well, well.'

'Old friend, I think we both got what we wanted,' Mr. Tsai said quietly.

'You are right Tsai-San. Come, let us go eat and drink to our forthcoming success,' the old man said. The thought that he had just been tucked-up by his old friend obviously erased from his mind. 'You won't mind if we keep your keys to this place?'

Han Choy Inc came into being on the 25th February 1982. Han Sen's intention for the title implying that all of his products would give their users the literal translation of the phrase: 'Heavenly Joy.' The date coincided with their first production run in the new factory. This was an order from Sunshine Trading Inc. for five thousand rotary salad tossers. Han Sen had learnt from the bucket episode that stacked items were much cheaper to ship, calculating that if he produced five thousand fully assembled salad tossers, they would fill four large shipping containers. Instead, he produced and supplied them in three parts - the bowl, the lid with the rotary mechanism and the basket that clipped onto the lid. This meant that all the parts would stack in tall boxes, thereby fitting into one large shipping container. He would also supply the purpose made packaging, so that Sunshine's distributors would have a relatively simple assemble and pack operation in the country of destination.

Han Sen literally worked day and night to make sure that disruption was kept to a minimum during the move. Once the company was fully installed in its new premises, he was able to catch up on cancelled appointments and start to spend more time at home with the family.

The first visitor to the new company was the insurance agent Mr. Veng. Great Uncle Sen had been dealing with the man for years and regularly sang his praises. Yet, Han Sen disliked his darting eyes and his avaricious appearance immediately. They briefly discussed all aspects of insurance cover held by the company, Han Sen listing the points carefully and finally deciding to continue with the most basic cover, making a mental note to find someone else for the next renewal.

A more interesting visitor was a sales representative from a Hong Kong based company called VSS Ltd. They were ostensibly suppliers of raw materials and the sales rep offered Han Sen very competitive prices. As Han Sen was showing him out of his office, the man said casually, 'We also distribute finished goods from various manufacturers into Europe and the USA,'

Being polite, Han Sen replied, 'Oh, what sort of products?'

The rep's face reddened noticeably, 'Well, it's not my specialist field, you understand, but they are toys of an adult nature. I can leave you a catalogue if you wish, just as an example of one of our suppliers.'

'Adult toys, eh? What, high tech gadgets, I suppose? Remote controlled cars and suchlike, no?' Han Sen asked, curiosity taking over.

'No, no. Ahem,' the rep looked around for non-existent eavesdroppers and mouthed the word 'Sex.'

Han Sen burst out laughing, 'Sex? Sex toys? You're kidding me.'

'No, no,' the rep was by now highly agitated. 'Stay there, I'll get you a catalogue,' he rushed down the stairs, startling the receptionist in the lobby in the process and returned breathless, handing over a glossy catalogue to the bemused Han Sen.

'Thank you, I'll have a read,' Han Sen said, smiling at the rep, 'I'll contact you if I see anything interesting.' He laughed again as they shook hands. 'Thanks for coming by and have a good trip home.'

He spent the next half hour at his desk browsing through the catalogue, eyes wide in amazement. He'd heard of such things from shop floor banter but this was the first time he'd seen anything in such vivid detail. A complete range of products dedicated to human sexual pleasure and gratification. Wow, now here was something that could seriously get his pulse racing. Still, he reminded himself as he emerged from his sex-toy reverie, that for the time being he needed to concentrate on his bowls, buckets and salad tossers.

He put the catalogue into his briefcase and went along the corridor to the buying office with the pricelist from VSS. His buyers would squeeze extra discounts from the already keen pricing offered by the rep. Yes, his was a worthwhile visit this morning he thought to himself, smiling inwardly.

Raya, Rao and Han Sen all knew that their unspoken love was built on unshakable foundations, yet their individual nightly encounters, although physically satisfying, were pushing fragile sensibilities to the limit. Despite his dependence on both girls for his own inner peace, Han Sen knew that if they carried on, there would be an irreconcilable breaking point. He had to act decisively.

Moral ruthlessness did not come easily to Han Sen. Instead, he preferred to rely on the teachings of the Buddha and attempt to banish suffering and despair in any way he could. He worried about choosing one girl over another. He sensed that Raya was being uncharacteristically reticent about speaking her mind on the situation. He decided to talk to her, she was the one who knew the answer to everything.

'Raya, I think you know this situation cannot continue,' he said to her one night as they lay in bed.

'Of course,' she said, stroking his chest.

'Tell me your thoughts.'

'Can we act first and talk later?' She vaulted quickly onto him. In one swift action she had him inside her, her breasts lightly brushing his face.

'Raya, please,' he groaned.

'I need you, Han Sen, I need you now,' she said, pulling his head between her breasts, slowly riding up and down on him.

He could only take her at her word, but he needed to be in control. He carefully flipped her over onto her back and slowly bought them both to a shuddering climax, their sensuousness somehow heightened by their earlier words. His unspoken thoughts echoed in his mind as they lay recovering. This sister: like an older sister to him - sensual, understanding, serene and graceful. Her younger sister, almost like a younger sister to him as well: playful, risky, energetic and challenging. He had to choose. But why? Most young men in his position would want to carry on, wouldn't they? But then most young men hadn't been through what he and the girls had been through.

Perhaps it was right to celebrate life in this way? No, intuition told him he had to make a choice. Han Sen, the great moraliser, or was that love-rat, or both?

Raya stirred. She grasped his hand. 'I am pregnant Han Sen,' she said softly.

He heard her speak, and saw Rao in his mind, glancing over her shoulder at him, smiling yet weeping softly. He saw both the girls in the camp near Ban Lung three years ago. He saw the hate in the eyes of the guard who had wanted to kill him. He saw the flesh and blood flow from the commander's head as he pulled the trigger against it. He saw the fear in both the girl's eyes as he emerged from the commander's office. He saw their recognition of what he had done, reflecting his own.

He clung to her, their sweat combined. He loved her, no doubt. He loved both of them, no doubt. 'That's fantastic, Raya. You have to tell me what we are going to do though, sister.'

'I will lose Rao as a sister, hopefully not forever. You will never lose her, she knows the ways of the Buddha. You ended our suffering in the only way you could.'

'We must stay together,' Han Sen said.

'No, Han Sen,' she said, sadness tinging her voice. 'We have gone as far as we can as three, now it is just you and I and baby Sen.' She turned him slowly onto his back in one movement sliding down his chest and taking his manhood fully into her mouth. 'We will tell Rao tomorrow, together,' she said as she licked and caressed him urgently into life. The decision had been made.

The next day was Sunday. Raya broke the news to her sister as they sat in Hoon-jin Park following their normal visit to the temple. There was a period of silence from Rao, then she stood up and screamed at her sister, 'You did this deliberately! You think because you're older, you have the God-given right to take him away from me. I love him more than you will ever know. I should never have said yes to sharing him. You bitch, you've cheated me!' she sobbed uncontrollably.

Raya tried consoling her sister, 'It was an accident sister, it could have been you.'

'It should have been me! Don't you understand? We were in love long before any of this happened. You told me to lay off him, remember? I should have told you to go away and mind your own business. I can't believe you've done this to me.'

'Rao, please, after all we've been through together, you can't talk to me like that,' Raya said in a despairing tone.

'No, you're right. I'm not going to talk to you like that anymore. In fact, I'm not going to talk with you at all, ever. I'm leaving here and don't try and stop me or find out where I've gone.'

Han Sen interjected for the first time, 'Rao, this was not planned, believe me. Please don't go, we love you too much.'

Rao looked at him for the first time, her bottom lip shook. She swept her gaze back on to her sister with a wild contempt in her eyes. 'I'll never forgive you for this.' She turned and ran towards the gates of the temple.

'Is it Mr. Sen?' The tall smartly dressed Englishman had made a beeline through the crowd of animated business people towards the slightly edgy Han Sen. They were both at the AGM of the Taiwan Manufacturers Association in the ballroom of the Grand Hi Lai hotel.

'Yes, that's me.' He was relieved to have someone to talk to.

'Please, allow me to introduce myself. Vernon Saunders of VSS Ltd in Hong Kong. Our representative Mr. Chet came to see you a couple of months ago?'

'Ah yes, I remember, you sell raw material and buy finished products. Pleased to meet you.' They shook hands smiling.

'He told me all about your business and your new premises. I think your buyer has contacted us recently to ask about discounts.'

'Yes, probably, I passed him the pricelist and told him to put the squeeze on you.' They both laughed.

'Well I'm sure we can do something on the prices, we publish a very competitive list, as you probably noticed. We tend to treat the material supply side of the business as a loss leader and make our money on the finished products.'

'So you may be interested in our range of household goods, then?'

'Well, actually not very much, and that's not taking anything away from the quality of your product,' he said quickly. 'We tend to specialise.'

'Sex toys, right?' Han Sen asked smiling again.

'Afraid so, yes,' the Englishman nodded showing an almost indiscernible coyness.

'Your Mr. Chet left me a catalogue from a Hong Kong based company. Their product range looked very good. Very comprehensive, too.' Han Sen was beginning to like the way that every time he talked about sex toys, he couldn't help smiling.

'Yes, Lanchau are very good. Lots of problems though,' he said, frowning.

'Problems?' Han Sen asked.

'Permanently late on delivery, expensive too. I struggle to compete, not so much in Europe but in America. That's where the really big market is and we'll never crack it with them.'

Han Sen's pulse was quickening as they spoke. There was something about this man, he looked as if he should be arrogant but wasn't. Han Sen liked his modesty and his candid nature. 'So if I were looking to produce something in that line, what should I be looking at first?'

'Oh vibrators, without a doubt. You need a three-inch handbag version, an intermediate five-inch and a big boy seven-inch. That's enough to cater for most tastes. Give them a quality feel and make them reliable. Then blow-up dolls and strap-on willies, probably in that order. Once you've got those three basics, the world's your oyster. It's all down to imagination after that.'

'So if I was able to come up with some prototypes, an idea of pricing and a reasonable delivery time, you would be interested?'

'More than interested, Mr. Sen. I'd bite your arm off,' the upright Englishman said, laughing.

Han Sen also laughed. 'OK, Mr. Saunders, I will get three prototypes made and come and see you in one month. I'll also bring some drawings of other products that I think we can produce, and the prices, of course. How's that?'

'Excellent. I could come here, if it's easier. It's only a short flight.'

'No, I will come to Hong Kong. I've been there once but didn't get to see much of it.'

'In that case, I'll give you a guided tour when we're through with the business discussions. Bring your partner, make a weekend of it.'

They shook hands, both comfortable in the knowledge that here was someone they could do business with.

Han Sen flew to Hong Kong and back on his own in one day, Raya preferring to rest and keep vigil for her sister.

Since his last meeting with the Englishman he had brought samples of the Lanchau vibrators and stripped them apart to see how they worked. He then assembled three prototypes using the Lanchau inside mechanism and his own best quality plastic finish with a chrome strip around the bases. His buying office quickly found suppliers for all of the electrical and mechanical parts and put prices together. The Han Choy finished product price worked out at about forty percent of the price shown in the Lanchau catalogue and Han Sen was pleased. This was where they should be, taking into account the cost of shipping and a distributor's margin. Yes, he thought. We can do this.

The Englishman's eyes lit up on seeing the prototypes for the first time, 'Absolutely first class, Mr. Sen. They look beautiful. Whose idea was the ivory finish?'

'Mine, I suppose. They need to be unique, don't they?'

'Yes, of course, and aren't they just? I think we can do a number on the packaging as well. What do you think of a hardwood case with satin lining and a brand-name, I don't know, something akin to Dunhill, with London, Paris and New York printed on the satin? The ladies wouldn't be able to resist. The respectable vibrator with exclusivity. We're onto a winner here, Mr. Sen.'

'The box will push the production cost up, and the shipping.'

'I know but people will pay top dollar for a bit of added value like a nice wooden case that would sit nicely on their dressing table.'

'I could make a very nice plastic case.'

'No, it's got to be wood. It will make the product look a million dollars and also give it a natural feel, compliment the ivory, know what I mean?'

'Yes, I'm sure you're right. You want the prices right?

'Hmm, the big question. How much?'

'Ex-factory, packed in cardboard boxes of fifty, the five-inch model will be $35, the larger one will be five-percent dearer, the smaller one two-percent cheaper.'

'Hmm,' the Englishman said, reaching for his calculator. Let's see then.' He tapped away furiously for a couple of minutes, scribbling numbers on a pad. 'What would your delivery be on 5,000 assorted sizes?'

Han Sen did his own mathematics in his head. 'Six weeks,' he said.

'If I were to give you an order now for 5,000 of these things, could we agree on a further ten-percent discount?'

'Two and a half-percent discount, with a ten percent down-payment and payment in full before the goods leave Taiwan,' Han Sen replied.

'Five-percent then. Same terms.'

'Three-percent is really all I can do, the price is like your raw material list – pretty much on the bone.'

The Englishman gave a slight frown and tapped some more numbers into his calculator, looking askance at the result, 'OK then, done,' he smiled and stood up, they shook hands. 'What do you reckon the wooden case would cost - ten dollars?'

'With the satin and the printing, probably fifteen,' Han Sen said.

'I'll sort that out, I need to think of a brand-name,'

'How about Han Choy in English?'

'Good Lord. Heavenly Joy! I think you may just have it, Mr. Sen. Has anyone ever told you you're a genius? Come on I'll run you to the airport, you'll be impatient to get back to that partner of yours. Any news about her sister?'

It was as if they had known each other for years.

15. *Industrial Inspiration*

Great Uncle Sen did not understand the sex toys at all. 'False penises,' he said thoughtfully during one of their Saturday afternoon business discussions. He had seen the first VSS shipment being prepared during the week and a strap-on prototype in the R&D centre. 'Presumably for people with disabilities, certain parts missing, that sort of thing?'

'No, just for pleasure, really,' Han Sen replied as casually as he could.

'What, so they can pretend to have one. Makes them feel better I suppose,' the old man said, nodding.

'No.' Han Sen was struggling to paint none too graphic a picture. 'They're mainly for ladies.'

'What, ladies who want to be men, with a penis and all?'

'No, ladies who don't have a man.' There would come a point where the old man would catch on, surely?

'Single ladies, who want to be men and you make the hand-held ones vibrate in case they lose them when they're doing the housework? Wouldn't an alarm be better?'

'No, no, they use them in place of a man.'

'Ah, so they like being single, but they like the idea of having a man around.'

'Well, not necessarily. They could have a man too for all I know. I suppose it depends on their lifestyle,' Han Sen said, shrugging his shoulders.

'They like being single and they want a man around, yet some of them have men too. Wouldn't some sort of educational process be better than a false penis?' The old man shook his head slowly, 'These women seem to be very confused.'

Han Sen decided to leave the graphic description for another day, or perhaps someone else would enlighten the old man. 'All I know is, they sell for $150 in America, and VSS are buying them from us in lots of 5,000 at a time. They're great business.'

'Sure, but even so, I won't be able to look a Western woman in the eye again without wondering what she's got in her underwear.'

Han Sen laughed. 'Best sticking to good old-fashioned Taiwanese ladies, eh, Great Uncle Sen?'

'Oh I'm too old for that, I take my pleasure in the Temple and the Gardens nowadays, and watching you run the business, of course. I'm worried about that girl though, where could she have gone?'

'Anywhere Uncle, I don't know. She is very strong willed. I know she'll be back though, we went through too much together for her not to come back.'

'It was the baby, wasn't it?'

'Yes. You guessed,' Han Sen said looking at him, surprised.

'I have good ears. I knew what was going on when all three of you were together, at least I knew towards the end. To start with I was just confused, one girl one night then the other girl the next night. If you don't mind me saying so, you were playing with fire,' the old man said.

'Yes, I know. We all were. We're paying the price now,' Han Sen said.

'I'm guessing you couldn't make your mind up and the baby forced the issue,' the old man ventured.

'Right again, Great Uncle, Raya knew her sister would take it badly, neither of us thought it would be this badly. She will be back. It's just a matter of when.'

'And pray she doesn't come to any harm in the meanwhile.'

'Yes, well we do that anyway,' Han Sen said, gathering the lunchtime plates. They went to the temple that afternoon and lit candles. They asked Buddha to shine a path for Rao's quick return.

Raya gave birth to Li Lai in September 1983 at the Kaohsiung General Hospital. Mother and child both survived the trauma of first birth, Han Sen holding Raya's hand, comforting and encouraging her throughout the seven-hour labour. Once mother and daughter had been examined and given a clean bill of health, the three of them sat together on the hospital bed. Raya held the swaddled infant to her chest.

'She is the most beautiful person I have ever seen,' she said, gently stroking the little one's nose. 'I knew all along it was a girl.'

'Yes, she is beautiful,' said the doting father. 'We have a daughter. Rao has a niece and she doesn't know it.'

'It's her own stupid fault, she shouldn't have run away, should she?' Raya's bitterness shocked Han Sen.

'I just thought it would be good if she were here to see Li Lai,' he said.

'I was relieved when she ran away. It means the three of us can get on with our lives in peace with no complications.'

'Raya, how can you say that? We love Rao, both of us, don't we?'

'She's my sister. Sisters don't always have to get on. Anyway, you love me. Li Lai is the proof of that.'

'Yes, of course but it doesn't mean we stop loving her, does it?'

'No, I'm just glad she's not here. I hope she's happy wherever she is, but now it's just the three of us and Great Uncle and Auntie Sen. Look, she wants food.' Raya pulled apart her top and offered a plump breast to the restless baby who settled down contentedly to feed once her mother's nipple was located. Both parents looked on in amazement. Han Sen looked on at Raya, he wondered whether he would ever understand this woman; she seemed somehow different without her sister around.

Within a year of placing their first order, VSS became Han Choy's single biggest customer. Although Han Choy had sales staff by this time, Han Sen preferred looking after VSS himself and was a regular visitor to their Hong Kong warehouse. He enjoyed spending time with the Englishman, they would have dinner together in one of the city's many top-class restaurants. His host seemed to know them all and would always insist on paying the bill, assuring Han Sen that he would be able to reciprocate when he visited Kaohsiung.

Their talks over dinner invariably touched on past experiences. The Englishman was shocked when Han Sen told him about his past in Cambodia.

'The Khmer Rouge got you to build their apparatus for torturing people?'

'Yes, engineers are in short supply in Cambodia. As soon as they found out I was one, they drafted me in.'

The Englishman was curious. 'Please, if you feel uncomfortable, tell me to stop asking questions but what sort of things did they get you to produce?'

Han Sen told him about the items he made in the Phnom Penh workshop, including the Multi-Stretch.

The Englishman's eyebrows raised, 'Well, well. That's interesting.'

Han Sen was surprised at his reaction, 'How do you mean?'

'You must have noticed in the Lanchau catalogue that they have a section of bondage equipment. Chains, shackles, that sort of thing, even whips and spanking paddles. We sell quite a bit of it, you know.'

'And you think Han Choy could produce better and cheaper, is that it?'

'I realise this could be difficult for you with your past experiences and all, but you do seem to make just about everything else better and cheaper, so why not?'

'You have a point,' Han Sen said, deciding to buy himself some time. 'I'll have to think about it.'

The Englishman leaned towards Han Sen and said in lowered tones, 'This is very much between you and me, but from your description, I reckon there's also a lot of potential for the Multi-Stretch.'

Han Sen was astounded. 'You can't be serious. Whoever would want to buy one of those?'

'You'd be surprised. There are two sorts of people, well three really. Let me explain.' He beckoned to the waiter for some more coffee.

'My previous experience as a General on the logistics side of the British Ministry of Defence has given me access into the world-wide arms trade. We get enquiries from my old contacts for all sorts of weaponry, from automatic rifles to aircraft-carriers. You name it, there is a government out there wanting to buy it. Now, included in these requirements are machines specifically designed to, shall we say, 'impart intelligence in a humane and controllable manner.'' The Multi-Stretch, given some up to date features, could offer the perfect solution.'

He poured some coffee, took a sip and continued. 'There's also a strong and growing market for auto-erotic equipment. There are some very strange people out there looking for the ultimate sexual thrill, a near death experience. If they could buy a machine offering this in a variety of different ways, the Multi-Stretch could offer them a perfect solution. There are also rental companies, on the West Coast of the USA, including the largest; Hert Rentals Inc., who supply kit like this for a daily fee.'

By the time the languid Englishman had finished, Han Sen was sitting back in his chair stupefied. 'It's unbelievable that we're sitting here discussing this. People would pay money to do this sort of thing? Hert Rentals? Spelt H-U-R-T?'

He smiled, 'No, it's a play on Hertz car rentals, H.E.R.T. The people that buy and rent these things are generally fairly wealthy. They've bought all the experiences that money can buy them, they often fancy experiences outside the norm, something more on the edge. It's the ultimate pleasure seeking principle - hedonism gone mad.'

'So I guess they would be prepared to pay a premium price for a high quality machine,' Han Sen could feel himself already rising to the challenge.

'I reckon for an all-singing, all-dancing Multi-Stretch with all the bells and whistles, you've got to be talking a sales price of $100,000.'

Han Sen couldn't help whistling softly through his teeth. 'That much?'

'Don't feel under any pressure, Mr. Sen. It's your decision at the end of the day but leaving aside percentages and margins and talking about pounds, shillings and pence, I reckon your costs to build something like you've just described would not be more than $15,000, even with some sophisticated control electronics. I would be willing to pay you something like $30,000-$40,000 per machine, ex-factory, packed in a wooden crate. I'll do the rest. We can both make some serious money at it if you're interested.'

'Wow,' Han Sen said, unable to think of what else to say.

'It's all true; I've seen what these things go for. Take some time to think about it, do your sums and if you're interested, send me a proposal for a basic machine with a budget price. The military version could come later - increase the thickness of steel, paint it green and double the price, eh?' he laughed. 'Seriously though, anything you send me will be treated as strictly confidential.'

This statement struck home with Han Sen. Were they breaking the law?

The Englishman sensed Han Sen's burst of apprehension. 'Don't worry, if you decide to go ahead, you would be able to build the machines completely anonymously, your company name doesn't have to appear anywhere; you'll just become part of the international defence industry. As for the private stuff, it's just one step up from some of the equipment you get in modern gymnasiums. It's like sporting therapy, really. That's what we'll sell it as, we just have to be a bit careful on some of the liability issues. I can guide you through that though, I've got a lawyer in Washington who worked in the Pentagon for a while. He's offered to draw up a bullet-proof set of Terms and Conditions for me if I ever need them. Safe as houses, trust me.'

And thinking about it in the limousine to the airport, Han Sen did trust him. Vernon Saunders was obviously a very good salesman. Full of relaxed charm and natural banter, and he couldn't help liking him. He paid when he said he would pay, he placed repeat orders and he treated Han Sen like royalty. More than that, he respected Han Sen and his values.

The old thoughts from Phnom Penh returned. Morally, could he do this? The private sales didn't bother him too much. If the market was mostly America, the more Multi-Stretches the Englishmen could sell there, the better. He could still see the B52s dropping bombs on towns and villages. Tens of thousands of Cambodians had suffered at the hands of the USA, this would be small scale revenge.

The military sales bothered him more. He imagined some despotic dictatorship intent on punishing his own people. But was it not better to have a machine that did the job neatly and efficiently than suffer the appalling amateur attempts at torture? It would go on without his machines anyway. You could argue that he was assisting the victims in providing some dignity to the ghastly process.

What about other manufacturers, say those who made cars? Their creations annually killed thousands in traffic accidents and pollution. Did that stop car-makers from producing and developing new models? Of course not. His creations would be on a minute scale in comparison.

The money was attractive in that he would be able to buy out his Great Uncle quicker than anticipated, but this wasn't his main driving force. He would pay Uncle Sen off eventually without the Multi-Stretch, no problem. As with most things he had accomplished in the past, he wanted to do the best possible job. He felt his pride start to overtake any moral argument. By the time he reached the airport, he knew he was going to go ahead with the Multi-Stretch project. His product would be the best. No compromises, not on quality, function or price. He would call it the MassageOmatic.

As engineering challenges go, the MassageOmatic proved to be the largest in Han Sen's short career. Admittedly he had the foundation of the design from Phnom Penh all those years ago, but when he drew what he remembered of the old design, it only made him realise how crude it was and how far he would have to go for it to be anywhere near a world-class, desirable product. Where to start? Probably more important - where to finish? He decided to draw up the basic machine with a long list of features and talk to the Englishman some more about it. Hopefully this would define the end product for him.

He spoke to several people about potential legitimate uses for such a machine so as to form the basis of his design. He started with sports and clinical therapists and found that there was a market for a general purpose machine that people with muscle injuries could lie on and be gently massaged. One tick in the box, he thought to himself. The next call he made was to a robotic specialist. He needed to check whether robot technology was sufficiently mature and could offer the strength he needed at an affordable price. The answer was a resounding yes on all counts. Lastly, he questioned a software designer who had done some work for Great Uncle Sen in the Sen Industrial days about the possibilities of making the machine do what he wanted across a wide range of parameters. The answer was again yes. He was set – the MassageOmatic was about to take shape.

He sat down one evening and drew the basic design. It was essentially an immensely strong steel table - strong enough to ensure stability and provide support for the mechanisms and controls that would be needed. The table top was like a bed of nails but instead of nails, the 400 or so upward pointing pieces resembled miniature padded-rubber boxing gloves on stalks. The master control panel was at the head end of the table, while a slave control panel was mounted on a flexi-stalk for user access, it could be put on either side depending on left-hand or right-handed preferences. Each panel featured a large red emergency stop button.

The intended setting parameters for the basic version of the MassageOmatic were fairly simple, from gentle to exhilarating vibro-massage with the boxing-gloves on stalks oscillating up and down in controllable frequency and in a random pattern. They could be grouped so that the user could have just certain parts of each limb or torso massaged or they could be set to oscillate in harmony so the user could experience mini-waves, either in groups, from one end to another or from side to side.

'Mr. Sen, you really have excelled yourself. What a fantastic creation, did you think this up all by yourself?' The Englishman looked on with excitement as they sat in the Han Choy boardroom going through the MassageOmatic design dossier that Han Sen had put together.

'I spoke to a few people before I started; there is a market for a machine like this in sports and clinical therapy markets. They tell me it could be quite a big market,' Han Sen replied.

'Is there? Well, well. If that's the case, it gives us the perfect opportunity to build this as the standard machine and then offer some options for our other target markets,' he winked at Han Sen.

'I can't wait to try it,' Han Sen said enthusiastically.

'Neither can I. If everyone else thinks it's as appealing as we do, we're onto a winner, aren't we?'

'Could be,' Han Sen replied.

'You're too modest by half, Mr. Sen. Now then, what tricks does it have up its sleeve for the military version?'

'Well, the machine will be built to be extremely strong to give it reliability, the motors we use and the force it could exert far exceed what is needed for a basic massage machine.'

'Hmm, so this thing could be adapted to beat people up while they lie there, is that right?'

'Yes.'

'You mean you could increase the force each stalk can exert and play around with the groupings?'

'Yes, from one single punch from one stalk, to a small group of stalks exerting gradual pressure say halfway along one limb. Oh and the groups of stalks will be able to stretch whatever is between them,' Han Sen said, preferring not to make any reference to people or victims

'Ouch, that's horrible. Mr. Sen, you are wicked,' he said, chuckling.

'The force thing will mean going into the software – we will set the safest setting here at the factory.'

'Good idea.'

'I decided not to pursue the attachments idea.'

'You know I did think about a tickling stick for the S&M market,' the Englishman laughed. 'No seriously, why not?'

'Just too amateurish, really. I wanted one single machine that does everything it needs to do. Besides, we couldn't make all these bits ourselves. Maybe it's something to think about for the future. Another idea for the future is a double decker version but it would be very heavy and very complex. That way you can just turn people over,'

'Hmm, but a double decker version would mean that we wouldn't have to fit straps or turn people over, wouldn't it?'

'Yes. It would be the best, the cleanest. But it would also practically double the weight and the cost,' Han Sen said.

The Englishman stroked his chin and frowned. 'Know what I think?' he said eventually. He didn't wait for a reply before continuing, 'Straps and turning people over won't work. We have to have something where the person on-board either titillating themselves or being interrogated are in the same position throughout the process.

As for straps, you said yourself, you wanted to get away from the old fashioned bondage type devices. Straps aren't exactly twentieth century, are they?'

'You're right. I guess we could make a single deck version for the therapy market where turning over is part of the process, and a double deck version for the military and the others.' Han Sen couldn't bring himself to use the phrase S&M. People who wanted to inflict pain or have it inflicted on themselves was not something he would ever understand.

'Bingo, just what I was thinking. The military love big, heavy, expensive things. The top brass think that the heavier a thing is, the less likely your average soldier is of breaking it. But let's face it, if you've got anything to do with it, it'll be unbreakable anyway. As for the sex- maniacs, if they can afford to buy one of these, they can afford to have their floor strengthened, can't they?' He laughed at his own joke.

'OK, single and double deck then. We can use all the same components, I'll get onto it straight away,' Han Sen said, feeling enthusiastic himself now with a clear direction.

'Excellent, the military version sounds like a truly monstrous machine, Mr. Sen. I look forward to seeing another Han Choy masterpiece. Now then, when can we see some prototypes?'

Han Sen had already anticipated this question. 'I've started to build two prototypes, one basic, one military. They will be complete one month from now, then we have to test them. The basic version I anticipate will require one month testing, the military version will take longer, say two months.'

'You're the boss. How much do you want up front for an order for five of the therapy and five of the military?'

'As it's you, payment for one of each will do. The basic version costs thirty-five thousand dollars, the military version will be around sixty-five thousand.'

'OK,' the Englishman sighed as he pulled his chequebook out of his inner jacket pocket. 'Are you sure that's enough?'

'Absolutely.'

'What's your margin?'

'100%.'

'That's good. More on the military version, right?'

'I'm aiming for 120%.'

'Excellent. We'll get you into that second factory before you know it, Mr. Sen,' he said, handing over the cheque. 'Send me an invoice when they're ready. We'll have to agree on a name for these babies, you know. I don't think Heavenly Joy will go down very well in military circles,' he grinned.

'MassageOmatic would be the simplest,' Han Sen said, hoping there would be a triumph of practicality over ephemera in their choice of names.

'They'll do for now,' the Englishman obviously had other things on his mind. 'Now then, where are you taking me for dinner tonight?'

16. Testing Times

It took Han Sen several visits to the Fo Guang Shan temple before he achieved an understanding of the Taiwanese Humanist form of Buddhism. A Buddhism that made allowances for life in a fast-moving, results-oriented culture. That recognised progress had to be made with the development of society in general, including family relationships, education, democratic politics, business and the care of the natural environment. This Dharma was appropriate to the lifestyle of most Taiwanese and gave them succour from the words and teachings of the Buddha in a context that was somehow sympathetic to the life they found themselves in. After reading several books by Hsing Yun, the Venerable Master, Han Sen and Raya were accepted into the temple. They joined Great Uncle and Auntie Sen and all of their old friends, it was as if they had been part of the congregation all of their lives.

Han Sen often thought of his old tutelary friend Hem Suvorn, and wondered whether he managed to find his way in the post Khmer Rouge mess that was Cambodia. Was he even still alive? Would Han Sen ever get back to Cambodia to find out? He seriously doubted it. He had found his niche here and there could be no looking back now. All of the pain and suffering that his family, friends and country-folk had endured in his homeland made it all the more likely that he would never summon the appetite to return.

As far as living his life according to the teachings of the Buddha, Han Sen had some issues that required some form of absolution. His guiding light so far in life had been Hem Suvorn: imagining what he would have said when faced with such dilemmas. One of the issues was the fundamental aim of the business. He remembered his conversation with the old monk about what he wanted to do with his life and the old monk's wise words in reply: 'There is nothing wrong with wanting to achieve an ambition, Han Sen, as long as you live in joy and in love.' As he was in the process of achieving his ambition, he welcomed a continuing source of moral and ethical guidance. Through the language of Humanistic Buddhism he found that Buddha would have broadly approved of what he was doing, his career was an honourable path to follow. The question was what purpose the money from the business served and how it should be distributed. There were several suggestions in the transcripts he read and he readily discussed them with Great Uncle Sen.

'One idea from Master Hsing Yun is that you give a fifth of all the money you make to the poor, one fifth to savings, one fifth for living and two fifths for the business,' Han Sen said. 'Then he quotes the Nirvana Sutra that says one fourth of all the money you make should be to support one's parents and family, one fourth for servants, one fourth for friends and relatives and one fourth for country and monastics. I think we have to split somewhere between the two. Servants? We don't have a house big enough to warrant servants, and we'd certainly never spend a quarter of Han Choy revenue on them. What do you say, Great Uncle?'

'I say wealth can be split between the very narrow sense of cash and the broader sense, things like health, wisdom, relationships, ability, trustworthiness, eloquence and lots of other intangible things. To the enlightened, money is quite a small part of being wealthy,' the old man sat back in his chair, smiling at his young nephew.

'How did you split the money that Sen Industrial made?' he asked.

'Oh, to start with we sent about twenty percent of our profit to the monastics and the poor people in the neighbourhood via the temple, of course. By the time you came along, we were doing really well, more than half the money we made was going to the temple. When your business does well, everybody should benefit, starting with the less fortunate, those that are not so wealthy, eh?' he smiled knowingly.

'Yes, I agree,' Han Sen said, sitting forward in his chair. 'I think we should start off by splitting the Han Choy profit four ways; one quarter to parents and family; one quarter to the business; one quarter on living; and one quarter to the temple. Each year we shall review it and change it as we think necessary. What do you think?'

'Han Sen, we do not need any more money; we have plenty, give it to others who are more needy,' the old man said.

'The money will go to your account whether you need it or not. I'm sure the Temple won't say no if you don't want it,' Han Sen said breezily.

'As you wish, it's a bit of a merry-go-round though,' the old man said with raised eyebrows.

'Ah, but if it makes us feel better, we've achieved something.'

'True, I'll increase my Temple payments; it'll certainly make them very happy.'

With the fundamental issues resolved in his mind, thanks to the teachings of Hsing Yun, Han Sen was able to go forward and focus on his plans for the new products. True he still had other issues to come to terms with; the killing of the two Khmer Rouge at Ban Lung had lived with him like an ulcer. It would either explode one day or it would recede slowly into the distance. The other issue was the MassageOmatic. Just how far did he want the project to go with the Englishman? The challenge of building the machine was something he couldn't leave alone, it excited him. The military version still troubled him but he knew that between them, they would reach a satisfactory conclusion.

'Oh yes! Oh this is incredible, ah, oh, ah, oh my goodness. The sensations! Oh my God, please stop - it's too wonderful.'

Han Sen and his Swedish quality controller, Sven, stood watching and smiling at one another in the small test pod specially constructed for the testing of the very first MassageOmatic. The Swede reached over to the control panel and tapped the stop command. The shirt-sleeved Englishman continued lying on the bed of the machine in his stockinged feet for a few seconds longer.

He sat up slowly. 'This machine is going to make you an absolute fortune, Han Sen. People will pay huge amounts just to experience that, and they will continue to pay good money, I'm sure it will be addictive. I can see a few disgruntled masseurs and masseuses already; they'll be put out of business by this baby! Wow, I feel different. My whole body is tingling. You've got to try it!' he said, getting gingerly to his feet.

Having both put themselves through several trials on the prototype already, Han Sen sat on the bed and lowered himself to a reclining position to demonstrate all the features. 'Try the first programme Sven, then switch through all six briefly, then Random and Jog settings, just to make sure they all work and so Mr. Saunders can see the programmes,' he said.

Sven and the Englishman positioned themselves by the controller at the head of the bed, and the Swede explained the workings. 'Each programme lasts for five minutes. Number one is the softest, number three is the roughest. You experienced number two. We both think that is the best if you're trying to impress someone. It is the default Demo setting. We're pretty happy with the whole table mechanism. Once it's proven and finalised, it won't change, the only changes we will have to make are to the controls; it will all be in the software, different versions for different applications.'

The Englishman was mesmerised. 'You people, you're so damned clever and so damned hardworking,' he gestured at the machine. 'Six weeks ago, this didn't exist, it was just an idea that we discussed over dinner one night, now we have a world class product. Unbelievable.'

'Almost world class,' the Swede interjected in his usual sombre tone. 'There's still a few things we have to do to make it perfect but yes, everything we do here is Han Sen's personal baby. If it's not right, it gets rejected, this attitude gives us an edge over our competitors.'

'I'll say. What else is there to do?' the Englishman asked.

'We have to finish off a further two weeks of testing to make sure it's reliable. We have some overweight people from the local slimming club lined up to come and do their worst on it, that's mainly so we're confident about the American market. Then we have to get it certified by an independent test house - this is important for the product liability insurance. Then we write a manual, work out the packaging and voila, production can commence.'

Han Sen hopped off the table. 'Hold it on a vertical number one wave, Sven.' They all watched as the boxing gloves on stalks rose up and down in a wave pattern from the head to the foot of the bed. 'Now horizontal.' The Swede touched the panel and the movement of the stalks changed to a sideways wave from left to right. 'Now put it on six and do the same thing.' The Swede tapped the panel five times and the stalks' upward travel increased dramatically. 'This is just to show you the variation in movement; number six is set at a maximum of fifty millimetres, anything more and you start feeling seasick. We reckon it's about equivalent to a Force Eight Gale!' he laughed.

The Englishman held his stomach and grimaced, 'You could probably sell it to trainee yachtsmen as a simulator. Call it the Multi-Puke. Hah! You think I'm joking,' he laughed at the two engineers. 'Come on then, we've got a lot to talk about and I'm disappearing this afternoon. Got a meeting tomorrow morning in Shanghai. There's a chap I know there in defence procurement who's itching to get his hands on something like this, the military version anyway. So what's for lunch?'

'We'll go to Hoo Yan's Gravy House and get a quick buffet,' Han Sen said. 'Sven, if you could carry on with the programme, give the slimming club a chaser.'

Over a snack of marlin fish balls and rice noodles accompanied by several cups of chai, they discussed progress and agreed some dates for the first shipment.

Then Han Sen moved the conversation onto the more delicate subject of the military version. 'What I'm going to suggest is something you may not like, but tell me, OK? I'm sure we can sort it out.' The Englishman looked at him with slightly raised eyebrows. 'We will produce the military version as a fully functioning, double-deck version of what you've just seen, on the dates that we've just agreed, OK?'

The Englishman looked mildly surprised now. 'Yes, what's the problem?'

'The problem is, Vernon, that I can't morally stand up in the temple in front of Buddha knowing that I have designed something that is going to injure people. Sorry, but there it is, I just can't do it. I did it once before and I still have problems with it.'

'But you have. You are, making a machine that could injure people.'

'No, I am making a mechanism that can be adapted for many purposes. We have started with the therapy version. And there's a wide market available. You mentioned yachtsman earlier, maybe as a joke but who knows? All kinds of simulators could use a large scale version. The possibilities are endless.'

'So where does this leave my order for five of the bloody things? All sold, with more orders expected, I might add.' The Englishman's expression was serious now.

'Don't worry, I will fulfil your order, you shall have your machines. The only thing I cannot do is write the software that you'll need to make it do what you want it to do. I think it would be a good idea if you offered your customers a standard type of software programme with a number of options. I will put you in direct contact with our software designer, he knows the basics of what you want.'

'How much is all this going to cost me?' the serious expression was changing to anxiety.

'Nothing as far as I am concerned. I will give you the plug in panel pre-programmed to do what you want it to do, within certain parameters, of course. These I have agreed with the designer, you just have to agree with him what needs to be done.'

'You're not stitching me up with some sort of liability or design right issue here are you, Mr. Sen?' The suspicious look had re-appeared.

'There are two things you have to remember, Vernon. One is the Khmer Rouge. You know what went on, you know what I did on their behalf. There are other things that I did in that era that I am equally not proud of. Things that no one is ever going to hear about. Two, I stand tall in the temple as a committed member of the congregation, I ask for forgiveness every day for what happened in Cambodia. I can't expect the Enlightened One to listen to me when I carry on doing what I was doing before.'

'I understand, Mr. Sen. I just wish you'd told me all this before.' The Englishmen looked resigned.

'You are getting a fine product, and with some additional input, it will be perfect for your needs, believe me. I trust this software designer, you will too,' Han Sen said testily.

'OK, OK, Mr. Sen, calm down.' A smile played on his lips as he held up his arms in mock surrender. 'When can I meet this man?'

Han Sen relaxed slightly. 'Next time we meet, next time. Now drink up, you have a plane to catch and I have a factory to run. There is a shipment of ten thousand vegetable peelers leaving this afternoon; I want to see them before they go.'

'Vegetable peelers? I thought you'd given that lot up?' the Englishman said, surprised.

'No, I can't,' Han Sen smiled, shaking his head. The only things that go up are the quality and the quantity. I make the best vegetable peeler outside of West Germany, only at half the price. I'll let you have one - they're fantastic!'

'Hmm, can't say I peel too many vegetables myself but you never know, I suppose,' the Englishman laughed. 'Thanks, Mr. Sen, very decent of you. You'll make a chef out of me yet.'

They left Hoo Yan's Gravy House together that afternoon, both in good spirits.

Raya watched in amazement as Li Lai took her first steps clinging onto the sitting room furniture. She clapped and looked on in delight as the giggling child looked up at her, obviously uncertain as to what all the fuss was about.

Raya loved Saturday mornings; Great Uncle and Auntie Sen were at the market, Han Sen was at work, and she would spend the whole morning with Li Lai. They would read books, make up games, play with toys and even watch a cartoon or two on TV. It took Raya back to her own happy childhood in Ban Lung when she would spend time with her mother and her sisters. Spending time with Li Lai was therapeutic yet somehow introspective for Raya. It seemed to be the only time she could focus on her innermost thoughts; the toddler seeming to inspire her with her unconditional dependency.

She was in an idyllic situation and her worst fear was that it was not going to be permanent. Her love for Han Sen was the most enormous thing in her life.

She also knew that greed, for this was the only way she could describe her feelings for Han Sen, was against the teachings of the Buddha.

Her love for Han Sen came before anything in her life. Li Lai was a much needed therapy for her inner despair, as should be the temple, but the goal of Nirvana had always somehow eluded her. As Han Sen was the biggest source of goodness and vitality in her life, so her younger sister was the biggest negative influence. Of course she loved her sister. As the sole remaining members of their family, they had a duty to love and share one another's troubles as all good sisters should. Those shared nights in this very apartment had taken them beyond the point of caring for one another and into the realm of competing for his attention. Guilt came easily to her. She thought sharing Han Sen was the right and fair thing to do at the time. How could they not share him? He had saved their lives. They would both be dead if he had not done what he had done. More, he had done things that only they would ever know about. Their lives would be inextricably linked forever.

If only she could love her sister without the threat of her taking him away. Her feeling of relief that her sister was not around saddened her to the point of a crushing despair, she saw it as a price she had to pay for this happiness, however temporary it was going to be.

In her mind's eye, she saw Rao and Han Sen walking away from her together, arm in arm, and she would think Li Lai would be enough for her, wouldn't she? The toddler was as much a part of Han Sen as she was of her. These thoughts always ended up with a resounding, screaming chorus of no, never. She had faced death before. She lived with the knowledge that she would face ending her life again if Rao came back into their lives. She sometimes found herself praying for her own life when she knew she should have been praying for the life of her sister.

'Granny, Granddad,' Li Lai called out as she heard Great Auntie Sen coming along the hallway, breaking Raya's reverie.

'Hello, sweetheart, your Granddad's gone to the factory to meet with your Daddy. He bought this, shall we have it with lunch?' She showed Li Lai her Granddad's special treat; a bowl of shaved ice topped with red beans and sweet taro. 'I'll put it in the freezer until then.'

Li Lai looked at her mother with an expectant look. 'We'll have lunch soon, darling,' Raya said.

Raya and Great Auntie Sen sat and drank chai with taiyang bing. They watched Li Lai clamber around the furniture with her new-found walking skills, eventually taking a break from her energetic romping to eat some of the freshly-baked suncake.

'Granddad wanted to talk with Han Sen about a prototyping machine - whatever that is,' Auntie Sen laughed.

'Oh, you can bet your life it'll be something to make them all more efficient down there. It nearly always is,' Raya said, smiling. 'If it makes him happy then I'm all for it.'

'He's not unhappy, is he?' Auntie Sen asked, looking directly at Raya.

'No, never. He loves us all; his life, his work, the temple. Everything. He's always happy, especially when he comes home to see you, monster.' She pointed at Li Lai as she said it and laughed. Cake covered the lower part of the little one's face.

'And you?' Auntie Sen asked. 'You're happy too?'

'Yes, of course,' Raya said. 'I worry about my sister, but then we all do. I don't have to tell you that.'

'No, we all miss her and worry that she's OK, Granddad especially. I've never known him to be so worried. He goes out during the day looking for her. He thinks she must be in Taipei or maybe Taichung, somewhere far away.'

'Han Sen is the same, he really worries for her,' Raya said, pursing her lips with her teeth.

'He loves you both very much, doesn't he?' Auntie Sen said, reaching across to touch her hand.

'Yes, he does,' Raya said, her voice shaking slightly. She felt her eyes welling with tears. 'He does love both of us, but only one of us can have him.' She broke down in tears.

Auntie Sen came and sat next to the sobbing girl and comforted her. Li Lai looked on, curious. 'There now, Raya, there, there,' Auntie Sen said. 'All three of you have been through so much together. You're bound to be closer than most.'

'I stole him, Auntie, I stole him from my sister. That's why she ran away. It's all my fault,' Raya's body wracked with sobs.' Li Lai clambered onto the sofa and did her best to comfort her mother.

'There, there, dear, she'll be back one day, you'll see.' Auntie Sen clung onto the girl and her granddaughter.

'That's what I worry about,' Raya said quietly, her sobs quelling.

'You're worried about her coming back, and...' the older woman suddenly realising what Raya was alluding to. 'Oh Raya, no. She wouldn't do that. Rao is a good girl, she loves you. No not at all, she would never do that.'

'She loves him as much as I do, Auntie, that's the problem.'

'Well, when she comes back, I'll sit her down and I'll tell her. We all love her to bits but she needn't think she's going to be carrying on with Han Sen. No, no, I'll put her right on that score, don't you worry. You just leave it to your, Auntie Sen,' the older woman said triumphantly.

Raya, with her head buried in her Aunt's shoulder, smiled to herself.

17. The Influence of Suzy Woo

'The union? Getting uppity?' Han Sen said to Sven in amazement. The Swede and Tom Huang, their new Marketing Manager, sat opposite Han Sen in his office. He'd wanted to enlighten Tom, on the intricacies of the Han Choy sex-toy test programme, 'I didn't even know they had a union, can we talk to them?'

'Yes, I would think so, they will have a leader, maybe even negotiators, I don't know,' the quiet Swede explained with Tom looking on. 'They are upset about the amount of time we took with the vibrator endurance testing apparently.'

'We paid them the going market rate, didn't we?' Han Sen replied immediately.

'Well, I thought so, but maybe the buying office drove too hard a bargain, they are pretty ruthless sometimes.' The Swede shrugged his shoulders. 'The girls seemed happy enough to me, but wouldn't you be?'

Han Sen turned to Tom, 'It seems we have to arrange a meeting with the prostitute's union, last time we made private arrangements for the girls to take the vibrators home and do some road testing on them. It seems the union are unhappy with the arrangement.'

'You use prostitutes to test the products?' Tom asked, eyebrows raised.

'Yes, of course, how else are you supposed to test a product with such an intimate interface? They fill in our questionnaire after 100 hours or so of use. We get good feedback and the girls get a few quiet nights in. It's easy money for them. Everybody wins. These things are going all over the world, Tom, we can't send things out untested or untried. Like they always say in quality control - the next test is the customer.'

'Wow, yes I see.' Tom said. His eyes bright in anticipation.

Han Sen reached for the phone and spoke to the buying office. 'Can you tell me what hourly rate we paid those women for testing the vibrators? Fifty dollars reduced to thirty five for 100 hours. Hmm, is that good value? Equivalent to 100 average customers in a fortnight and they're at home tucked up in bed. Doesn't sound bad to me. Do you have a contact with the union? Yes, ring me back please, thanks.' He put the phone down.

'So, Sven,' he said, getting back to the point of the meeting. 'We are designing a new product that will basically cool a gentleman's schlong so he doesn't orgasm prematurely. Can you put some thought into how we test it?'

'Yes sure,' the Swede replied, deep in thought. 'Do you envisage using the prostitutes again or is this something we could hand out to the men in the factory and tell them to take notes with their wives or partners?'

'Impartiality is the key, Sven, we need impartiality. We will get some feedback from the guys in the factory but it won't be impartial or particularly thorough with notes and timings etc. No, we will have to make up some test sheets and employ people to test the product scientifically. We should be aiming for data that can be analysed and verified. Anecdotes are not enough.'

'OK, but what about the men, should we use volunteers? If we advertise, we will be deluged. I can get you a dozen within about five minutes from the Swedish ex-pats club.' Sven smiled delicately.

'OK, OK. Credible people only, though. Handpicked by you. You have to produce meaningful test results for us. I will let you know the quantity once I have spoken to the union and Tom and I have worked out the budget. Thanks for coming in.'

The phone rang as the Swede left the office; it was the buying office with the contact name and number for the street-workers union.

He rang the number straight away, 'Miss Wu? Hi, this is Han Choy Inc, the vibrator people? We will have some more business for your girls but we need to work out a budget. No, it'll be real work this time, not vibrators. Yes I know we need to agree a rate. A meeting? Yes of course, how about tomorrow at 9.30, here at our offices? OK, fine, see you then. Ask for Tom Huang.' He nodded up at Tom. 'Thanks, bye.' he put the phone down. 'We'll work the budgets out tomorrow, I'll come in on the meeting briefly. See you in the morning.'

'OK, boss,' Tom said, excitement showing. 'See you tomorrow.'

Han Sen smiled to himself, looked like his young marketing protégé was going to have a meeting with his first ever prostitute.

He spent most of the evening studying Tom's marketing brief and putting his own thoughts down on paper. To be effective this thing had to be as small and unobtrusive as possible, flexible too, to grip the base of the penis but not to restrict it in any way. He thought of male condoms; the Ardourator would have to emulate the way they fitted. All in all, quite a challenge. He went to bed, his head buzzing with thoughts.

In the morning, his desk phone rang just after ten. Tom had Miss Wu in the meeting room. They had agreed a rate following a brief interjection of pressure from one of the team from the buying office. Did he want to pop by just to say hello? He stopped what he was doing, strode down the corridor and entered Tom's office.

He knew, and he could see straight away that she knew. Despite the fashionable western-style clothes and the outrageous died-blonde hair, her face was instantly recognisable to him. It was the large dark-brown almond shaped eyes with long lashes. He stood and gawped. She was still the most beautiful girl he had ever seen. She busied herself putting pad and pen into a clasp bag.

'Rao, it's you,' was all he could say.

'Hello Han Sen,' she looked up and smiled directly at him. Her familiar easy smile made him feel suddenly weak.

'Sorry, Tom, we're old friends. We grew up in Cambodia together.' He couldn't help himself, he walked slowly around the table towards her and she stood up in anticipation. He threw his arms around her and she reciprocated. He hugged her, smelled her, felt her, and never wanting it to end. Eventually, still holding one another as if they were scared to let go, they leant back and each examined the other with a smile and a slight awkwardness.

'I'll leave you two to catch up,' Tom mumbled as he gathered his things and left.

'It really is you, after all this time,' Han Sen said, his voice breaking slightly.

'You've been busy,' she said, gesturing around them.

'You know me. Always keen for a challenge.' He couldn't stop looking at her.

'Yes, thank God,' she said shakily before bursting into tears. She wept silently on Han Sen's chest as he stroked her hair. He struggled to stop his own tears from flowing. He had to stay strong for her.

'Promise me never to leave again,' he said gently. 'We all love you and miss you. We've never stopped worrying about you.'

'Oh, Han Sen, I can never come back, I have my own life now,' she said quietly.

'Rao, no matter what your circumstances, you must at least keep in contact with us.' His voice was as steely as he could muster under the circumstances.

'How is the little one, and my sister and Great Uncle and Auntie?'

'They are all fine, Li Lai is two. She may have driven us apart but she is a treasure, a fountain of goodness and joy. You will love her.'

'We have to talk Han Sen, I mean really talk. I can only come back into your lives on certain conditions. I would rather you don't say anything to anybody until we have spoken. I have to go now, when can we meet?'

'Now we have met, I don't want to let you go again, Rao,' he said hurriedly. 'I want to see you straight away, as soon as we can.'

'Tonight then, call me when you're ready.' She kissed him on the lips just imperceptibly longer than friends normally would, brushed his cheek with the palm of her hand and she was gone.

Han Sen felt drained and empty. He smiled sadly to himself as he walked back to his office. She always did have that effect on him.

Rao went straight back to her small apartment on the other side of town. She pulled the telephone lead out of the wall socket, made herself some chai and sat down in her only armchair. She couldn't believe what had happened to her that afternoon. She had walked straight in on the one man in her life she had ever truly loved. Damn, why did it have to happen like that? She wasn't ready, she was far from ready.

She remembered that afternoon in the temple garden when she had screamed at her sister. She could still feel the shame she felt in front of Han Sen and in the garden of all places, the garden of the Enlightened One. She saw Han Sen's shocked face and his pleading eyes, don't leave Rao, don't leave. She had seen it again that afternoon and she hadn't wanted to but she had forced herself. To put on the mantle of dignity that had become her second skin since she had been away.

Life on the streets was desperately hard, much harder than starving to death. No dignity. No pride. Just dirty filthy sex and dirty filthy money to drag yourself out of the gutter with. To get you somewhere where you could stay alive. Away from the constant danger on the streets. Her talent for controlling her own destiny was spotted by the other girls, they asked her to start a union for them all. They paid her money to represent them, to stand their corner. She did it to the utmost of her abilities. She was a tough negotiator; she wasn't scared to go to the Chief of Police and demand protection from the triad gangs muscling in on the only way these girls could support themselves. She stood in front of the City Council and told them that girls did a valuable service to the community, that they deserved decent working conditions.

As much as she didn't want it, she had become a minor celebrity in the sex-worker field. She couldn't leave her girls though. They had to have her support, without her continual snapping at the heels of authority, the conditions would go back to how they were.

How could she go back to live on the decent side of town? Back to a decadent lifestyle where money wasn't an issue and comfort was a byword. She couldn't. Sure, they all worked hard but didn't everybody? They went to the temple too, that was one thing she did miss and told herself one day she would return. Han Sen was there too, with her sister and their baby. She still felt numb about the whole episode. Why she had agreed to share him in the first place was still a mystery to her. She needed time to think, but what was there to think about? Only Han Sen, and she couldn't live with him in those circumstances. She would have to have him as he would have to have her. That was certain. This afternoon was proof, their longing was too powerful, more powerful than either of them would be able to control.

Her sister knew this. It was as clear as night following day. She knew.

Darkness fell. Still she sat in her armchair, occasionally sipping cold chai. Thinking, thinking. Can I be the decent, giggly, carefree sister, great niece, auntie to the little one and lover? Raya would know the minute the thought entered my mind in front of her, so what was the point? Perhaps a loving threesome, all enjoying a nightly romp between the sheets, all the fun of the fair. That was probably what they should have done before, kept emotions out of it, all three of them just screwing each other senseless. She laughed with heavy irony, it would never have worked.

In her mind she despaired. She couldn't go back, she just couldn't.

There was a soft tapping on the door.

'Who is it?' she called out in the darkness.

'It's me, Rao - Suzy. Are you OK?'

Rao flicked the light on and went over to the door, she opened it. 'Come in, Suzy, of course I'm all right. Sorry, I've got the phone unplugged, there's someone I'd rather not talk to at the minute.'

Suzy Woo was one of Rao's street girls, one of the first to ask her about representing them. 'Anyone I should know about?'

'No, just someone from the past. He wants to see me tonight, I was trying to think the whole thing through but just ended up going around in circles as usual. Sit down, I'll make us some fresh chai.'

'Sounds like you love this person, no?'

Rao laughed as she washed the cups. 'Yes. Always have, always will. He is the one who grew up with our family and rescued my sister and I in Cambodia. We always had a soft spot for each other from way back when. He and my sister had a baby together, that's why I had to get away.'

'You love your sister?' Suzy asked the question, then part-answered it herself. 'You must do!'

'Yes, of course. I still blame her for taking him away from me though. That's why I cannot go back.'

'He is a good man? He sounds like he is, rescuing you and all.'

'Suzy, he is the most beautiful man, in body and in spirit. He is the only man I could ever love.' Rao set the fresh pot of chai and the two cups down on the small table.

'And your sister loves him?'

Rao waited for Suzy to answer her own question. It never came. 'Well yes, I guess she does,' she stumbled over the words.

'Not as much as you do though?'

'If you ask her she would say she loved him more. The problem is they are partners and a woman will nearly always stand by her partner no matter how much she does or doesn't love him.'

'Hmm, in some cases. The way I see it, if he loves you and you love him, you should go back there and claim what's yours. Your sister will come around eventually, she knew about the feelings you had for each other before, didn't she?'

'Yes, she did. But Suzy, I can't go breaking up their relationship,'

'Look, Rao, you amaze me. You can stand up in front of top government and council officials and get exactly what you want on our behalf but when it comes to your own life, you're a straw in the wind! Come on now, if it means getting out of this shit-hole and looking after tarts like us, then you've got to do it, haven't you?'

Rao stopped, mid-thought, with the tea-pot half-way to the cup. 'You're not tarts, you're respectable women. Anyway, it's just too painful. She will be completely distraught, I'm not sure what she'll do.' She resumed pouring the chai.

'And you haven't been, and aren't now? Distraught, I mean.'

'Well, yes, of course, it's the biggest regret of my life.' It was the truth.

Suzy reached forward and pointed towards Rao with her outstretched index finger. 'You go and see him, girl, and you tell him: never mind my sister, it's you and me again, just like it was before. Give him the best seeing-to he's ever likely to have had in his life, bit of pillow talk afterwards and Bobs your Uncle, your whole life's back on track. Simple.' She sipped her chai noisily, looking up at her friend.

Rao laughed, 'Oh Suzy, you make it sound so simple.'

'Well it is, isn't it?'

'Yes, I suppose you're right.'

'Plug your phone back in my girl, you talk to him, do you hear? I've got to go now, thanks for the chai.'

'You're welcome, any time, Suzy. Thanks for the pep talk tonight, I won't forget what you said.' They smiled and hugged one another. Rao closed the door as her friend left.

The phone rang five minutes after she plugged it back in. They arranged to meet.

Their lovemaking was high-voltage. Single caresses set off quivering reactions and shimmering eddies of aching tenderness through their bodies. A dark, thirst-quenching passion filled the air around them and from their frenetic, first coming-together to their post-coital torpor, the realisation that they were finally together and complete again hung heavy in the air.

Neither spoke. They held one another, looking, smiling, caressing and savouring their closeness. Eventually voices returned and Han Sen's mind turned to Rao's missing years, 'Rao, tell me.'

'Oh, where to start, Han Sen, where to start,' she said stretching, looking up at him, smiling. He could never tire of that beguiling smile. He felt himself succumbing, her charm overwhelming him suddenly and completely. They made love again, slowly, leisurely this time. Their first night together after years of not knowing would be spoilt by reality Han Sen thought to himself. He gently bit her straining neck muscles, softly withdrew from her and teased her with his manhood, keeping her on the abyss of orgasm, delighting in her aching pleasure.

They awoke together in the early morning, sunlight just beginning to give the small apartment some brightness. She showered, and he watched as she dried herself and searched for clothes. He bit her bum playfully, they made love again, she was late, and neither cared. They arranged to meet one night during the week. They would be serious that night, no sex, just talking. After she'd gone, he let himself out of the apartment and went straight to the factory.

It was Saturday. Another day, another dollar.

He hungered for her.

'How was Hong Kong?' Raya asked as he came home that lunchtime.

'Oh, same as usual. Vernon the Englishman sends his love to you and to Li Lai,' he said, bending down and picking up the toddler. 'A big English kiss is what he said to give you, young lady.' He blew a long raspberry on her cheek, she squealed and giggled.

Raya laughed in mock outrage, 'They don't kiss like that in England, do they?'

'No, but this is how they kiss in France so they tell me,' he kissed Raya, his tongue entering her smiling mouth. Li Lai still in his arms, watching with curiously.

'Don't you get any ideas, little one,' she said looking at Li Lai. 'Daddy's a naughty boy.'

'You know the other thing the Englishman always wants to know?' Mother and daughter both shook their head. 'What's for lunch?'

They sat down in the dining room, the three of them together with Great Uncle and Auntie Sen. When they had finished eating, the women withdrew to the lounge, leaving Han Sen and his Great Uncle to have their traditional Saturday afternoon discussion about the business.

'So, how are things?' the old man asked as he always did.

'Couldn't be better, Uncle. The household goods grow and grow. Larry Han is doing an excellent job, I'm thinking about giving him a bigger stake in the business.'

'You think he should become a director?'

'Yes, he more or less runs that side of it anyway. He works very hard, we pay him well but if he were to own some of the company, this would be a far greater incentive for him to perform even greater things.'

'Yes, he is a good man, I agree. It is only fair that his hard work brings him a greater reward. What about this new industrial venture, you're building some impressive machinery? Have any been delivered yet?'

'Yes, the first five therapy machines left for Hong Kong this week and I'm expecting another order for ten from the Englishman anytime now. He is our best dealer by a long way, we have a good relationship.'

'Hmm, be careful. He is exploiting your talent.'

'Yes, but it is making the company grow, our employees all benefit both in security and in their pay packets.'

'And this heavy duty version?'

'The first prototype is in the test cell now, we're ready to start testing.'

'What exactly is this machine designed to do?'

'Well, we're building it to the Englishman's specification; he has ordered five of them, and he reckons there is a huge market for them in the private and the military markets.'

'And?' the old man was not going to be smoke-screened.

'It's a little bit stronger than therapy. It's for people who are seeking a little bit of punishment.'

'Go on,' he probed further.

'Some people like living on the edge, he says. The military have a need to push people to the edge. All soldiers do anyway.' Han Sen decided to try and end the conversation. 'Great Uncle, I honestly don't care. I build high quality machinery, if someone wants to buy the machinery and adapt it for their own purpose, what concern is that of mine?'

'It will be a concern,' the old man said in a very measured way, 'when the insurance inspectors come knocking on your door and tell you that one of those machines has killed someone.'

This took Han Sen by surprise. 'Great Uncle, that won't happen. For a start, it's never going to kill anybody because the controls won't let it. And secondly, the liability for the product is being handled by the Englishman.'

'Who is programming the controller?'

Han Sen thought about lying, deciding against it, 'Freddie. He is doing it directly for the Englishman. Han Choy is not involved.'

'Freddie is a capable man but he is greedy. He would sell his wife and children if the price was right,' the old man said in his normal candid way. 'So as far as product liability is concerned, it is the Englishman's product. Is that correct?'

'Yes, absolutely. Han Choy is effectively a sub-contractor,' Han Sen said, relieved by his own new-found definition.

'Even though Han Choy is producing ninety-nine per-cent of the product?'

'The important thing is what's on the paperwork and on the ID tag. I'll make sure that our name doesn't appear anywhere. You're worrying too much, Uncle.'

'Maybe but the stakes have never been higher. I can show you several examples of firms that have closed overnight due to US product liability laws. Once those lawyers get their teeth into you, they don't let go of you, my boy.' The old man sat back; the conversation had exhausted him and he was ready for an afternoon nap.

'Don't worry, Great Uncle, I'll take care of everything,' Han Sen said. He patted his Great Uncle on the shoulder affectionately and helped him towards the lounge. The old man may have passed his best, but he still knew a thing or two, he thought to himself.

18. Setting Three, or Five?

Han Sen and Rao talked during the week over a takeaway dinner in her small apartment. She told him about life on the streets, learning from the other girls how to turn a trick to be able to eat, eventually being able to afford somewhere to live. How she had been outraged at the way the prostitutes were treated by officialdom. So much so, that being literate and determined, she fought on their behalf, formed the Union, joined with their sisters in Taipei, Chenggong and all over Taiwan. No one was going to walk over her girls, be they an over-exuberant randy seaman, or the Mayor turning a blind eye to his officials dipping their wick. She would see them banged to rights whatever their role in life. Most men sickened her. She had even turned towards lesbianism and had experienced a couple of unsatisfactory affairs. Her current beau lived in Taipei and was high powered in the Government. She had to keep the relationship going to get what she wanted for her girls.

'Sorry, Han Sen, that's how it is. That's why I can't come home, my work is not finished, in fact it's just beginning.'

'You have to come home,' he told her. 'Raya, Li Lai, Great Uncle and Auntie Sen, they're not the same without you around. You light up all of our lives. We all worry about you. Not knowing is the worst thing, whether you're dead or alive. Rao, you must.'

'My sister and I cannot share you,' she replied. 'The minute she sees me, she will know that we are lovers. It is best that I stay missing, and that you say nothing.'

'I am living a lie. Being deceitful.'

'No, you are managing your life the best way that you can. You love both of us, the same way that we both love you.'

They broke their agreement and made urgent love. Later that evening they couldn't help having a slower, more leisurely session. They capped things off in the early morning sunlight with a playful, boisterous romp, that made both of them late. They parted, and Han Sen worried that he would not see her again, despite Rao telling him she loved him too much to forsake him now.

'We both have responsible positions now, neither of us are able to disappear completely,' she said.

Han Sen went through his reception area in a trance-like state that morning. He was happy, spiritually and emotionally. He was delighted that he had found Rao, but nervous that she would disappear again, and anxious about his relationship with Raya. He was worried what would happen if she found out about Rao, or more likely *when*. He would have to tell her, not just yet though.

'Good morning, Han Sen,' Angelique said as she entered his office. 'Mr. Veng and another insurance gentleman are waiting for you in the meeting room.'

'Good morning Angelique, can you get me the insurance file please?' He had looked at it briefly last night but the thought of meeting Rao overshadowed everything. He really hadn't gleaned all that much from it. This was unlike him; he liked to be prepared for meetings. He would just have to let his intuition take over and get the facts from this Veng character whom he didn't like much anyway.

'Morning, Mr. Veng, what can we do today for you?' he strolled in to the meeting room purposefully and shook hands formally with the brooding insurance salesman.

'Good morning, Mr. Sen. I'd like to introduce you to Mr. Chan from Hong Kong, he represents a large London insurance firm called Liechtenstein Re. Now, this company are looking to further their interests in the region and consequently are offering some very competitive premiums. We are in a position to offer Han Choy much cheaper product liability insurance than I quoted before as long as it is part of your overall package.'

'Very good. What are the rates?' Han Sen asked.

'We can do the whole policy including the £10 million product liability for just $100 more than what you paid last year.'

'I've not heard of this company before, are they reputable?' Han Sen asked.

Mr. Chan spoke for the first time, 'Mr. Sen, I have been dealing with them for thirty years, I personally know the company founders, David Collins and Edgar Edwards, they are old friends of mine. They are greatly respected in the city of London. Liechtenstein Re has 600 employees and currently has assets covered to the value of over £5 billion. I can personally vouch for the fact that they are a bona fide company who mean business.' He handed over a glossy brochure containing all the information.

'I thought the Re meant re-insurance,' Han Sen said, leafing through the binder.

'Yes, this is how they started off but they have now got to a size whereby they act as a main insurer now,' Mr. Chan replied.

'Hmm, very good. Do these two guys still run the company?' Han Sen asked, still looking at the brochure.

'Edgar is the Chairman now and David is the Managing Director, but he wants his son, Roger, to take over the business. He will do a good job of running the company,' Mr. Chan stated. He knew this touch of family continuity would appeal to a Cambodian more than most.

'How old is his son?' Han Sen said.

'I think about twenty-seven,' Mr. Chan replied.

'Wow and he's going to inherit a City of London company with 600 employees. He'll be doing better than me. We'll have to watch this one,' he said, laughing.

The two older insurance salesmen laughed with him. 'He will have plenty of very experienced people around him,' Mr. Chan replied. 'Don't you worry, it is an extremely sound company.'

'OK, Mr. Veng, Mr. Chan. I guess you sold me on the Liechtenstein Re people. If we can make it for $100 less than last year, we're ready to sign,' he waited for their response.

They looked at one another, and then Mr. Veng said slowly, 'Mr. Sen, it's very kind of you to make us this counter proposal, if we were to agree on the same premium as last year then I'm sure that would be acceptable to all involved.'

'Done,' Han Sen said immediately. 'I'll bring our admin guy in, he can do all of the form filling and paperwork for you, I'll do any signing that is required later.' Mission accomplished, he thought to himself, and guessed they would both be taking a hit on their commission.

'Thank you, Mr. Sen,' Mr. Chan said. 'If there are any other associate companies that you think would benefit from our very attractive rates then please let us know.'

'Actually, VSS in Hong Kong buy quite a lot from us and ship it all over the world, I think they would be quite interested,' Han Sen replied on his way out of the room.

'Do you have a contact name there please, Mr. Sen?' Mr. Chan stood poised with pen and notepad in hand.

'Yes,' Han Sen paused. 'The person you should talk to is the Managing Director, Jamey Woo. Vernon Saunders is the CEO. He's English, you'll like him but he's hardly ever there, best talk to Jamey. Gentlemen, thanks for coming by. I'll see you before you go to sign the forms. Can I assume we will have immediate cover?'

'Yes, of course, we will leave a signed temporary certificate,' Mr. Chan smiled at him.

'Thank you!' Han Sen saluted them with his characteristic flat palm and was gone.

*

Han Sen's next meeting that day was with his production team. It seemed that demand for Han Choy products was at an all-time high. The household goods section was struggling to meet their production targets, with Larry Han arguing that he had lost people who had been seconded to the MassageOmatic lines.

'Yes, Larry, you are right and I apologize,' Han Sen said. 'We are struggling with orders on that side too. The therapy machine and its variants are proving very popular out there. Now that they are in full production I intend to step back from the MassageOmatic group and concentrate on organizing the business. Don't worry, you will have my full attention.'

'But then you get wrapped up in new product development like the Ardourator. I hear there is a special chair in development too. We need you to concentrate on running the whole business Han Sen, or else we'll start to lose all of our good people. There is no shortage of firms ready to snap them up around this region,' Larry said.

'Okay, answer me this. Would you prefer that I remain as I am, someone who oversees the product development and engineering, or someone who organises the business?' Han Sen said.

There was silence. All of the people sitting around the table knew what a key question this was. Han Sen was the man behind all the products. From the humble plate drainer right up to the 20th Century sophistication of the MassageOmatic machines, he was the man who made sure they worked and would carry on working. Some would call it over-engineering, at Han Choy it was just the way things were and it was all down to Han Sen.

Larry Han spoke up eventually, 'You are a first class engineer, Han Sen, you *are* our product range. It may be better to bring in an MBA person to manage all of us.'

'A Managing Director,' Han Sen stated, looking for responses from around the table but primarily from Larry, he was the most senior person present.

Several nodding heads ensued, Larry spoke up again, 'I think it would be for the best, boss.'

'OK, I'll talk with my Great Uncle and we'll do it. Now, let's get on with the real business of the meeting. Can we make the Ardourator in house or do we get someone else to do it? We'll talk about the sex-chair later,' he rubbed his hands together, eager to get on.

They had worked out the amount of cooling that was actually needed to bring about a slowdown in the gentlemen's arousal process by combining some research into blood flow-rates and thermodynamic engineering principles. They then designed a tiny Peltier-effect cooling device. On one end was a micro-processor with the very smallest pancake lithium battery and two tiny touch-sensitive switches that acted as a simple controller. The whole assembly measured just two inches long, half an inch wide and three sixteenths of an inch high.

A local condom manufacturer was then called in to discuss the possibility of integrating the device into a suitably durable, double-skinned membrane that would wrap comfortably around the base of the gentleman's member. There were six prototypes in the middle of the table all employing differing rubber thicknesses and jointing methods.

Sven was the first to speak, 'We've done some preliminary thermal testing just with the device sandwiched between an inner and an outer condom layer. The tests have been on a one to one basis so they can't be too objective. My boys say it definitely slows them down but the real test will come on the endurance trials - full scale orgy testing. On the physical side, my test boys looked at the prototypes this morning and they say they can't deal with any sort of ridge at the front end; it needs to be joined without the ridge, like this one.' He picked up one of the Ardourators and held it up so they could all see. 'This seemed to be their favourite, purely from knowing what the device felt like previously, these are all untried as of now.' The Swede looked around the table with his normal enigmatic expression.

'Thanks, Sven, can you give us some feedback by next week's meeting on that prototype?' Han Sen asked, pointing at the rubber skinned device that was now doing a round of the table, being stretched and pulled at.

'Yes, I think it would be better if we were to organise some group sessions, the results will be more meaningful,' the Swede replied.

'Yes, I see what you mean. I never envisaged telling one of my staff to get on and organise an orgy but if that's what you've got to do, then do it. Make sure you let the Union know what you're up to. I'll let you have the telephone number.'

Following a short debate, it was decided that the assembly of the Ardourator into its rubber sheath was best left to the experts. Han Choy would make the device, ship it to the condom company who would encase it and ship it back to Han Choy for final testing and packing. Han Sen instructed the buyer present at the meeting to get prices from the condom company so they could look at costs for the next meeting.

Han Sen then asked Sven for an update on the sex chair, this was another suggestion from the sales group based on feedback from the dealer chain. The chair was designed for the purpose of having sex and would open up a whole new dimension of available positions for the discerning 1980's couple. Han Sen had applied his imagination in consultation with the Swede and they had simply passed over a pencil sketch of a multi-level chair to the model shop instructing them to make up something from welded steel and padded vinyl. The Swede had taken this away to his secretive off-site test-house for evaluation.

He replied in his usual laid back manner, 'Yes, we are making progress with the preliminary model. I have a meeting with Peter,' he pointed at the model shop head further down the table, 'later, to discuss some modifications. After some more testing, I think we will be ready for a pre-production prototype. It's looking good, Han Sen.'

No one could ever accuse the Swede of not loving his job, Han Sen thought to himself, 'OK, thanks Sven,' he said. 'Keep up the good work, oh and tell your boys to just, well, keep it up.'

Amid laughter all round, the meeting closed. Han Sen went onto his next session with the sales group, briefing them on the last meeting and telling them to prepare for the Ardourator launch in a few weeks and the to follow shortly sex chair.

'Oh and by the way, we need a name for this new chair…'

It was mid-afternoon by the time Han Sen got back to his office. He had several messages, among them one from the Englishman and one from Freddie Chen. He guessed Freddie's call was technical and decided to respond to that one first. 'Hello Freddie, you called?'

'Hi Han Sen, we're just finalising the programme for our first MassageOmatic. I wanted to ask you about the strength settings. Obviously the Military version will be full strength, what limit should we put on the S&M version?'

'That's a leading question, Freddie. I told Vernon I didn't want anything to do with the controls for your versions.' Han Sen hoped he sounded suitably exasperated with his old sub-contractor.

'OK then. On a scale of ten, I think you said your therapy version was limited to number three. I was thinking about limiting the S&M version to number five. Will that do what we want it to do?'

Han Sen chose his words carefully. 'Freddie, this can only be answered by running some tests.'

'This one ships this afternoon. And besides, we don't have anyone here to test it on.' A slight air of panic was coming down the phone line.

'In my experience, something that sounds sensible does not always give you the result you are looking for,' Han Sen said, always the diplomat. 'I would delay the shipment until you are satisfied.'

'Come on, Han Sen, you've run tests on these things. If we increase the strength are people going to hurt themselves?'

Han Sen could tell the programmer was in a bit of a spot. 'Undoubtedly. But I thought these people wanted to hurt themselves?' Han Sen replied.

There was a momentary hesitation from the other end. 'Thanks Han Sen, that's the answer I was looking for. I'll talk to you later, bye.'

'Bye Freddie,' Han Sen said to the dead handset. I should have expected this, he thought to himself. Selling sophisticated equipment to cowboys. He respected Freddie but his Great Uncle was right, he was in it just for the money.

He looked at his post for ten minutes, then called the Englishman out of courtesy. 'Hello Vernon, you called.'

'Han Sen! Thanks for ringing back,' he said as if they hadn't seen each other for years. 'How are you, old chap? Busy, I'm guessing. How're all of those new products of yours coming along?'

'They're coming along nicely. We're doing some final testing on the Ardourator and the sex chair as we speak. Actually, we need a name for the chair, you're normally quite good at that sort of thing.'

'How about the Tally-Ho chair?' the Englishman responded straight away.

'Tally Ho? What does that mean?' Han Sen said.

'Back in England, when the gentry go hunting on horses with their packs of dogs, they generally cry Tally-Ho and blow bugles and rush about in a frenzy of excitement whenever they spot a fox or anything else worth chasing for the dogs to rip apart,' he made an extremely loud bugling noise down the phone line.

'OK, OK.' Han Sen gingerly returned the phone to his ear. 'It is supposed to be a pleasurable experience, using the chair that is.'

'Pleasure? You obviously don't understand the English upper-class, Han Sen. Anyway, enough about Tally-Hoing, you're obviously not too impressed. Changing the subject, I gather you've spoken to Freddie and re-assured him of the correct settings for our first MassageOmatic that we're sending out this afternoon?'

He had guessed this would be the subject of their conversation. 'Yes, I have spoken to Freddie.'

'And?'

'What do you mean, and?'

'Are you happy with what he is proposing to do?'

'I said to him, the only way of establishing whether it is correct or not, is to carry out some tests.'

'You're sitting on the fence on this one then.'

'Vernon, the mechanism I have made for you is a first class, proven piece of engineering. It will not let you down. The control of the mechanism is down to you, that is how we agreed to proceed with both the Military and the other versions.'

'But you agree in principle that the S&M version should be roughly half the strength of the Military, don't you?'

'If you see that as an appropriate scale for your customers then I see no reason to disagree with you.'

'OK,' the Englishman talked slowly. 'I see. I'm all on my own with this one then?'

'No. If you have a problem with the mechanism that is my problem. You are not on your own. We have spoken about this before, you know my position,' Han Sen said with an air of finality.

There was a pause. 'Yes, I understand completely. Thanks, old friend. We're sending the first one out this afternoon to a customer in the UK, I'll let you know of any feedback we get. Even if you don't want to hear about it,' the Englishman said with a sardonic ring to his voice.

'OK Vernon, I'll be pleased to hear your feedback. If we can improve the mechanism, then we will.'

Han Sen put the phone down with a sigh. He shouldn't have allowed himself to get into this position. The other sex toys were fun and whimsical, this was a big leap into the unknown for him and for Han Choy. He was nervous.

His perspective of the MassageOmatic range had changed over the weeks they had been building them in the factory. The basic version was a first class Han Choy product that would sell in its thousands. Likewise, the Military version didn't bother him too much;

the Englishman was merely fulfilling a commercial need. The version aimed at the other market was the one that bothered him. This machine was going out to the general public. Deviants they may be, but they were unskilled and untrained users. He was certain there would be some fallout. Still, it was all down to the Englishman and nothing seemed to bother him, aside from making more money.

These were the thoughts in Han Sen's mind as he walked through the busy factory to oversee the preparation of the first large shipment of all three variants of the MassageOmatic. His production teams had been working long hours for the last three months to make the quantity of machines on this order. The shipping department was crammed with large wooden crates piled up three-high and ready for packing into shipping containers destined for Europe. On a smaller scale, yet still managing to spill out onto the factory walkways, were the Military versions, ready for shipment by truck and ferry to VSS.

He looked at the mountain of hardware and marvelled that this was all due to one conversation in a restaurant four years ago. Here he was sending out over 11 million dollars' worth of Han Choy product in one shipment. It staggered him, it staggered everybody in the business. They would soon need a third factory.

He arrived home later than usual that night, exhausted. Raya was waiting for him as she normally did, everyone else was in bed. She poured some fresh chai for him and made a small bowl of noodles to go with the prawns she had saved from earlier.

He ate the dish as she told him about their day. 'Your daughter is the most curious person; she wants to know about everything. Questions, questions, questions; she wears me out. Today we went to Shoushan to see the monkeys and she was telling people off for feeding them. She went straight up to one older gentleman and said, `Please don't feed the monkeys it makes them aggressive.' He stuffed his bread into his bag and walked off, I think he was a bit embarrassed, I was too,' she laughed. They laughed together.

'The thing is though,' Han Sen said between mouthfuls, 'is that she's nearly always right.'

'I don't know where she gets it from,' Raya said, still smiling.

'I do, she's just like her mother used to be,' he said, looking up at her from the bowl of noodles.

'Used to be? Does that mean I'm not right any longer?' Raya looked at him with one raised eyebrow.

'Yes, of course, I'm only joking.' Not the time for conflict, he thought to himself.

As he lay in bed that night, he sighed inwardly. Why did every conversation have to be so loaded? They both knew it was because of Rao. Neither could raise the subject any longer. Would their relationship just decay to a point where it was unsustainable? He shuddered when he thought about what would happen when Raya found out about her sister and him. He wondered how long he could keep up the pretence. Something would happen sooner or later, or should he force the issue?

He dozed in and out of consciousness with thoughts about the two sisters and him living together again, being able to share their lives together. His last thought before the final oblivion of sleep was that perhaps not all dreams are impossible. Surely?

Part 4. 1982 - 1990

19. Extradition

Quentin chuckled as Roger opened Hilary's first letter at the small table and passed over the picture for his approval. 'She's real cute. I feel like I know her already, if you know what I mean.'

It had taken almost five weeks for Roger to receive a reply to his letter. But she *had* written back. A small photo was neatly folded in between four pages written in a handwriting style that was instantly recognisable as 'girl'. The dot above the 'i' in her name was a little squashed oval, and there was even a single kiss at the end! Roger read the letter three times.

Quentin was perplexed. 'She's mighty pretty, buddy,' he said, looking at the small picture of the blonde, smiling Hilary.

'Yes,' Roger gushed. 'She used to die her hair, she's natural now.'

Quentin leered at the photo. 'What, all of her hair?'

'No, of course not. She shaved too often for that,' Roger lied. Quentin's bedtime stories had all sorts of sexual embellishments, chief among them being a recurring fantasy of his imaginary girlfriend's nether regions.

'You'll have to get her to send a bigger one next time. Maybe persuade her to take one without so many clothes on.' His cell-mate pouted, still looking at the small picture.

'She says here that her Uncle imports dildos from the Far-East. She's going to set up in business with him!' Roger said. Was she making this up?

'Wow. Pussy heaven,' Quentin said dreamily. 'Ask her if she could send us some freshly used ones.'

'You are gross,' Roger grimaced. He started to read the letter for the fourth time.

Roger's predicament of being put in a cell with the slightly unpredictable yet cuddly Quentin, as he described him in letters home, was a very large slice of good fortune. Prison life outside their cell was barbaric and dangerous. He often thought back to the words of the woman who introduced Roger to the prison and how right she had been. Ignoring everybody else and everything that went on around you was probably the best way to survive. There were some inmates who resented him merely for having an English accent, mostly this took the form of impolite joshing which Roger was able to laugh along with, and in some cases give back as good as he got. He soon learnt that misjudging the situation or overstepping the mark was a dangerous business.

King of the pile in E Wing was Tony Oliuzi. Sicilian born, he was related by marriage to the Carpetta family, who had drug dealing and extortion networks in all the major US cities. Oliuzi spent most of his time in his hardly-ever-locked cell, his Cosa Nostra cronies doing all of his legwork, and would venture out occasionally for recreation surrounded by his bodyguards. It was said that he controlled his business interests on the outside just as effectively and probably in greater safety from the inside. The warders on E Wing were mostly all on his payroll, so nothing was out of the question. Nothing apart from one thing. Oliuzi was a sex maniac and there is only one way a sex maniac can get his kicks in an all-male prison. Freshly inducted young inmates were his favourite prey. A fresh, young English inmate particularly appealed to Tony's warped mind.

'Hey, McDonald. Come out here,' a warder called out as he unlocked the cell door just after their evening meal. As Quentin disappeared out of the door to see what the warder wanted, one of Oliuzi's thick-necked cronies slipped into the cell and said to Roger in a threatening voice, 'Mr. Oliuzi is coming to see you now. You be very polite to him, you hear?'

Roger looked up from the book he was reading and smiled questioningly at the serious looking, olive-skinned inmate. 'What is he, a social worker? Prison visitor, that sort of thing?' he asked with reckless irony.

The Sicilian thug looked at Roger with venom in his eyes. Oliuzi swept past him into the cell, removing a calf leather glove from one hand, an overcoat slung across his shoulders, every inch the Mafia Don.

'You could say I'm a prison visitor, Roger,' he said, standing very close to the still-seated Roger. 'Except, I don't do it voluntarily. There's always a price to pay when I come visiting our newer members.'

Roger shook his head and went to carry on reading. Oliuzi's ungloved hand stroked Rogers face whilst the thug continued to stand by the cell door.

'Do you mind Scarface?' Roger asked, looking up at the Italian for the first time. 'I hope you washed your hands recently,' he said, wiping his cheek and frowning.

'Think you're the clever Englishman, don't you, boy? I'm not here to listen to your wise-ass comments, I have people to do that for me, like Luigi here,' he said gesturing at the thug standing by the door now brandishing a flick knife. 'No, I told you there was a price to pay and here it is,' he pulled his coat apart and brandished his full blown erection within inches of Roger's face. 'Suck it now, boy. Wank me 'til I come over you, bitch!'

Roger had been attempting to read a large, hard-backed copy of an aptly titled library book called *Sailing close to the Wind*. He looked with frowning disbelief at the inflated organ, casually picked the open book up hymnbook style and snapped it shut vertically, trapping the unfortunate Sicilian's erectile between its heavy pages. Oliuzi howled and bent double, the thug immediately rushed towards Roger, flick knife raised. Roger ducked under the rushing thug who continued on at speed, ramming into the small table and his still doubled-up employer simultaneously. Roger rushed out onto the landing. Quentin, hearing the commotion, was running along the landing towards him, the warder who had called Quentin out of the cell following behind.

'What's going on?' the warder asked, looking into the cell.

'Mr. Oliuzi got a bit over excited in the bell-end region,' Roger said, looking over the warder's shoulder at the two Mafiosi picking themselves up from the floor.

'You're gonna die, punk!' Oliuzi snarled, holding his coat round his nether regions.

'I'll cut it off next time, you jerk-off queen,' Roger replied. Looking to his left he saw another olive-skinned Oliuzi crony rushing along the balcony towards them, and instantly regretted his words.

Quentin stepped between Roger and the oncoming Oliuzi follower, holding up a big black hand like a traffic cop directing a rush-hour queue. 'Now then, boys,' he said. 'We going to sort this out real calm and collected, you hear?' The potential assailant slowed to a stop. The big inmate continued in measured tones, looking at the crumpled face of Oliuzi who was now limping out of the cell, followed by the glaring Luigi. 'I thank you two gentlemen for vacating our premises. And if you,' he glared directly at the warder, 'could do the job that the government pays you to do, we could all get back to what we should be doing, where we should be doing it.' He ushered Roger into the cell and followed him in, nodding a smile towards the watching Mafiosi.

'You're gonna die, nigger.' The Sicilian said.

Quentin glared at him and his two compatriots. 'If I die, greaseball, my black brothers in here can guarantee you will be meetin' yo' maker within 24 hours.' With a final widening of the eyes at the small Mediterranean gathering on the landing, he slammed the cell door shut.

From that point on, as far as the Sicilians community in E Wing was concerned, Roger was a marked man. Denying Don Oliuzi his conjugal rights was an offence punishable, at the very least by serious injury. The taunts Roger received at meal breaks and during recreation made it all too clear that they were out to get him.

In the context of daily prison life, this was no big event. There were fights and stabbings almost on a daily basis. Arguments amongst the inmates would arise from the tiniest, most trivial incident; a look at the wrong moment, a slight bump between passing inmates in a corridor, someone seen to get extra privileges, or being seen to not participate in a protest or a riot. All were potential killings waiting to happen.

When Roger thought about it, usually at night when Quentin had dozed off to sleep, he became completely terrified. The whole prison environment was balanced on a knife edge. Minor fist fights, if allowed to get out of hand, could develop into a full scale riot where people would invariably die. This really was hell on earth. Sooner or later his luck would run out and he would be raped or stabbed or worse, or was that better under the circumstances?

And Quentin couldn't always be there for him.

He had nightmares about doors. Hundreds, thousands of doors. All locked, never open. He would bang on the doors until his hand hurt and his voice became hoarse. Everywhere he went, there was a corridor, or a landing, always a door.

Then he would be on the toilet, and there was no door. Strangers would walk past, looking at him and commenting. His Mum, sometimes, upset: 'Roger, please, we don't all want to see,' she would say. Then his cousins Pip and Amy would sometimes stand and stare, sniggering to one another.

A good dream would be about solitary.

Solitary confinement was a week for a minor infringement, or a permanent status for the serial killers. Quentin had done a couple of solitaries for asserting himself in minor skirmishes. He described them to Roger as spells of nothing. Nothing but four walls and your mind. No daylight, no recreation, no books, no paper. Just nothing.

He heard rather than felt the first stiletto blade as it entered his right lower back. A tearing, piercing noise as it made its entry. A scything, sliding noise as it was withdrawn. The second blade entered his left groin area as the first one was being withdrawn, the immediate pain of the second insertion shocking him into a temporary paralysis. The third entered his left buttock as he was coming down from the plateau of shock, about to double over, still holding his dinner tray. As this final blade was withdrawn, Roger collapsed, his dinner tray scattering across the tiled floor. He felt his hot blood slowly embrace the lower part of his body and began to feel the searing high temperature pain of being badly cut. He writhed on the floor, groaning, feeling sick, his arms and legs gathering automatically into the foetal position. Please, no more, he thought.

Life around him became very confused as he slipped in and out of consciousness; people were rushing in all directions, someone was looking into his swimming eyes, voices were shouting close by, too close. Go away and shout somewhere else, can't you? I'm trying to die here peacefully. Finally there was no more, the shock and the blood loss overpowered his struggle against those around him and he slipped into an all-enveloping blackness.

He woke up in a green room with one window. He somehow knew he was high up, he could see clouds, heavy, rain-filled clouds, close up. The closest he'd seen clouds other than in an aeroplane. Was this heaven? His memory recoiled at the detail of what had happened. He wondered whether he remembered it so clearly because he had been expecting it. He wasn't in pain any more but he did remember the pain, the violation of knives going in and even worse, the coming out. He flinched involuntarily.

First there came an attentive, smiling nurse, followed by a doctor. He would be OK and would make a full recovery, his injuries were not life threatening, he'd lost some blood but the flow had been stemmed by quick reactions from the prison staff and he was immediately brought into the hospital. They had scanned him for internal damage, the lower back stabbing had just missed his kidney. They had stitched him up, given him a drip and he had slept. Slept for a day and a half.

Then one of the guards came and took a statement. 'Did you recognise your attacker, or attackers?'

'No,' Roger answered. He wasn't protecting himself or anybody, he had not seen any of the people who had attacked him.

'You suspect anyone?'

'No.' There was no point in even mentioning the Sicilians.

After the guard departed, Roger thought through the whole incident, replaying in his head what he should have said to the guard's second question. 'Yes I do, Officer. Four months ago, Mr. Oliuzi tried to rape me. I defended myself and following this incident, in all probability, Mr. Oliuzi issued instructions to his Sicilian thugs that I was to be damaged, rather than killed. This leads me to think that he views the attempted rape as unfinished business and would like to have forcible sex with me at some time in the future. The triple stabbing in the food hall must have been meticulously planned. Two armed assailants behind, one in front, and a further two decoys to distract Quentin. They knew that food was Quentin's downfall, his attention span would be at a minimum when queuing for dinner. There you have it, Officer. Now you can go and arrest Mr. Oliuzi and his chums and bang them all to rights, there's a good chap.'

He would exact his revenge on the queer Sicilian himself one day.

On his father's next visit, the only reference Roger made to the incident was, 'I got into a bit of a scrape with some of the Italians. They've moved them now; they were causing everyone a lot of trouble, Mafia you know.'

His father continued visiting monthly, always alone. Roger was unsure whether this was his mother's choice or something his father insisted on, he never spoke about it. The only excuse his father gave was that she was unable to cope with the emotional trauma of seeing her son in such constant danger. She sent him long, sealed letters via his father and Roger got into the practice of writing long replies. They stayed in good contact and David was happy to act as postman between the two of them.

It was two years almost to the day since he first set foot in the South Miami Federal Correction Institute when the cell door was opened unexpectedly one afternoon and the guard said to Roger, 'There's someone here to collect you. You're going home.'

Roger looked at Quentin, unsure whether to laugh or cry.

'This is great news.' His large cell-mate rose to his feet, beaming. 'I'm sure going to miss you and that girl of yours.'

'I'm going to miss you too, Mr. Q. Roger said. 'I'll write. I'm still going to be in a prison you know.'

'Yeah, I know. At least you'll get to see your ma, though,' Quentin said, scribbling his home address on a torn-off piece of newspaper. 'Here, just in case they release me on parole for being a good nigger. Ha!'

Roger finished packing his small bag of meagre belongings and Quentin gripped him in a fearsome bear hug, 'You take care, you hear? I'll come to England one day, the three of us can have tea and scones together.' they laughed.

Roger left the cell and was escorted down to the prison store where he changed into his civilian clothes and collected his fifty dollars. He left the prison in a yellow cab bound for the airport, handcuffed to a warder wearing the uniform of Her Majesty's Prison Service.

Roger finished his stay in the US Prison with a bear hug from his old cellmate, and started his prison sentence in the UK with another, slightly gentler coming together with his delighted, tearful mother. He had arrived at HMP Coldingley early on a Sunday morning having travelled overnight from Miami handcuffed to the warder, his only reprieve being the toilet breaks. Margaret Collins was first in the queue outside the prison gates for visiting time that afternoon.

'Mum!' he called out as he entered the visitor centre, rushing over to her. 'Oh God, it's so good to see you. I'm so pleased you came.' They hugged. Roger remembered their last hug two years ago, her hair and her perfume smelt the same, this time there was no travel smell.

'It's so good to have you home, Rodge. Well, not home exactly, but you know what I mean,' she said, tears still in her eyes. 'You've got to tell me all about it someday. Not now, you're tired. Have you slept?' she asked breathlessly, wiping her eyes with a handkerchief.

'No, you recover from jet lag quicker if you don't, apparently.' They sat down opposite one another, refusing to let go of the other's hand.

'Yes, that's what they say,' she laughed. 'You won't know the hours in here yet, they won't be the same as Miami, will they?'

'Induction tomorrow morning at seven, I'll find out then.'

'Dad sends his love.'

'He's been good to me, all that time he spent travelling to come and visit. Make sure I was all right. Not that it made any difference but all the same, it was great to see him.'

'He really wants to retire,' his Mum said with a hint of sadness.

'Does he? He never told me,' Roger said, genuinely surprised.

'He spends more and more time at the church, it's his new passion. He bunks off work to give himself more time there.'

'What does he do?'

'He's a lay preacher, I bet you didn't know that either?'

'I didn't, no. He told me he fancied having a go.'

'Well he's gone and signed up on a lifetime contract with the almighty, as he puts it.'

'You're not worried are you?' Roger asked, struggling to understand why his mother appeared to be so worried about his father. He wondered whether the jet lag was affecting his judgement.

'No, look, we'll talk about this some other time. I brought you this.' She fished in her bag and pulled a tin out, taking the lid off. It was a freshly baked, golden-brown sponge cake. 'Baked this morning, with butter icing in the middle,' she said, smiling.

Roger's mouth watered. 'Thanks, Mum, that's wicked. You didn't put a file in it did you?'

'Well if I did, I'd probably be joining you in the next cell. They put it through an x-ray machine.'

'Ah, it'll be well done on the inside then.'

The first few weeks in the UK prison were almost surreal for Roger. The American jail had been a frightening experience with the harsh conditions and the continual violent atmosphere. Coldingly felt like a holiday camp in comparison, just without the cheery atmosphere or the amusements. The warders were a bit like everyone's Dad: wanting to be your friend and lead a quiet life. It was a total contrast to the hard-men in the US, where you never knew quite what their agenda was, whether they were in the pay of Mr. Big.

Roger had a single cell this time and the single-cell life suited him; he read books from the reasonably well-stocked library, watched his own small, screwed-down portable TV and wrote letters to all of his past associates, notably Charlie, Quentin and, of course, Hilary. He no longer wrote to his Mum as she came to see him twice a week and his Dad came on Sunday afternoons. His first visit from Hilary came when he'd been in the British prison for about three weeks.

The warder unlocked the door and shouted, 'Collins. Visitor.'

Roger walked into the visitor centre to see Hilary sitting demurely at the small table, blonde and smiling as he always remembered her. 'Hilary Saunders,' he managed to say. He sat down awkwardly. He felt humbled.

'Hello Roger, surprised?' she asked, her slim hands planted firmly, palm down on the table.

'Of course I'm surprised, it's so lovely to see you,' he said, thinking this must sound rubbish. 'How did you get here?'

'My Uncle, he's waiting outside,' she replied.

'Your Uncle Vern? From Hong Kong? What's he doing here?'

'He's over here quite regularly. He wanted to introduce me to some of his contacts, so I'm spending a week or so with him. We're travelling around the UK in his Bentley, staying at the best hotels. It's great,' she giggled.

'Wow, and you had time to think of me? Hilary, you're mad,' he said, unusually self-deprecating.

'Roger!' she said sternly. 'Come on, you're stronger than that. Those letters you sent me were great, I can't believe they sent you to prison, let alone what sounded like Alcatraz!'

He smiled. 'I bet your Uncle doesn't think much of you coming here, does he?'

'Funny that, he thinks I'm mad too. I said to him, if you can't support your friends when they need you, then what's the point of having friends?'

'There's no answer to that,' Roger said, feeling flattered.

'Ah you don't know my Uncle. I won't tell you what he said. Anyway, how much longer have you got in here?' She was back in business mode, back to the point. This was the Hilary he remembered.

Roger sighed, 'I really don't know. I'm in my third year of a seven and a half year sentence. My Dad says the Yanks like to see justice done, especially for a convicted drug trafficker like me.'

'Oy. Stop putting yourself down.'

She was telling him off – wow, she really was on his case. 'Sorry,' he laughed. 'I've got an appraisal coming up next month, they should be able to give me an idea of what my chances of parole are.'

'Well, tell them from me, you're innocent. You should be released straight away.' She was fishing in her bag for something.

'OK then, Miss Saunders. I'll put you down as a character witness,' he replied.

'Of course,' she said seriously. 'Look, I bought you this. This is what my Uncle and I have set up – it's our business.' She passed a thick booklet over to him, with a mysterious smile lingering on her face, 'Some light bedtime reading for you.'

He flicked through the booklet in disbelief. It seemed to contain either dark, mysterious girls in seriously sensual underwear or cheeky blondes with even less on, having fun with vibrators. As for the men's section, Roger was lost for words, 'You're not in this, are you?'

'No, of course not,' she replied indignantly. 'What do you think I am, a harlot? I choose who gets to see my body, thank you very much!'

'But this is all; sex.' He flipped through the pages.

'Toys, Rodge. In polite company they're called marital aids. They're the future, you know, I've done the research. Increased leisure time, growing single population. My Uncle wants me to develop the UK market and pay me a commission on every sale. It's working out fantastic. I've got two people working for me back at the office.'

'Wow,' he said looking at the cover again. 'HP Sauce, that's fantastic!'

She laughed coyly. 'Rodge, sorry I've got to go. Uncs will be getting impatient. I'll come again, on my own next time. Let me know if you want any orders,' she said, laughing and pointing at the catalogue on the table.

'Oh yes, a dozen blow-up dolls, I could hire them out in here,' he joked. 'Bye, Hilary. It was really good of you to come. I'll write.'

'Yes, that would be excellent. I do keep all of your letters, you know. There'll be a book of them one day. Bye, Rodge, take care.' She pecked him on the cheek and strode off towards the visitors room exit. With a final smile and a wave, she was gone. Roger sat down at the table for a few minutes, looking at the front cover of the catalogue. Hilary Saunders. She had always been like an unexploded bomb in his younger life. She continued to be just that.

'Wow,' he said again under his breath.

20. Final Stretch

By 1985, David and Edgar's firm, Liechtenstein Re, was in its twenty-sixth year of business with over 400 employees and an annual turnover of over £300m. David had watched with astonishment as Mrs. Thatcher's Conservative Government decimated the country's traditional industries, sold local authority housing, slashed higher rate taxation and abolished credit restrictions. The government's ambitions seemed limited to making the wealthy wealthier and the poor own their own homes.

David and Edgar were millionaires many times over by this time, Edgar being the more enthusiastic about the new found financial freedom in the country, David ever sceptical.

'It'll all end in tears Edgar, you'll see,' he said one day in response to one of the Irishman's frequent bouts of swooning praise for Mrs. Thatcher. 'We'll never be able to compete against the likes of Taiwan and Korea. You watch this country implode on itself - in twenty years' time there'll be no manufacturing industry to speak of and there'll be massive consumer debt.'

'Who cares David, wherever the industry is they'll still need insurance,' Edgar replied, eyes glinting as normal.

'These are our customers going down the pan, don't you have a conscience?' David was never able to admit defeat in their frequently combative discussions.

'Of course I do. That's why we changed our sales strategy, remember? Our worldwide associates do all that now, we just do the clever stuff, underwriting it all,' Edgar said.

David couldn't resist mentioning the one thing that separated the two partners. 'So you're going to change residency and move your money back into a British bank?'

'Certainly not. Forty percent is still a hell of a lot of money to be paying the taxman,' Edgar responded, his jaw set firm.

'A hell of a lot more than nothing, you mean.'

'Oh David. How many more times? We should know each other well enough by now. You pay the taxes, I pay the accountant a little bit extra to squirrel it away overseas. We should leave it at that, you know?'

They had been for a meeting with one of their institutional investors that morning and had stopped at Enrico's in Finsbury Circus for lunch. As the plates were being cleared away, David decided to tell Edgar something that had been on his mind for some time. 'Edgar, I want to tell you this in absolute confidence. You are the first person I've mentioned it to,' he said as he stirred his espresso. 'As soon as Roger gets out of prison and we get him settled into the business, I'm going to retire.'

'You what?'

'I've had enough. The world of finance isn't the challenge that it once was for me, I'm surprised you haven't noticed. The call of the Church is overwhelming me at the moment, and while I've still got the energy, I want to make the commitment.'

'David, I can't believe you're telling me this. You're only fifty-six, we're making more money now than either of us thought possible when we set this thing up. You can't leave now, it wouldn't be right,' the Irishman said, sounding hurt.

'Roger reckons he has just over two years in jail, I'm telling you this so we can at least prepare for me leaving, and Roger taking over my position.'

Edgar spluttered into his coffee, 'Roger? Take over your position? But he's got no business experience. I'm going to need someone with a business head on, at least. Whatever makes you think Roger can do your job?' Edgar looked at David, bemused.

'I know, he won't be able to take over straight away, of course, but I've spoken to the Governor at the prison and he's going to set him up with a correspondence course so he can learn about some of the industry and something about commerce in general.' David said.

'David, if you really are leaving, I'm not going to need an apprentice. I'll need a senior exec with clout. Someone at least as good as you are from day one. Don't give me someone with L plates, because if you do the business will go down the tubes.'

'OK Edgar, I take your point. Roger will run the business one day when you and I are both out of it, but maybe he should start as a junior partner. Don't worry, I haven't mentioned anything to him yet so he won't be disappointed. You must have thought about retiring though?'

'Yes, of course. I only have five years to go until I'm sixty, that's when I'm going. The business is on a roll, David. We've worked too hard to give up now, you should reconsider.'

'I haven't got the passion for making money any more. My faith is my new passion. I thought about studying theology in the early days but didn't, and it's always been a regret. The lay-preaching I've been doing over the last few years is great, but it's not enough. I've got to do it Edgar, I'm sorry.'

'I respect you for it, David and in a way I'm jealous; I wish I had something as good besides work. You always were a lucky devil!'

David laughed, 'There's you with your fast cars, your string of girlfriends and your millionaire lifestyle, envious of a silly old duffer like me giving it all up to go and worship God. I don't believe you.'

'It's not all it's cracked up to be, you know,' Edgar said, smiling. 'Listen, about Roger, it's nothing personal, you know.' He swirled the remains of his Frascati.

'Of course not,' David replied cheerfully. 'He might appear to be a bit offish, but he'll pick things up quickly, you'll see.'

Roger's appraisal was a non-event. There was no suggestion of an early release from the two serious-looking, middle-aged men and the one tweedy woman on the other side of the desk. They seemed more interested in his experiences in the US than his immediate future in HMP Coldingley.

'Did you get visitors in Miami, Roger?' The tweedy woman who had introduced herself as being from the Association of Prison Visitors asked starchily.

'Yes, my Dad used to come over once a month. It's only because he's rich though, someone without his money wouldn't have been able to afford it,' Roger replied.

'And your Mum?'

'No, she only came the once when I was on remand. She couldn't bear to see me in prison, she would get too emotional. We wrote to each other regularly though,' he said.

'Has she been to see you here?'

'Yes, she was here the first day. She comes once a week, sometimes twice.'

'Roger, as part of the extradition process, we have to report back to the US Prison Service on your progress. Do you think you're better off in a UK Prison than in the US institution?' One of the middle-aged men interjected.

'Oh, yes,' Roger replied. 'It was horrible out there. Like the middle ages compared to this,' he said enthusiastically. The man frowned and looked down at the document in front of him.

'It says here that you got in a bit of bother in the prison there,' he looked up expectantly.

'Yes, a mafia boss tried to rape me in my cell one night, and because I defended myself, I got stabbed three times by his gang. You could call it a spot of bother,' he added.

They all looked at him intently. 'You're all healed up now?' the woman asked. The man looked across at her impatiently.

'Yes, sitting down is still a bit painful though,' he squirmed in his seat for effect.

'Look, Roger,' the irritable second man interjected. 'You're in here because you committed a crime, regardless of where it happened. It's our job to try and ensure that when you leave here you will be fit to reclaim your position in society again. No longer a criminal, in other words, fully rehabilitated. I would like your reassurance that this is what you want too.'

'Well, yes, of course.' Roger struggled to respond to the open-ended statement, aware that three pairs of eyes were on him. He continued, 'Firstly, I didn't commit a crime. I was a completely innocent participant. Secondly, I don't need to commit crime to survive. I'm going to take over my Dad's business as soon as I get out of here so I know I'm not going to need anyone else's money. Thirdly, I think all prison's suck, whether it's Alcatraz in the US or an easy life like this one, so I'm not ever going to be coming back. I don't need rehabilitating, is what I'm saying.'

They looked at one another as if unsure how to respond. The second middle-aged man eventually responded in an offhand, abrupt manner, 'Thank you, Roger, I think we all know where you're coming from now. Do you have any questions?'

'Only the inevitable really,' Roger said. 'When am I getting out?'

'You've served two years and three months of a seven and a half year sentence. You will be eligible for parole in two years and three months' time, that's July 1987. If you keep your nose clean between now and then I don't see any reason why you won't be released.' The man stood up as he tidied his papers.

He would be twenty-five by the time he was even eligible for parole. Bollocks, what a waste of time he thought gloomily. A solitary warder escorted him back to his cell.

Two years and three months. Twenty-seven months sounded better. Looking at the HP Sauce calendar in his cell and extending the dates forward on a sheet of paper, it worked out to be 112 weeks from now. 2,688 hours he worked out using almost forgotten long multiplication. So, how was he going to spend his time? On the same sheet of paper he wrote *Plan for the future* and drew up a checklist:

- *Learn about the insurance industry*
- *Learn about business*

- *Draw up a plan for a boat*
- *Get Hilary to make a pledge to marry me*

He couldn't think of anything else.

He remembered Quentin's description of solitary confinement in Miami, life in HMP Coldingley was a bit like that, he thought – a nothing. He missed the large black man. He had represented life, warmth and challenge to Roger. There was nobody in the UK prison that he wanted to get close to. There was nothing for it, he would have to get on with making his own life, sod everybody else.

Routine became a watchword for him. His mum would always visit on a Wednesday and a Saturday, his Dad would come on Sunday afternoons. Hilary was the exception, her visits were completely random. This at least gave Roger a small thrill every time there was a knock on the cell door – he guessed that was why she did it. The development of their relationship led to a certain amount of frustration on both sides. Roger, although he struggled to contain his natural ardour with her in such close proximity, sometimes had the feeling that he was a convenient outlet for Hilary.

'I hate being in here with you, we need our own space,' he said to her during one of her visits. He was squeezing her hands.

'Oh, I don't know, Rodge, this is great being here with you, just chatting,' she said dreamily.

'Come on, Hils, you want more out of this, don't you?' Roger rasped.

She looked at him with one of her coy expressions. 'You know what I think?' She waited as he rolled his eyes. 'Well, I'm going to tell you anyway. The stuff that I sell, do you know who my biggest group of customers are?'

'No, of course I don't,' he said, losing patience with her.

'It's people who are scared of losing their sexual drive, people who are in danger of burning themselves out, people who started too early. I group them all under one umbrella. They're all sad losers, Rodge.'

'Hilary, you said yourself, they're toys. Have you had a bad day or something?'

'No, not at all, I'm just getting a bit more realistic about the whole thing. People don't need toys to have a fulfilling sex life, you need love and respect and a little bit of magic, like what I think we've got,' she said, leaning forward, smiling.

'You sound like my father. He wants to be a vicar, you know,' he said.

She looked in his eyes with that honest, heartfelt look she had sometimes. 'Good for him,' she said. 'Do you know what I think?'

'No, but then I never do,' he replied, honestly.

'We should have a Tryst of Celibacy,' she declared triumphantly.

'What's one of them when it's at home?'

'We agree that we don't have sex until we're married.'

'Like we've really got a choice on *that* one, me being stuck in here,' he said.

'Yes but when you get out too. We carry on, I think it's a great thing. You'd be marrying an unsullied woman too.'

'Carry on? Unsullied?' Something wasn't quite right here. It suddenly hit him. 'What about Pat Barry and the other boys at school?'

'Hah! They wouldn't have dared, I'd have cut their whatsits off if they'd tried it on with me. Bit of a snog now and again, that was it though,' she said, a trifle smugly he thought.

He sat back and looked at her, aghast. His perception of Hilary changed that afternoon, it did a complete flip. His plan to ask her to marry him made a dramatic lurch forward in his mind. He had to stop himself asking her there and then.

'Hilary Saunders,' was all he could say.

'Yes?' she asked, eyebrows fluttering.

'Magic.'

'And?'

'Respect.'

'And was there something else?'

'Love,' he said, genuinely astonished to hear himself say the word. If he was standing up, he was sure his knees would have buckled.

'Mutual,' she grinned, offering both hands to him. They stood up and hugged. The warder on duty peered over his paperback, and raised his eyebrows, only to return to the book when the obviously delighted Hilary looked directly at him over Rogers shoulder and winked.

Their Tryst of Celibacy was enshrined as part of their relationship. Although Roger worshipped the ground she stood on, he still had the vague suspicion that perhaps the celibate thing was a convenience to Hilary, an escape for her, because her daily life was so wrapped up in the sex industry where he imagined seediness, lack of respect and exploitation were the norm. Anyway, he loved her and she loved him and that was that. So she liked controlling the relationship, he could live with that. He had no idea how, but it would be different when he got out.

His experiences in the US Prison made the daily grind of life in HMP Coldingley seem mundane and boring. He didn't fraternise with any of the other inmates. He didn't care if he was seen as aloof or too conceited to join in with the others. The words of the woman who introduced him to the US Prison still reverberated within his memory banks – 'don't do any favours or accept any favours and you'll do all right.' He guessed he was seen as the poor little rich boy with his rumoured extradition from the US Prison and his succession of well-to-do visitors.

The business correspondence course that his father arranged for him was interesting to a point. He read the course text books avidly, making notes in pencil as he went. Unfortunately most of the exercises set by the course tutors were based on investigations and analysis of the student's workplace - Roger, for obvious reasons, was unable to do them. Developing a good theoretical understanding of how to run a business was enough for him at the moment – it had to be. He read through the exercises and politely ignored attempting them, even though the head warder, at the behest of Roger's father, offered him a chance to carry out his assignments based on the prison as a model business. To Roger, this meant getting involved in other people's lives, which he had programmed himself to avoid.

His father sent him packages of information on the insurance industry. This was some of the most boring and turgid drivel he had ever seen. After the first one arrived, he only had to see the franked image of Liechtenstein Re on the envelope and it would be dispatched almost straight into the waste-bin. He did actually open them just in case his father had enclosed some money, or include a handwritten note that would make life difficult if his father asked him about it. The thousands of words written about items such as actuarial standards, reliability statistics in the engineering industry and networks of liable parties only had one effect on Roger – they sent him to sleep.

As he whiled away the hours, days and weeks of his remaining sentence, Roger did manage to tick-off some of the items on his wish list. The boat of his dreams took shape on a sketch pad with hundreds of sketches and design notes detailing the features he wanted. He promised himself that one of the first things he would do on taking over Lichtenstein Re would be to commission the build of this boat.

There was now certainty that Roger would be taking over Liechtenstein Re. David was pleased that his son was going to inherit and hopefully grow what he had started, and would enable him to take up what he saw as his life's ambition; the full time worship of God. Roger was pleased because he would be wealthy. Yes, stinking rich. He couldn't wait.

Roger celebrated his twenty-fivth birthday in HMP Coldingley, and Sunday afternoon visiting saw both his parents arrive brandishing gifts.

'Thanks Mum and Dad, you shouldn't have,' Roger grinned at them as he finished knotting the silk tie. 'This feels great, I need a mirror.'

'It's not very big, but it's better than nothing,' his Mother said as she offered him the make-up mirror that normally adorned her dressing table from her handbag.

'Wow, fantastic,' Roger said as he held the mirror at full stretch with both arms and slowly moved it up and down.

In anticipation of his release they had bought him a suit, a shirt, a tie and a pair of black leather shoes. His mother had insisted on buying some new underwear for him too, the unopened pack of boxers lay on the desk, ready for later.

'It's for your release, and hopefully for your first day at your father's company,' his mother said, beaming.

'What do you mean hopefully? It's going to happen Mum. Isn't it Dad?'

'Yes of course it is, son,' his father said. 'We've already got a training course set up for you.'

'Training course?' He looked at his father askance. 'I thought all the stuff you've been sending me was training.'

'Well, yes it is, the course you'll be going on is specifically about the company, how we operate, who's who, that sort of thing. We run it for all new employees,' his father said.

'Employee?' Roger was suspicious now. He was hearing all the wrong words. 'I thought I was going to be in charge.'

'You will be, son, don't worry, you will be. You just need to know a bit about what you're going to be in charge of, that's all,' his father said. 'This is a company with interests all around the world, Rodge. You can't just walk in more or less off the street and take over, you need to know the basics at least. Edgar will be able to show you some things, I'll be in the background as well, but a basic understanding is essential.'

'OK,' Roger said begrudgingly. 'As long as Edgar realises that I'm going to be in charge.'

'Did anyone else send you a present or a card?' David asked, tactfully changing the subject.

'Yes, I had a brilliant card from Hilary. She says she's going to bring my present along, probably later.' Although he wasn't actually certain when or if she would arrive.

'You two seem to be getting quite close,' his mother said.

'Yes, she runs her own business so she's quite busy, although obviously not as busy as I'm going to be when I'm out. It's good that she comes to see me while I've still got the time in here really.'

'Not that close then,' his mother replied.

On the day of his release, Roger emerged blinking into the sunlight of the vast outside world, his figure dwarfed by the bleak, stone gatehouse of HMP Coldingley.

He was carrying a small paper bag containing a few papers from his Dad's business, Hilary's letters, an almost new tube of toothpaste and a travel clock; a present from his Mum.

Margaret had been waiting patiently for him in the car since early morning, rushed over and threw her arms around him. They remained motionless for almost a full minute, eventually pulling apart and slowly walking back to the car.

She chattered nervously on the way home whilst Roger sat in silence.

It had been five years since he'd been home.

It really did feel like a lifetime.

21. Coming of Age

'Marry me, Hils, you'll never have to work again,' Roger groaned, looking down at Hilary with a pained lust in his eyes. They were kissing on the sofa, following her parent's eagerly-awaited departure to bed that night.

'No, Roger. Not yet, we've got plenty of time, we're still young. I don't know about you, but I've still got a lot to do before we get married.' She looked up at him and kissed him, as if to soften the blow.

'Oh, yeah? Like what?' He licked his poised lips.

'Like HP Sauce achieving a million pound turnover. Like flying first class in Concorde, like buying a Jaguar, like having a Geoffrey Archer penthouse overlooking the Thames.' She looked at the ceiling dreamily.

'If I just give it all to you, would you marry me then?' He somehow knew what the response would be.

'No. I need to do it myself, Rodge, you know that. Besides, where are you going to get all that money from?'

'Ah come on, Hils, I'm rich. OK not right now, but as soon as I take over Lichtenstein Re I will be,' he said with growing confidence.

'On paper, sure, you'll be a millionaire based on the value of the shares that you hold. You start earning real money when the company grows and your share value increases. Once the shareholders see that you mean business, you'll be able to pay yourself a fat-cat salary. Until then, technically you're an employee, paid by the company to do a job.'

Bloody hell, he thought, she knows all the answers. 'Whose side are you on?' he said.

'I'm on your side, of course I am. Have you ever thought about doing a business studies course? For real I mean, not just reading the words.'

'Bloody hell, Hils, I've just spent five years in jail. I read those books from cover to cover, I know enough about business. I'm not going to waste any more time learning stuff, I need to get on, make up for all those wasted years,' he pulled away from her.

'I'm sorry, Rodge,' she said sitting up, wrapping her arms around him. 'We'll get there, we just have to be patient.'

'Patience, my arse,' he shouted, tearing himself away and stomping over to the fireplace. 'Fuck it, Hilary, you've got no idea what I've been through, have you? I'm impatient, he's impatient,' he said pointing at the large swelling around his groin area, 'and all I get from you is, we have to be patient, Rodge, we have to be patient. Well I've had enough, I'm going to take over the company and I'm going to be rich. If you don't like it then I'll find someone else who will. It's as simple as that.' He stared hard at the fireplace, fuming.

After a short while, she called to him, arms outstretched, 'Roger, come here, please. For Hilary, come on.'

He glanced over his shoulder. Oh God she was so beautiful, and she loved him. He felt ridiculous with his bad temper and his big hard-on, but what was he supposed to do?

'Come over here and we'll do something about him.' She pointed at his straining trousers.

'But what about the tryst?' he asked, stunned.

'There's ways around that. C'mere,' she said, gesturing impatiently.

He felt his heart miss several beats. He walked over to the sofa, unsure what to expect. There was no point in trying to hide his painfully obvious erection. In fact, a glimmer of pride showed itself in his mind at that moment. Hilary perched on the edge of the sofa looking squarely at the bulge with a determined expression. She applied both hands to the task of freeing Roger's straining manhood. Once it sprang free, she gasped and his mind went back to their previous conversation in Coldingley about her lack of experience. She grasped him inexpertly with both hands and slowly forced his foreskin back. Roger, feeling his juices rising, was unable to control his excitement and exploded. Hilary was showered in the white, hot, salty fluid. It was everywhere; creamy, cloying and glutinous. She looked around in shocked disbelief for something to wipe both of them with, holding onto Roger's penis as if it were unexploded ordnance, liable to go off again at any moment.

Roger, momentarily thinking along the same lines, suddenly felt a sense of panic sweep over him. He had to do something, 'Oh God I'm sorry Hils, I'm really sorry darling, hold it there, I'll go and get a towel.' He raced off to the cloakroom, tucking himself in as he ran. On his return, he kneeled in front of the still shocked yet smiling Hilary and tenderly wiped what he could of the rapidly cooling mess from her face and hair, gentlemanly turning the towel over in half before handing it to her so she could wipe herself.

As she handed the towel back to Roger, he kissed her fleetingly on the cheek. 'You OK?'

'Of course I am. Just a little bit more control next time, eh, Mr. Collins?' she smiled up at him.

'Hils,' he said sheepishly.

'Yes?' she replied suspiciously.

'The towel. What are we going to do with it?'

Hilary laughed. 'I'll have to tell my Mum that you had an unexpected explosion in your trouser department.'

Roger looked on at her, a disbelieving look crossing his face. Hilary struggled unsuccessfully to hold back further shrieks of laughter.

Roger found day to day life with his parents just about tolerable. The house was big enough for him to comfortably live his life without any real intrusion from them. He had his own large bedroom with an en-suite on the opposite side of the house to his parents. The only areas that he would spend any time with them, through choice or otherwise, was the lounge and kitchen downstairs.

He busied himself in the first few weeks of his new-found freedom, organising a driving licence, buying clothes for work and, with his mother's help, getting things just right in his bedroom with half an eye on furniture that would go with him once he had his own place.

The question of his role in the company had not been discussed. His father seemed completely relaxed about the whole thing, just happy to have Roger back home again. They agreed that Roger would have a month at home to get acclimatised and would then start learning the business with his father. To Roger it felt like the summer holidays, a pleasant time doing what you wanted to do with some trepidation about the end of the holiday, never sure whether it would be good or bad. Looking back, those September new-term schooldays never seemed to be that bad, so Roger was full of unqualified confidence that things would work out fine.

Roger guessed, correctly as it turned out, that the insurance documents he found lying around the house had been left by his father in the hope that he would develop an intuitive understanding of the insurance industry. He still had the prisoner's instinctive hunger for information, so he did pick them up and glance through them occasionally. Subconsciously, it worried Roger that nothing he saw or read about the insurance industry interested him in the slightest, but he shrugged this off as something that would be surpassed by his interest in making money. Surely that was the more important instinct at the end of the day, wasn't it?

As his first day at Liechtenstein Re approached, he began to feel nervous. Nervous about his father's expectations, Hilary's and not least from the 400 or so employees of Liechtenstein Re. Was he up to it? The sanctity of life in a prison cell was harshly in perspective and he felt doubly bitter about the wasted years.

So it was an immaculately coiffed and suited Roger waiting for his father in the hallway at seven twenty-five on their first Monday morning. His father appeared shortly after, fresh from having his normal breakfast of porridge, orange juice, coffee and a glimpse through the Financial Times. Roger envied his aura of confidence and well-being as they strode together across the driveway to the garage and the waiting Jaguar, his father breaking almost a lifetime of tradition in deciding to drive to the office for Roger's first day. They chatted in the car, for once feeling relaxed in one another's company, his father complaining about the unbelievable volume of traffic. As they got closer to London, the conversation turned more towards work and what Roger could expect in his first days and weeks in the business.

'I've been thinking about this day since before you were born, Rodge. It's an important day for both of us, you probably realise that though,' his father said, smiling.

'Of course I do, Dad. I'm really nervous. I thought I'd be able to take it in my stride but I'm not so sure anymore,' Roger felt himself opening up to his father in a way he'd never done before. And the realisation that he'd had almost a whole lifetime of non-communication with the man who had raised him suddenly hit him.

Sensing his son's apprehension, his father said, 'The most important thing to remember is that nobody is ever going to insist that you do this. If you don't like it here or you feel uncomfortable in any way then go and do something else. I want you to take over the business because I've enjoyed every minute of being involved in it, and I hope you do too. At the same time though, I realise that maybe you won't, enjoy it that is. So don't feel under any pressure. Understand?'

'I think so,' Roger was about to explain that what he had read about the industry so far was not very interesting, but thought better of it. It probably would not be a good idea for this new found openness to go that far. 'I don't want to let you down.'

'You won't be letting me down, son. Listen, there's people out there,' he said pointing to the towering city skyline on their right hand side, 'who would give their right arm to buy a business as profitable and as well organised as Liechtenstein Re. Edgar and I could sell this business tomorrow if we really wanted to.'

'Wow. How much is it worth then?' asked Roger, genuinely shocked. He knew his Dad was rich, but it was beginning to sound like he was seriously rich.

'Oh I don't really know, we've never had it valued. This year we should make a net profit of about £40 million. It's unheard of in our industry. In fact, I don't know any other industry where you can hope to achieve anywhere near 10% of your turnover as net profit. We don't declare all of it, Edgar always wins that argument. He has all sorts of ways of avoiding paying tax, personal and corporate. I leave all of that to him, you'd probably have to ask him about the value of the company, I'd be guessing at around the value of our turnover plus property and stock.

Roger turned the numbers over in his mind. 'But that's going to be over half a billion pounds,'

His father laughed, 'Yes, probably. It's only a means of exchange though, Roger. They're only pieces of paper issued by the bank that say, I promise to pay the bearer the amount in the top right hand corner, that's all.'

'Presumably Edgar is a lot different to you,' Roger said. He knew they were poles apart, he'd heard his Dad complaining about Edgar sometimes.

'Yes, we're chalk and cheese. If I was like him we'd probably be sitting on a company worth five or six times as much. But then again, we probably wouldn't be together after twenty seven years or so, that's more a measure of how successful we've been in my eyes.'

Despite himself, Roger was beginning to get interested. 'So if Edgar looks after the money, what is it that you do?'

'I'm the underwriter in chief. I decide what we insure, how we insure it and how much we charge our customers. We base it on the amount of money it would cost us if things go wrong and we have to pay a claim. I have to do a hell of a lot of other things too, but that's it in a nutshell,' his father said.

'I guess I'll learn from both of you,' Roger said. This was a side of his Dad he never knew existed.

'Yes, that's the plan, son. These first few days you'll be with both of us.' His father brought the car to a halt at the entrance to the car park below the Cheapside offices and, using a swipe-card, raised the barrier. 'Then I want you to spend some time in the various departments - underwriting, sales, claims, administration and so on. That way you'll get a feel for how the business runs.'

After parking the car, they entered the lift. His father used the swipe-card again to take them directly up to the executive suite of offices on the top floor. Roger was immediately impressed by the opulence before him. Luxury carpet, real wood, bright white lights recessed into the ceiling and artworks, paintings and pictures almost everywhere you looked.

'Yes, I know, there's an awful lot of artwork,' David said resignedly. 'I keep saying to Edgar we need to think about a gallery somewhere, we're running out of space. They're investments, all catalogued and valued regularly. See that one,' he said, pointing to a large picture of a man riding a horse. 'That's an original oil painting by George Stubbs from 1863, you wouldn't believe how much that one's worth. That's Edgar's pride and joy.'

There were eight glass fronted offices around the periphery of the top floor with a central island in the middle containing four workstations. They walked through an anteroom into one of the larger end offices with a spectacular view over London and the River Thames from the full height window, 'I chose the South facing view, Edgar preferred the other end, it's closer to the old country,' his father said, taking his jacket off. 'Come on, I'll show you your office. Ah, here's Edgar now.'

The congenial Irishman was still clad in his raincoat. 'Hello Roger, you're here at last, welcome on board, it's great to see you. You do look very smart,' he said, straightening Roger's tie and brushing his suit shoulders.

'Hello Edgar, it's good to see you again,' Roger said. They'd met several times throughout Roger's life and he, like most people, couldn't help but like the slightly eccentric Irishman.

'Let me think now, the last time I saw you, you'd been scrumping next doors apples!' Edgar said slapping his thigh in amusement. 'You're embarrassed, hah! No need, son, no need. You were showing a true entrepreneurial spirit. You're going to be a success here, I just know it. Now has your old man showed you your office yet?'

'I think he was just about to,' Roger said, bemused.

'He was all set for putting you in the basement, you know? I said to him, David, I said, your own flesh and blood, how could you? The least you could do is give him an office on the same floor as us, make the lad feel a bit important at least. Now then, what do you think of this?' All three walked into the room.

'Wow, this is great, I wasn't expecting this,' said Roger, impressed.

'I chose this one for you so you didn't get the feeling your old man would be keeping an eye on you all the time, know what I mean?' He winked broadly. 'The view's not too great, mostly Fenchurch Street station, but you can see the East End and some of Essex on a clear day. I thought something a bit modern might give you some inspiration.' He pointed to the large Lichtenstein that dominated the flank wall. 'If you want to change it feel free to choose, just get Louise or Pauline to arrange it.'

'I love it already, Edgar, Dad. Thank you for all of this,' Roger said, looking around. He felt like a child in Santa's grotto.

'Now then, I'm going to leave you to get acclimatised and I'll see you later, if you need anything, you just whistle.' He waved as he headed out of the door in the direction of his own office.

Roger sat down behind the desk in the large leather seat and swivelled around to take in the panoramic view across the busy London skyline. He felt an overwhelming sense of power. He was born for this. He had reached his destination in life.

With David's impending retirement, the two partners decided that Edgar would become Chief Executive Officer with David in the role of Chairman. Edgar's first task as CEO was to appoint a new managing director, recruited from a rival firm with a wealth of experience in the insurance industry.

'But that's my job,' Roger said huffily to Edgar on being told of the new arrangement.

'Rodge, don't worry, one day this will all be yours,' Edgar replied. 'You're doing a great job of learning the business. It's just that I need someone with experience. I only do the deals, I can't run a company the size of Liechtenstein Re; this guy can.' He laughed, 'We know he can because he's been doing it at LGR. Hopefully they're really going to miss him.'

That night, Roger went home in a black mood. His mother and father were just finishing dinner when he arrived home.

'What do you mean giving my job to someone from off the street? You went behind my back, *oh you'll get the company one day, Rodge, you're our man.* Yeah like fuck.'

'Roger. Language,' his mother said, shocked.

'You're part of this too. You just do what he says.'

'Don't you dare talk to your mother like that,' his Father roared.

'I just did, didn't I?' Roger replied, goading his father.

'You don't come into this house and insult both of us. If you've got a problem, let's talk about it,' his Father said.

'Yeah, I have got a problem with that bloody stupid Irishman and you two, scheming up ways to sideline me into some poxy clerk's job.'

'You are not being sidelined, we are giving you the benefit of experiencing all of the departments in the company. Most people would be grateful for the experience. You can't just walk into managing a company the size of ours, you must see that.'

'Ours, not mine then,' Roger replied.

'It will be yours one day,' his Father shouted, 'how many more times? God help us, why are you so impatient? We're paying you a good wage, you have a fantastic lifestyle. What more can we give you?'

'Err, Liechtenstein Re?'

'You are a greedy, selfish, grabbing bastard,' his father was red-faced and struggling for breath. 'How the two of us ever produced someone as downright evil as you, I'll never know. The way you're carrying on, I'm ready to disown you. You can go live on the streets for all I care, forget the bloody company, aghh...' David suddenly clutched at his chest, slumped back onto his chair and then forward still holding his chest, groaning.

'David!' his mother screamed, rushing around the table, kneeling at his side, 'Roger call an ambulance. Now!'

'Yeah, yeah,' Roger replied, heading for his room.

'Roger, please! Hurry!'

'OK, OK,' he went into the hall and dialled 999. On hearing the operator answer the call, he put the phone down and ambled slowly up to his room. Typical, he thought, his parents would try and get the better of him by coming up with some stupid stomach-ache scheme, mind you his old man seemed to be in a fair bit of pain, serve him right, let them sweat on it a bit. There was no way he was being done out of the Liechtenstein Re inheritance, he'd go to the high court if necessary. He threw his jacket onto the bed and started loosening his tie, looking around for the TV remote. His mother's scream focussed his attention.

'Roger! Help me, please!'

He went downstairs to the kitchen and found his mother frantic. 'I can't find a pulse, I think he's had a heart attack, when are they coming?'

'Oh, ten minutes or so, they said,' he lied.

'Help me with him, we've got to try and do something, don't you have to try and pump the heart or something to get it going?' They lowered him onto the kitchen floor. His father was a dead weight and completely still, his flesh clammy and grey in colour. His mother loosened his shirt and started rhythmically pushing onto his chest with both palms.

'I'll go and get a blanket and some cushions,' Roger said, leaving the kitchen. He raced to the phone and called the ambulance again, for real this time, 'Ambulance please, you'd better come urgently. It's my father, I think he's dying from a heart attack. Thirty-two Acacia Avenue, hurry please, thank you.'

'Oh Roger it's not working, ring the ambulance again,' his mother was in tears still pumping his chest when Roger re-entered the kitchen with cushions and a bedspread. 'Oh God, please don't take him away from me like this, not now, he's a good man, he doesn't deserve to die.' She was crying frantically.

'Mum, let me, the ambulance is on its way,' Roger said, helping his mother up and taking over with a heavier slamming of both hands onto his father's chest.

Margaret felt for her husband's pulse, still crying, 'The doctor told him to stay away from stress, 'she said, sobbing. 'That's why he wanted to retire, that and the church. Oh David, I love you so much, please don't die.'

The doorbell rang. 'Thank God,' she said rushing out of the kitchen. The paramedics bought in a defibrillator machine, connected it up and made several attempts at restarting his father's heart, his lifeless body twitching with each surge of voltage.

After the third attempt, the pulse monitor spluttered into life, slowly settling into producing a regular audible beep, 'Oh thank you, thank you,' his distraught mother said to the two paramedics. They carefully loaded him onto their wheeled stretcher and covered him with a red blanket.

Roger consoled his distraught mother as best he could, his mind spinning. He'd nearly killed the old sod, he shouldn't have delayed the 999 call. Still, perhaps now, the old man would see sense and retire, passing his shareholding over in the process.

Then the crazy Irishman was all that stood in his way.

22. Inheritance

Over the three month period of David's convalescence, husband and wife agreed that he would step down from the business with immediate effect. The obvious benefactor of his shareholding was Roger but this needed to be discussed with Edgar. The meeting between the three of them took place at Enrico's one lunchtime.

'Well, I for one, am just so pleased to see that you're still here, David,' Edgar said as they waited for food to arrive. 'Nothing else matters now, you've had your warning, you need to de-stress your life.'

'Yes, I know. I'll miss the business, but this fellow won't,' David said, patting his chest.

'David, you'd be an eejit if you carried on, right enough. You just forget about everything now, it's in the past, you hear? The new MD is doing a great job, not as good as you, but hey, you can't have everything in life. He'll certainly see out my last few years in the firm. I'll just carry on doing what I've always done and the profits will continue to roll in. No sweat.'

Margaret smiled, 'Edgar, sweety. Can I ask you how Roger is doing in the company and where you see him, say in five years' time?'

'He's doing OK. My honest opinion is that he has an awful lot to learn, but he is picking things up slowly. On the down side, he hasn't got the passion that your David and I had at his age. I think at the moment we need someone to just keep an eye on what he's doing. He's not ready for any full responsibility yet. He's a non-executive board member at the moment which he doesn't like; he wants power and control. The MD, me and the other non-execs have to keep a pretty tight rein on him at board meetings. He can get a bit, shall we say, hot under the collar, when decisions are made that he doesn't like.'

David and Margaret looked at one another, 'Sounds like Roger,' Margaret said, nodding.

'But now we have to talk about the shares, don't we?' After pausing for agreement, he said, 'I'm going to give you an outline of how I see things. Tell me if you don't agree, OK?'

'We're relying on you to tell us like it is, Edgar,' David said.

'Right, you have three choices. First choice is to sell the shares to the highest bidder, second choice is to sell them to me and third choice is to give them to Roger.'

'I think you know my thoughts on the first two,' David said. 'A big pile of money is not my objective here.'

'I'm not particularly in favour of the first two either, our institutional shareholders won't like it if we just sell them. It would also leave me vulnerable to a takeover with that amount of shares coming onto the open market. If I buy you out they'd see me as having too much control and, to be perfectly honest, I don't want that amount of responsibility now I'm in me dotage. Twenty years ago I probably would have had them off you. So, it looks like the best option is to gift your shares to Roger. One thing's for sure, he isn't going to want to carry on as a non-exec, we'll have to give him a role with some controlling power. That's my problem.'

'OK, so what would you say his main strength is?' Margaret asked.

'I would say business development is the area where he's shown most promise, but he's not a people person, as you know. He can spot the opportunities, but then I usually go and do the deal. I don't mind that but I have to think a few years hence when I'm not around anymore. I'm thinking Sales Director, he probably won't like it much but I can put it to him in such a way that he'll see further opportunities when I'm gone, if you get my drift. Either way, he'll be a millionaire, at least on paper, and earning a six-figure salary. You'd think he wouldn't have that much to complain about, would you?'

'Oh, Roger will always find something to complain about,' David said, smiling resignedly.

'I think the Sales Director role will be good for Roger, if he sticks at it. There's a certain amount of admin involved, you know, analysing the figures, writing reports etc, so he won't be at the sharp end all of the time which will suit him. I think it will either make him or break him. What do you think?'

David took a sip of water and said, 'I'll tell him later today that we've put the share transfer in place if you talk to him tomorrow about the job. I'll make it clear to him that I don't have any input on the decision regarding his role with the company, OK?'

'Grand. That'll do,' he said looking around, 'now where's the food? I could eat a horse.'

The conversation between Roger and his father that night was low key, as his parents insisted all their dealings with Roger had to be since his father's heart attack. Roger was surprisingly sombre. He shook hands with his father at the end of the conversation and kissed his mother, then said goodnight to both of them, he was off to see Hilary.

In the car he pondered his position. Based on his father's estimate of the company value and with his father's shares, he would now be worth about £125m. It was still only a quarter of the company. He knew that institutional shareholders owned about half of the company's assets, with Edgar owning the other quarter. The Irishman was saying he was going to retire in about five years, which seemed an age away. He'd have to try and oust him before that and collar his shares. It certainly did give him plenty to think about. He went into work the following day in the same thoughtful mood, just as Edgar called him into his office.

'So Roger, how are you feeling this morning?'

'OK, thanks Edgar, why?'

'You did have a conversation with your Pa last night, didn't you?'

'Yes,'

'And he told you that he's going to be giving you his shareholding in the company, did he?'

'Yes. I take it you two had discussed it?'

'Of course. So how are you feeling about it all?'

'Well, I'm pleased obviously. Does it mean I get a real job now?'

'What you're doing at the moment is a real job, Roger,' the Irishman laughed. 'But yes, it is only natural that a major shareholder should become a director with voting rights on the board.'

'That's what I thought, so what kind of Director?'

'That's what I called you in for, I want to share my thoughts,' Edgar walked around the office to the whiteboard on the inner wall and sketched out an organisation chart showing a level string of boxes with names inside including his and Rogers, and one box on top with David's name in it.

'That's how things are at the moment; you, me and the MD together with the institutional boys and a few other non-execs from outside basically run the company. Your father is the Chairman, he has the final vote on everything we do. Now what I'm going to put to the board at the next meeting in two weeks' time is this.' He rubbed out David's name, 'Sorry my old mate, don't take it personally.' He inserted his own name, 'I become Chairman and CEO.' He rubbed out Non- Exec in Roger's box and put Sales Director. 'And I want you to take responsibility for all sales. What do you think of that?' he said, returning to his desk.

'Sales.' Roger looked at Edgar with a blank expression.

'You've worked in the department, you know how it works, you know the people, you've said to me before that this is the area that interests you the most.'

'Yes I know, but that was Business Development,'

'The sales role is one of the most important in the company. New business is our lifeblood, we won't survive without it. A few years in the sales job will give you a unique insight into the opportunities that are there to exploit. I retire in less than five years. I know you don't like the idea of biding your time but there's no reason that you shouldn't step into my shoes when I go after a few hard years at the coalface. You can do all the business development you want then, and you'll still be in your early thirties. Think about it, Rodge, let me know whether you want to accept it or not.'

'It sounds like everything I do is some sort of test, do this well, Rodge and maybe in five years you could be doing this,' Roger said. The smile on his face contradicting the sentiment in the statement.

'Life is a test, son. I am the most senior figure in this organisation yet everything I do is scrutinised. Institutional investors want to know about the insides of a duck's arse at every turn. They'll want to know about your appointment, they'll ask me why I've appointed this guy, how much experience does he have, etcetera. I'll have to justify it all right, Roger. I'm relying on you to do a good job for me.'

'If I do accept the sales job, not that I seem to have much choice, who do I report to and who sets my targets?'

'If I said I'm putting you in charge of underwriting or the actuaries or administration, what would you say?'

'I'd tell you to get lost.'

Edgar spread both palms and raised his eyebrows. 'Exactly. And you' be reporting to me. I have an interest in everything you do. I know you probably won't like it but that's how it's got to be. If I was you, the thing I'd keep at the forefront of my mind is that in a few short years, you could be running the whole show. Keep that in mind and you won't go far wrong.'

'OK Edgar, I accept, and thanks, I won't let you down.' Roger shook hands with the Irishman.

That'll do for now he thought, you just wait you son of a bitch. Sales Director? Who did he think he was?

Roger eventually persuaded Hilary to marry him. The negotiations were good-natured but lengthy, the Tryst of Celibacy hung over Roger's head like a phallic sword of Damocles. His principle demand to Hilary was to give up HP Sauce and spend her time looking after him and their future family. Hilary refused to abandon the business she'd spent two years getting off the ground.

There were also other barriers that had to be overcome. 'Of course, I want our marriage to be open, on my side anyway,' Roger announced one day. They were in the midst of making plans for the wedding day.

'Of course, my love,' Hilary replied, smiling. 'As long as you understand that if you go with another woman, I'll have your manly parts removed.'

'That's not fair,' Roger sniffed. 'When you're earning as much money as me, you shouldn't expect me to be monogamous. Women will be falling over themselves to have sex with me, you can't blame them.'

'No, you're right, Roger, I wouldn't blame them. It's just that you wouldn't have a penis anymore because I'd have had it cut off and pickled if you so much as fingered a gusset,' she replied.

'Oh, I see what you're after,' he said grinning lewdly. 'All right then, I'll let you sleep around too. How's that?'

Hilary's indignation bristled, 'Roger, are you mad? Is all this self-abuse making you somehow deranged?' she asked, outraged. 'Marriage is for one man and one woman to live with one another, to share a home, bring up a family and be faithful to one another. That's what the bible says and that's what we're going to do. If you don't like it, then forget it. Find some other dim-witted trollop to have your open marriage with.'

'Look,' he persisted, 'Mrs. Queen of the Vibrators. What's it going to look like if it comes out that you only have sex with your husband, that you're not actually a raving nymphomaniac? Bad for business, I'd say.' He grinned, thinking he'd made the killer punch.

Her withering look almost said it all. 'You are mad, I thought so. Look, I am in the sex industry, admitted; you know what keeps me sane? I'll tell you - a sense of moral value. I keep my dignity when everyone else is losing theirs, that's what keeps me sane. A jewel in a bed of thorns, a beacon in the primeval swamp, that's me. Does it not mean anything to you, the fact that I've saved myself for you? Do you really think that knowing me the way you do, that I really want to sleep around? Most other girls in my position are at it like rabbits just to keep their fiancés happy. These are *my* principles, Roger. Just show me some bloody respect.' Anger simmered in her eyes.

Roger had the good sense to reply with a placatory interjection.

'Hilary, darling. I love you, remember? I respect you and yes we are magic together. Even this conversation we're having is a bit magic. I'm me, and you're you, though. We're different. Maybe that's what makes us good together. This no-sex thing though, it's a bit of a hot potato. Can we put it on hold, Hils?'

'No, hot potato, Rodge, it's very clear; one sniff of an open marriage and your reproductive organ is in a jar.'

'All right, all right,' he pulled a sour expression, holding his crotch. 'No chance of another hand job, I suppose?'

'No there bloody isn't,' she scoffed. 'Open marriage indeed.'

Another vexating issue for them was the question of where to live. Roger was beginning to tire of life with his parents and was itching to buy a riverside apartment in London whilst Hilary was keen to continue living in Surrey, close to her business and family. They eventually agreed that they would go and see an example of their dream home together, the idea being to compare notes and perhaps reach a compromise. 'Wow, Roger. This is unbelievable,' Hilary said as she walked through the split level lounge onto the wide balcony overlooking the Thames.

'You can see Greenwich to the left and the city to the right. On a good day you can see the tip of the LR headquarters in Cheapside. I'll be able to keep an eye on our prize asset.' Roger held Hilary's waist with both hands as she leaned on the balcony railing, admiring the view. 'We could both entertain our clients here, impressive or what?'

They inspected each of the three en-suite bedrooms and the vast kitchen before Hilary eventually returned to the balcony. Sitting down on one of the teak dining chairs with a slightly dazed yet thoughtful look on her face, she asked, 'How much is this place again?'

'They're asking £850k. But I reckon I could talk the developer down to eight. It'll be worth a couple of mill' in a few years. These places are great investments, all the city boys are buying them up.'

She swallowed, 'It's huge. Do we need three bedrooms straight away?'

'We may as well start as we mean to continue. When we have kids we'll just get somewhere bigger. Money is never going to be an issue Hils, trust me.'

'That's not the point though, Roger. We want a comfortable, safe environment for our kids to grow up in. No disrespect to the people of

Bermondsey but I don't see many pastoral landscapes around here. Once you're outside of this apartment block you're in inner-city concrete and tarmac, can you imagine what the schools are like and what it feels like to have your car firebombed by resentful locals?'

'So we send them away to boarding school and keep the car in the secure underground car park,' he said, sensing further opposition.

'And what do we do with them before they go to school, and when they come home between terms? This is no place for kids, Rodge, absolutely not.' Then, as if she was going to meet him halfway, said firmly, 'Look, I'm impressed, but I don't think it's for us, that's all. Don't be disappointed. Remember, we're doing this so we can agree on a place to live.'

The discussion continued as they drove back to Surrey in the Aston Martin. Roger could see his dream apartment disappearing. 'OK, so I work in London, I want to be close to my business too, certainly at some times during the week I'll be entertaining clients and won't want to drive all the way home. We could buy a biggish house in Surrey and a smaller flat in London. I might even be able to get the company to pay for it. How does that sound?'

'It sounds like we need to see what we can get in Surrey for a starter. We get married in less than four months.' She punched him on the shoulder excitedly. Roger rolled his eyes to the heavens.

They eventually settled on a four bedroom country home nestled in a secluded woodland in a quiet Surry backwater, Hilary having fallen in love with it straightaway, Roger seeing the potential for twentieth-century improvements and the room for his intended collection of sports cars.

'What do you mean you're pregnant?' Roger said. It was two months after their honeymoon.

'What part don't you understand? I am with child. I have a bun in the oven. I'm up the duff. Aren't you happy about it then?' Hilary said.

'Well, yes, of course, but your business, you'll have to sell it or something.'

'Roger, I'm having a baby, not changing religion. I'm perfectly capable of working while carrying the child and looking after it when it's born, as well as running the business. I'm a woman remember, we can do these things.'

'I thought you were on the pill anyway.'

'Yes, well, I didn't fancy it. I decided on keeping myself in an oestrogen-free zone. If we want birth control after it's born you can have your tubes garrotted.'

'I'm not having that done, it's un-masculine.'

'Suit yourself, we'd better not have any sex then.'

'God, you're a bully. You're trying to repress my manly urges. Don't you enjoy sex then?'

'No, no, can't you tell? It bores me senseless.'

'I hope you're being sarcastic Mrs. C, or you're going to be the one on rations from now on,' he said reaching out to her, a lustful expression on his face.

'Even with only half of you in it, our child is going to be a raving lunatic.' Hilary ducked his attempted embrace and giggled. She shrieked as Roger lunged after her and chased her up the stairs to the bedroom.

23. Sam, Julian and Tania too

Hilary felt uncomfortable with the piped music, crisp white uniformed nurses treating patients like customers and wallpaper on the walls. She was used to the more utilitarian surroundings of the National Health Service.

It was a perfect birth. Both babies were in the ideal head-down position in Hilary's womb. After a four and half hour labour, Samantha was the first to emerge and Julian followed seventeen minutes later. The smiling nurses rushed around making sure that their charge with her new arrivals was happy and content. Her Mum and Dad fussed around her, taking pictures and delighting in being grandparents for the first time. David and Margaret, both joyful at the arrival of the twins, alternated between the ward and the corridor, reluctant to get in the way whilst Roger cosseted Hilary and fussed around the children the whole time.

'Two for the price of one, eh, Hils?' Roger joked, sitting on the side of the bed, smiling down at Hilary.

'More like double the cost of everything, isn't it?' She looked up at him with an uncertainty.

'Money's not a problem, darling. You know that,' he said, still smiling. 'We'll get a nanny and they'll both be off to boarding school before you know it. They won't get in the way for long, don't you worry.'

'In the way of what?' Hilary asked with an appalled expression.

'Well, your business. And mine, come to that. Life mustn't come to a halt just because of these little beauties, eh, my darling?' He smiled inanely at the cooing grandparents.

'No, but we have to alter our lives to accommodate them, Roger,' Hilary said firmly. 'They need love and attention from their parents, we've had this discussion before.'

'Yes and they will have all of that, my sweet, I promise you. Now, I've got to go. I'm going to leave you in the capable hands of the nurses here, and your parents, of course.' Seeing the look of exasperation on Hilary's face he added quickly, 'I'll be back later, there's just a few things that need sorting out at the office.'

'You promised me you'd have some time off,' Hilary said.

'I'm going to, darling. I'm on light duties for the rest of the week. I've told Irish Edgar I won't be around much.'

'You haven't forgotten I'm going to the Dealer Conference in the Far East the month after next, have you?' It was almost certain that he had, she thought.

'No, darling, of course not, how could I forget that?' He quickly kissed her and waved cheerily at the assembled Grandparents. 'Back in a few hours, see you all later!'

Hilary looked at her parents with a patient, resigned expression. Inwardly she seethed. Who did the bastard think he was, abandoning her like that? She was still in pain from giving birth to his children and he was off, back to the city. Most of the time, he couldn't care less about work, almost resentful that his father had got him involved in the first place but the moment she needed him, he was suddenly full of interest and enthusiasm. She couldn't help noticing that things were still difficult between father and son.

Not that she was all that surprised. Things were always difficult with Roger. She had her own way of dealing with him though, mostly disdain laced with some ridiculous motherly affection. But she had wondered whether this would change with the arrival of the children.

She looked on with wonder at her two new sleeping beauties.

'OK, sweetheart?' Her Dad interrupted her reverie. 'You were miles away.'

'Yes, Dad, I'm fine. I was just thinking about the future, you know, our future.' She continued looking dreamily at the sleeping babies.

'They've got you as a Mum, they'll both be wonderful people, and I'm not biased. Much.' He swept her hair back and kissed her lightly on the cheek.

'Hmm, that's what worries me. You know, the percentages.' She looked at him directly.

'Yes, I know what you mean,' he replied. She could see the familiar unconditional love in her father's eyes. She also saw something less familiar, a look of concern.

As he rushed back to the office in the Aston Martin, he pondered why Hilary had been so upset with him at the hospital. He did have a business to run and he was adamant that the arrival of the children was not going to interrupt him. She was surrounded by her family who were obviously besotted with the little ones. His mother and father were also there, so it wasn't as if he'd abandoned her. Especially as there was much more important business to attend to. The car phone rang, it was Louise, the director's executive secretary.

'Roger, there's been a man on the phone from a boat company. He needs to talk to you urgently,' she said coolly as always. 'I hope you don't mind, I've given him your car phone number.'

'No that was the reason I was coming back, I'm expecting his call. Bye,' he put the handset back into the cradle. It rang two minutes later.

'Hello Mr. Collins, this is the Tegwin Boat Company about the boat, just a reminder that you need to send us the forty per-cent stage payment today and finalise the internal décor. If you don't do it today we may miss the delivery slot next year.'

'OK, I'm just on my way back to the office, I'll send you a fax copy of the cheque that will be in the post later and confirm the décor. Is that OK?' Roger said.

'Yes, I'll ring to confirm receipt, thanks and bye-bye,' the salesman put the phone down.

Cocky git, Roger thought to himself. Here's me with a wife just given birth this morning, racing back to the office to deal with the boat and he's harassing me. I'll give him a hard time when it comes to making the final payment. This boat was going to be the most perfect boat that had ever been through their premises. He'd make sure of it.

'Well?' Louise asked from behind her reception workstation as he stepped out of the lift into the director's suite of offices.

'Well what? I spoke to the man from the boat company, if that's what you mean,' he replied, looking blank.

'Hilary, what did she have and are they both OK?'

'Oh,' he laughed. 'Sorry. Yes we've got twins and yes they're fantastic and Hilary's just fine. Thanks.' He smiled awkwardly and continued on his way to his office.

'Congratulations, that's fantastic. Have you chosen names yet?'

Bloody hell, what is it with women, he thought to himself, they're never satisfied. 'Yes, the girl is called Samantha and the boy is called Julian.' There, satisfied, you nosy bitch?

'Ahh, that's sweet, I'll get them something at lunchtime, and you can take it when you go later.'

How do you know that I won't be going to the pub later instead of the bloody hospital? 'You shouldn't bother, Louise, they've already got loads,' he mumbled as he keyed in the security code to his office.

Roger sat down behind his desk and looked at the pile of correspondence. He flicked through it quickly - a selection of the normal whinging problems from their worldwide agents; the targets you set are unreasonable, I need a bigger commission from these policies, it's not fair that you withdraw commission when the customer cancels. Can't they deal with this shit themselves, he thought wearily as he abandoned the pile and reached into his bottom drawer for his boat file.

He smiled as he looked at the image of the boat he had ordered at last year's Boat Show. His smile broke into a grin as he imagined being on the flying-bridge with 2,400horse power at his command from the twin-diesels as the dark-blue 70 foot hull cut through the heavenly azure-blue of the Caribbean. A trio of heavenly beauties would be sunning themselves on the aft deck, preparing themselves with body oils for him to ravish them later when the sun sunk below the yard arm and the gin began to loosen those inhibitions...

Now all he had to do was pay for the bloody thing. He found the sales contract in the file and winced as he did whenever he looked at it. He had paid a ten per-cent deposit at the show of just over £100,000. The dealer was now looking for another 40% as the engines had been installed and the top and the bottom of the boat had been joined irrevocably as one. This second payment amounted to just over £400,000. He winced for the second time. He had briefly mentioned to Edgar that he was about to buy a boat and would it be all right if he put it on the company? Edgar had nodded dismissively mentioning something about a director's loan account. Roger had taken this as firm commitment and gone straight to the Boat Show, his corporate Gold Card burning a hole in his wallet.

He grabbed the file and stood up, pushing his chest out. Fuck it, he thought to himself, this was almost my company, I'm not having the Chairman stand in my way. I'll do what I like, with what is very nearly my money. He strode from his office in the direction of Edgar's.

The Irishman was just about to leave his office and was clearly delighted to see his younger junior partner. 'Ah, Roger, I didn't realise you were coming in, so tell me all about it.' He looked at Roger, eagerly expectant.

Oh God, Roger thought, not again. He put on a smile, hoping it looked genuine. 'Twins, Edgar. A boy, Julian, and a girl, Samantha, mother and children all well and healthy. I'll be going back there later.'

'Splendid! Congratulations, my boy. You be sure to send my love to all three, especially that lovely wife of yours. Tell her I'll come and see her when she's back home.'

'I'm sure she'll appreciate that, Edgar, thanks. Can I see you for a minute?'

'Yes, of course. It must be important if it dragged you away from the hospital,' he said, returning to his desk.

'Well actually, it's about the boat. Remember I said I would be buying one, on the company?'

'Yes I remember, I assumed you'd been and done it.'

'That was only a ten per-cent deposit at the Boat Show. They want the second payment today.'

'Ah and you want some more money, is that it?'

'Yes, rather. £400,000 actually. Just over.'

Edgar coughed. 'How many more payments are there?'

'Just one more, same again.' Roger said quietly.

'How many boats did you say?'

'Just the one, it's fairly large.'

'Bloody hell, Roger, a boat costing the company a million pounds? Without board approval? Are you mad?'

'£1,029,411 actually. Oh and another £100,000 for a two year berth in the South of France, it's all part of the deal. Plus the VAT, of course.'

'When you said you were buying a boat, I assumed something more reasonable, but this is 1.25 million pounds that you don't have. You've signed a contract, I take it?'

'What do you mean money I don't have? I own a large chunk of this company. What's one million pounds to Liechtenstein Re? Nothing,' he said, answering his own question.

'Yes but expenditure like this has to be authorised. We can't go and spend the company's money just as we wish.'

'Well if you're not going to give me your signature, we'll just have to let the Tegwin Boat Company sue us. There's a boat being built right now on the other side of the world with our name on it.'

'Jesus, Roger, you are the limit.' He reached into his drawer and withdrew a chequebook. 'Here, you write it. We'll have to think of something good for the board meeting next week.'

'OK,' Roger said. 'If any of you want to borrow it, you can.'

'Yes, that'll be bound to swing it,' Edgar said ironically as he signed and dated the cheque.

Roger was grinning as he left Edgar's office. A celebratory visit to the local hostelry was in order this lunchtime. A lobster salad washed down with some Dom Perignon would go down very nicely. After that, a visit to the yacht chandler in St Katherine's Dock. He wanted one of those dark- blue skipper's hats with the shiny peak. The ladies liked a man with an air of authority about him, he thought, imagining himself driving his very large, brand new boat into the marina to admiring glances all around.

*

Roger drove Hilary and the twins home three days later. He carried Samantha and Hilary carried Julian across the threshold of their Surrey home. During Hilary's stay in hospital Roger had dispatched Louise on a madcap shopping spree to buy another one of everything; cot, car-seat, steriliser and more sets of baby clothing in pink. The single pushchair got traded in for a twin version, and even the decorators got called in to give the nursery a touch of pink femininity.

Roger had wanted one of the spare bedrooms hurriedly converted to make another nursery but Hilary overruled him, claiming there was plenty of time in the future for giving them their own bedrooms and they wouldn't object at this early age.

On this occasion, Hilary was wrong. Once they were in the swing of living together as a family, they found that one hungry baby woke the other one up. They moved Julian into one of the spare bedrooms after two days. Roger's told-you-so was immediate and often-repeated.

After interviewing several potential nannies well before the birth, Hilary had appointed a young Swedish girl called Inge to look after the children in their absence. Hilary was adamant that she was not going to start full-time until Inge had spent at least a month with the children on a one to one basis. Or one to two as Roger reminded her. Inge did visit two or three times a week for an hour or so at Hilary's suggestion to get to know the babies and their routine, and for the little ones to get comfortable with this new person in their young lives.

By the time Hilary was ready to go to the Han Choy dealer conference in Taiwan, both Sam and Julian were sleeping most of the way through the night and Inge was ready to move in full time. Hilary herself had some catching up to do on events in the business and prepare herself for the conference. She looked forward to travelling again but the thought of leaving her babies made her apprehensive. She deliberately kept the trip short as a result. Against Hilary's instincts to take the economy option, Roger insisted she travel business class. She smiled to herself as the plane climbed away from Heathrow that night above the mass of South-West London lights. She stretched out in the comfortable leather seat with a pre-dinner glass of champagne. She had to give him credit; there were some things that

Roger did that were just unerringly right, and this was one of them. Mind you, she was not complacent about money like he was. She would have been in the back-half of the plane almost by default if she hadn't married this slightly wacky heir to the Lichtenstein Re fortune she thought as her eyelids began to close.

She stirred awake, the stewardess smiling down at her, offering the evening meal menu. It was only after reading the menu, that she realised lunchtime had been over nine hours ago and she was ravenous. She tucked into the hearty four-course dinner, drank a small bottle of Burgundy, watched a bit of the movie with a blanket wrapped loosely around her and promptly fell asleep again. The stack of business correspondence and things that she had intended to look at lay in her briefcase in the overhead locker, untouched. She awoke in what felt like the dead of night, the cabin lights dimmed, people all around dozing or asleep, the constant drone of the 747s engines a reminder that they were making progress through the cold night air towards Hong Kong. She gave up on the idea of doing any work, put the headphones on and read the book that she had bought hurriedly at the airport, savouring the peace and the solitude.

The plane landed in Hong Kong on schedule at four-fifteen local time the following afternoon. Uncle Vern was waiting for her as she entered the terminal building and enveloped her in a fearsome bear-hug.

'Hilary, it's so good to see you, my dear. You look wonderful! How was the flight?' He stood back, still holding both her arms.

'It was fine, Uncle, thanks.'

'And how are the little ones?'

'They're great. There's nothing to it, this having babies stuff. It's over-rated.' She giggled. 'I think it's a case of us women trying to talk ourselves up over you men, you know.'

'You don't have to do that as far as I'm concerned, Mrs. Collins. You're head and shoulders over any man that I know.' He took over pushing her luggage trolley and proffered his arm for her to tag onto. They began a slow walk to the terminal exit. 'And how is Mr. Collins?'

'Scheming how to get richer, as usual.'

'Please tell me you brought pictures of the two little cherubs.'

'Yes, of course, I have an album to show you when we get home.'

'Talking of which, you don't mind staying at my place tonight? I can soon book you into the Regent Palace, you know, but it would seem silly as we have so little time together.'

'As long as no one is going to talk about us, of course not.'

'Well actually, I think my standing in the community could be bolstered by having someone as pretty as you staying with me.' He straightened his back and preened as they walked through the afternoon crowds of travellers in the busy terminal.

She batted him across the shoulder with her free hand. 'Uncle Vernon, will you behave yourself,' she said, laughing. 'You really are getting worse as you're getting older.'

'Sorry m'dear,' he said. 'I'm just so proud of you. I tell everyone that you're my bestest niece, you know. Honest.'

A short plane ride the following morning found them at Kaohsiung Airport. A taxi took them to the factory where they were greeted enthusiastically in the reception area by a team of smiling Han Choy people. Uncle Vern seemed to know all of them by their first name and insisted on introducing Hilary to every last one. Amid much bowing and nervous laughter, she delighted in shaking all of their hands, Uncle Vern translating for her as they went.

Out of the corner of her eye, Hilary noticed a good-looking, medium built man in a simple business suit, a stark contrast to all the people in reception who were in casual clothes. He came down the spiral staircase slowly, a smile on his lips. She sensed this was Han Sen. But he was so young! Although Vern had talked about him during the course of their previous evening together, she immediately sensed that there was something special about him. His boyish good looks framed with longish black hair, his warm handshake, enquiring politeness and his easy, sincere smile. He reminded her of somebody but she couldn't think who.

The two day conference went by in a blur for Hilary. She loved every minute of it - meeting other business people from all over the world, seeing how things were made in the factory and getting to know some of the workers was a whole new world for the girl from suburban England. It inspired her and she gushed with enthusiasm.

The first morning saw the group taking a tour of the production areas dressed in white dust jackets and safety glasses where she was invited to have a go at assembling one of the vibrators on the production line, then she drank chai with a group of smiling women production workers on their break in the canteen under the serene gaze of the Buddha. She had her picture taken with them which would later be heavily featured in press releases of the successful Han Choy conference. The beautiful English lady with the flowing blonde hair and the perfect smile on the shop floor with the workers in a Taiwanese factory was a PR dream. Hilary had unknowingly become a symbol of the Han Choy ethos - of taking great joy in creating perfect products for our customers all around the world.

By the end of the second day, Tom Huang had finished with his presentations on new product pipelines and sales-target pie-charts. Han Sen had given his thanks to all the delegates for attending and continuing to support the efforts they made each day in the factory. It was time for the conference to close. Factory staff were on hand to present small immaculately wrapped gifts to each delegate. Hilary carefully opened hers to find a beautiful hand-carved Buddha. She hugged Han Sen tightly, slightly overwhelming the young industrialist but she couldn't help herself; he had influenced the course of her life and no doubt, she hoped, would continue to do so into the future.

The pair from England went to a night market for their last night in Kaohsiung. Somehow sitting in a restaurant didn't seem the right thing to do after the euphoria of the last two days. The busy stalls lit by bright lanterns and the throb of people coming and going was the perfect antidote to Hilary's slightly sagging spirits. Of course she wanted to go home to be with her babies but she loved this place. She looked around her and at Uncle Vern as they sat on high stools drinking chai at a noodle stall awaiting their Danzi Mian.

'Tell me, did Han Sen build all of Han Choy up himself?'

'Yes, with the help of his Great Uncle Sen. He had a business here for many years and Han Sen took it over and transformed it. All of the production and all of the products are Han Sen's creation.'

'Maybe next time I can meet his Great Uncle.'

'He's a very astute old man,' Uncle Vern said as the bowls of hot steaming noodles with pork, egg and shrimp were placed in front of them. 'Hmm, smells wonderful. Xiexie,' he said to the stall holder.

'I bet he's a fountain of knowledge,' Hilary said as she picked up her chopsticks, savouring the rich aroma. As she took the first mouthful it suddenly came to her, the resemblance she had picked up on meeting Han Sen, it was David Collins, Roger's father. It was obviously not physical, but the mannerisms, the modesty and the enquiring mind. They were both full of graciousness. That was what it was. She smiled and looked at Uncle Vern.

'What?' he smiled back.

'I was just thinking, I keep bumping into people who inspire me as I go through life, especially out here.'

'Presumably that means the people back home don't? Inspire you, I mean.'

'Yes, you could say that. Apart from my Dad, of course, he's my rock.'

'Well you know my opinion on that husband of yours, he's had it all handed to him and still he's got some chip on his shoulder about, well, I'm not sure what about. He's a cold fish. I don't think I'll ever like him. Money aside, I don't get what you see in him, my love. There I've said it, sorry in advance. I'm not accusing you of being a gold-digger either.'

'I know, I know. He has got something special though, Uncle Vern. I thought I'd coaxed it out of him, but now I'm not so sure. He thinks money is everything, money and material things.'

'Maybe he needs to spend some time out here. Get to know the value and the meaning of life. Get to know the Buddha a little bit. That would help.'

'He thinks all foreigners are out to get him for some reason,' a thought suddenly struck her. 'You're not Buddhist, are you?'

He stopped eating, 'No, I'm far too heavily involved in making money. I do understand why so many people believe in what he taught though. There's a real powerful aura in all of the temples here. You can feel it. Maybe I'm one of Buddha's followers deep down.'

'I think we all are. We need to spend time thinking about what he taught and we're all too wrapped up in our own lives to do it,' she said. 'You live with Buddhism, you probably understand more than most westerners.'

'True. You'd love to come and live here, wouldn't you?'

'Yes, but if I came out here you wouldn't have an agent in the UK, would you? It would be like cutting your own throat.'

'We could soon find someone else, not as good as you obviously,' he said quickly. 'But we'd find somebody. We could build the business together, I am looking to retire soon, you know.'

'If it wasn't for Roger, I would do it, Uncle Vern. I feel I need to almost compete against him to keep him in line. Otherwise, he'd walk all over me. The business is my protection, my sanctuary.'

He looked at her with a determined look in his eyes. 'Maybe one day?'

'I'm sorry, Uncle.' She played with the remainder of the noodles with her chopsticks. 'I don't mean to burden you with my problems, or raise your hopes. Please.' She touched his forearm lightly. 'Forgive me. Can we take one step at a time?'

'Your daft old Uncle's just getting a bit ahead of himself, darling, that's all,' he said, pouring the remainder of the chai into both their cups. 'You don't have to worry about burdening me though, Hils. If you get any problems at all,' he said with a concerned look in his eyes, 'I want to be the first to know about them.'

She felt embarrassed that she'd told him too much. 'Yes, of course. Thanks. Thanks for everything.' She really did feel close to her Uncle. Perhaps too close, she thought.

24. Attractions of the East

The board of directors didn't have much choice. With Roger conveniently away on paternity leave, a way had to be found to pay for the boat that the founder's son had inexplicably bought with company money. Eventually, after many raised eyebrows and questioning looks all round, a consensus was reached. A director's loan account would be set up, and Roger's performance related bonuses would pay this off over a five year period. Simple really, and by way of an added bonus, Edgar announced with heavy irony at the end of the meeting, that they could all use the boat. Looking at the polite smiles all round, he knew that no-one actually would. If these wealthy individuals had any interest at all in boating, you could be sure they would have a boat of their own.

Roger's role as Sales Director at Lichtenstein Re was comparatively easy during the heady days of the late 1980s when the UK economy was enjoying unprecedented boom times under the free-market approach of Mrs. Thatcher's government. Roger's sales team was one step away from being a call centre, the sales people only had to pick the phone up, quote the person on the other end of the line, and then proceed to write the business. If they didn't get business from that call, there would be another one along in a few minutes. It was an easy life and Roger envisaged no problems achieving the sales targets Edgar had set.

Except that during the early months of 1990, the phones stopped ringing.

The economy had slid into an almighty recession almost overnight. Interest rates, raised by the government to try and dampen excessive consumer demand were at an all-time high, and inflation was rampant. The houses that people had been encouraged to buy by Mrs. Thatcher were suddenly worth less than the mortgages they had taken out to buy them. Mortgage lenders were re-possessing homes on a grand scale. Central London saw its first rioting since the Gin Riots of 1743 thanks to the Poll Tax which the Conservative government hastily withdrew just months later.

It slowly dawned on Roger that unless he upped his game and found some new markets, he would struggle to meet his sales targets. This would endanger his profit share bonus and consequently the final payment on the boat, not to mention the upkeep of his large house in Surrey, plus his intended London riverside apartment and collection of sports cars. Something needed to be done.

Edgar and Roger had several discussions about the changing state of the market and Roger was finally convinced that his sales team would have to hammer their overseas agents for all they were worth to make up for the rapid slowdown in the home market. He employed a consultant who advised him on where they were most likely to make up the shortfall in the coming years.

Reading the lavishly overpriced consultant's report, it occurred to Roger that Lichtenstein Re had only one agent in the whole of the Far East. Yet these were the so-called Tiger Economies, the countries around the Pacific Rim. He was drawn to Hong Kong because it was still British. Looking at the neighbouring countries, he ruled out communist China, considered Korea, discounted Thailand and noticed Japan. These countries were where the world's industry was. You name it, they made it, normally in vast quantities, too. Ships, motorcycles, cars and masses of consumer electronics. This was where they needed to be. He immediately summoned the single Lichtenstein Re representative in the Far East to London.

Edgar, as was his way, greeted Mr. Chan like a long lost cousin. It was seventeen years since Edgar and David had set him up in Hong Kong and he had grown up with Lichtenstein Re in his blood. The two of them had a lot of catching up to do, the Irishman insisting on entertaining the Chinaman for the duration of his short stay in London. Roger insisted that his young family needed him to be at home that evening and declined Edgar's invitation to join them for dinner, instead delegating a junior Sales Manager to accompany them.

The message that Roger got across to Mr. Chan at their two hour meeting the next morning was clear and succinct. Mr. Chan had to produce more business quickly but how was he going to do it?

Despite Roger's lack of international business etiquette shining through as a brusque indifference bordering on rudeness, Mr. Chan maintained his dignity throughout. He was aware that the wheels had come off the UK economy and that Roger was probably under a lot of pressure to perform for the company. He went back to Hong Kong with his tail slightly between his legs, tasked with producing a business plan to double the volume of insurance business within a three year period. It didn't matter that he had been one of the top performing Lichtenstein Re agents in the world for most of the last fifteen years, Roger had decided that he wanted more. The consequences of Mr. Chan not providing the extra business remained unsaid, however the young sales director made it clear with his attitude throughout the meeting that nobody was indispensable in his quest for more business.

Mr. Chan had been successful in business by being very selective about the people he dealt with, preferring quality to quantity. Roger was forcing his hand into expanding his network to encompass people he had no respect for but who nonetheless sold insurance. On returning home Mr. Chan and his sales manager sat down and reluctantly drew up a plan. They decided that they would take no commission on new business written by the new associates for the first year. This would be a powerful incentive for the new associates as they would get all of the available commission. It would be up to them if they wanted to discount premiums to get new customers on board. The trick was then hanging on to the business in the second and third years as the premiums increased, but that was always a challenge. Not earning commission on new business was a bitter pill to swallow but it had to be done if they were to keep the new sales director happy.

Roger called individual meetings with all of the existing worldwide Lichtenstein Re agents and told them all the same thing. He managed with some difficulty to avoid entertaining any of them, leaving this to the gregarious Edgar who was in seventh heaven seeing old friends turning up on almost a daily basis. Roger's stock excuse to Edgar was Hilary and their new born babes.

The only exception that Roger did make was the agent from Norway, a perfectly formed, dark-haired beauty from Trondheim called Freya. She was standing in for her father who ran the business. Her English was faltering and this was her first time in London, so Roger took it upon himself to show her the sights of the capitol. Of course she was impressed with this dashing young director, his large office and the Aston Martin. So impressed that after dinner on her second and last night in London, she asked the by-now completely besotted Roger if he'd like to come back to her hotel room and help her pack. Roger, feeling it would be churlish to refuse, spent the night with the modestly self-termed Norse Goddess of love and beauty. She in turn, perhaps with knowledge imparted from her spiritual husband Odin, the God of War, taught Roger a thing or two about rape and pillage.

As they kissed outside Heathrow Terminal 1 the next morning, neither of them noticed the elegantly dressed older gentleman waiting for a taxi with an expression of abject shock on his face. Vern, on his way to a meeting with a defence procurement agency in London, thought some very dark thoughts about Roger that morning. The scumbag was playing away with his precious Hilary. At that moment, he avowed there would be some tragic revenge exacted on her behalf.

Roger used the strategic importance of entertaining their overseas agents as his excuse to Hilary for staying away. He even went on to say the Norwegian agents might need some special coaching in business development which would require him to go over there once or twice later in the year.

'Good at that now, are you?' Hilary asked, turning towards him in surprise. They were in the kitchen whilst Hilary cooked dinner and Inge took care of the children.

'Yes, well, it comes naturally now I'm responsible for all of the sales,' Roger replied casually.

'So what technique do you use?' Hilary was genuinely interested; her own business was suffering just as much from the recession.

'Oh, nothing specific, increased market penetration via agents mainly. Especially in parts of the world where the economy is good like the Far East, and Norway, funnily enough. Anywhere other than the UK, at the minute,' Roger said, sounding pleased with his new found expertise.

'Any suggestions for my business then?' she asked, part curious, part challenge.

'Yes, pack it in and look after our children,' he replied without hesitation.

She ignored him and served the dinner. They carried on their discussion as they ate. 'So what is the problem with me running a business? And don't say you're worried about the children because I know you're not. I've also seen you panting after Inge so I know she's not the problem either,' she said.

'Panting? That's a bit strong, Hils. I'll admit she's a bit of a stunner. Any man with an ounce of spunk in him would find her attractive,' he said defensively.

'Hmm, so what then,' she pressed.

'I don't see the point. I earn more than enough for both of us and I know what you're going to say about your bloody emancipation and all that feminine independence bollocks. And while we're talking frankly, I don't like that Uncle of yours either.'

'Uncle Vern? How could you not like Uncle Vern?' she asked, shocked.

'Because he's slippery,' he said, avoiding eye contact with her. 'The way he looks at me sometimes, gives me the willies. And he slimes all around you.'

'Because he loves me! And he cares for me. Maybe you could learn a thing or two from him. You are crass sometimes, Roger, completely crass,' she thought of storming off but it wasn't in her nature to give him that satisfaction. She could see that Roger was becoming increasingly uncomfortable.

'Oh come on, Hils, let's stop this can we?'

His pleading only infuriated Hilary further, 'Listen, I picked you up from that jail because I saw something in you. This inheritance has changed you completely, you're cold with me and you're cold with the kids. It seems like we were a passing interest, well fine! If that's the way you want it then you just carry on doing your thing. Just don't ever tell me how to do my thing!' She had never been this angry with him before.

'Maybe we should have a holiday,' he said in an unusually placatory tone. 'I've bought a boat. Maybe we could go somewhere on it, somewhere hot.'

'A boat? What sort of boat?'

'A big one. Eighty-five footer, luxury. You'll love it,' he said, 'it's got a children's playroom on board, they'll love it too.'

'Where is it?' She had visions of a grey English Channel, ferries, sea-gulls.

'Antibes in the South of France, near Nice. In a beautiful marina.'

'How much did that cost then?'

'What? The marina?'

She had to laugh. 'No, the boat, stupid.' It somehow broke the steely atmosphere.

'Just over a million,'

'A million quid? But you don't have a million quid!' she spluttered.

'Very shortly I will, Hils. Several tens of millions, in fact. Besides I'm a Director. Directors of large wealthy corporations can do things like that. They have a duty to, buy boats, I mean, to entertain their friends and clients. Impress people.'

Hilary was literally speechless. She started clearing the dinner things away. There was no point in arguing with him, she had made her bed and she would have to lie in it. She would prevail though, she knew that much.

'Well, what do you say?' he asked hopefully.

'Do you know how to drive the thing? Safely, I mean, from one place to another. Navigation and all of that stuff?'

'Yes, of course I do, but we won't have to bother with that,' he said lightly.

'No?'

'No. It's got a permanent crew, well a skipper and a stewardess,'

She sighed inwardly, just what had she got herself into?

Roger leafed through the business plan from Mr. Chan. It was the first to land on his desk and he was pleased with what he saw. The Chinaman had increased his network dramatically, an unpronounceable company had been appointed for Japan, Hi-Star Associates in Korea, Veng & Co in Taiwan and so on. Another fifteen associate companies, in total. Why hadn't the old fool bothered with any of this lot before, he wondered?

He read on. They were also going to split the associate's commissions for new business in the first year. This was music to his ears. So what if the old man didn't make as much money, he'd done well out of Lichtenstein Re up to now, he should be prepared to forego a little to fund this expansion of his. And to think of all that new business flooding in!

Roger applauded himself. What a fantastic idea it had been to get the agents to increase their networks. He couldn't wait until the board meeting that afternoon, his fellow directors would be beside themselves with all this new business about to flood in. He couldn't wait - he could already see the swanky Docklands apartment and his collection of sports cars starting to accumulate.

The phone rang, it was Louise. 'Mr. Chan for you, Roger,' she said with a slight hesitation, she knew he didn't like talking to foreigners very much.

'Ah excellent, thanks Louise, put him through,' Roger said into the handset.

The surprised Louise patched the call through.

'Mr. Chan!' Roger said, enthusiasm personified. 'It's lovely to hear from you. And how are things in Hong Kong this morning?'

'Well it's seven in the evening. The sun is just going down over Lantau, and in London?' the Chinaman enquired politely.

'Cracking, Mr. Chan, cracking. I'm actually just reading your report, it's excellent. You've done very well and exceeded our expectations. I look forward to seeing the fruits of your labour!' Roger boomed into the phone.

'Yes, thank you. Actually, that is why I rang you. You will maybe have noticed one of our new associate companies, Veng & Co, in Taiwan?'

'Yes, I have indeed,' Roger confirmed.

'Well they will bring us a lot of industrial business. They have one very hot prospect at the moment, a manufacturing company. Their insurance is up for renewal. Mr. Veng has been to see them, they have agreed a price and he has issued a temporary cover note. It's obviously very important that they have the cover straight away, but there is just one issue.' The line went silent.

'Yes?' Roger asked, trying hard not to sound impatient.

'Well, they make household goods,' the Chinaman continued. 'You know, peelers and can openers, things like that. They also make sex toys and specialist therapy machines. They export a lot of their output to the USA. Mr. Veng was wondering, as he's never dealt with this sort of product before, if this was a risk that Lichtenstein Re is happy with, from the product liability point of view that is.'

Roger frowned in puzzlement, then laughed out loud. 'What, in case some randy housewife tries frigging herself with a can opener or peeling the spuds with a dildo, that sort of thing?' Roger replied, sensitive as ever.

'Ha-ha, no. It's just the vibrators and the therapy machines because they have such, how shall we say, intimate interfaces. The vibrators for obvious reasons, but he has seen one of the therapy machines and he says they are quite amazing things. You lie on them and the thing vibrates your whole body or whatever part you want treated. He was just worried that if one of them malfunctions, they could probably do quite a lot of damage, that's all.'

'Come, come, Mr. Chan, you know the pack-drill on this one by now? As long as these products have been tested independently and have some kind of approval, then of course it's no problem. We put a limit of liability on the policy anyway don't we?'

'Yes, $10 million, that's the reason for the call, is that enough?'

A more diligent person. A person not in as much enthrallment about the prospects of new business coming in at any cost as Roger was, would have referred Mr. Chan to the senior product liability underwriter who sat two floors below. This highly-skilled, highly-paid professional would have carried out a rigorous analysis of the risks involved, probably involving a trip to the manufacturer's premises and to the independent test house to see the test results for himself and verify their correctness and authenticity. Only once the results of the investigation were cleared and signed off at board level would Lichtenstein Re have issued a policy including the product liability cover to a stated maximum amount. 'Make it $50 million, if you like, Mr. Chan,' Roger said casually. 'That should cover it, shouldn't it?'

'Why, yes. Of course. Thank you,' came the somewhat startled reply.

'Good. Let Mr. Veng know and we look forward to receiving his proposal documents. Please make sure that all the documents you send to us are marked for my attention. I will get the policies issued without delay.'

'OK, Mr. Collins. Thank you and enjoy the rest of the day,'

'You too, Mr. Chan. Good-bye.'

Roger sighed as he put the phone down. These bloody foreigners are a bit slow to catch on sometimes.

'Therapy machines? What sort of therapy?'

Roger sighed inwardly for the second time that day. Questions, questions. Why did they expect him, of all people, to know these things? 'Sports injuries and the like, sports clubs will be the biggest market for them, physiotherapists too,' he said, his imagination taking over.

'Presumably these machines have had some form of medical assessment and been through rigorous testing, have they?'

Fuck me, this was tiresome, Roger thought to himself. 'Yes, in Taiwan, where they're made. Of course they have.'

'And we've seen the results and the certificates, have we?'

'No, but we will get them with the proposal documents when they come,' Roger looked at the Chief Underwriter with an expression of incredulity and contempt.

The Chief Underwriter had a hushed conversation with the man sitting next to him at the board meeting. What now, Roger thought to himself, he had only given them the Chan case as an example to give them a taster of just how much business was going to be coming their way thanks to all his efforts, and this guy had the effrontery to jump down his throat in front of everybody. Now he was having a private discussion. The bloody cheek.

The Chief Underwriter turned to him and said hurriedly, 'Carry on, Roger, we'll talk afterwards, sorry.'

'Well, thanks,' Roger said sarcastically, looking at the rest of his audience with a half smile as if to say, who is this idiot? He got no response from the assembled Directors. 'As I was saying, this is just one early example of the efforts our agents are prepared to go to in order to increase their levels of business. The Far East is one area that I'm certainly very positive about, the other is Scandinavia, the offshore oil and gas industry in Norway in particular. I shall be spending some time over there in the coming months to work with the agent to maximise the opportunities. I am confident that this export-led sales strategy will result in an upswing in new business that will equal, if not better, the volumes of business that we've lost in the UK due to the recession. Thank you,' Roger sat back with an air of smug finality.

Edgar looked up. 'Thank you, Roger. I am sure some of you will have some questions. Yes, Bill,' he gestured at the Chief Underwriter.

'While I think this is an excellent effort, Roger, which I wholeheartedly support, by the way, and believe it is in all our interests, at the same time we have to be very careful. We're entering new territory, taking on risks that need careful analysis. We're industry people at heart, we've always gone out of our way to understand processes and techniques used by our customers, that's why we've been successful in the past by working closely with them. In the scenario that Roger has just described, two things concern me. One, we are relying on agents to do that job for us. And two, our end customers could be working in areas that are new to us.

'I know this is your first response, Roger, and I don't wish to sound defeatist but the company in Taiwan is a good example. We have a new agent and a manufacturing company with what sounds like a very diverse range of activities. All I would say is that we should exercise extreme caution and diligence in dealing with this sort of arrangement. We have to underwrite all the way upwards starting from the sales process. We may have to spend some time, as Roger is valuably suggesting, with the agents, to get to know how they work and quantify the risks to Liechtenstein Re. That's all I wanted to say, thanks Edgar, Roger.'

'OK, Bill, I think we all get the message. If nobody else has got anything else to say, I declare the meeting closed.'

Roger certainly got the message; it brought back a memory of the American trial judge sentencing him to seven and a half years in prison, and the pain of being stabbed three times by the Mafia. He looked at the Chief Underwriter and hated him intensely. He would show the miserable bastard a thing or two about underwriting from the sales process upwards. His sales strategy was going to work, come what may. Everybody else could go and hang themselves, he thought as he walked out of the boardroom and back to his office. It was four-thirty in the afternoon, he knew he shouldn't really go but he'd had enough. He threw everything he needed into his briefcase and made for the car park, ignoring everybody on his route down to the basement. He opened the door of the Aston and threw his briefcase onto the passenger seat. He similarly threw himself into the driver's seat and slammed the door, feverishly groping with the key for the ignition switch.

The sound of a semi-automatic pistol being cocked as cold, hard steel made contact with the back of his neck made Roger think immediately of Hollywood. Had he made it big? Was this his big break? Where were the cameras? To compound his anticipation he even looked in the rear view mirror and yes, it was a dark-clothed, extremely fearsome Chinaman looking him square in the eyes.

'Leave the keys in the ignition and get out of the car slowly, very slowly,' the voice from the back of the car said.

'Let me guess, Candid Camera?' Roger asked, smiling.

'It's up to you whether you live or die,' the Chinaman hissed. 'Now if you want to live, get out of the car.'

'Come on, you're a Stripagram, right?' he looked right and left, looking for signs of discarded underwear or policemen's hats. It was as his head returned to the central position that he felt a tremendously powerful *thunk* from behind his right ear and noticed that almost simultaneously, the front and rear windscreens of the car just opposite had exploded into a million pieces.

'Get out of the car now, or you really will die,' the voice said calmly from the rear.

Roger got out of the car in a daze. The Chinese marksman nimbly flicked the driver's seat forward, got out, leapt into the front seat, started the engine, slammed the door and gunned the car ferociously in a deafening cacophony of screaming tyres and smoke, heading towards the car-park exit barrier. A few seconds later Roger heard the barrier disintegrate as the car smashed its way through the exit and out onto the road.

Roger felt a warm trickle running down his neck, he put his hand to his ear. His earlobe seemed not to be there any longer, 'Fuck,' was all he could say. This was the last sentiment echoing in his mind before his knees buckled and he fainted into almost the perfect CSI silhouette on the car park floor.

Part 5. 1990 - 1992

25. Party Time

Hilary did her best to look composed. The sights, smells and sounds of so much sex going on around her was hard to take in. Here was the human, animal form at its basest. Naked and semi-naked bodies standing, lying down, writhing, gyrating, pulsating. A curious mixture of facial expressions: expectant, hypnotised, ecstatic, some gargoyle-like with tongues flickering. It was a genital fest. Polished, rampant cocks and glistening honeyed pudenda competing for gratification. The pushy and the adventuresome skirmishing with the available and the willing. Private thoughts and feelings shrouded in stimulation, penetration and masturbation. Earnest couplings, and frenzied copulation like naughty pets in the park, compliant openings held in anticipation, greedy eyes staring, busy hands and fingers, the occasional shuddering orgasm.

'Goodness.' Hilary turned and smiled upwards at the tall moustachioed man by her side. 'It's all happening here then,' she heard herself say. She sounded like the Queen, she thought, or should that be Prince Philip?

'Yes this is the main orgy room, I'll show you the specialist rooms upstairs later,' he gestured. 'Can I get you a drink?'

'A soft-drink, please.' She wondered whether alcohol was actually on the menu at an event like this. Probably early on, not later though. Not now, surely.

'Good turnout tonight then, Marty?' she deliberately kept her voice upbeat, despite her shock at the scene before her. Was she really in this line of business? She didn't feel like she should be if this is what they got up to.

'Yes, excellent,' he replied in his deep Welsh accent. 'There's no Match of the Day at the moment. They're always better in the summer anyway - I think the higher temperature gets them going more.'

Hilary chuckled. 'It certainly looks like it.' She followed the Welshman over to an annex area where there were sofas and soft music playing. There were other clothed couples here, some chatting, some petting. Marty was one of Vern's new industrial dealers, she had met him on their first round of visits in the UK. She had just happened to phone him during the week about a vibrator order and he'd told her all about the arrival of the new MassageOmatic machine, and about the swinger's party at the weekend that she was welcome to attend if she wanted. She had thought about bringing Roger along. Not for very long though. Their previous discussion about open marriages and his incessant wandering eyes stifling the idea almost instantly. He would have been completely insufferable at an event like this. More than normal, she thought sadly. He was in Norway anyway, doing his educate-the-plebs act.

Marty got the drinks from a well-stocked cabinet. 'This is the respectable area. They can get warmed up in here but definitely no sex allowed. I paid a lot of money for these sofas and carpets, don't want them ruined,' he said, smiling.

'Yes, I can imagine it's quite a messy business. Not something you'd normally think about,' Hilary said. More like the Princess Royal now, she thought.

'Come on, I'll show you upstairs.' She followed him out into the large hallway and up the curved staircase, couples coming and going as they went. 'This is our *pièce de résistance*, not many establishments can boast they have one of these. We call it the Dewhurst Room. It's basically for people interested in toilet training, let me just check there's no one using it,' he poked his head around the door. 'No, we're all right.'

A shiver of panic went through Hilary. It must be bad in here if he thinks I'll be shocked after seeing what's going on downstairs, 'Wow,' she said as they stepped into the room. It was simply a vast expanse of tiles, the floor, the walls, the seating areas, everywhere.

Marty was obviously proud of this creation. 'Basically it's a large wet-room with superb drainage all round, and low level shower heads for washing away. That's where they do the number-ones,' he said pointing to the periphery of the room. 'In the middle we've got the area for the number twos. The glass-topped table with a central channel and built-in water jets, everything is washed down to the drain there when they're finished,' he said pointing to a large grate in the floor.

Hilary looked on in awe at this monument to depravity. She wasn't going to ask what happened on the glass topped table. It was just too horrible to comprehend, 'Why is it called the Dewhurst Room?' she asked, ever the polite royal visitor, she thought.

'After the bloke who designed it, old Ron. He loved this central feature. It's a bit of a pseudonym now, you know like hoovering? Yes, if you fancy going for a Dewhurst, this is the place to come. I think it's pretty unique actually, it's hygienic and extremely well ventilated,' he said proudly, pointing to the shower area and the large ducts on the ceiling. 'Come on, I'll show you the other rooms.'

Marty then showed her the dungeon complex which was actually four inter-connecting rooms: the dominatrix wardrobe, the tool cupboard and the torture chamber. He explained about their house rule, how women were allowed to torture, abuse and humiliate men all they liked but not the other way round.

The fourth room contained their newest investment.

A couple were waiting to have a go on the shiny, white, purposeful-looking machine. Marty took over, 'Please, allow me to show you the wonders of the MassageOmatic,' he said gesturing at the male to get on the table. 'Come here, missus,' he said to the girl, 'and I'll show you how to operate the controls.' Her partner climbed onto the lower deck and lay down on his back. 'Now, it's quite simple, just press start.' She did so and the upper deck arced down slowly, locked into place on its upright supports and came vertically down to just above the incumbent male. The hundreds of what looked like miniature boxing gloves on stalks settled themselves around the man's contours for the complete length of his body. The girl gave a short giggle of anticipation.

The Welshman continued, 'Now, you have a variety of options. You can see the outline of your partners profile on the screen so you can choose the area of the body you want to concentrate on. I suggest all over first.' He watched the screen and blocked on with the roller ball cursor all over the human outline. He pressed enter with a flourish. 'If you scroll through the display, you can choose vibrate, punch, squeeze or stretch. Don't worry the controls are pre-set in the factory to a maximum force of five, you can't do any serious damage, it won't let you. Let's have vibrate to start with, select, set, now strength, select one. OK, ready? Then press start and we're away.' He stood back.

The male groaned as the upper and lower boxing gloves on stalks began pounding away gently over his whole body, 'Oh that's wonderful, so good.'

Marty stepped up to the control again. 'Increase to two, how's that?' he asked.

'Oh even better, excellent,' came the reply.

'Increase to three, how's that?'

'Whoah,' came the slightly strangulated reply.

'Increase to four, you OK?'

'Bugger, it's starting to hurt,' the voice was now tremulous.

'Feeling like a man?' Not waiting for a reply, Marty increased the strength, saying in his best train-station announcer's voice, 'Increase to five.'

'Shit, agghh, stop the bloody thing,' the voice was now synchronised in harmony with the miniature boxing gloves on stalks as they rammed in and out of the man's body in a cacophony of violence.

'OK sorry, back to two,' Marty looked at the shocked girl and winked.

'Ahhh,' came the now steady, relieved voice from between the decks. 'That's better.'

'Now then, we'll stop that and put it onto say, punch. You can have a single stalk punch right in the middle of the stomach set at say number two like this.'

'Oogh, bloody hell,' came the shocked voice from within.

'Or you can have a grouped punch, again to the middle of the stomach, say set at number four, like this,' Marty's fingers were a blur on the control pad.

'Ooph,' Breathless gasps were now coming from the machine.

The girl looked at the Welshman, only very slightly amused now, 'You winded him.'

'He'll be OK,' he said casually. 'Now we'll put it onto squeeze, again whole body, factor two, start.'

'Wohoh, bloody hell,' the breathless incumbent gasped.

'Now we'll set the squeeze setting and put it on to stretch, factor two, start,' he said, excited now. This was the machine's *coup de grâce*.

'Oh, oh, oh, oh, this is bloody unreal! Get me out of here!' the angry voice from within shouted. The boxing gloves on stalks were squeezing and stretching simultaneously.

Marty looked at the speechless girl, 'Does he normally swear this much?'

'No, he doesn't,' she replied dazed, 'this thing is awesome.'

'Ought to be for the money it cost,' he turned to Hilary. 'Well? What do you think? Good or what?'

Hilary was frozen, momentarily speechless. Her mind was spinning but the words would only come slowly. 'I think if I were one for this lifestyle, I'd prefer the orgy.' She hoped she didn't sound churlish or disappointed. Or willing.

'Yes, well, we try and cater for all tastes,' the Welshman concurred as he helped the groaning party-goer from the bed of the machine. 'Come on mate, you'll be OK.'

As she watched the ashen-faced male limp away with the help of his girlfriend, Hilary gulped. He was a young man and he had only been on the machine for a very short while. She wondered what could happen to someone older, not as fit. Especially with someone at the controls who harboured a grudge, against the person, against people in general, maybe. She shuddered. She now knew what Vern meant by his 'industrial' side of the business. This was a big step on from titillation. This was hurting people for real and she was silently horrified.

Hilary had arranged to have lunch with Marty the following day. His company Party-Mart was well known throughout the sex toy industry, partly due to the highly partisan nature of their advertising slogans. 'Putting the Cwm back into Cwmbran,' and 'Bringing Randy to the Rhondda,' being two of his recent high-profile campaigns. Hilary wanted to know what made this man tick, and if there was anything she could learn from him. After the horrors of the previous night, she felt she had an inkling of what the conversation would be about.

'Hello Hilary, I apologise if I'm late,' he said as he came into the pub slightly breathless. 'Had to do a bit of clearing up after last night. I'm sorry we didn't get a chance to speak much either. I've been looking forward to lunch. How are you after last night?'

'Oh I'm fine, thanks Marty. Just to clear one thing up, you weren't expecting me to join in, were you?'

'No, no of course not. I mean look at me - I never do. I guess you could call me a facilitator. I organise, put things in place, clear up afterwards. Someone's got to do it and it might as well be me. I'd rather be making money than screwing weirdoes.'

'You must get tempted, surely?' Hilary asked in surprise.

'No, never, not in public. Couldn't do it. See that?' he asked, holding up a limp little finger. 'That's me with no clothes on in public. Shameful it is, shameful.'

Hilary couldn't help but laugh. 'Well, I'm relieved I'm not the only one who thinks that our customers are a bit weird,' she said. 'What gets me is that they keep coming back for more. You'd think they'd learn that stable relationships are better for you than orgies and wife-swapping, wouldn't you?'

'Dyed in the wools, they are, once a swinger always a swinger. As long as you can keep a stomach for it there's money to be made. Long may it continue is what I say.'

'And I thought I was pushing my luck selling a few mail-order vibrators.'

'Tip of the iceberg, missus, tip of the iceberg. Some of them will stop at nothing. You know, there's people at that party last night who've re-mortgaged their houses to keep coming to my parties, that's how desperate they are.'

'I shall go away this afternoon rejuvenated,' Hilary said, smiling. 'You've restored my faith in human frailty and weakness in all its forms. Here's to them and happy days for us,' she laughed as she raised her glass. 'Cheers.'

The chat continued over lunch about business in general, eventually getting onto the subject of the MassageOmatic. She admitted to him that she was shocked at what she had seen. 'At the dealer conference they said they were bringing out a therapy machine. What happened?'

'Well my understanding is that's how it started off. I think your Uncle somehow managed to convince Han Choy that there was a market for a machine that could be used by the military for extracting information. The auto-erotica version is a de-tuned spin off.'

'Extracting information? That means torture, doesn't it?'

'Yes, I think so. Your Uncle didn't go into too much detail. I know he's selling a lot of them though. The one you saw last night was taken at the last minute from a mixed shipment of 100 destined for the USA.'

'A mixed shipment. That sounds dangerous, I hope they got the labels right,' she said.

Marty burst out laughing, 'Yes, they'd end up with a really pissed-off military and a lot of dead swingers, wouldn't they?'

'Don't laugh, it could just happen. You haven't seen my Uncle's stock-control methods, have you?' she said, struggling to suppress a giggle.

They finished lunch in good spirits. Marty went home to finish clearing up in readiness for what he coyly referred to as his specialist week-night parties whilst Hilary drove back to Surrey in a thoughtful mood. Notwithstanding the moral and ethical arguments, would she be able to carry on if it was true that Han Choy and VSS, her two principle suppliers, were building and exporting weapons of torture?

She would have to speak with Vern about it, but if it was true, she really couldn't see how she could possibly continue.

The vibrators were an excellent product, but knowing that the same company produced machines that would hurt or even kill people. That was something else. Starting another line of business was not really an option either, what with her family commitments.

Maybe Roger's wish that she give up the business would come true, after all.

Vern sounded unusually troubled by Hilary's direct questions regarding the MassageOmatic.

'No, absolutely not, my dear. You should know by now this is a legitimate business I run here. I'm not some shady back street arms dealer who surfaces at air-shows to sell to dodgy dictators and gangs of mercenaries. It just so happens that I get military enquiries from old connections and the MassageOmatic is a perfect solution for some of them. Governments have a need to extract information from certain people intent on causing trouble. I am merely fulfilling a need and making some money in the process, you can understand that, can't you?'

'What governments?'

'Hilary, I can't tell you that. I've signed contracts and the secrecy element is always one of the biggest clauses. Sorry, my dear, I'd love to tell you but I can't.'

'I thought Han Sen was building a therapy machine, does he build these for you as well?'

'His MassageOmatic is a fantastic machine; you saw one at the Dealer Conference. Han Sen has said to me in the past that he doesn't want anything to do with coercion, he was involved in it a long while ago and it sickened him. The truth is, Hilary, I get Han Sen to build the mechanism and I use someone else to programme the controls for the two versions, one is purely for military use and the other is the auto-erotica. Marty has one of the first ones. Fantastic piece of kit, don't you think?'

'Frighteningly powerful though, they can really hurt people.'

'Yes, my dear, but as I said, I am filling a hole in the market. I already have pre-orders for eighty or so from my worldwide dealers. That tells you something, doesn't it?'

'Marty said his was taken from a US shipment of 100 mixed, presumably destined for the US Military?'

'Hilary, please stop asking questions about the military equipment or I'll end up in all sorts of trouble, there's a love.'

'They look expensive, how much are they?'

'The one you saw cost Marty about £70,000. I let him have it at a good discount as he's hoping to sell some more.'

'The military versions are a lot more?'

'Yes.'

'So you're the only one driving this whole MassageOmatic how-much-pain-can-you-take thing?'

'Yes.'

'How do you protect yourself, I mean if one of the victims comes looking for you.'

'All of my deals are protected by a confidentiality agreement, I only sell to people I trust. You are my niece and business partner, I obviously trust you to be discreet about this, unlike Marty,' he said with a trace of annoyance.

'To be honest, Uncle Vern, I'm not sure I can carry on being your business partner. Knowing what you do. The whole thing sickens me.'

'I understand, my love. I really don't want to lose you as a niece and a friend, but I've invested far too much money in this to back out now.'

'I realise that, and no, you won't lose me as a niece or as a friend. You're my Dad's brother, we are flesh and blood after all.'

'That's nice, thank you. I'll talk with Han Sen. If you want, he'll be able to supply you direct with the sex-toys. You'll probably get a cheaper price but he may want to ship in larger quantities.'

'OK. I'll think about it. Goodnight, Uncle Vern.'

'Goodnight, my dear, sleep tight.'

Hilary put the phone down. Maybe she wouldn't be giving the business up after all. He was a sad old git though - couldn't he just be content with what he'd got? Or was it a case of once a soldier always a soldier? The word coercion sent a quiver down her spine, and she thought back to the hapless couple on Saturday night. OK, so the male was a bit of a drip, but she could still hear the terror in his voice. If that was a de-tuned version, she dreaded to think of the damage a fully-fledged military version could cause.

The trouble was, it was the person at the controls who was the dangerous one. That person was the final link in the pyramid of paranoia that would trigger the government to buy the machine in the first place. OK, so the auto-erotica thing was almost a necessary evil.

Everyone knew it went on, sad people having sex while strangling one another with bits of rope or plugging each other in to the mains to fulfil some weird kind of fantasy. But even if Uncle Vern had sold one slightly stronger version to an old military mate as a favour, let alone marketing the thing, however discreetly, she would still not feel comfortable continuing a business relationship with him.

As she drove home, she wished she had someone to talk to. The problem was that everyone knew her Uncle. She had no wish to compromise him. She was no whistle-blower either; he was family, nothing justified tearing the family apart.

As for Roger, he was in a permanent state of blissful ignorance when it came to moral dilemmas. She gritted her teeth as she pulled into the driveway; he was the last person she could talk to about this.

Roger was in the kitchen making cheese on toast as Hilary came in the front door, dumping her overnight bag in the hall.

'Hello, my love, did you have a good weekend?' he enquired politely, walking across to meet her at the kitchen entrance. They hugged. He kissed her on the cheek.

'Yes, excellent, thanks. Kids in bed?' she asked.

'Yes, Inge took them up. She's gone to the pictures with the boyfriend.'

She touched the remains of his right ear-lobe delicately, Roger flinched. 'Oh Rodge, he really did shoot you, didn't he? Is it still sore?'

'Yes, it bloody is. If I ever catch the fucker, I'll cut his balls off. The worst of it is, the car was back there the next day. Right as rain, not a scratch on it. They'd even washed and valeted it. It's almost like someone's taking the piss out of yours truly. The bit I don't understand though,' he said, feeling his ear, 'threats of violence, yes - but actually shooting someone and taking out the Chief Underwriters windscreens at the same time, that's not funny. Well, it would be if it was just the windscreens, I suppose.' He took a large, noisy mouthful of the toasted cheese sandwich.

'They returned the car washed and valeted? You're kidding me,' she said.

'None of my tapes were missing either. I didn't check, maybe they'd upgraded my collection for me - I wouldn't be surprised.'

Hilary couldn't help laughing out loud. 'How very odd. What did the police say?'

'They've never seen anything like it either. They suspect someone wanted a mould to make a kit-car but they normally just go and hire one for a day. They can't find any evidence of the glass fibre that they normally use, but it does explain the washing. Either that, or it's friends having a laugh by using a contract hit-man, the shooting bit being an unfortunate mistake.'

'Who needs friends like that?'

'Exactly. It's a ridiculous theory.'

'You poor thing,' she comforted him before slowly breaking away. 'I'll just go and tuck the kids in.'

'Want tea or toast or anything?' Roger asked as she was halfway up the stairs.

'Tea please,' she called down. As she entered Sam's room, she looked at the sleeping girl, the familiar motherly instinct tugging at her emotions. She knelt by the side of the bed, stroked her hair lightly and watched her sleeping. After the horror show of the weekend this was really where she wanted to be, snuggling in the pureness of her children. There were no dark thoughts here, just unconditional love and dependence, and she suddenly felt fulfilled. This was her real life, the business wasn't all that important. These two needed her, more than those weirdoes out there with their strange habits. Where had she gone wrong with it all? It was all so clear before these two came along. She felt like she was going through life on a train that she couldn't get off. She pulled the duvet up and tucked it around the two-year-old's shoulders and slowly left the room, picking up clothes as she went, pulling the door to so that some of the light from the landing spilled into the bedroom. After visiting Julian and tucking him in, she closed his door completely, knowing he liked the darkness. More like his father, she thought as she came down the stairs.

'How was Norway?' she asked, taking the mug of tea he offered.

'Cold and wet, as usual. I brought you back another spectacularly ugly troll for your collection. Oh and this, it's from Lapland,' he said pushing a small bag across the table in her direction.

She took the wooden box out of the bag and removed the lid. 'Oh Roger, thank you, it's beautiful.' It was a wood and leather hair grip encrusted with multi-coloured gem stones.

'I bought a smaller one for Sam and a toy car for Jules, they love them too,' he said, smiling.

'Thank you,' she said, kissing him on the cheek. 'When did you get back?'

'Three o'clock this afternoon, spent a bit of time with the kids which was nice,' he replied.

'They OK?'

'Perfect. Inge is great with them and they seem to like her,'

'And you're managing to instil some business sense into those Norwegians, are you?'

'Yes, they're very receptive actually. I'm learning quite a bit from them too.'

'Good,' she said, looking at him. There was something odd about Roger lately that she couldn't quite put her finger on. She wondered idly, as she sipped her tea, if he was having an affair. She found her inner reaction to this thought quite puzzling, she was almost quite pleased for him.

26. An Enlightened Decision

As Han Sen had predicted, the first fall-out from the VSS MassageOmatic didn't take long to materialise. A mildly surprised-sounding Vernon Saunders rang him five weeks after the dispatch of the first major shipment.

'First casualty I'm afraid, Han Sen.'

Han Sen was shocked. 'Someone's hurt?'

'Dead actually. It happened over the weekend. He had a weak heart apparently, I think we're covered by the words we put in the manual on health and safety, you know, suggesting that asthmatics and pregnant women and the like are not recommended etc. I'm also sure we put something in about anyone with a history of heart disease shouldn't be using it.'

'What was the cause of death?' Han Sen asked slowly.

'The squeeze function apparently. The programme was on random and when it came onto blanket squeeze on a number five setting, it sounds like the duration was too long for this bloke, and his heart stopped. They tried reviving him but no-go. You know what these swingers are like, all right at frigging each other senseless, but bloody useless at anything practical like first aid.'

'Was he American?'

'Yes,' the Englishman replied cheerfully. 'I was saving that for last, thought that might cheer you up. One down, only 259 million or so to go eh, Han Sen?'

'Vernon, this is not the time for jokes. This man's family, what do you think they're going to do?'

'Not a lot they can do, is there? The coroner's verdict was death by misadventure. They can't do much without coming out publicly and admitting their man was a cheap pervert who liked hurting himself and others for kicks.'

'And if they don't mind? Admitting their man is a pervert, that is, and it becomes a court case? They could wipe you out, Vernon.'

'Han Sen, I can't help noticing that I'm using the word 'we' in all of this, and you are using the word 'you'. You are going to back me in all of this, aren't you?'

'Yes, of course I am,' Han Sen replied, his mind flicking back to the $11 million that entered his bank account that morning. Not to mention the two further orders, both bigger than the first one, that were currently keeping his factory order book at record levels.

'Good. Well if it all goes pear-shaped for us, Hert Rentals are insured, we're insured, we just let the insurance companies carry the can. We pay hefty enough premiums, don't we?'

'Yes, we do. Did you see those guys from Liechtenstein about your product liability?'

'Yes I did. I've been meaning to thank you for that, Han Sen. Yes, they quoted me an extremely keen premium so I got myself signed up pretty much straightaway. $50 million cover for every machine that leaves here, fantastic or what? Where would the world be without insurance companies, eh?'

'You did tell them all the details about the machines, didn't you?'

'Of course, of course. Don't you worry. Safe as houses. Money in the bank, old chap. Toodloo for now.' And he was gone.

Old chap? Now where did that come from, Han Sen thought as he put the phone down. It was probably another archaic, condescending phrase originating from England's days as a world power.

Perhaps it was the Englishman's military background, but he seemed to be so blasé about everything, not just human life. Han Sen knew this would not be the last call from Hong Kong with sad news. At least sad as far as Han Sen was concerned.

For the first time ever since starting Han Choy Inc, he went home early that afternoon. He called a surprised Raya and told her he would pick Li Lai up from school. He had a bursting desire to spend some time with his daughter. Of course they spent time together at weekends; Saturday evenings and Sundays at the temple, but they were hardly ever on their own, just the two of them.

Angelique was slightly bemused as he told her to take messages, and that he would be back in the morning. 'Sorry Angelique, I only realised today that I have never picked her up from school, isn't that terrible?'

'You do work very hard, San Sen,' she said with a reproachful expression. 'Enjoy your afternoon.'

He drove home in his small commuter car, reflecting on his family.

'Li Lai will be thrilled to see you.' Raya said when he came through the door. 'You should do this more often.'

'We'll go to the zoo. We do need to spend more time together,' he said, unbuttoning his work shirt and heading for the shower.

'Don't get her too excited,' Raya called after him, ever the concerned mother.

'Why not?' he called from the bathroom.

'OK then, just this once,' she replied.

When Han Sen emerged from the shower, they made slow, passionate love. Han Sen was oblivious to any of his feelings about anything outside of the bedroom and outside of his relationship with Raya, the mother of their child. She was still beautiful, still extremely desirable, still very wise and he did love her a great deal. They lay for a long time in each other's arms afterwards, teasing and cajoling one another. Life couldn't be more perfect for both of them. They agreed between them that an afternoon in bed occasionally ought to be mandatory for all consenting couples. They got up eventually and after some chai, Han Sen went off to collect Li Lai from school.

Li Lai's face turned from an uncertain search for a familiar face amongst the crowd of parents outside the school gates into a disbelieving grin as she spotted her father.

'Daddy, daddy, you came to school!' she called excitedly, rushing towards him, arms outstretched.

He scooped her up and kissed both cheeks, 'Yes, my darling, they said I could come home early from work and I gave Mummy the afternoon off, too. Shall we go out somewhere?'

'Can we go to the zoo?'

'What a great idea,' he grinned.

'And we can see the panda bears and the hippopotamuses, I can't wait!'

This was how life should be, Han Sen thought as he bundled his excited daughter into the passenger seat; just the two of them, having fun. Why did life have to be any more complicated?

As if he knew that further difficulties with the MassageOmatic lay ahead, Han Sen threw himself into work at the factory with renewed energy and commitment. He became almost obsessively involved with the everyday and the mundane. Everything from fixating on minute engineering detail on new and upgraded products to kick-starting creative meetings with the sales group for fresh ideas, from finding a new business manager to harassing the buying office into finding new and better suppliers. Everybody involved in the business became much more wary than normal when Han Sen was around.

He took refuge in the temple, applying the same level of fastidiousness as he was doing with the business. Enquiring, pursuing, uncovering and eventually determining a sequence of events that would tie in with the core beliefs that the Buddha had taught.

He only knew one way of analysing problems, and that was as an engineer would do it. He started at the very basic teachings by drawing a table and commenting against each one of the four noble truths as taught by the Buddha.

Noble Truth One. Dissatisfaction and suffering exist and are universally experienced.	*I try very hard to make people's lives a little better with products that work well and don't cost the earth.*
Noble Truth Two. Desire and attachment are the causes of dissatisfaction and suffering.	*I only desire my family to be fed, housed and clothed and my workers to be happily employed. I am attached to nothing more than my family, to the ones I love and to the way I make my living.*
Noble Truth Three. There is dissatisfaction and suffering.	*We must all strive to find our own way of ending any dissatisfaction and suffering.*
Noble Truth Four. The end can be attained by journeying on the Noble Eightfold Path.	*By understanding the noble eightfold path, one can attain the end of dissatisfaction and suffering.*

Satisfying himself that he had commented as truthfully and as best he could, he then set out another table to make comments against all of the noble eightfold truths. This confessional was harder and took him a lot longer than he expected.

One.   Understanding   and Attaining   The   Right   View. Understanding the Four Noble Truths. See things as they truly are   without   delusions   or distortions   for   all   things change.   Develop   wisdom   by knowing   how   things   work, knowing oneself and others.

I see things without delusion or distortion and recognise in family and in business and all around us that things change. I   make   it   my   business   to understand how things work, I know myself and can sum up other people's qualities very quickly.

Two. Correct Thinking. Decide to set a life on the correct   path.   Wholehearted resolution and dedication to overcoming the dislocation of self-centred craving through the development of loving kindness, empathy   and   compassion.

From my days in Cambodia, I have tried to live my life in accordance   with   the teachings of the Buddha. There have been moments of weakness in doing what I did for, and against, the Khmer Rouge. I also contribute to the making of machines that can harm, this could be easily misunderstood as exploiting the weaknesses of others for gain. It is better explained as doing the best job possible to enable dignity on both sides because we are powerless to prevent people who want to do this to themselves and/or others.

Three. Correct Speech. Abstinence from lies and deceptions, backbiting, idle babble and abusive speech. Cultivate honesty and truthfulness; practice speech that is kind and benevolent. Let your words reflect your desire to help and not harm others.

I believe I communicate sufficiently with everyone around me those words that need to be communicated. I love two women, women who are sisters and shall never accept that one should have my love to the exclusion of the other. I love them all the more knowing that to be the case and pray for resolution and a sharing of our love.

I do not harm others, my machines help those people achieve what they want to achieve in a clean, consistent and controllable way. The parameters of the control are set by others, perhaps it would be more straightforward if I were to be in complete control.

Four. Correct Conduct.

(Following the Five Precepts) - Practice self-less conduct that reflects the highest statement of the life you want to live. Express conduct that is peaceful, honest and pure showing compassion for all beings.

I work hard to please others. My family and my workers benefit from my hard work, I strive for compassion in all that I do.

Five. Correct Livelihood.

Earn a living that does not harm living things. Avoidance of work that causes suffering to others or that makes a decent, virtuous life impossible. Do not engage in any occupation that opposes or distracts one from the path. Love and serve our world through your work.

With the benefit of first-hand experience, the self-made alternative to my machines is a truly horrific spectacle. Han Choy machines are enablers of dignity.

All Han Choy products are reliable, consistent and are designed to give people satisfaction throughout their long lifetime.

Six. Correct Effort.

Seek to make the balance between the exertion of following the spiritual path and a moderate life that is not over-

This table is an effort to restore family and work balance. It will show where I could be going wrong, I am over-zealous with my workers

zealous. Work to develop more wholesome mind states, while gently striving to go deeper and live more fully.

sometimes. I need to be consistent as I think I am with my family.

Seven. Correct Mindfulness. Become intensely aware of all the states in body, feeling, and mind. Through constant vigilance in thought, speech and action seek to rid the mind of self-centred thoughts that separate and replace them with those that bind all beings together. Be aware of your thoughts, emotions, body and world as they exist in the present moment. Your thoughts create your reality.

I am careful with thought, speech and action. I strive with my thoughts and deeds for the betterment of the human condition.

Eight. Correct Concentration. Deep meditation to lead to a higher state of consciousness (enlightenment). Through the application of meditation and

Only on Sunday at the temple can enlightenment be properly attained. Hardly ever during the working week. Business is no excuse,

mental discipline, seek to extinguish the last flame of grasping consciousness and develop an emptiness that has room to embrace and love all things.

just a practical block, we at Han Choy should all strive for more communication with the inner soul, a shrine to the Buddha in the canteens is not enough, I will talk to the priest to see if he can do more for us.

He read back his words and was relieved, they showed he lived his life in sympathy with all of the basic tenets of Buddhism. He was sure Hem Suvorn would have approved.

One thing that leapt off the page at him was the issue of who sets the control parameters for the MassageOmatic, the issue that had been dogging him since the first discussion with the Englishman. If the strength of his conviction was that strong, then he should stand by his product and not duck into the background on the issue of responsibility. Han Choy would be responsible from now on. There, he had made a decision, a forthright decision based on analysing whether he lived his life in accordance with the teachings of the Buddha or not. Well the answer was a resounding yes, the Buddha would approve of the basic principle behind the MassageOmatic.

He phoned the Englishman to tell him the good news.

'Nice of you to ring for a change, Han Sen. Another one of our mutual clients met an untimely end yesterday on one of your machines,' the Englishman said with his normal exuberance.

After all the good work he'd done in answering all of the doubts he'd had about his lifestyle and the positive outcome, Han Sen suddenly felt sick. He remained resolute in his decision to stop this going any further.

'Vernon, we've had this conversation several times already. Unless you take notice of what I tell you, this problem won't go away. Your only hope of getting out of this situation is by either having a product recall, or getting Freddie to go to each machine and lower the strength settings. I know it is going to be expensive for you but at the end of the day you bought a product from me that works. You ignored my advice about testing your modifications before you shipped them. You can't afford to ignore me anymore.'

'Han Sen, may I remind you that you build the machines with sufficient strength to be able to seriously harm, even kill people. You have an equal responsibility here, if not greater than I do,' the Englishman responded.

'When they leave here, they are double-deck therapy machines. They couldn't kill a fly if it was sandwiched between a pair of its stalks and you know it. The strength is merely a by-product of the reliability we build into the machine. It's the modifications that you and Freddie do that cause these problems.'

'Freddie swears you told him that the five setting would be OK for the MassageOmatic.'

'It's very simple, Vernon. Freddie is lying.'

'OK. What about a technical bulletin, send it to the dealers, let them do it. They made money on these things, let them share some of the pain.'

'It won't work. It's not enough, you will still have rogue machines out there that won't get modified. Besides the dealers aren't qualified to re-programme the circuitry in those machines. You'll have a worse nightmare on your hands if you let unskilled people loose on them, no matter how good Freddie's instructions are.'

'Well, if it comes to it, we can point to the technical bulletin as proof that we did something about it. If the owner chooses not to take the dealers advice that's down to him, isn't it?'

'If it's just a paper exercise you want, then it's your choice, you get on with it. I want nothing more to do with this batch. From now on, if you want a MassageOmatic, I will take charge of the test programme and I will tell Freddie what strength the settings need to be instead of finding out by killing your customers. That's ridiculous, Vernon, you should have known better.'

'Now hold on, Han Sen, what are you saying? You're going to produce the complete machine for me, is that right?'

'Yes, if you are still in business after this batch.'

'Well that's fantastic news. What brought about the change of heart?'

'What do you think, Vernon? I'm in business to try and make the best product I can. I can't bear to watch other people take one of my products and just, well, mess it up completely!'

'Good lord, I do believe that's the first time I've ever heard you nearly swear, Han Sen. Jolly good, old chap, let it go. Bottling it up is the very worst thing, you know.'

'So, I believe we have some orders to fulfil for VSS. I think we need to discuss just how we are going to proceed. When are you coming over?'

'Forthwith, young man. I'll be on the plane tomorrow morning. See you about eleven-thirty.'

He thought about ripping up the order for the MassageOmatic machines in front of the Englishman when he arrived. But no, the challenge had been set, and he would fulfil what he had been asked to fulfil. They would just have to think about getting some volunteers for the test programme. Sven's boys were up to whatever they normally got up to with the Ardourator and the sex-chair tests. He just wasn't sure if they would be that interested in doing this sort of real pain thresh-hold testing. He would talk to Rao about it, she probably knew of a client or two who would enjoy the experience.

'Ninety-four out of ninety-six of that batch were MassageOmatics for the S&M market. Just thought I'd cheer you up first thing,' the Englishman said cheerily as he stood in the office the following morning. 'Oh, and Freddie rang me this morning, he's going to retire.'

From behind his desk, Han Sen looked at the tall, physically imposing presence of Vernon Saunders and tried to bite back his frustration. He was beginning to tire of the man's florid verbal style and his whole attitude towards the MassageOmatic crisis. 'No matter what contempt you feel for these people, Vernon, they will have mothers, sons, daughters who will care about them. They will also want to come after you with the very best lawyer in town if they even suspect that your machine has a design defect or is unsafe.'

'Even if it says in the manual in very large letters; *this machine can cause injury or death, read this manual thoroughly before use?*'

'If it can be proved that the settings on the machine can squeeze to a point where people's organs stop working and break bones or dislocate joints, then it doesn't matter what you print in the manual, that machine should not be in the public domain.'

'How else are people going to hurt themselves? This is a product that is designed to fulfil a demand. You don't understand, these people want to get hurt, they're not like you or me, like normal people, they don't get their thrills from seeing a pretty girl or looking at nice countryside. No, these are sadists, masochists, monsters who put on black leather masks with zips and chains and hurt one another, this is a breed apart, old friend. These are serious, big-time weirdos, believe me. These people deserve the MassageOmatic, they've got it coming to them.'

Han Sen saw the light at this point in the conversation. He saw the chink in Vernon's armour, the zealous glint in his eye, the slight foaming at the corners of the lips, the almost imperceptible nervous twitch. They were all on show today. It was becoming obvious that he was on a mission; a mission to destroy everything he disliked about these people.

Eventually Han Sen spoke, 'Have you had a bad experience somewhere along the line, Vernon? Have one of these people upset you or one of your family?'

'No. Absolutely not. I wouldn't have anything to do with them in the first place, so how could they?'

'Just asking. You seem fairly passionate about it.'

'Passionate?' The Englishman laughed, as if realising that he'd let his defences slip. 'No, not really. I know what side my bread's buttered, I just like making money and this seems to be a pretty good way of doing it. To be perfectly honest, the odd casualty here and there just adds to the excitement, keeps me on my toes, if you know what I mean.'

'Bit like your old job, eh?' Han Sen asked with a small smile.

'You could say that.' The Englishman raised his eyebrows, acknowledging Han Sen's observation. 'Except nobody's trying to kill me. Yet.'

'Well, my friend, I think the first thing we have to do is establish just what the MassageOmatic can or cannot do in terms of damage to its users. Then we can make a decision about the units in the field and then the units going through production at the moment.'

'You're absolutely right, Han Sen, as usual. I'll see if we can get some volunteers to put the thing through its paces, we'll rent a small unit in Hong Kong, no need to upset the neighbours with the screams, is there, what? I'm sure we can sort this out before long and get back to boring old business as usual, eh? It's good to hear you use that word 'we' again.'

27. The Forged Papers and the Dancing Bear

Roger suddenly became childishly excited when Louise dropped a large, thick envelope onto his desk with a Hong Kong postmark. He sat back in his executive chair and rubbed his hands. He could already hear the cash registers ringing up his year-end bonus. He would have the apartment overlooking the Thames and yes, maybe another car for the New Year. He was beginning to get bored with the Aston, maybe a Bentley next time or possibly something Italian, or even both. The future was certainly looking bright he thought to himself as he tore open the envelope and laid out the documents.

Besides a covering letter from Mr. Chan requesting the earliest possible policy issue, backdated as per their discussions, there were five completed proposal documents in the envelope. Mr. Chan hinted in his letter that these five would be the first of many from his new network of associates.

Roger was uncharacteristically determined to make sure that these early fruits of his labour were going to get priority treatment and that he would stick to his word and get Mr. Chan's policies out to him as soon as he possibly could. He briefly looked at the completed forms and immediately recognised one as being the firm in Taiwan that made the dildos and the therapy machines.

'Someone's got to make them, I suppose,' he muttered aloud.

He asked Louise to find existing clients in their database who closely matched these new businesses in terms of turnover, the number of employees, the type of business and their risk profile. He was looking for an underwriting checklist and a numbered risk assessment all stamped and signed by the Chief Underwriter. Then he spent most of the day practicing their signatures.

That night he made sure that everybody in the building had gone home before taking the lift down two floors to the underwriting department and making straight for the Chief Underwriters office. He quickly found what he was looking for; a stock of blank forms and the department's rubber stamp of approval.

He photocopied the original risk assessment documents from the existing client files, cut out the text from the copies with scissors and glued the text onto the blank forms. He then photocopied the glued together form, stamping each new document and signing on top with his almost perfect Chief Underwriter's signature.

By eight-thirty he was finished, and quickly tidied up the mess of surplus paper and cuttings, took all of the completed documents back down to his office where he completed a blank check list by hand and pinned the newly created documents onto the proposals. He left them on Louise's desk with a note asking her to drop them into the policy issue department in the morning.

Satisfied he would have his policies out by next week, Roger felt distinctly pleased with himself. He had no intention of by-passing the underwriting department every time the Chinaman sent him new business proposals, just this once to get the relationship off to a flying start. Oh, and to get this bunch of policies registered for his year-end bonus, of course. And they were only backdated by a couple of weeks, what harm could it do?

He smiled to himself as he walked through the entrance lobby and waved at the security guard. Of course there was always the satisfaction of sticking two fingers up at the Chief Underwriter. If this wasn't underwriting from the sales process up, he didn't know what was.

Since the incident with the trigger-happy Chinaman in the Lichtenstein Re car-park, he had taken the precaution of parking in the local public multi-storey, never on the same floor or in the same space for two consecutive days. Despite the fact it cost the company thousands of pounds per year in parking fees, he felt safer and didn't mind the five-minute walk to and from the car every day, it was the only exercise he ever did.

As he walked north along Cheapside in the direction of the multi-storey with an obvious spring in his step, he was so engrossed in thoughts about his future success at Lichtenstein Re that he failed to notice the limousine with blacked out windows, parked just outside the exit to the car park. Not surprisingly, he also failed to notice the shadowy oriental occupant of the limousine, and the conspicuously large remote control device sitting on the passenger seat next to him.

As he headed south in the car across London Bridge and into the South London sprawl, he called Hilary on his car phone, 'Hils, fancy eating out?' It was nine-thirty.

'No, Rodge, it's far too late. Have you just left?' her voice registering surprise.

'Yes, had a bit of a rush job, new customers and all that. If you don't fancy it, I'm just going to pop over to the golf club, I'll get something to eat there. Don't wait up, I may be a bit late,' he said cheerily.

'OK, be careful, the police are getting hotter on the drink driving.'

'Don't worry, I'll see you later.'

As he put the phone back into its cradle he glanced in the rear-view mirror, noticing the limousine in the distance for the first time.

He emerged from the golf club bar two and a half hours later having had two pints as an 'aperitif,' a solitary meal with a bottle of red wine and several shots of brandy with coffee afterwards. He drove home thoughtfully, still pleased with himself. Of course he'd taken a big risk in forging the documents but what was the likelihood of anything going wrong? One company made dildos and therapy machines, another one he just happened to glimpse at as he photocopied the documents supplied raw materials and sold finished products, some that they modified to suit different markets, so they were basically an import-export agency. Nothing particularly specialist, so how high was the risk, really? Besides he was a director, he had the right to make decisions about whether to take them on or not.

The golf club was set deep in the rolling Surrey countryside about eight miles from home. He drove along the dark country lanes with the brash self-confidence of a drunk. As he approached one of the tiny villages along the way, he noticed the limousine again parked in a lay-by with its lights on. Just as he was wondering if the car had broken down, there was a small muffled bang from the Aston's engine.

He instinctively took his foot off the accelerator pedal and looked down at the dashboard instruments, but everything looked fine. Maybe he'd hit a bird or some other animal.

By now he was approaching the village too fast. He braked, the brake pedal going to the floor, but nothing. Then, the engine note changed from virtually ticking over to that of full power and the car started accelerating towards the sleeping village. Roger was in a blind panic. He tried the clutch to disengage the drive, but this pedal too went straight to the floor with no effect.

The car hurtled faster and faster past the rows of neat cottages, he had nowhere to steer the car to safety, he had to keep going. There was a bend fast approaching in the middle of the village and there was no way he was going to make it. He glimpsed at the speedometer, seventy-five mph and increasing rapidly. He wrenched the steering wheel in an effort to get the car around the bend. He knew it was a lost cause. Effectively driverless, the car careered through the front roadside garden of the village pub, wooden chairs, tables and umbrellas airborne, as if being inexpertly juggled by some supernatural force. Totally unhindered by the garden furniture, the car smashed head-on into the front wall of the pub, the high speed impact of the two-tonne sports car against the rather insubstantial 1930's brick and timber structure sending a sonic boom across the rooftops of the sleeping village.

In the collision, the front of the car crumpled, mercifully causing the engine to stall and cease delivering power to the rear wheels. It came to rest in the approximate centre of the pub bar in a swirling maelstrom of cascading building structure, splintered furniture and all-enveloping dust. There was a loud hiss of escaping steam from the punctured radiator of the by-now barely recognisable Aston Martin, one of its front lights casting a ghostly hue across the scene of devastation.

Not that Roger would ever know it, but the landlord of The Dancing Bear Pub would tell the tale of that night to many of his regulars for years to come. In the midst of a splendidly twitchy, post-coital snooze alongside his girlfriend of six months, he was startled awake on hearing and feeling a tremendous explosion, as loud and as close as if someone had detonated a thousand pound bomb downstairs in the bar. The other major telltale sign that told him something was seriously amiss was the blood-curdling scream from his girlfriend as she disappeared, complete with duvet cover into the void left by the disappearance of most of their bedroom floor.

He briefly thanked his lucky stars that he'd politely ignored her requests to position the bed in the front bay of the bedroom, instead, putting it off to one side against the party wall. Funny that, she wasn't keen on the net curtains either. He had wondered briefly whether she was showing signs of being a bit of an exhibitionist. If she thought he was going to be performing coitus or any other sexual activity ending in 'us, in full view of the houses opposite she'd have to think again. Not that he'd said that to her yet of course.

Having checked with his feet that there was going to be somewhere to land on his side of the bed, he leapt out and began feverishly looking for clothes and footwear in the unaccustomed and eerie half-light from the street below. There was dust everywhere, simply breathing made him cough. He grabbed a handful of tissues and held them up to his mouth. They were cold, soggy and tasted of sex. He dropping the tissues and used his vest instead. He hopped around, unable to balance properly, eventually struggling into a pair of boxer shorts. He slipped into his slippers and edged gingerly across the room. It was strangely reassuring to find the bedroom door still there, with his dressing gown still hanging on its hook. As he made his way downstairs, he didn't know what to expect. Gas explosion? The IRA? An earthquake? In Surrey?

A sports car, coupe style, sat in the middle of what had been the Public Bar. It had taken out almost the complete front of his pub, and came to rest with its nose against the bar. His girlfriend was lying on the back end of the car, her breath coming in gasps and wheezes. The car's single remaining front light shone a white-blue haze towards the back of the pub, whilst a red light from the intact rear lights shone across what was the front of the pub, spilling out onto the now visible pavement.

The phone was still in its place behind the bar, he dialled 999 looking warily at the remaining ceiling above him. He felt distinctly unsafe. The operator asked him to stay on the line, he refused saying he wanted to get to his girlfriend and get them both out of danger. He looked in on the driver of the car lying comatose in the driver's seat and decided to ignore him - he looked comfortable at least, being completely swaddled in white, cloud-like airbags.

Approaching his girlfriend, it appeared that the duvet had cushioned her fall, probably saving her life. She was semi-conscious and now groaning, which he supposed was a good sign. As there was nothing obviously broken he decided to take the lesser risk and lift her bodily, duvet cover and all, out of the danger zone of potential falling masonry and out onto the pavement.

He stood on the pavement with his girlfriend in his arms as the emergency services arrived. The paramedics immediately put her onto a stretcher and into the back of the ambulance where they carried out their assessment. The fire and rescue teams started preparing their safety support mechanisms to shore up what remained of the first floor.

No one at the scene noticed the black limousine as it drove slowly up to the knot of fire tenders, ambulances and police cars outside the wreckage of the pub. It stopped, sat for a short while, then reversed slowly backwards, turned around and drove off into the darkness.

Roger was struggling to breathe, the massive pain in his chest preventing him from taking anything but the shortest breaths. He felt himself drifting in and out of consciousness, like sleeping-in late. He distinctly recalled the sickening, bowel-emptying feeling of the hugely powerful engine accelerating the vehicle in a straight line collision course with the front of the pub, having come perilously close to bouncing off one of the cottages on the opposite side of the road. In what seemed like a lifetime but was probably only a second or two, he established that the car was accelerating wildly and inexorably towards the pub, on its own, totally beyond his control, and he had the brake pedal fully down to the floorboards.

He couldn't recall the impact.

Those arses, he thought, struggling to breathe under the pressure of the airbag on his face that kept falling forward because of the pain in his chest. The sales info he'd picked up from the dealers told him all about the racing pedigree and the exceptional performance and stability. He hadn't thought about the safety aspects. It's a tin box on wheels that crashes, just like any other fucking tin box on wheels.

That's when he blacked out completely.

The fire crew decided that the roof of the £200,000 sports car was going to be cut off in order to extricate Roger without additional injury. The members of the team involved in getting Roger out of the Aston took rather longer in setting up their equipment than normal. They made sure each cutting edge was flawlessly honed, and painstakingly cleaned all of the hydraulic connections so they would mate perfectly with one another. They were going to comfortably take the record for cutting up the most expensive car in the history of their watch tonight, and they wanted a perfect job. The knowing looks exchanged by the members of the team suggested that a certain amount of pride was at stake.

In the event, the roof came off quickly, with disappointing ease. One of the crew grumbled that he had seen stronger, more resistant Fords. They took some solace in having to destroy most of the walnut-trimmed dashboard to get the multiple airbags out of the way. This enabled them to hack out the Connolly leather driver's seat. Roger was then lifted, still strapped in the seat, out of the car and onto safe ground outside the pub where the medics checked his overall body condition. They then carefully extracted him from the seat and transferred him onto a stretcher. The car and all of its dismembered body parts was winched onto a recovery truck and driven away to the local police station.

Roger awoke with a start, immediately aware of his hospital surroundings. The pain in his chest concentrated his mind as he fought against the drowsiness. Slowly, he recalled some of what happened last night. Was it last night? He assumed so. The feeling of being in a nightmare, bracing himself for the crash and not remembering the impact. It would be funny if it weren't so serious, thought Roger, after all, the car had cost him £200K. He must get someone to phone his insurers. They should phone him for God's sake, he employed them.

'What happened, Roger?' Hilary leaned over him, the voice of calm and compassion in Roger's muddled head.

'The brakes failed, Hils. I'm not sure who's going to believe me but the car seemed to be driving itself. It was definitely accelerating towards that pub, I couldn't stop it. I don't remember the impact at all. Did I kill anyone?'

'No, some injuries, but no one's dead,' Hilary said sternly.

'What about me?' Roger asked.

'The car's at the police station for investigation,' she carried on, ignoring him. 'They reckon about six months to carry out structural repairs on the pub. The landlord's girlfriend is in the next ward with severe shock and lots of bruising. She was lucky, the paramedics reckon the duvet she was wrapped up in saved her.'

'Yes, yes. But what about me?' Roger asked, spluttering slightly.

Hilary gave him one of her disdainful looks and said, 'Shock, mainly. The doctor here suspects a couple of broken ribs, they want to x-ray you later on just to check there's no internal damage.'

'Is that it? I was in so much pain. I thought I'd broken my back or something.'

'Shock manifests itself in a lot of different ways, Roger,' Hilary reassured him. 'You're a very lucky man. They're aiming to have you out of here later today.'

'Oh,' Roger said stiffly. 'That's good.'

Hilary put her book into her bag and stood up with a look of finality. 'Your clothes are on the chair over there. I'm going to go home. Inge's looking after Sam and Jules and it was supposed to be her weekend off. Do you want anything?'

'Only you,' he said, arms outstretched. He was amazed, he really did need her.

She pecked him reservedly on the cheek. 'Oh, by the way, the police came by earlier. They want a statement, they'll probably come back later on.'

The police, Roger thought with some alarm. What would they want? How do they go about establishing levels of alcohol in unconscious crash victims? Alcohol. He knew something didn't quite fit in the back of his mind. He did have quite a lot to drink before and after the meal. But his brakes hadn't worked. And he distinctly remembered putting his foot all the way down on the brake pedal. Surely when they inspected the car they'd find the brakes had been tampered with? But then if the car had been tampered with, who had tried to kill him? Maybe the Chief Underwriter was responsible, or the mad Irishman. Maybe even the Miami mafia. Well, bollocks to the lot of them, thought Roger. Better luck next time.

He closed his eyes and thought about naked thrashings with birch twigs on the snow covered shore of the fjord; they were approaching the season for it according to his Norse Goddess. He was looking forward to his next visit to Norway with just a tiny amount of trepidation.

Hilary drove home contemplating what had happened. Had he been drunk? She had certainly noticed he'd been drinking a lot more recently. But if his brakes had been tampered with, that meant someone wanted to kill him. She wasn't aware of any particular enemies Roger had created over the years since they'd been together. He told stories of life in the US prison where he had upset the local Mafiosi, surely they wouldn't hold a grudge against him for this long? Would they? If they did he probably wasn't the only target. In the movies, at least, they went for families too. She made the decision to be extra vigilant from then on.

She got home to find a message on the answerphone from Uncle Vern, who was unexpectedly in the UK. She called him back.

'Hilary,' he said in his normal surprised yet always delighted way. 'How are you, my dear?'

'I'm fine thanks, just back from the hospital, actually. Roger's been in an accident.'

'What sort of accident? Is he OK?'

'They think he's fine, maybe a couple of broken ribs. He was lucky; he drove into a building at high speed. His brakes failed and he reckons the car accelerated towards the pub.'

'Good lord, a brake failure and something wrong with the throttle. Pretty unusual, isn't it?'

'Yes, the police are investigating the car at the moment.'

'The police, eh?'

'He almost destroyed the whole building!' she said. 'It's an old pub quite near here, The Dancing Bear. They reckon six months to rebuild it.'

'Crikey, must have been quite spectacular. He's lucky to have just a couple of broken ribs.'

'Yes, he is. Anyway, what brings you to Blighty?'

'Well, my dear, I'm on a little bit of a world tour. I'm in London at the moment attending to a bit of business, and off to see Marty tomorrow. Then I'm off to the States; our West Coast dealer seems to have struck gold with the massage machines. People are falling over themselves to get hold of them. I'm just going over to see what the secret of his success is.'

'Are these the ones that hurt people?'

'Er, well, some do, yes. On the way back I've also got to call into Washington. Then home.'

'The Pentagon, I'm guessing? I suppose they buy the ones that really hurt.'

'Hah! If I could tell you, Hilary, I would. You know that.'

'I wish I was as good at keeping secrets as you are,' she said provocatively.

'Not my secrets, old girl, I'm merely keeping them for others.'

'Not so much of the old. When are you coming to boring Surrey?'

'Afraid I can't this time, darling. Why don't you come over to Hong Kong when I'm back? Bring the kids, they'd love it as much as you do.'

'I'll talk to Roger about it. I'm not sure what's happening at the moment; I know he was planning a trip to Norway fairly soon. Whether he'll still go or not I don't know.'

'OK then, well I hope to see you soon.'

'Yes. Oh and Uncle?'

'Yes, my dear?'

'Don't let people hurt themselves on those machines, will you? Can you have a word with Han Sen and just get the control settings lowered or something? I lay awake at night worrying about those damned things.'

'Well, funny you mention that. Han Sen has just agreed to organise some testing for me in Hong Kong, I think he's sending his man over next week.'

'What, you mean the machine has never been tested?'

'Yes, of course it's been tested. The mechanism from Han Choy has been through all sorts of testing. It's even got certificates. No, I think they had a problem finding volunteers for this batch so they're doing it at my place. Anyway, don't worry my dear. It's all in hand.'

'I can't believe some of the things you get up to, Uncle. If I didn't know you as well as I do, I probably would have pulled out ages ago.'

'Oh, come on, Hilary, it's only business. We've all got to earn a living somehow,' he said dismissively. 'I promise, we'll get together soon and get our heads together on this business of yours. I'm not far off retiring, you know, we have to plan for the future.'

'Han Sen seems perfectly happy supplying me direct. Even though the shipping costs are higher, I can still make a good margin.'

'He wouldn't do that for just anybody, Hilary,' he said as the gentlest reminder that he was still the one with the influence.

'No, of course and I understand why, I'd be the same,' she said. 'Anyway, you know you are always welcome Uncle Vern, no matter what the business is doing.'

'Thank you, my dear, I really appreciate that. I look forward to seeing you wherever it may be, hopefully soon.'

His voice had an unconditional tone that always put Hilary at ease. Damn him, she thought. 'OK Uncle, take care on your travels,' she put the phone down with a sigh. It was a mistake going into business with family, no matter how much of a leg-up he had given her. The whole relationship had clouded her judgement on what should have otherwise been clear cut decisions.

She wouldn't say as much, but she looked forward to him retiring. Things would be a lot simpler then.

28. A Family Re-united

It was Han Sen's thirtieth birthday. Han Sen, Raya, Li Lai, Great Uncle, Auntie, Emic and Raj Sen who had flown in from Taipei for the weekend went out for a meal that night to celebrate. They let Li Lai make the choice between *Mrs. Meatball* at Sankuaicuo or the *Hamasan Black Marlin Fish Ball King* on Gupo Street. When she had stopped giggling, she chose the fish, it was her favourite. They took a taxi downtown.

Although business talk between the two men was forbidden by the ladies, the future of the business did come into the family discussion over the meal. Great Uncle Sen was, as ever, in a contemplative mood.

'Raj, I wish you would come back into the business. We are desperate for people with your management experience. You could work with your brother and Han Sen and when you come to retire it would be passed onto your children. It is a large concern now, my son, we employ 150 people and turnover some $15 million dollars.'

'Wow, how have you grown to that size in such a short time?' Raj looked across the table in surprise at his father and Han Sen.

'By making products that people want to buy is about the only explanation that I can think of.' Han Sen smiled at his great-nephew.

'Still household goods?'

'Yes, although a large part of the turnover increase is due to the high value therapy machines that we now build. Our agents sell them to all sorts of people, sports clubs, physiotherapists, even governments who buy the military version.'

'Military version?'

'Yes we have an agent in Hong Kong who specialises in them. He takes our basic machine and modifies it.' Han Sen said, not alluding to the inner turmoil this decision was causing him.

'But you have an accountant, right?' he asked looking at Han Sen and his father.

'Yes we do, my son, but there is always room in the business for you. You know that,' his father replied quickly. 'You may not start off as a senior manager but at least you will be playing a part in the family business.'

'Do you still give a proportion of your profits to the temple and the poor?'

'Yes, of course, it's about half at the moment. We started off at about a quarter but we have been increasing it. You'll see the temple tomorrow, it is quite magnificent. The neighbourhood is also much improved. We no longer have any homeless people. Of course, that's not solely down to us,' the old man said, pride showing on his face. 'But every little helps, my son.'

'Could I come and have a look around the factory, maybe tomorrow before I go back to Taipei?'

'Of course, we'll go early tomorrow, before we go to the temple.'

And so having seen the pristine new factories and spent time with the family at their temple over the weekend, Raj finally agreed to come into the business. They discussed Han Sen's plans to bring him into a management role once he got to know the company and the products. Great Uncle Sen was delighted.

'The best move you've ever made, my son. You'll not regret this,' he said cheerfully to Raj as they said their goodbyes at the airport that evening.

As the two men drove home, Great Uncle Sen flicked through a copy of the Taipei Times newspaper that Raj had left behind. 'Han Sen!' the old man gasped. 'Look at this, look!'

'Uncle, I can't see, get off,' he said, batting the newspaper to one side.

'Look, Han Sen, stop the car, you've got to see this!' the old man persisted.

'All right, all right,' he bought the car to a juddering halt on the hard shoulder of the busy airport expressway. He looked at the picture of a young woman being interviewed outside a courtroom and quickly read the article. 'Rao. Oh fantastic, it's her. Thank God she's alive. She looks great too, doesn't she?' He peered closer at the article. 'Rao as a union leader? Who would have believed it?' he said, hoping he sounded genuinely surprised.

His Great Uncle was close to tears, 'Oh, Han Sen, I'm just so glad she's alive. Come on, let's get home and tell your Auntie, she will be thrilled.' He looked at the picture again, now sobbing quietly. 'Look at her, she is so beautiful. How could she?'

Han Sen was quiet for the rest of the journey. He had not seen Rao for the last few weeks. She had mentioned a court case in Taipei that she was heavily involved in. How was Raya going to react? How was life going to be with the two women in his life together again. He decided there was no purpose in worrying, fate was going to win out yet again. What would happen would happen.

Raya was as thrilled as her Great Uncle and Auntie, even volunteering to contact her first thing Monday morning via the newspaper. Li Lai couldn't remember Rao, yet she was just as excited. She went to tidy her bedroom in honour of her soon to be returning Auntie.

After the double-high of the weekend, it was back to business as usual for Han Sen on Monday morning. He organised a meeting with his morose test manager Sven to see what could be done about testing the MassageOmatic.

Han Sen recalled one of the Englishman's phrases as the Swede sat down in front of his desk. 'Sven, there's no point in beating around the bush. Do you know any people who, erm, like to get hurt and like to hurt others. I think they call it S&M, don't they?'

The Swede's eyes lit up momentarily before returning to their normal downcast position. 'Well, I used to when I lived in the UK but I don't know anybody over here that does that sort of thing. Why, what do we want to test?'

'You know the Englishman modifies the MassageOmatic machines to make military and S&M versions?' Han Sen said, interested to find out if the Swede did know.

'I did wonder what happened to them when they left here,' the Swede admitted.

'Well, there have been one or two injuries on the S&M version. Now this doesn't affect us because we're not the supplier, but I've agreed to supervise some tests so we can establish what the machine is capable of.'

'If we supervise them, don't we then become responsible in some way?'

'No, we are still technically a sub-contractor. We carry out the testing in the same way that we supply VSS with the mechanism.'

'I see,' the Swede replied. 'We're not going to do it here, are we?'

'No, in Hong Kong.'

'Ah in that case, we can find some volunteers among the Brit community over there. They love all that S&M stuff, something to do with deprived childhoods or something.'

Han Sen decided not to pursue the Swede's obvious interest in English childhood psychology. 'Good, I'll tell the Englishman to place some ads in the English language newspapers. I'll let you know when we have some volunteers.'

'OK. This is legal, isn't it?' The Swede asked as an afterthought as he stood up to go.

'As far as I know it is. They are volunteers, after all. I'll check with the Englishman, he'll probably get them to sign something. Thanks Sven.' He waved at the departing Swede as he picked up the phone and dialled the VSS number. He really didn't want to be doing this testing but no one else would.

'Mr. Saunders is currently in America on business not returning until next week,' the receptionist at VSS said politely. 'Can I take a message for you, Mr. Sen?'

'Yes please, tell him to call me when he gets back.'

'OK, I will. Thanks, bye.'

If he was in the States again, he was probably selling more of those damned machines, Han Sen thought. Sometimes he wished he had run for the hills the day the Englishman had introduced himself. But then he looked at the amount of business he had bought to Han Choy, and so the argument would go around and around in his mind. It was like being on a treadmill that he couldn't get off. One day he would concentrate on making really useful things, he kept telling himself.

His phone rang, the voice of Angelique coming over the speaker, 'There's a Mr. Threadgould on the phone. He's a lawyer, says he wants to speak to you.'

'Did he say what it was about?'

'About some machines in America?'

He knew this would be something to do with the Englishman. 'Put him through Angelique, thank you,' he paused while she connected him. 'Hello, can I help you?'

'Hello Mr. Sen, thank you for taking the time to talk to me. I have certain information that could be of benefit to you. If I could just explain?'

'Yes go ahead,' Han Sen said, business-like, impatient.

'There are some machines called MassageOmatics that are imported into the USA by several companies but they all originate from a Hong Kong based company called VSS. You are aware of this?'

Han Sen was immediately cautious, 'Should I be aware of it?'

'Ah-ha, yes. The reason I'm calling you is that there have been a number of fatalities and serious injuries on these machines, and we think from what we've seen that there are likely to be more. We heard today that a certain law firm on the West Coast with a big reputation for successful class actions is sniffing around with a view to claiming substantial damages for the loved ones left behind in all of this.'

'How did you get my contact details?' Han Sen asked.

'Well forgive me, but our firm Threadgould, Threadgould and Santacruse, are reasonably well known in the sexual-aids industry. One of the US distributors of the product contacted us to get our views on how they should defend themselves against this potential class action. I'm simply coming back up the tree to offer our services. We know how these things work, we have fought against this law firm before and have a pretty good handle on how they do things.'

'You mentioned VSS earlier, I think they are the ones you will need to defend. They are the producers of the equipment, our company only makes the mechanical sub-assembly. We sell it to VSS who then produce the various versions of the machine.'

'Ah, OK, that's interesting. Mr. Saunders from VSS mentioned that they only programme the machines, they are entirely your production.'

'Well, if Mr. Saunders is saying that then he is mistaken. I sell him a machine that could not press wild flowers; they are advanced therapy machines when they leave here, nothing more, nothing less.'

'Can I ask you, Mr. Sen, do you have product liability insurance and if so the name of the firm?'

'Yes of course, it is a London based insurer, I am waiting for the policy to be issued at the moment. They are called Liechtenstein Re, I believe.'

'That's good, it sounds like you have nothing to worry about,' the American replied casually.

'Mr. Threadgould, you have just told me that one of my products has been adapted in such a way as to injure and kill people. You think I should not be worried about that?'

'I'm sorry, Mr. Sen, I was talking purely from a legal and financial standpoint,' came the immediate reply.

'How many casualties are we talking about here?' Han Sen asked.

'Well we know about two deaths for sure, and a reported eight serious injuries, mainly crush problems. We know there will be more because that's the nature of the industry. There will be people who get injured or killed and the relatives will be too embarrassed to admit the true circumstances of their death. The other law firm will go to great lengths to uncover these people with the promise of untold riches. Trust me, there will be more and they will mostly all testify.'

Han Sen had heard enough, 'Thank you for your time, Mr. Threadgould. I will pass you back to Angelique now, she will take your contact details. We may speak again.'

Han Sen was close to swearing when he put the phone down. He might have known the Englishman would do the dishonourable thing. He was probably swanning around America telling his dealers that none of this was his doing. He could hear his suave voice from the other side of the Pacific, 'Yes, some really clever Cambodian guy is the brains behind all of this. He's an expert at torturing people, you know. He's just made the thing a tad too strong this time, don't worry though, they're only perverts, no great loss.'

The bastard, Han Sen thought bitterly. It was time to do an immediate assessment of the scale of the damage so far and prevent any further casualties. He walked briskly downstairs to the production office. This was not part of the plan at all.

Raya tracked down her sister with the help of the newspaper reporter who had written the article. The two sisters had spoken on the phone and it had been arranged that Rao would come round on Saturday afternoon. The atmosphere in the apartment prior to her arrival was tense. Great Uncle Sen was beside himself with excitement and was getting on everybody's nerves, 'Do you think she'll stay? Where can she sleep? Li Lai you must make sure your room is tidy in case she wants to stay and we have to put a bed roll down.'

'Now just calm down, my husband,' Great Auntie Sen spoke. 'The girl will find us as she finds us. If she chooses to stay, which I very much doubt, she is most welcome but our apartment was fine and comfortable for her in the old days and it will be again. Do not worry.'

'As you wish, my love,' the old man said. 'I'll make us some chai.' He disappeared into the kitchen, glad to have something to do. Li Lai followed him, arranging the cups on a tray.

Raya went to the door when the doorbell finally rang. The two sisters embraced and held onto one another for a long time. They both wiped away tears as they released one another, but they couldn't help themselves and embraced again, both laughing gently this time.

'My sister,' Raya whispered. 'My sister, after all this time. Seven years, Rao. You have been away for seven years.'

'I feel bad enough about it, do not make me feel worse. I had to go away, my sister, for my sake and yours. I did not think it would be as long as this.'

'You are doing the right thing in coming back,' Raya said. 'We have all missed you so much. She looked over her shoulder at Li Lai, who was peering cautiously around the kitchen door. 'This is your Auntie Rao.'

The girl skipped forward and smiled nervously at her "new" Auntie. Rao bent down and kissed the ten-year old on both cheeks and held her for a short while. 'You're just like I imagined, a little bit of your Daddy and a little bit of your Mummy.' She pinched her nose gently. 'I brought you a special present from Taipei. Don't eat them before dinner or I'll be in trouble.' She handed the girl a small delicately wrapped present.

'Thank you, Auntie Rao,' Li Lai said excitedly.

Rao hugged Han Sen like a returning sister would to her brother, 'How are you, Han Sen?' she asked.

'I am fine, Rao. We're all so pleased to have you back in the family. We've missed you terribly,' was all Han Sen could think to say. He thought the word 'we' was better than 'I' under the circumstances.

She hugged Great Uncle Sen next. 'You haven't changed, Uncle, you look very fit,' she said with a smile.

'Fit for whiling away the days doing nothing in particular,' he said grinning. 'Eh, Auntie Sen?'

'I keep him on his toes, don't worry,' Auntie Sen said to Roa as she took her into her arms and smothered her. 'It's good to have you back, my girl.' Auntie Sen's tears rolled down both cheeks as she held onto the younger woman. 'Promise us you won't go away again. I couldn't bear it. Please?'

'I won't, Auntie, I won't,' Rao replied as she surrendered to the warmth and love of her Great Auntie.

They drunk chai and ate some suncake around the dining table. Rao told them all about her life since she had been gone, as a working girl then as a union leader, how she had coped during the low moments and how she really had missed them all. She told them all about her partner in Taipei, how she had thought about bringing her along today but re-considered at the last moment. She needed to be on her own to meet her family again. Li Lai plucked up the courage to ask her Auntie why she had dyed her hair blonde.

Great Auntie Sen looked at the little girl in mock outrage, 'Li Lai, you shouldn't ask things like that.' She looked at Rao and smiled expectantly.

'I'll tell you later,' Rao said, winking at Li Lai. 'Can we go to the temple now? I can't wait to see it again.'

'Yes, let's take Auntie Rao to the Temple,' Li Lai said excitedly. 'We can light candles!'

Their combined joy and relief at the returning Rao didn't make it the best of times for quiet contemplation. Nevertheless, it was a memorable afternoon for all of them. Giving thanks to the Buddha was the only obvious conclusion, his serene perfection humbled and inspired the whole reunited family.

Great Auntie Sen had been right, Rao didn't stay over. She left after the evening meal, promising to return the following weekend with her partner. Li Lai was in the kitchen with her mother, bursting with a question she had not dared ask Rao.

'Mummy, how comes Rao has a woman partner?'

'Because that's how she chooses to live, darling, we're not all the same, you know.'

'But she is supposed to have a husband, a man, isn't she?'

'Not necessarily, Li Lai, women can love one another too.'

'But they can't have babies can they?'

'Not like a man and a woman have babies, no. But they can adopt children if they wanted to, I suppose.'

'Or perhaps a man could give them a baby. She would really have to love the man of course. That way it would really be theirs. As long as her partner agreed it would be OK, wouldn't it?'

Raya looked at her daughter as if a light had suddenly come on. 'Yes, you could be right, maybe something like that could happen.' She continued clearing up the kitchen, turning her young daughter's words over in her mind, marvelling at her innocent yet far-reaching insight.

After the great day of Rao's return and for the first time in his Han Choy career, Han Sen was not looking forward to going in to work. Over the weekend he had come to the conclusion that he had to regain control, he could no longer tolerate the situation whereby the Englishman dictated the future of his company. He had to go back to being in control, even if it meant closing lines down and laying people off. He had to be firm and incisive. No more Mr. Nice Guy.

The scale of the problem was plain to see. There were ninety four MassageOmatics out in the field either already in use or in dealer warehouses awaiting shipment to the end user. The Englishman was the only one who could verify where they were geographically and the only one who could initiate any action. Han Sen carefully drafted a letter to VSS, aware that using the wrong words could incriminate Han Choy.

VSS Ltd
Hong Kong
Attention Mr. Vernon Saunders

Dear Vernon

Re: VSS Modifications to MassageOmatic Machines

Further to our recent communications regarding the machines that you have modified and are already in the field, in the interests of customer safety, I strongly recommend that you undertake either of the following at your earliest opportunity:-
1.   An immediate product recall
2.   An engineer visit to each customer site and bring each machine back to its factory default settings.
Unless either of the two actions identified above is carried out, I regret that Han Choy Inc. will no longer be in a position to fulfil any current or future VSS order for MassageOmatic machines.
Please let me know if you need any assistance in carrying out any of the above.

Yours sincerely

Han Sen
For and on behalf of Han Choy Inc.

There. Short and to the point. He supposed a lawyer should look over the letter before he sent it but he was the only one who knew about the arrangement between Han Choy and VSS. He suspected that the Englishman would not do anything about it, in which case it would be clear that the relationship was over. He sent it through to Angelique to type up. He felt relieved; now he could get on with some real work.

He buzzed Tom Huang to come and give him a debrief on where they were with the various product launches, Tom looked relaxed as he came into the office.

'Tom, sorry I've been a bit preoccupied with some of the therapy machines lately,' Han Sen said, looking apologetically at the young marketing man. 'Where are we with everything?'

'Things are just great, Han Sen, the Ardourator test results make it look like it's going to be a winner. Sven has put it through three orgies now and the guys are lasting all night with a variety of different, ahem, activities. It's going to become the must-have gadget for all male orgy-goers. Now that we've proved the male version, I think we should look at one for ladies.'

'Hmm, maybe, we should get a gynaecologist on board for that one, and possibly a psychologist too for the marketing angles, it could get complicated. Remember, we're just simple engineers, Tom. Men can handle our indulgences and almost encourage us to go further. It's a bit of a different story with women. Anyway, I heard there was a question of whether the Ardourator is throwaway or not, what's your thinking on that one?'

'Well we're looking at a retail price of roughly fifty US dollars. We think that most guys would buy new at that price. That would give us the volumes we're looking for. We could double the price and make it slightly more durable but I'm not keen, this should be a one shot product.' He laughed at his own joke.

'I agree, one shot for the product and hopefully just the one shot for the customer. Hah!' They both laughed. 'Do we have a date yet?'

'We aim to press the button on production next Friday, we're all set.'

'Excellent. How about the sex chair?'

'Sven's test results are telling us that the ladies really love this one, they just can't get enough of the different positions you can achieve on the thing. We're just in the process of changing the seat material from black vinyl to brown suede. We could push go later this week if you give the thumbs up. There will be a finished one downstairs for you to have a look at later today,' Tom gushed with enthusiasm.

'How about a name?'

'The latest, and one I think sums it up nicely, is best: Perfect Roger.' The younger man looked at his boss for a reaction.

Han Sen thought about this for a moment, then he laughed gently. 'Hmm, I see what you mean. I'll come down and have a look later. Thanks, Tom. Good job.'

Ah, the impetuousness of youth, he thought to himself. It had literally been a lifesaver in his younger days and he was pleased to recognise this vitality in others.

He felt better now, dealing with real issues that he was in control of. This was what he thrived on, the reason he had started Han Choy.

29. Perfect Roger

'Roger J Collins: I am Police Constable Regan from Godalming Police Station. We conducted a routine blood test at the hospital after your collision last night. Your blood sample contained 168 milligrams of alcohol. You are therefore under arrest for the offence of drink-driving. You do not have to say anything, but it may harm your defence if you do not mention when questioned, something that you later rely on in court. Do you have anything to say?' The police constable stood by the side of Roger's hospital bed having requested the duty nurse to pull the curtains to give them some privacy from the other ward patients.

'Yes, my bloody brakes failed and the car was driving itself!' Roger blustered. 'That accident was not my fault. When you've inspected the car, you'll see it's been tampered with.'

'We will be looking at the car in due course, sir. Do you have any idea why someone would have tampered with your car? Have you had any disputes with anyone recently either personal or business?'

Even if I did know who it was I wouldn't tell you just yet, Roger thought to himself. 'No, Officer,' he said, shaking his head slowly. It was then that it dawned on him. 'Wait a minute, my car was stolen last month and returned in better condition, maybe that's when it was tampered with.'

'Better condition, sir?' the PC was obviously struggling with the concept.

'Yes, washed, valeted, tapes all put in order that sort of thing. The City of London Police know all about it, I can let you have the reference number. Chinese fellow, shot my ear off in the process,' he said, fingering his ragged ear lobe.

The PC raised his eyebrows quizzically and continued making notes, 'He shot you?'

'Yes, in the car park just around the corner from my firm, he was waiting for me in the back of the car. Said if I didn't get out and give him the keys he'd shoot me. I didn't straightaway, so he did.'

The PC finished taking Rogers details and instructed him to report to the police station as soon as he was released from the hospital where bail conditions would be arranged pending a court case. He would also have to hand in his driving licence.

He'd need a chauffeur for the next few months then. He mused as to what car would be best as he watched the PC stride out of the ward with his helmet held under his arm. Probably a Jaguar saloon: yes just about the right level, he thought to himself, those big BMWs are a bit, well, German aren't they?

Following a body scan and a bedside visit from the doctor, Roger was discharged from hospital later that day with three cracked ribs. The airbag had just failed to inflate quickly enough to prevent his chest colliding with the steering wheel. Despite his protestations, Hilary drove him straight to the police station where he gave them Edgar as a bail guarantor. He then spent the rest of the weekend moping around the house, pondering on what had happened, anxious for the police to do their work and find out just who was trying to kill him.

The Doctor advised Roger to have some time off to allow his ribs to knit together. Complete rest, no lifting, no exercise, and he'd be all mended in a couple of weeks. Roger had other ideas and decided he was going to Norway the next day. He'd had enough of being in the house avoiding the children and getting an erection every time he saw Inge.

'But Roger, the doctor said complete rest,' Hilary said when he told her.

'Oh come on, darling. I can't work so I might as well do the coaching bit, get it over and done with, then I can concentrate on real work when I get back. It's only reviewing their processes and encouraging them really. I'll be all right, don't you worry,' he said magnanimously.

'What about your bail conditions? You're not allowed to leave the country,' Hilary said.

'Sod 'em. This is important work. Besides, it's only a few days and they've got my telephone number, they're not exactly going to put me in the Tower for it, are they?'

'No but they might extend your driving ban,' she said.

'I'll just have to manage a bit longer with a chauffeur then, won't I? That'll be hard,' he said witheringly.

Hilary looked at him with her usual mixture of disbelief and scorn.

So after advising Louise of his enforced spell of convalescence as a result of the accident, he got her to organise his travel arrangements and went off to Norway, the return flight scheduled for the following Saturday. His Guardian of Valhalla had insisted he stay for the Friday. According to Norse legend this day was named after her and her brother Freyr, who was not only King of the Elves, she reminded him as they spoke on the phone at the airport, but also the horned God of

Fertility. Roger trembled slightly as he pressed the red button on his mobile phone. There was definitely something very scary about this woman. He would have to tell her to go easy on him with his broken ribs and his, well his after-shock, yes it had been a very shocking experience for him. He really hoped she would understand.

Although she would never show it, Hilary was pleased Roger had decided to go away. He was not the stoical type with ailments and she knew he would milk them for all they were worth, insisting that people run around doing things for him. Without him pestering her night and day, she would be able to concentrate on the two things that gave her inspiration in life; her children and her business.

She realised she was privileged in having the ideal set-up. A business she ran from home in a large outbuilding, and a Nanny to look after Sam and Julian during the day. Her increasing discomfort with Roger as a husband made her determined to keep growing the business. She was steadfast in refusing Roger's demands that she close the business and become a full-time mother. The children had her around the whole day if they needed her, Inge was well paid and did a good job, despite Roger's complaints. If it ever looked like her two were suffering as a result of the situation, she would give it up straightaway and knuckle down to being a compliant wifey. Meanwhile, she would remain proudly independent and enjoy life to the full.

These were the thoughts going through her mind as she sat down with her first cup of coffee at her desk on Tuesday morning. Uncle Vern, the other man in her life was travelling also, so she really was able to get on with things.

Her warehouse manager came into the office, 'This was in the latest Han Choy shipment, Hilary, it's addressed to you.' He handed her a large flat package.

'Thanks James,' she said, opening it carefully with her desk knife. 'Oh, it's the picture they took in the factory at the dealer conference.' She carefully withdrew the picture from its packaging. 'Oh my God, it's fantastic. Look James, it's in a beautiful frame, too!'

They both looked at the picture of the beaming, overall-clad Hilary surrounded by Han Choy production staff. 'I love it. Would you mind hanging it for me right in the centre of the wall there?' she said, pointing to the wall behind her desk. She handed the picture to him and opened the envelope that had dropped out of the package.

Kaohsiung
11.11.1992.

Dear Hilary
You may remember having this picture taken. My staff were all so impressed when they saw it in our newsletter and the local newspapers that they suggested we should get one framed and put it in our reception area. So now it hangs very close to the picture of my Great Uncle Sen who founded the original business. I decided that you should have one too, as you are the star of the shot.
Please accept this with all of our best regards and my personal compliments.
We all look forward to receiving you again in Taiwan, and hope that it is not too long until your next visit.
Yours sincerely

Han Sen
For Han Choy Inc.

'Oh, how thoughtful,' she said, reaching for a tissue and blowing her nose. 'He's such a good man. He has an aura around him and so do all of his staff.' She looked longingly at the picture again.

James covered his slight embarrassment at seeing his employer close to tears by saying, 'His products are good, too. Nothing from Han Choy has ever been returned to us. I've never known a fault, actually. I wish we could say the same for all of our other suppliers.'

'You're right, he's a very clever man. I'd like to get to know him a bit better but he's always so busy,' she said as she turned to the paperwork on her desk whilst James went off to get some tools to hang the picture. 'Maybe next time.'

With the picture taking pride of place in her office and acting as further inspiration, Hilary was able to plunge back into her work with renewed vigour. She was halfway through a letter to accompany a mail-out when her office assistant put a call through to her.

'Edgar,' she said, pleased to hear from him. 'What a pleasant surprise. How are you?'

'Oh, I'm fine, Hilary, now that retirement is just around the corner, I'm better than I've been for a long, long while.'

'I'm surprised you're still there,' she said.

'Well, I'm just, what you could say, protecting my asset, making sure the team are going to do a good job. Someone's got to fund my retirement,' he said jokily.

'If I was you, I'd sell your shares and disappear over the horizon,' Hilary said mischievously.

'Well, we'll just have to see how it goes,' said the Irishman ambiguously. 'The reason for my call is to find out how Roger has been just lately. I heard he was in an accident last week?'

'Yes, he had just the one night in hospital, three broken ribs. It was quite a bad accident, he could have died, but luckily he came through it.' The caring wife coming out in her, she thought.

'Does this have anything to do with his car being stolen?'

'The police are looking at the car this week, I haven't heard anything from them yet,' she replied. 'It was a bit strange though, wasn't it?'

'You're telling me. I think there's more to this than meets the eye,' he said, his tone suggesting to Hilary that all was not well.

'It sounds like you know something,' Hilary said, curious.

'Well, only that we're getting reports there may be some heavy claims about to hit us on a couple of new policies,' Edgar said, sounding rattled.

'Oh. You think Roger may be able to assist?'

'Hilary, look, this is not your worry. I'm sorry to have even alluded to it. We'll thrash it out with Roger next week when he's back from Scandinavia,' he said apologetically.

'OK, if I can help in any way, I will,' Hilary said, putting the phone down and returning to her mail-out letter.

The Ardourator looked like it would be a sure-fire winner. She laughed to herself as she imagined Marty having to extend his opening hours to accommodate all of the extra intimacy enabled as a result of Han Sen's new device. As for Perfect Roger, the sex-chair, it was a shame about the name, but it did look absolutely wicked. She felt a stirring in her loins just looking at the thing. Maybe if she were to get one in, she may be able to entice her somewhat disinterested of-late husband to regain an interest in matters of the bedroom.

Or someone else?

The thought surprised her. Although it went against her principles, the idea of having an affair was all of a sudden, quite appealing. And there was one very obvious candidate in Taiwan she knew she could fall wildly in love with. Uncle Vern had told her about the two sisters from Cambodia. That relationship sounded complicated enough without a white woman staking a claim.

Get back to your mail-out you silly woman, she scolded herself.

Gentle by the Norse Goddess's standards was probably akin to being mugged once or even twice a night, thought Roger as he sat exhausted on the homeward-bound plane. He knew it had been a mistake going away so soon after the accident but he just couldn't help himself.

The naked cavorting on the fjord earlier in the day had been extremely painful, especially the bit where Freya and her buxom friend, Gerda the Jotun, had tossed him around in the waist-deep snow like he was their very own plaything. Mind you, between the two of them, they had certainly made amends in the sauna afterwards, he just hoped he would be able to remember something other than the constant pain of his broken ribs. The two girls had competed with one another for his attentions and their own voluminous gratification. They represented all of his lifetime's sexual fantasies rolled into one sweating, heaving, orgasm-tasting, dream-like romp.

He wished someone could come up with a device that slowed down the arousal process. After what seemed like a very short while he had become a spent force in the ejaculation department, the throes of fluid-less climaxes making the pain in his ribs unbearable. He may even have lost consciousness at some point during the proceedings. What a way to go though, he thought to himself as he drifted off into a fantasy-filled sleep, the dinner-serving Scandinavian stewardess going unheard and unseen.

'You look knackered, Roger,' Hilary said as he walked into the lounge and threw himself down into one of the armchairs.

'Yes, sorry love. A bit too much of the Schol last night with the boys from the office, they could certainly teach us Brits a thing or two about drinking. They're mad for it over there, costs a fortune too, four pound a pint, thirty quid for a bottle of wine. Amazing.'

'You had a worthwhile trip then?' Hilary asked politely.

'Yes thanks, love, I think we made some progress. Everyone OK here?'

'Yes. The kids are in bed, Inge has got the weekend off. We're all fine, have you had dinner?'

'No, I'll just get something,' he went into the kitchen and as he walked past the microwave, he noticed the two HP Sauce press releases laid on top. He stood and read about the Ardourator in disbelief.

'Like it?' Hilary asked, surprising him as she came into the kitchen noiselessly.

'What? Oh, yes. Does it work?' he asked, trying to sound casual.

'Apparently yes,' she said brightly. 'Actually it comes from the firm in Taiwan so yes, everything they produce is the best quality.'

'Perfect Roger?' he announced indignantly looking at the second sheet.

Hilary laughed as much at the double-entendre as at Roger's reaction. 'Thought you'd like it. Looks fantastic, doesn't it?'

'You can't market it in the UK with a name like that,' he said outraged. 'It's a slur on my name and every other Roger in the country.'

'You could say all of the Rogers in the world actually, unless of course, they've got a sense of humour,' she replied impishly.

'Whoever thought of that as a name wants shooting,' he said sourly.

'Tom Huang is your man. He's got a masters degree in business and marketing from Princeton, they don't come much cleverer, Rodge,' she said.

'Well if that's what they teach them over there, I'm glad our kids are going to be educated in this country. Perfect Roger indeed,' he said huffily.

'Fancy a go?' she asked with her best saucy smile and a raised eyebrow.

'No, I bloody don't. Not until they or you change the name of it,' he said emphatically.

'What about the Ardourator then, you have been known to take a lady by surprise in the past,' she asked, obviously warming to the theme.

'Look, Hils, I'm not acting as a bloody Guinea Pig for your stupid bloody gadgets. I've just come home from an extremely tiring business trip, my ribs still hurt and yes I am bloody knackered, so don't bloody take the piss all right? I'm going to bed, don't wake me up.' He stormed out of the kitchen and up the stairs to the bedroom.

Hilary stood with her hip leaning against the worktop, arms folded, shaking her head with a rueful expression. What a complete arse, she thought to herself, what did I ever see in him? She angrily scrawled a note on the notice board to say Edgar called and then poured herself a glass of wine.

Roger hated Edgar's office. Probably because whenever he was in there, it normally meant that something had gone wrong or he wanted something badly enough to have to ask the crazy old Irishman for it. Like more money for his boat, something he would have to discuss with him in a few weeks' time. He pushed the thought to the back of his mind.

'Morning Roger, how are the ribs?' Edgar was bright-eyed and bushy-tailed this morning, Roger noticed, groaning inwardly.

'Ah, still a bit sore, Edgar, but they're on the mend, I think,' Roger smiled reluctantly.

'And how were things in Norway?' the older man asked.

'Very good, we've got an excellent relationship now, and the agent seems to be making inroads into the industrial markets over there,' he replied, hoping he at least sounded enthusiastic.

'Good, good. We need some more customers like that, don't we?'

'Yes, it is something I will be concentrating on over the coming months,' Roger replied. Pushy old git, he thought to himself.

'Excellent. Now Mr. Veng, our most recent associate in the Far East. What do you know of him?'

'He's an old friend of Mr. Chan, and is well connected in Taiwanese industrial circles,' Roger said, trying his best to sound authoritative. 'Why?'

'While you were away I took a call from a US lawyer. He told me there is a rival law firm in the States gathering data for a possible class action against one or possibly two of Mr. Veng's clients,' Edgar said, looking directly at Roger.

'Insured by us I take it?'

'Yes, in fact very recently, the policies only went out to both of them last week.'

Roger's heart missed a beat. 'Do we have any details of the class action?'

'Only that there have been some serious injuries and fatalities on a machine produced by both or either of these companies,' Edgar said gravely.

'How many?' Roger asked cautiously. If the Irishman knew about Roger's by-passing of the underwriting system, he wasn't letting on.

'He didn't say. We can only assume that if a class action is being considered there must be more than just one or two. One of us will need to go out there and try and establish just what is going on, who builds these machines, who sells them etc. I suspect there may have been some ambiguous information presented to us on the proposal forms.'

Roger was silent. The Far East was the last place he wanted to go. The place was full of foreigners. 'How credible is the information from this American lawyer?'

'Our US associates have checked them out. They are a reputable firm. We can't afford to ignore what we've been told, a successful class action could wipe us out, Roger. I've seen it happen before. When can you go?'

Roger panicked, if he suggested one of the underwriters go they would spot immediately that they had never seen the proposal document. Unless they knew already. He was unsure how to play this one.

'Me? Well I've just got back from Norway and my ribs aren't properly healed yet, I would prefer to send one of my senior sales guys.'

'You are a senior director, Roger, your shareholding gives you the best incentive in the world to get this one sorted out. I do think the experience would do you good but I can understand your health concerns,' Edgar said, nodding thoughtfully.

'I think someone should go with him,' Roger said at last, more for something to say than anything else, to show he was still interested.

'OK, I suggest someone from the claims department investigation team, they can generally smell a rat from 300 yards,' the Irishman said with a sad smile.

Edgar was on top form with his instant decisions. It made Roger nervous. He wondered if the old fool was playing for time. Had he spoken with his father about it? If so, that would mean both of the old sods against him. All for the sake of getting some God-forsaken new customers on the books. What were these daft Chinese buggers up to though, lying on the proposal form? That was typical underhand behaviour. These were the sort of people who stole cars from under the noses of their owners in Central London. Or were they? Was there some kind of connection here?

The claims department manager was another Liechtenstein Re old hand who had been around in the days of David and Edgar. His attitude was cold, bordering on hostile at Roger's request for a senior claims administrator to accompany his sales manager on a trip to the Far East on urgent company business.

'Well I don't have people waiting around just to go at a moment's notice,' he said tetchily into the handset.

'It's next week, they can go out Tuesday and come back on the Saturday, how much notice do you need?' Roger was growing exasperated. Why was everything so hard around here?

'Why so senior? Couldn't you take a clerk? It's not that difficult, this investigation work, you know?'

For God's sake, Roger thought. He decided to pull rank. 'Look, we have some reports from the US that there is a possible class action being bought against one of the companies out there that we provide cover for. It is in all our interests, including yours, that we send our very best people out there so we can refute any claims made. Is that simple enough for you to understand?'

'Very well, you can have Miss Scant for four days. She is our senior claims manager on the liability side. She'll put them all straight,' he said with obvious satisfaction.

Roger groaned inwardly. He imagined his sales manager travelling with a matron-type spinster with baggy stockings and a sour expression doing her knitting in business class for the twelve hour flight.

30. Flying Visits

Han Sen and Sven could not help looking on in admiration as the trim young Englishwoman, Miss Scant, eased her heeled business shoes off and sat down gracefully on the lower bed of the MassageOmatic machine, taking great care to position her posterior centrally. Once happy with her location, she held onto her suit skirt and swung both shapely legs up onto the bed, smoothed any wrinkles out of her skirt and lowered herself so that she was lying perfectly flat on her back.

'OK, ready,' she called out demurely, eyes closed in anticipation, lips slightly parted.

Sven pressed the start button and the top deck manoeuvred slowly and silently into place, the miniature boxing gloves eventually forming themselves around the young woman's body with perfect symmetry as if recognising and reflecting her meticulous positioning and the stylish way she had climbed onboard.

Sven put the machine through a short demonstration programme on the number two setting and there was a series of gasps and moans from between the beds. Han Sen smiled at Sven and at the young Liechtenstein Re Sales Manager who was also looking on. He couldn't help feeling good about someone so obviously enjoying themselves with one of his products. 'We'll give you a short blast on the highest setting, hold on,' the Swede called out. The moans quickly turned to breathless shrieks of delight as the boxing gloves drove into the young girl's body with a whisker more force. 'This is the invigoration setting,' the Swede called out, grinning.

She lay on the bed patiently, not moving until the upper bed had reached the very end of its upward travel. She then carefully repeated the opposite movements to those she had made when climbing onboard. When she was at last standing in stockinged feet, she turned to the two engineers and said, 'Mr. Sen, Sven, thank you. That was simply breath-taking. Slightly more than breath-taking towards the end, but phwoah, brilliant. Chris, you have a go,' she looked at the Sales Manager and then to Han Sen, 'Can he?'

'Yes, of course,' Han Sen gestured for the Sales Manager to step up.

'No, I'm OK. Thanks anyway, I think Julie has shown us all what the machine can do,' the Sales Manager said, looking slightly embarrassed.

The small party walked back to Han Sen's office. 'If you don't mind Mr. Sen, we'd just like to ask you a few further questions?' Julie Scant asked.

'Please, go ahead,' Han Sen said, smiling.

The English couple left an hour later. Han Sen would have liked to offer the young Englishwoman one of their classy vibrators in the wooden case but was too embarrassed to propose it. The vegetable peeler in the beautiful wrapping would serve as a reminder of her visit to Han Choy Inc. The Sales Manager was presented with a discreetly wrapped Ardourator.

Over a drink in the hotel that night, the two insurance professionals agreed that the underwriting risks associated with a company like Han Choy were absolutely minimal. A positive for the Sales Director's strategy so far, they concurred. The Claims Manager swallowed her disappointment at seeing her colleague's splendid gift, she had really fancied one of those classy looking vibrators in the wooden case but was too shy to ask.

They flew out of Kaohsiung the next morning on the short flight to Hong Kong and the taxi pulled up outside the VSS premises at ten thirty. The receptionist looked harassed, 'I'm sorry,' she said, looking at them apprehensively. 'Jamie Woo, he not here, he said to tell you very sorry, had to go to China. Urgent business, be back next Tuesday. Really sorry, you want tea?'

'No thank you, does he have a phone?' the Claims Manager asked.

'No, sorry,' said the receptionist with a crestfallen expression.

'Does he call in then?' she tried again.

'Sometimes he does, sorry.'

'Is there anybody else we can see,' she checked her file. 'Vernon Saunders?'

'No, he's in America, really sorry.'

They discussed what to do, finally deciding that they would come back later after speaking to London.

'OK sorry, see you later. Bye-bye,' she said, full of apologetic smiles.

They came back at five, only to find the place locked-up with not a single car in the car park. The Sales Manager reported back to Roger on his mobile as they stood outside the deserted industrial unit. 'I'm sorry, Chris but you're going to have to hang around till someone turns up. Try and get in the place and see what he does in there. When they're open, obviously,' Roger told them.

They booked themselves into a very nice hotel and had a lovely time on company expenses for a few days. They called VSS on Tuesday to be told Jamie Woo would be in the next day.

They showed up bright and early. 'Sorry,' the receptionist said, looking at them nervously. 'He go to Australia this time, urgent business, really sorry.'

They flew home that night frustrated. Why was the management of VSS Ltd being so damned elusive?

Han Sen was becoming concerned. Where was the Englishman? Previously when he had been in the USA, he had called Han Sen almost daily with snippets of market information and stories of new sales contacts. To coin another one of the Englishman's phrases, he'd gone to ground.

He called Tom Huang into his office.

'Tom, Foo the accountant is giving me hell about the amount of MassageOmatics downstairs. We need to push them harder though the dealers, VSS seem to be going through a bit of a sticky patch at the moment. Any ideas?'

'If we reduced the price by twenty-five percent, they would go almost overnight,' Tom said confidently.

'And we'd still make a decent margin?' Han Sen asked, thinking of Great Uncle Sen and his magical forty percent.

'Yes, I'll confirm it but I think about fifty percent.'

'In that case do it. We need to shift inventory to get Mr. Foo off our backs.'

'OK, boss,' the young man replied enthusiastically. 'Straight away.'

The phone rang, 'Thanks Tom,' he said as the young sales manager disappeared with a very big spring in his step. Angelique informed him that Mr. Saunders was on the phone.

'Vernon, long time no hear. How are you?' He said with a mixture of anxiety and relief.

'I've been better, Han Sen,' came the stark reply.

'What's wrong?'

'The death count is up to twelve and growing. I really don't understand these people, they seem to be using these things as death machines. Just because the things have the strength to do damage, they seem to think they have to use it.'

'They want their monies worth, Vernon, it's human nature,' Han Sen said calmly.

'It's blood lust too, Han Sen. I've heard that some of the deaths have been innocent people dragged in off the street. I was targeting the sexual thrill people, but over here it seems everyone is a closet-murderer. No wonder our machine sells so well. The bloody lawyers are involved too. One California firm in particular is proposing a class action against us, for God's sake.'

'I take it you're still in the States?'

'Hmm, I was coming to that. Yes I'm on police bail, they won't let me leave,' he said, sounding grim.

'You're under arrest?' Han Sen was genuinely shocked.

'Yes, no charge yet. At one time they were talking about corporate manslaughter but it's probably going to be criminal negligence or some such.'

'Do you have a lawyer?'

'Yes, I'm using my guy in Washington. We've got the preliminary hearing on Thursday, they'll set a date for the trial then.'

'Is there anything I can do to help?'

'Thanks, old friend, but no. I just wanted you to know what was happening. I gather the insurance company have been sniffing around?'

'Yes, they were here last week. They were going to your place afterwards.'

'They need to see me really, I'm the only one at VSS who knows what goes on. Did they say anything at your place?'

'No, they just had a go on a MassageOmatic. The girl loved it. They asked a few questions about our other products then went. It was nothing really.'

'Well, you're clean, aren't you? It's me they suspect. I saw your letter, I'd do the same in your shoes. Can you get rid of all those machines I ordered?'

'Yes, don't worry. I've just had a conversation with Tom, we'll be discounting them through our dealers. Tom reckons they won't be around for long.'

'Good, I'm pleased. Sorry, Han Sen, I've gone and buggered things up for us somewhat.'

'We all learn as we go through life, Vernon, we can sort it out when you get back. Just the therapy machines in the future though, eh?'

'Titillation not torture, eh?'

'Yes, you can buy me a beer on the strength of that one next time you're here.' He made a note of the Englishman's US contact details. Han Sen frowned as he put the phone down. Contriteness was not something he had ever heard from the Englishman, he hoped his friend would pull through it all with his head held high. If it were true that some of the deaths were caused wilfully, then perhaps his role in all of this could be put down to a certain level of naivety? Or perhaps he was just trying too hard to see the good in everybody, including the judges.

The Englishman's wretched tone during their telephone conversation continued to bother him throughout the day. He thought about going to California. He may not be able to do anything other than provide moral support for him but wasn't that what friends were for? He had never been anywhere outside Taiwan other than Hong Kong in the twelve years since arriving on the island. Nor had he had time off in the ten years since starting Han Choy. The thought of crossing the Pacific made him nervous, the thought of being in the USA made him even more nervous. Despite everything, he decided to go. Angelique organised the twelve hour direct flight from Taipei to Los Angeles.

The dry heat of California hit him for the first time as he stepped outside the air-conditioned terminal building at Los Angeles International Airport.

Once installed at his hotel, he called the Englishman to announce his arrival and took a taxi to his downtown apartment.

Han Sen was shocked by what he saw. Vernon Saunders had obviously lost weight. He looked gaunt and was unshaven. Shaking hands didn't seem to be the right thing for either of them under the circumstances. With a joyful expression the Englishman threw both arms around Han Sen and gripped him tightly.

'Han Sen! It's so good to see you. Surely you didn't come all this way just to see me?'

'When we spoke on the phone earlier in the week, you sounded, well, the most miserable I've ever heard. I thought maybe if nothing else, I could at least cheer you up,' Han Sen said, smiling.

'You've done that already, old friend. But you've had a long journey, you must be tired,' the Englishman said as he showed him into the bare apartment.

'Yes, and hungry too. Where are we going for dinner?'

'Hah! I know just the place,' he said, finger in the air. 'I'll get showered, shaved and smartened up and we'll go to the local Gravy House. You'll love it!'

So over a mass of spicy meat and seafood sauces, breads, potato mash and vegetables, the once again animated Englishman told Han Sen all about his recent experiences in the Sunshine State.

'In hindsight, I shouldn't have been taken in by it all,' he opened up candidly. 'Me, of all people, used to the iron discipline of the British military, lucky enough to be living in a beautiful part of the world surrounded by beautiful people, and Buddha. I stand to lose everything now, all because I was lured by the US dollar. Filthy lucre, Han Sen, that's what drove me here. Drove me to take stupid, unnecessary risks. You warned me, I should have listened to you but no, I was convinced I was right.' He nibbled at the same vegetable as he talked, 'Putting an untested machine into a market as weird as this one was asking for trouble.'

'It's funny, when we had the Englishwoman from the insurance company at the factory last week,' Han Sen said, tucking in to the food. 'We gave her a go on a MassageOmatic and she absolutely loved it. Mostly number two setting with a short blast of number three where she got a bit breathless, but the whole point is, we know that the number three setting can't do any damage. It's a great machine, you've just got to know where you are with it.'

'Yes, well, I figured that a number five setting would hurt people just enough to give them what they were looking for. And it was true, it did. The trouble is, it seems that these people can't stop themselves once they've got their juices flowing. Something that hurts a bit over say a couple of minutes will kill someone if you do it over four or five hours which is what these lunatics have been doing.'

'Tell me.' Han Sen stopped eating. 'What strength setting is the military version?'

'Unregulated. No limit. It's probably equivalent to ten, or even more.'

Han Sen winced, 'How many, and to who?'

The Englishman slowly crunched the remainder of the broccoli piece he had been nibbling at since the food arrived. 'Strictly between you and me, only about a dozen. Mostly the CIA so I don't honestly know where they are now, could be anywhere. A couple went into the Balkans, those Serbs love killing anybody who's not Serbian these days. If I hadn't lost the stomach for all of this, I would have probably carried on because it's easy money.'

'Easy money, difficult on the conscience though,' Han Sen said.

'Exactly, my old friend. You know these things though, I should never have talked you into it.' He looked at Han Sen with a hangdog expression.

'Vernon, I have a world class product in the MassageOmatic which, I realise, I wouldn't have had without you suggesting it in the first place,' Han Sen said. 'It's strength makes it reliable and if you leave the controls as they are when they leave the factory it will last a lifetime and never hurt a fly.'

'Thanks for that,' the Englishman said ironically with a half-smile playing on his lips. 'It comes back to the old argument though, if it doesn't hurt, how can you sell it as something that does? I know I know,' he held both hands in the air. 'I know what you're going to say - don't.'

'You're learning, Vernon, you're learning.' Han Sen resumed tucking into the food.

The Englishman's facial expression suddenly changed. 'There's something else I did too which I'm regretting.'

'What, on the MassageOmatic?' There was more? Han Sen panicked slightly.

'No, I tried to kill my niece's husband.'

'Your niece Hilary?'

'Yes. She's married to a complete loser. They don't get on that marvellously, I was convinced he was knocking her about. That and the fact that she would really like to move out to Hong Kong and he was standing in her way. I got Freddie to knock up this electronic control device and had him install it on the husband's car. It basically killed the brake and clutch hydraulics and gave the throttle remote activation. Freddie's UK guy set it off when Roger was on his way home one night, heading straight for a village where he was bound to hit something hard at more or less top speed. Trust my luck though, the idiot survived with just a couple of broken ribs.'

Han Sen was incredulous, 'So not content with killing off half the adult population in the USA, you tried to kill your niece's husband. Does anybody else know apart from Freddie?'

'No.'

'Well, you need to tell Hilary,' Han Sen said strongly.

'Tell her?'

'Yes, the poor girl must be scared it's going to happen again or that the whole family might be a target.'

'Hmm, never thought of it like that,' he nodded. 'I'll tell her but I'm not quite sure what her reaction will be.'

'You must promise me something, Vernon,' Han Sen said looking at him. He had stopped eating again.

'What?'

'I know you used to do it for a living but you've got to stop killing people. It's not something you need to be doing. It brings you nothing but trouble.'

'Yes, I know, and you're right. It's a mug's game,' the Englishman conceded. 'Let's get all of this behind us, and I'll go back to earning a legitimate living. Pure titillation from now on, I promise.' His expression changed suddenly again. 'There is one thing I need you to do for me though, Han Sen.'

'What's that?' he asked, with a spring-roll halfway to his mouth.

'I'm going to need the test results for the MassageOmatic,' the Englishman looked at him hopefully.

'What, the results of the test that we never actually got round to doing?'

'Yes. It's the only way I'm going to get off here. I need to be able to prove that this machine on the half-strength setting can't do any permanent damage to people.'

'Not sure how we go about doing that. I'll have to have a word with Sven,' Han Sen ruminated aloud. He knew what was coming next.

'Perhaps some extrapolation of your previous test results, just extend the lines a bit more, can't you? How would anybody know that you hadn't gone that far?'

'I'll see.' Han Sen felt distinctly uncomfortable even thinking about producing falsified test results. The Englishman was probably right though, if he couldn't show them in court, how else could he prove his innocence? 'I'm sure we can come up with something,' he said finally.

'Thanks, Han Sen, I knew you would save my bacon,' the older man said.

They finished their meal, the Englishman dropped Han Sen off at his hotel where he slept another deep, dreamless sleep. The following day they attended the preliminary hearing at the downtown courthouse. The judge announced that the Federal Grand Jury had already decided there was enough evidence for a trial on the charge of criminal negligence, and a prosecuting attorney had been appointed. Vernon Saunders was going to be held to answer and the date for arraignment would be one month from today. Han Sen would be called as a witness for the prosecution as would Freddie Chen and HERT Rentals. A jury was going to decide the Englishman's fate.

Han Sen didn't enjoy the experience of Los Angeles, its physical size daunted him and its lack of soul saddened him. The people he came across seemed full of false bonhomie and brash self-confidence. It seemed to him that people lived their lives focussed on an anticipation of greatness, maybe the local film industry had rubbed off on everybody, gave them all a blinding ambition, whether they wanted one or not.

He looked out of the taxi window on his way to the airport as they passed block upon block of humanity. Theirs was a struggle without respite, the dollar bill their sustenance, their hopes and dreams wrapped up in uncertain ambition. He ached for the sanctity of the temple, for the wise words of the Buddha and the perfection of the living landscape he grew up in; sunlit forest clearings, waterfalls and simple villages with happy, smiling people. He would go back to his home country he decided, soon. He would take Li Lai to the top of the mountain and show her his country as Hem Suvorn had done with him all those years ago.

The test results would stay unaltered despite his last conversation with the Englishman. He could not bring himself to contemplate falsifying them, his friend would have to meet his fate according to the will of the jury and of their Gods at the end of the day. He felt like a coward.

As he watched the sprawl of Los Angeles disappear from view through the aeroplane window, he smiled to himself. There was something therapeutic about travelling, or maybe it was just that he had time to reflect and contemplate. Home life was unexpectedly harmonious nowadays. He didn't miss the lovemaking with Rao, he saw it as a natural expression of their need for one another at the time, something that neither of them had any control over.

As Raya's anxiety over the return of her sister diminished, so too had his lack of understanding. Love had conquered over all in the Sen household. He was lucky. He had got away with playing with fire, twice. He and the girls would survive anything now. He laid the seat back and closed his eyes as he made himself comfortable for the long flight home.

31. Edgar's Last Stand

'So, where do we go now?' Edgar asked as he looked across his desk at Roger. 'It seems that VSS are the people we most want to talk to in all of this, and they don't want to talk to us. Doesn't that strike you as a bit strange?'

'Yes, it does,' Roger said. 'The owner is in America, and the Sales Manager is in Australia. We need a list of associates or dealers in those countries, then we could track them down. We need to get Mr. Veng to ask the people in the factory to get it for us. I'll talk to him.'

'Yes, good idea. Our priority is the American list, we need to talk to the owner, this Vernon Saunders fellow.'

'Vernon Saunders.' Roger stifled his shock. Surely not Hilary's Uncle Vern? From Hong Kong as well. It had to be. He noted the name down as casually as he could.

The sharp-eyed Edgar spotted Roger's pondering, 'Do you know him then?'

'No, no, it's Hilary's family name, that's all. There's nobody in the family called Vernon, though,' he lied. Blimey, he thought, if it was him, what was the old sod up to?

'What we need is a telephone number; I'll talk to him if you can get it. Let me know as soon as you've got something,' Edgar said as Roger left the office.

Roger called Hilary as soon as he got back to his office. 'Where's your Uncle Vern at the moment?' he asked as casually as he could.

'Last time I spoke to him was a couple of weeks ago, he was just off to America. I would think he's back in Hong Kong now,' she replied. 'Why?'

'Oh nothing, I think we might have him and his company as a client through our Far East agent. Edgar wants to talk to him about some market information he heard on the legal grapevine. Nothing important. You wouldn't have a phone number for him in the States, would you?'

'No, but I can let you have his West Coast dealer's number,' she said. 'What sort of market information?'

'Something about a class action against him,' he said, being deliberately non-specific.

'A class action, that's pretty serious, isn't it?' she said, beginning to cotton on.

'Look, Hils, we just want to talk to him, OK? Please don't tell anyone about this. We don't know enough about anything yet, just the number please,' he said, struggling to keep his patience.

'OK, here it is, they're called Hert Rentals.'

'What as in Hurt, H.U.R.T?'

'No Hert. Like Hertz car rentals without the Z,' she said.

'Oh.' He took a note of the number. 'That's California for you, I suppose. Thanks, see you later.'

As he put the phone down, Edgar strode into his office. He was clasping a pile of papers together with the FedEx packaging. 'It's arrived,' he said grimly.

Roger looked at him. 'What has?'

'The lawsuit, the class action from those bloody lawyers in the US. They're claiming damages for eighteen deaths and twenty-five serious injuries. They are reserving their rights to increase this if anybody else dies. This could wipe us out, you know, Roger. We don't have the assets to be able to cover this. Heads will roll when I find out who underwrote this risk without proper bloody investigation!'

Roger gulped. 'How much are they claiming?'

'On average, 50 million dollars per death and 25 million dollars per serious injury. It amounts to over half a billion quid. And it's got our name on it. Jesus!' The older man's bottom lip was shaking.

Roger thought the Irishman was going to cry. 'We can contest it, can't we? Out of court settlement, that sort of thing?' he offered in a placatory tone.

'Oh yes, we might get it down to a third of a billion. Whoopee, you don't get it, do you, Roger?' he was shouting now. 'We're fucked. The end of the line. Bust. Up the Swanee. Bankrupt. Insolvent! I can just hear the words of the official receiver, 'the company is no longer able to meet its liabilities and must cease trading.' I am personally going to have to sack everybody. Some of these people have been with us from the start. It's going to be hard, son. Fucking hard.' He threw himself into the chair in front of Roger's desk with his head in his hands.

He *was* crying now. Roger was speechless. Anything he said now was pointless, he went outside and borrowed a box of tissues from Louise. The secretary looked on, knowing there was something seriously wrong. She had never heard Edgar swearing before.

'Here, come on, Edgar,' he said, proffering the box of tissues, 'It might not be as bad as all that. I've got the number, let me talk to VSS.'

'Ring him now,' Edgar said, staring at the floor in despair.

Roger dialled. 'Hello, I wish to speak to Mr. Vernon Saunders, please,' he said. 'Do you have a number I can get him on then?' He noted another number down. 'Thank you,' he put the phone down and dialled again. 'Mr. Saunders? This is the Liechtenstein Re insurance company from London. Are you able to talk? OK...'

Edgar reached across the desk and snatched the phone away from Roger's hands, 'You bastard, you fucking bastard,' he screamed into the handset. 'What the fuck do you think you're doing, killing and injuring all those people? Our company is facing ruin because of you! 500 people out on the street! What have you got to say to that, scumbag? Come on, say something, or I'm going to come over there and punch your fucking head off! Just stay there, I'm on my way. Lawsuit or not I'm going to knock the bejesus out of you. You'll wish you hadn't been born when I'm finished with you, you fucking idiot!' He threw the phone down on the desk and stumbled back into the chair, clutching his chest and uttering cries of agony. Louise rushed in to Roger's office at the sound of Edgar shouting and swearing just as he collapsed into the chair. She comforted Edgar as best she could and shouted for someone to call an ambulance.

Roger turned away from the melee in the office, his own heart pounding in his chest, 'Mr. Saunders?' he wasn't sure he was still on the other end.

'Please let the gentleman know that I'm really sorry. Truly, I am,' came the response.

'I'll call you back, stay on this number,' Roger put the phone down. It *was* Uncle Vern after all. Shit.

They found blankets for the now still, grey Edgar and lay him on the floor. Roger, remembering his father's heart attack, felt for a pulse. There was nothing. He frantically ripped the old Irishman's tie off, loosened his shirt and started to pummel his chest. He bounced up and down with flattened palms for all he was worth and felt like crying with desperation. Up until now he had wanted him dead, but now he was trying to save the old bugger's life. Don't leave me now Edgar, you're the only one who can save me, he pleaded wordlessly. Without the Irishman around, he would be out on his ear without a penny, he was sure of it. Say what you like about the old duffer, he was his only guardian angel in Liechtenstein Re.

'Please don't die Edgar,' he said as one of the freshly arrived paramedics gently eased him away, the other bending down with defibrillator pads. There was no response to the shock therapy and so the prone Irishman was bundled onto a stretcher and rushed out to the lift and the waiting ambulance.

Roger looked at Louise uncertainly; she was holding her hand in front of her mouth. He needed comforting as much as anyone round here, he decided. He walked over and held her in his arms, feeling her body shaking through the sudden release of her tears.

Louise eventually recovered sufficiently and went to the hospital to see what could be done for Edgar. Roger sat down heavily at his desk and dialled the USA number again, 'You're Hilary's Uncle Vern, aren't you?' he said as soon as he heard the older man's voice on the other end.

'Err, yes, and who might you be?' the voice replied.

'This is Roger, her husband. I run the Liechtenstein Re insurance company,' he said, although under the circumstances he really wished he didn't have to say that.

'Roger! I had no idea,' came the reply.

'No, neither did I,' Roger said calmly, surprising himself. 'I need to ask you some questions about VSS.'

'What do you need to know?'

Roger looked at the original proposal form, 'We have it on record that you buy and sell raw materials and finished goods. You also carry out some modifications to the finished goods with the manufacturer's consent to be able to sell the goods in various market segments. Is that correct?'

'Yes it is. That is exactly what we do.' Roger imagined the old Major standing ramrod straight, perfect suit, polished shoes.

'Do you know why people have been suffering serious injury and death on these finished goods of yours then?'

'I imagine this conversation is going to be on the record?'

'Yes, of course, these are significant events. We tried to talk with you last week in Hong Kong but you weren't there and none of your staff were available,' Roger said, still calm.

'I apologise for that, I'm currently under house arrest in Los Angeles and will be standing trial shortly, so the lawyers are telling me,' he said, his tone flat.

'Can I ask you on what charges?' Roger asked, not sure where this was going.

'Criminal negligence.'

'Off the record now, do you intend pleading guilty?' From the firm's point of view it made very little difference at this stage but he knew it would influence the outcome of the class-action.

'Most certainly not!' he replied indignantly, 'I am innocent in all of this. Used responsibly, these machines are as safe as houses. Our manual states clearly how they should be used, I am not responsible for any deaths or injuries. These people over here, if you'll pardon the expression, they're all fucking crazy, natural-born murderers, the lot of them. They're the guilty ones, the users.'

'Machines?' Roger asked. 'What sort of machine?'

'They're therapy machines, you know, intensive massage all over the body or you can just do selected bits if you want, fantastic product, you need to see one to appreciate it.'

'I'm guessing these are the finished goods that you modify,' Roger said. It was a statement.

'Only slightly. The machines are inherently very strong to make them reliable. By fine tuning the controls, we allow a little bit more of its strength to be used, that's all.'

'Why would you want to do that?' Roger asked, sensing this was a critical part of the conversation.

'Sadomasochism, Roger,' he said, using Roger's name for the first time. 'Heard of it?'

'Hmm.' He had visions of picture-postcard Norway and those two terrible women. 'That's where people hurt and like to be hurt in a sexual context, isn't it?'

'Bingo, got it in one,' came the schoolmasterly reply. 'And that is the market segment we concentrated our efforts on.'

'Were these machines tested at all?'

'Tested to death, not literally of course, ha-ha, but yes, of course they were.'

He was beginning to sound more like the Uncle Vern that he knew. 'And we can see the results, I mean, on real people so we can assess just what these things are capable of?'

'Yes, I can make that information available to you,' he said.

'We'll need all the other documentation relevant to the machines as well. Where and when can we access this?'

'Next week in Hong Kong, I'll tell my people to expect you.'

'They're not going to be buggering off to various parts of the world again then?'

'No, no, I'll talk to my Sales Manager today. He'll be there.'

'You're still trading then?'

'Yes, of course we are. Why ever would we stop trading?'

'Just curious, as you're under arrest.'

'Oh, this is just a blip, I'll be away from here after the trial. I tell you, I'm innocent in all of this.'

'Well, I hope for all our sakes that you are,' said Roger.

'Give my love to Hilary and I hope that other chap of yours is OK, is he always that excitable?'

'No, actually he's not. He's just a bit concerned about the amount of money being claimed for these so-called victims of yours.'

'Victims, my arse. You'll see at the trial. I'm innocent, you won't have to pay out a penny. Trust me,' he said with a laugh.

Roger sighed as he put the phone down. He was a madman. Sadomasochism? Did he really think he could get away with supplying something designed to hurt people? Perhaps he could, who knew? One thing was for sure though, Liechtenstein Re would be up shit creek without a paddle if the lawsuit against them was successful.

An ashen faced Louise came into his office later in the afternoon and sat down in the chair in front of Roger's desk. He didn't have to ask and for the second time that day, he comforted the young secretary.

'He's dead, Roger,' she said quietly as he held her, her voice quivering on his shoulder. 'He was only sixty three, just about to retire, worked hard all his life. He didn't deserve to go now, not like that. The doctor said it was a stroke brought on stress. He died here, right in your office.'

'I'll take you home, Louise, you can't carry on working like this, come on.' He helped her up and they walked slowly to her desk where she tidied things away and switched her computer off. Roger went into the MDs office, briefed him on the situation, then took the lift down to the car park with an unsteady Louise and drove her home. Outwardly Roger was the face of calm, but his mind was in turmoil; this was his company now. But for how much longer?

'You've seen one? Where?' he asked as Hilary served their dinner that night.

'In Wales at that party I went to last year,' she said matter-of-factly. 'There was a couple having a go on it and it really scared me, made me wonder what I was getting mixed up in.'

'Did they try it on the maximum setting?' he asked.

'Yes, the guy came off shaking like a leaf. It was only on number five for about thirty seconds. I think he may have shat himself. Mind you,' she said, a smile playing on her lips. 'It wouldn't have been a problem at that party, if you know what I mean.'

'Bloody hell, Hilary, what are you mixed up in?' he said, not bothering to take Hilary's excretionary references further. 'Did your mad Uncle supply that machine?'

'Yes, of course he did. His UK industrial dealer bought it as a demonstrator,' she said, tucking into fish pie and peas.

'Industrial? What the hell does that mean?'

'I'm the UK agent for the sex toys. Marty in Wales is the dealer for the machinery side of things. Uncle Vern just calls it industrial, that's all.'

Roger forced himself to stay calm, her blasé attitude wasn't helping. 'Look, today we received a lawsuit from an American firm that could cost us £500 million. As far as I can tell, it's all down to people killing themselves and their weird chums on that machine that your Uncle is selling, seemingly all over the world. Wales? What the bloody hell are they doing with a thing like that in Wales?' his calm was rapidly disappearing.

'I'm not surprised,' Hilary said, calmly ignoring the geographical aspect of his question and pouring herself a glass of wine.

'What do you mean you're not surprised? Look around you, Hils,' he said sweeping his hand around animatedly. 'This could all be a thing of the past. If this lawsuit goes through, we'll be living in a hostel. It's certain ruin for our company. Oh and by the way, Edgar died today.'

Hilary choked. She looked at him, her hand in front of her mouth desperately trying to find her voice. 'Roger, you bastard,' she coughed. 'You tell me all about the bloody lawsuit then you tell me Edgar died as if you'd forgotten to get the bloody milk on the way home,' her fury mounted. 'You're an uncaring, ungracious, rude, self-centred,' she struggled to find a word strong enough. 'Dickhead!' She stood up angrily, tears in her eyes and went into the kitchen, dinner half eaten, wine glass still full.

Roger hadn't touched his dinner, the events of the day had taken his appetite. Now this. He thought briefly about continuing the discussion before realising it would probably do no good. He wished he did have some control over his priorities in life, he thought sadly, but he couldn't help the way he was. Unusually, he decided to apologise; if there was one thing in life he would need in the coming months, it was the support of his wife.

Hilary was sitting at the table in the kitchen and he could feel her anger. She was devilishly attractive when she was angry though.

'I'm really sorry, Hils, I didn't forget, it's just that such a lot went on today.'

'You are such an arse sometimes, I just can't believe how cold and uncaring you can be,' she said shaking her head. 'How did he die?'

'A stroke apparently, in my office. Talking to Uncle Vern, well, shouting at him actually. His was a very quick ending, there one minute, gone the next. Scary really. I tried saving him, you know, the old heart massage?'

'It was all to do with the lawsuit, was it?'

'Yes. All his life he'd spent building up Liechtenstein Re and one man's folly could bring it all tumbling down.' Actually make that the folly of two men, he thought sadly, wishing he could go back and stop himself for blatantly ignoring the risks. His knees weakened at the prospect of being found out, he really would be out on his ear, even if the company survived.

'It's just too sad,' Hilary said. 'He was such a lovely man.'

'Yes, he was,' said Roger with false empathy, trying hard to ignore his overwhelming desire to be comforted by this fantastically attractive wife of his. Eventually he gave up. 'Come on, Hils, let's go to bed. I'll never be cold and uncaring to you again, I promise.' He held his hand out to her. 'Let me make it up to you,' he said pleadingly.

'You go up, I'll just clear up here,' she said looking around, frowning at the mess on the worktops. By the time she had finished loading the dishwasher and gone upstairs, she could hear him snoring from outside the bedroom door. She went back downstairs and made a cup of tea; she wasn't disappointed.

Edgar's seat at the board table was conspicuously empty. The members held a minute's silence before commencing the emergency meeting. Once the silence was over and the meeting was underway, the atmosphere in the elegant boardroom remained quiet and sombre, the passing away of one of their founders casting a pall over the proceedings.

Roger stared into the middle distance as the Managing Director briefed everyone on the succession plan. As Edgar had no family to speak of, his shares would revert to the Collins family.

The last few years of striving for this moment were now over. Lichtenstein Re was now his, institutional investors notwithstanding. Would there still be a company though? Shit, shit and double shit, he thought, why on earth had he forged those policies? The bloody Chinaman could have waited – at least he would have got some sort of year-end bonus, now, who knows? What a bloody catastrophe. His inheritance looked like it was going to disappear in a puff of smoke.

The Managing Director moved on to the issue of the law suit. He explained in brief and concise terms what was being claimed by the US law firm. A startled hush came over the room as the implications were digested by all present. The Chief Underwriter was the first to speak. Roger looked around at him.

'We will conduct a thorough examination of the facts in this case. If it is found that my department was at fault I shall of course tender my resignation. I can't at the minute explain how something like this slipped through the net. Off the record, I suspect that someone has not told us the truth. Misled us about the real intended purpose of these machines. We'll find out in the next day or so.' He sat down with a sigh and a grim expression.

The Managing Director thanked him and announced that the meeting was over, at least for the time being. They would reconvene in a week's time unless events demanded a shorter timescale.

Roger was the last to rise, his knees seemed permanently weak these days. On paper he was probably worth over £300 million now. Some of the non-executives came over and offered congratulations tempered with commiseration at the company's great loss.

He muttered bland acquiescences in response to their blatant networking and watched with dread as the Chief Underwriter strode out of the boardroom, talking with a colleague in a highly animated manner, no doubt formulating plans for his investigation. Roger's mind turned to ways of getting out of this dreadful situation. Unusually, he couldn't think of anyone he could sacrifice. Bugger, he thought darkly.

32. Claim On

'Mr. Sen, you design and manufacture the MassageOmatic machine, do you not?' asked Vernon's defence attorney in the brightly lit, air-conditioned courtroom.

'My company; Han Choy Incorporated does, yes, sir,' Han Sen responded.

'I wonder whether you could clear something up for the jury, Mr. Sen. Why is this machine called a MassageOmatic?'

'The machine is designed to gently massage the muscles, to therapeutically ease pain or injury. The 'omatic refers to the machine's ability to cover any specific area of the body that you programme into it,' Han Sen replied.

'Mr. Sen, you are from Cambodia originally, aren't you?'

'Yes, I am.'

'You at one time worked for the Khmer Rouge, did you not?'

'Yes, sir, I was forced to work for them. I had no choice.'

'Can you please explain to the court and the jury exactly what your role was in the Khmer Rouge?'

Han Sen had expected this, but not as soon or as direct. 'I was at school in Ban Lung when I was captured and sent to one of their detention camps close to my home town. I was there for a few months, they forced everyone to work long hours and fed us on thin soup, everybody was hungry, and...'

'Yes, answer the question, Mr. Sen, please,' the young attorney interjected.

'I was sent to Phnom Penh to work in the prison there,' he said falteringly.

'Doing what exactly?'

'I had grown up as an engineer and...'

'Answer the question please, Mr. Sen.'

'They forced me to make devices. They used these to extract information from the prisoners.'

'You mean torture, Mr. Sen, don't you?'

'I mean devices intended to extract information, sir,' Han Sen responded.

'What sort of devices, Mr. Sen?'

'Mangles, clamps, brackets, that sort of thing.'

'When you say that sort of thing, was there anything else specifically?'

'Water features, fire grates.'

'I won't ask,' the Attorney grimaced at the jury. 'And?'

'They asked me to design a machine that would kill up to 1500 people a day.' There was an audible gasp from the courtroom, even the young attorney was visibly shaken. 'That is when I made my escape. I could not do it,' Han Sen said calmly.

The attorney composed himself. 'But there was something you made that has a specific connection to this case, Mr. Sen. Could you please enlighten the court as to what it was,'

'It was a device called a Multi-Stretch,' Han Sen admitted finally. 'They gave me no choice. They would have killed me if I had not co-operated.'

There was a quiet stirring amongst the crowd in the courtroom. The attorney continued. 'I put it to you, Mr. Sen, that your experiences with the Khmer Rouge whetted your appetite for torture. Now that you are a free man, so to speak, you decided to pursue this previous interest of yours from where you left off in Cambodia. You are a self-styled designer and manufacturer of equipment used for torturing people! No further questions, Your Honour.'

The rather more sympathetic prosecution attorney led Han Sen skilfully through all of his previous experiences both in Cambodia and Taiwan, carefully ensuring the jury got to hear about his self-justifying motives whilst being forced to work in the Phnom Penh prison. He then moved on to Han Choy and how he had built a large manufacturing company virtually from scratch through sheer hard work and determination. Eventually, they reached the key point of the trial. 'Now Mr. Sen, can you tell me what the maximum strength setting is on the MassageOmatic when they leave your factory?'

'The strength setting is set to an absolute maximum of three,' Han Sen responded.

'The machine has been tested at this setting on people and you have records to show that it cannot cause any physical harm. Is that correct?'

'Yes sir.'

'If the strength setting were increased, what would be the result in your opinion?'

'I would imagine there could be some injuries, especially if someone wanted to cause injury.'

'And if the person on the machine were to have some form of weakness, i.e. heart complaint or a weakened constitution in some way, in your opinion, what would happen then?'

'Objection your honour!' the defence attorney shouted. 'This is prejudicing the expert witness statements.'

The judge looked over his half framed glasses at the attorney. 'Over-ruled. The witness has a right to state an opinion, he has more experience in this field than anyone here, by the sound of it! Continue.'

'If the pressure were exerted all over the body for long enough, then I guess the person could be injured. If it went on for long enough then that person could die. It all depends on who is operating the machine.' Han Sen made a point throughout the whole process of not looking at the Englishman who sat alongside his defence attorney.

'Mr. Sen, have you or has anyone to your knowledge carried out any testing to ascertain what would happen if the strength settings were increased?'

'No, sir. My original tests stopped at the point where the average sized person became uncomfortable. We like to call the maximum strength setting the invigoration setting,' Han Sen said.

'Is it an easy task to change the settings on your machine, Mr. Sen?'

'No, sir, you need specialist knowledge. More specifically, you need a laptop with a programme that can talk to the Eprom controller.'

'Thank you, Mr. Sen. No further questions, Your Honour.'

Vernon Saunders sat staunchly, the British army officer throughout. He was imperiously defiant during his time on the stand. The way he physically conducted himself and the way he spoke, subliminally screamed at the jury that here was the most honest and decent a fellow that they would ever have the good fortune to meet. The defence attorney's strategy was to guide the jury towards the operator of the machine as being the guilty party. After all, he explained, they were the ones that had gone looking for this type of machine, our defendant was merely fulfilling a need. How could he rightly propose offering them a machine that did not live up to expectations by *not* hurting people. It would be like buying a knife without a cutting edge, or a gun that could not shoot bullets. The manual explained explicitly that care should be taken when at or near the maximum strength settings. Medical evidence in all the cases of injury and death pointed to usage that was outside of the explicit instructions in the manual.

In his summing-up, the judge explained the two charges. 'You have to make a decision, members of the jury, on two separate charges. On the one hand, we have a case whereby these machines were supplied by the defendant with the express intent of causing harm to the citizens of California. We have seen the prosecution evidence relating to the horrific injuries, some fatal, that the users of the machines have experienced. We have seen the evidence presented by the defence concerning the documentation supplied with each machine to enable the user to make a decision about how the machine should be used and what level of strength should be applied. Now, we have to be mindful of the fact that the person in charge of the machine's controls obviously has a very large influence on individual outcomes. These people will be judged separately. The jury in this case have to decide whether the defendants, VSS Ltd of Hong Kong and Hert Rentals of Sacramento, California, have been criminally negligent in supplying these machines.'

'On the other hand,' the Judge continued, 'the defendants could be seen as merely fulfilling a need by certain members of the community. Perhaps, in fulfilling that need, he is doing the community a service by providing recreational activities for those who may otherwise fall into the practise of harming by some other means? In this case, the defendant does not face any criminal charges, but has to face the lesser charge of supplying unsafe goods. Again, I would point you to the evidence supplied by the two counsels particularly concerning two points. One, are you satisfied that the users had sufficient information as to the proper and safe use of the machine from the documentation supplied. And two, are you confident that the suppliers were fully aware of the capability of their own machine.'

The jury were out for just over two hours. Vernon Saunders and his co-defendant were found not-guilty of criminal negligence but guilty of supplying unsafe goods.

In his sentencing, the Judge sought to deflect some of the almost gleeful attitude shown by the local press towards his case. 'Far from being a trial on the social nefariousness of some of our, shall we say, less inhibited citizens, this case highlights a deeper malaise that affects our community when we, as guardians of the greater good in society, avert our gaze or look the other way. Let there be no doubt as to the seriousness of this offence. I am sentencing both defendants to a five year prison term, suspended for two years. I will also recommend that the State of California act to ban the sale of these machines in future; we have to be seen to be protecting our citizens, no matter how troubled their circumstances.'

Vernon was quoted in the unchastened press afterwards saying that it was the judge's comments about the knife and the gun that made up the jury's mind. He flew home to Hong Kong almost immediately, glad to be returning to a normal way of life.

*

The day after the jury's pronouncement on Vernon Saunders in the LA courtroom, the second emergency meeting of the Liechtenstein Re board of directors took place. Roger had resisted the temptation to put on two pairs of underpants that morning; his stomach had been churning for the last week with the dread of being found out. He steeled himself as he entered the meeting; he was the last to arrive. He felt all eyes on him as he took his seat.

'Ah Roger,' the Managing Director announced. 'Now you're here, we can begin. There are only two items on the agenda this afternoon, firstly the results of the investigation into the underwriting of the VSS policy followed by a review of how we respond to the lawsuit received from the US law firm. Bob?' he gestured at the Chief Underwriter to proceed.

Crunch time, thought Roger as the rather harassed looking underwriter stood up to speak. Roger found himself thinking of Hilary and the kids. He did love them all dearly, and he hoped they thought the same of him. He made a promise to himself to spend more time with them all.

'Gentlemen, I have carried out a thorough review of the case. All the paperwork is in order, the proposal document has been completed fully and accurately, even describing the modifications that are carried out to the machines in question. There is however one major issue that I am unable to resolve.' He looked around the table, his eyes lingering on Roger for just a fraction longer than anyone else. 'No one in my department has ever seen the proposal form.' He paused for effect. 'This only leads me to one conclusion. Someone in this organisation has gone out of his or her way to make sure that we never did get to see this document. Regardless of that, Liechtenstein Re now faces a legal challenge of considerable magnitude and the fact is that my signature is clearly on the sign off slip, therefore I must shoulder the responsibility and tender my resignation to the Managing Director with immediate effect.' He sat down heavily.

Blimey, Roger thought with shocked elation.

The Managing Director looked at the Chief Underwriter with a puzzled expression. 'You say that someone in this organisation prevented you from seeing the document?'

'Yes. In normal circumstances the system should be foolproof. We get to see each and every proposal that comes into the building.

No one in my department has seen this document and I stand by all of my staff in this.'

The Managing Director looked perplexed. 'OK, this is obviously not yet concluded. I shall consider what we do next. If it means a criminal investigation, we shall get to the bottom of it somehow. I will not accept your resignation until we do.' He looked at the Chief Underwriter. 'Meanwhile we have the second item on the agenda which could override everything, so let's move on.'

The Financial Controller explained to the board that they were able to accumulate all of the money given time. The reality of the situation however, was that without any cash or money invested, it would not be able to meet its current liabilities. This meant that the regulating authorities would have no choice other than to order Liechtenstein Re to cease trading and put itself into the hands of an administrator. These were the cold hard facts. Legal costs could tip them over the edge into abject bankruptcy. An out of court settlement was their only hope.

The Managing Director closed the meeting having elected a three-man team to fly to the US the next day and negotiate with the law firm. Roger declined the invitation to join the party, his skills as a negotiator in these situations were limited. He would rather stay at home and put pins into an effigy of Uncle Vern, he thought bitterly.

The board reconvened at the end of the week. The team had spent two days in the US locked in discussions with the law firm. The managing director announced the final agreement; they would pay $20 million per death and $8 million per serious injury. Any future deaths arising as a result of serious injury would be payable at the pro-rata higher rate.

The Financial Controller had the busiest week of his career organising the payment of $560 million in the largest single claim in the British insurance industry's history. Investments had to be cancelled with the corresponding early withdrawal penalties, shares had to be sold at whatever price could be got for them. According to the rules of the insurance regulator, an asset register was set up and those assets that could be sold quickly were. Those that could not be sold quickly were set aside as collateral and possible future disposal should the need arise. Included on this list was Roger's almost finished boat. Much to Roger's dismay, it was decided that the final payment on the boat would be paid only for the boat to go on sale immediately. And 495 of the 552 company employees were released without much hope of redundancy payments. The firm needed cash to remain solvent.

Once the news of the extent of the company's difficulties became public knowledge, the Lichtenstein Re share price plummeted from 700 pence to 28 pence almost overnight. The last board meeting was called to hand before the running of the business was passed to an administrator who would keep the business going until a buyer could be found. Roger was asked to partake in a management buyout but didn't have the appetite to take on this monster he had caused to crash with such enormous consequences. Liechtenstein Re was finished. It's future destiny likely to be as a few dusty files in the back office of a much larger insurance firm.

Hilary was stunned that night, 'You mean it just doesn't exist anymore?' she said, looking at him across the dinner table in disbelief. She knew the company was in trouble, but not this much trouble.

'Yep, afraid so. Stony broke, not enough money to meet its liabilities,' he replied with a glum expression.

'But there must be some money,' Hilary said.

'There is, but it's been ring-fenced by the administrator as a fund to meet potential claims. We can't touch it. Besides, when all of the existing policies finish, there's a list of creditors as long as your arm. The Inland Revenue probably the biggest - any redundancy payments will be a long way off, if at all.'

'You mean all those people lost their jobs and got nothing?'

'They got the promise of something when the claim has been paid and all of the current liabilities have been met, in other words, they're at the back of the queue,' he said starkly.

'Those poor people,' Hilary said, looking into the candle.

'Oh come on, Hils, these are industry professionals, they'll be snapped up by the other insurance companies in the City.'

'What about you, us, what are we going to do?' she asked.

'We'll have to draw the horns in quite substantially, old girl. No more six figure salary to waste on fripperies. We'll be OK in the short term. Believe it or not, I had started saving some money over the last few months. I was going to spend it on a few extras for the boat, but I won't be doing that anymore.'

'Oh yes, the boat. What's happening to it then?'

'The firm made the final payment and it's just been delivered to Antibes. They want to sell it to release the capitol. It's funny, I was talking to the broker this afternoon, and he says he's looking for someone to run their office down there. I was thinking of applying. What do you think?'

'What about the kids and the business?'

'The kids would love it down there. They're young enough to pick the language up quickly. You could sell the business and start something up down there if you wanted,' he said, wondering where this sudden optimism in him was coming from.

'Let me think about it,' she said to him, both a smile and a frown flickering across her face. He struggled, as usual, to guess what she was thinking.

'I'm going down to Antibes tomorrow. The broker says he's got some chap from the Far-East interested in looking at the boat. Reckons I'm the perfect guy to sell it to him,' he said brightly.

Hilary didn't reply.

'Uncle Vern's turning up tomorrow from the US,' she finally said, changing the subject. 'He got a suspended sentence. He's staying for a few days.'

'He's the cause of all this, you know,' he said. 'If it wasn't for him, we would still have a company. It's just as well I'm going away for a few days. I'd want to strangle him if I bumped into him now.'

'He's not doing those machines any more. At least not the modifications,' she said.

'I'm sure the grieving relatives will be pleased to hear that,' he said. 'The lawyers will be disappointed though.'

'Well, I keep him at arm's length these days. And if I'm going to sell the business then it's bye-bye Uncle Vern anyway,' she said.

Roger felt a tingle of elation at what she had just said, 'So you might say yes and come to Antibes?'

'I might,' she said with the half smile again, this time without the frown.

'Oh Hils,' he said, rushing around the table and holding her for all he was worth. 'You are just the best. We'll do this together, darling, me, you, Sam and Julian. Just us, no more crap insurance job for me, no more seedy sex toys for you. I'll be different, we'll all be different. It'll be brilliant, you wait and see.'

'Seedy?' she said quietly. 'You didn't really mean that did you?'

'Course not, darling," he replied hurriedly. "No, of course not. I'm sorry.' He hugged her ever tighter and nibbled her earlobe affectionately, he knew she loved that. She really was his rock now. He'd been weak, he thought to himself but he would be strong from now on, strong for all of them.

33. Hilary's Longest Day

'What do you mean you tried to kill my husband?' Hilary and her uncle were sitting at the kitchen table the following morning, drinking coffee. He had just made the confession that he had promised Han Sen in LA.

He looked at her, clearly startled. 'I thought you'd be pleased, my dear.'

'Pleased?' She stood up and walked over to the sink, biting the skin on one of her fingers. 'Whatever makes you think that?'

'Because I care about you, Hilary. I knew you were having problems with him and you wanted to get away. Let's just say I had the wherewithal to be able to do something about it and make it look like an accident. It nearly worked too,' he said, looking disappointed. 'I was trying to help you, Hilary.'

'I wouldn't call killing my husband, the father of our children and the breadwinner of our household, exactly helping me. More like helping yourself. Fuelling that bloodlust of yours. I can see it all now. Other people don't matter to you, do they? The people in that pub who nearly died and lost their livelihoods. The people who got seriously injured and who died on your dreadful machines, none of them matter to you, life is cheap in your eyes.

'Well, I hope you are satisfied because Roger and I have lost everything because of you. Roger's insurance company, which his father started in the 1950s, had to pay all the liability claims from those machines of yours. Over half a billion pounds! It's bankrupted the company. We now have precisely nothing.' She walked back over to the table, her fury gaining momentum. 'How do you feel about that then, Uncle Vern? You must be really pleased with yourself. You come here expecting sympathy from me when you tell me you were just trying to help? Get out!' she screamed at him, pointing her finger at the front door. 'Get out of our house now and don't ever come back. I'll be sending all of your stock back tomorrow, I don't ever want to deal with you again,' she walked back to the sink again, angrily ripping a piece of kitchen roll off the reel to wipe away her tears.

'Hilary, look…' he started to say.

'Just go. I can't deal with it any more. I'm tired. I just want you out of my life,' she said, ice cold.

Vernon picked up his flight bag and unzipped the zipper. Feeling inside, he withdrew two small wrapped parcels. 'For the kids, from LA.' He zipped the bag up again. 'I know, I respect you enough to know that what you say is what you mean. All I want to say to you Hilary is that I love you deeply, more than I've ever loved anyone in my whole life. One day I will put things right between us. I will make amends for this because you mean so much to me,' he picked the bag up and walked over to her. He pecked her on the cheek. 'Bye, Hilary, I'll write to you.' And he was gone.

She stood by the sink looking at the kitchen floor for a long time, calmness descending on her. She struggled to grasp the concept. Her Uncle had tried to kill her husband. He tried to claim it was because he loved her. Could she believe it? Should she believe it? Either way, she felt complete disgust. Uncle Vern had finally shown her his true colours. She was lucky to have her husband still alive.

'No more sex toys,' she said aloud. This would be a clean break. Roger was right, there was definitely a seedy side to it all. She shivered with disgust as she recalled the party in Wales.

She wondered what France would bring them. Could this be a new beginning?

The local Surrey Police Force could not quite believe what they had stumbled on in the case of The Dancing Bear incident. The investigation into what had caused the crash revealed that some extremely sophisticated electronic circuitry had been fitted to Roger's Aston Martin. The circuit board that over-rode the car's own electronic control box had been fitted very neatly to the underside of the car. The investigating electronics engineer could not believe his eyes when he uncovered that the circuit board not only contained an infra-red receiver but also disabled the car's braking, transmission and hydraulic steering systems by a series of interlocking solenoid valves.

This meant that someone could take control of the car from a distance, the driver rendered completely helpless, effectively a passenger at the wheel.

A telling moment in the investigation came when the electronics expert noticed that each of the solenoid valves had serial numbers – they were traced from the German manufacturer to a wholesaler in Hong Kong who confirmed the valves had been supplied to a company called Chen Electronics Ltd. This is where the trail stopped dead – according to the Hong Kong Chamber of Commerce, the company had ceased trading some months ago.

The bullet that tore Roger's earlobe clean off, and destroyed both the front and rear windscreens of the Chief Underwriter's car had been recovered by the City of London police. The bullet was of Chinese manufacture, proving nothing, but pointing towards some Far East villainy, linking the car-jacking in London to the Dancing Bear incident.

As Hilary was the only obvious link between Roger and the Far East, two detectives, one from each force, knocked on her door that afternoon. 'Thank you for seeing us at such short notice, Mrs. Collins,' the younger City of London detective said. 'We have some questions concerning your husband's two unfortunate incidents recently.'

Hilary looked at them calmly. 'It was my Uncle.'

Both detectives froze. 'Sorry, Ma'am?' the younger one said with a look of disbelief on his face.

'Mr. Vernon Saunders. Lives in Hong Kong: Number 481 Chang Khai Shek Tower, Kowloon Island. Do you want his phone number?'

'Are you saying you know the person that attempted to murder your husband?' the older, slightly more composed detective said.

'Yes, of course I know him, he's my Uncle,' she said indignantly. 'It's a shame, you only just missed him. He told me all about it this morning.' She almost couldn't believe what she was saying.

'Ma'am, I'm sorry to appear rude,' the younger detective said, 'but I have to ask you to accompany us down to the station to make an official statement.'

'Sure,' she said breezily. 'I'll get my coat.' Probably the luckiest day of their careers, she thought. There would be no going back on this decision. Not for the first time, she wished her Dad was here, he would know what to do.

'Bloody Freddie Chen.' Vern kneaded the bridge of his nose with two fingers. 'I told the idiot, make it simple – no electronics. 'What does he do? Builds bloody Silicone Valley, just to make the car crash.'

The two English detectives looked at one another in surprise, was this a confession? It certainly sounded like one. They'd tracked Vernon Saunders down to his hotel and promptly arrested him on suspicion of conspiracy to an assault, stealing a car and attempted murder. 'I have to ask you to come down to the station and answer some questions,' the younger policemen said.

'I'm getting used to this. First it's Dirty Harry in Los Angeles, now it's The Professionals. All we need is Jackie Chan to turn up.'

'Been in a spot of trouble elsewhere, sir?' the older policeman said as he slipped the handcuffs over Vern's wrists.

'No, not really. I just happened to sell some therapy machines to some Americans. I didn't know they were going to murder one another with them, did I? Could understand it if I'd invented a new gun or something,' he added acidly.

'I'm sure you're right, sir. Watch your head,' the policeman said as he bundled Vern into the waiting patrol car.

The detective's hunch was correct; the arresting interview did turn out to be a confession. Vern had wanted to kill his nephew-in-law because he was cheating on his wife, it was as simple as that.

The ever co-operative Hong Kong police were tasked with looking for Freddie and his gun-toting sidekick. Vern's theory was he had gone to ground somewhere in the vastness of the Chinese hinterland. With the small-fortune he'd earned from the MassageOmatic programming, there was no doubt he was being looked after by a bevy of compliant young ding-dong girls. It was possible he would come back to Hong Kong, but only if he had forgotten something.

The vexing issue for Vern was Hilary. He felt bad enough about upsetting her in the first place but was insistent that she should never find out about her errant husband's infidelities. The policemen said they would ask the court for leave to issue a restraining order on media coverage but, they told him, this could have the reverse effect in actually arousing the interest of newspapers and TV.

Hilary called Han Sen.

Angelique apologised. 'So sorry, Mrs. Collins. He is away in Europe right now.'

A momentary shiver of excitement passed through her at the thought of seeing him. 'He's not in England, is he?' Hilary said.

'No, he's gone to France to look at a boat.'

'A boat? I didn't know he was interested in boats.'

'Oh, it's not for him,' the young secretary giggled. 'It's a long story, and forgive me for your phone bill, but he has been looking for a boat for some time now. It's going to be an extension to the temple, somewhere for the families and the older folks and the needy to go at the weekends. Han Sen reckons they will be able to find their aquatic Nirvana there.' She giggled again.

'Sounds a great idea,' Hilary said. 'France though? You have lots of boatbuilders there, don't you?'

'Yes but Kha Shung, who built this boat, is a friend of Han Sen. They go to the same temple. He said this is the perfect boat for his needs. That is why he has gone to France.'

'Oh Angelique, I'm sorry,' Hilary said, sensing the young girl's awkwardness at having to explain her boss's whereabouts in such detail. 'I don't mean to be nosy – it is pretty unusual for Han Sen to be in Europe though, isn't it?'

'You are right. It is his first time. And Mrs. Collins, please, you ask as many questions as you want – it's a privilege to hear from you.'

'Oh, Angelique, thank you.' She had that same overwhelming feeling she had when she was in Taiwan. 'Please tell Han Sen I called. Maybe we can speak when he returns?'

'Yes, of course, Mrs. Collins, I'll tell him. Have a great evening.'

'And you, Angelique. Bye-bye and thanks again.'

Where else in the world would you have that sort of conversation with the secretary of someone you were trying to contact? In America maybe, but there you got the feeling it was always done for a reason. In Taiwan, it was somehow unconditional and completely genuine.

She thought of Han Sen and the look in his eyes when he spoke to her. Stop it, she said to herself forcibly. He's like that with everybody. She was being ridiculous; she was a grown woman with responsibilities. She'd married Roger for good, sound, practical reasons and she would stay married to Roger, despite the fact that some of those good, sound, practical reasons came off the rails sometimes. They did in any marriage, didn't they?

The phone rang, startling her. 'Hello, darling,' Roger said warmly.

'Hi, Rodge,' she said, playing for time and trying her best to shake off any thoughts about Taiwan and her unrequited love.

'You OK?'

'Yes. I'm fine thanks. It's been a long day. I was just thinking about a bath and a glass of wine,' she lied. She was still playing for time, wondering whether she should tell him about Uncle Vern.

'Phwoarrr,' he said. 'I wish you were here, we could share my Louis XIV style bath. I'm in the Ambassadeur – it's absolutely fantastic.'

Normally she would have criticised him for wasting money, especially considering their current situation, but this was not normal. 'It was Vern,' she said.

'What was?'

'Your accident.'

'The car accident?'

'Yes.'

'Your Uncle tried to kill me?'

'The police arrested him today.'

'Why the hell did the old sod want me dead?'

'Because he thought you were treating me badly, and he wanted me to move to Hong Kong and take over his business. He thought you were standing in my way.'

'Why didn't he just get them to shoot me?'

'He wanted it to look like an accident.'

'Bloody hell, Hils. I can't believe it.'

'Neither can I.'

'How did you find out?'

'He told me this morning.'

'Told you? What did you do?'

'I threw him out. Told him I never wanted to see him again.'

'That's my girl.'

'Then the police came round.'

'The police?' he sounded surprised. 'How did they find out?'

'I was the link between you and China – Chinese electronics, Chinese bullet, Chinese gunman.'

'What and you told them? What Vern told you, I mean.'

'Yes.' She wanted to cry. She did cry.

'Hilary. Please, love, it will be OK. I'll be back tomorrow. Darling, I love you so much. Nobody else would have done that for me. You are beautiful, Hils – Hils? Speak to me, darling. Is everything else OK? How are the kids?'

'They're OK,' she whispered finally. 'You've got a court summons here. It's the drink driving thing.'

'Oh that's OK – I'll just lose my licence for a while, that's all.'

'What are you going to do in France then?' her practical side was taking over again. 'Assuming you get the job, do you know yet?'

'Yes, I just have to sell the boat tomorrow and I'll carry on selling boats for them – purely on commission. I'll have to get a bike for a while.'

'Don't you need a licence for that though?' she said, regaining her composure.

'No, course not. Just a stripey shirt and a string of onions,' he said. Hilary laughed. 'You are coming, aren't you? To France, I mean. It's beautiful down here. I know you'll love it.'

She thought of her Mum and Dad, and England, and rain and the springtime greenery. 'Yes,' she said. It was only a short hop across the channel. Probably best not to think about the 900 odd miles to Antibes, she thought.

'And the business?' he said, sounding if he were about to burst.

'I'm going to put an ad in Daltons Weekly tomorrow.'

'Yes! You beauty!' he whooped. She imagined him fisting the air like Charlie used to.

She smiled for the first time that day. She would go and see her Mum and Dad tomorrow. Now for that bath, and the glass of wine.

34. Tania too

'Oh shit, get a bloody move on, can't you?' the young Master of the Motor Vessel 'Kitchener Bay' shouted angrily as he paced from one side of the navigation bridge to the other. He stopped only to glance impatiently through his binoculars towards a position on his port bow where a Moroccan ferryboat was struggling across the angry, grey waters of the Straits of Gibralter. 'Why is he going so slow?' he shouted to the officer of the watch.

The Skipper's impatience was the culmination of twelve days of frustration since leaving their last Far East port of Kaohsiung fully laden with some six-thousand containers. Everything that could go wrong had gone wrong on this short trip. Engine failure off Sri Lanka held them up for a day and a half, a knife fight on the aft deck between two Phillipino crewmen, both of them now locked-up down below, a hurricane-force gale as they rounded Cape Horn and of course the inevitable aftermath: a huge Atlantic swell square on the beam that drove everybody on board crazy on their northward journey up the African coastline. To cap it all, he was getting reports of serious fog conditions in the Mediterranean to slow them down even further on their route to Genoa, their first European destination.

Given the opportunity, he would have gone and punched the Captain of the ferryboat.

Here he was, ninety-three thousand tonnes of container vessel capable of twenty-seven knots, now doing just under six, almost tripping up over a two-bit ferry. 'This is the Kitchener Bay. Turn to starboard. Repeat, turn to starboard. I am in a separation channel and have priority. Over!' he shouted into the VHF radio handset.

A garbled, heavily accented Arabic-English voice mushed over the speaker. Neither the Captain nor the officer on watch were able to understand what was said although they did pick out the words 'engine problems.' The Skipper went back to pacing up and down across the bridge. On his first return he noticed a slight movement to starboard by the embattled ferry. 'He's turning! OK, Chief, full speed ahead. God, at last,' he called out to no one in particular.

The Chief Mate slid both engine telegraph handles fully forward and both men felt the full force of the 84,000 horsepower main engine accelerate the huge ship gently forward, faster and faster until a minute and a half later, the speed-log registered twenty-eight knots.

'Steady as she goes,' the Skipper called out. He would settle her back to a more economic cruising speed in an hour or two. They needed to make up lost time. Bollocks to the fuel consumption, he thought, the fog would be slowing them down pretty soon anyway if the weather forecast proved to be right.

He took a quick backward glance with the binoculars through the rear bridge windows and watched the ferryboat struggling to change back to its original course against the huge wake made by the Kitchener Bay. He felt a pang of conscience. He picked up the radio handset and called 'Kitchener Bay here. Thank you skipper. Thank you. Bon voyage. Over.'

There was no reply.

The last stretch of the Kitchener Bay's journey was an east-north-east course from Gibraltar to just past the Spanish Balearic Islands and then a north-easterly direction to Genoa, an 1800-mile journey. The Skipper calculated that at 25 knots this would take three days. If they got a berth straightaway, he should be able to make dinner at Anjio's restaurant in the old quarter of Genoa for Wednesday evening. The home-made pasta and pesto sauce there was to die for. They would then be off again, probably early on Thursday, back out of the Mediterranean and northwards up to Southampton, Felixstowe, Hamburg, Antwerp and then back to Oz. The thought of Christmas day on the beach again, gave him a flurry of excitement as he peered through the binoculars into the gathering foggy gloom.

The patchy fog persisted throughout the daylight hours. The French headland of Toulon showed itself on the radar early on the Wednesday morning. As they ran almost parallel with the French coastline, the combined landmass of France and Italy seemed to make the fog thicker, the visibility shorter. He reluctantly nudged the engine telegraph back a touch. Bugger, he thought.

It was dusk as the aircraft banked to the East and began its final descent into Nice airport. Han Sen looked down at the dark blue Mediterranean Sea between breaks in the cloud, admiring the Riviera, the rugged coastline with its inlets and bays and marinas stretching into the distance towards Monaco and the Italian border.

He stayed in the hotel that night, going to bed straightaway, too travel-weary to eat. After breakfast the following morning, he caught a taxi to the yacht broker's office, the young French girl greeting him in heavily accented English, 'Good morning Mr. Sen, I hope you had a good trip, can I get you a tea or coffee?'

'No, thank you,' Han Sen said politely, the French coffee was far too strong for him.

'In that case, I will drive you straight down to the yacht. Our Mr. Collins is already there, he is going to show you around.' She hung a closed sign on the office door and drove them down through the old town to the harbour in a very old Renault 5. They pulled up on the quayside adjacent to the gleaming dark blue-hulled boat instantly recognisable as one of Kha Shung's creations. Kha was right, from the outside this looked to be the perfect boat, not too ostentatious but solid looking, like it had been built to last. The name on the transom read 'Tania too.' Han Sen smiled, he even liked the name. It seemed almost a shame to have to change it.

They boarded the boat via the stern gangway onto the perfectly-finished teak decking. The young girl opened the large, polished stainless-steel patio door. 'Hello Roger, are you there?' she called out.

'Yes, just coming,' came the reply from inside. They waited. Han Sen warmed himself in the early morning sunlight, content to look at the detail on the aft deck and at the view of the old town that overlooked the harbour.

'Sorry, I was in the engine room,' Roger said as he came through the saloon, emerging onto the aft deck. 'Pleased to meet you, Mr. Sen. I'm Roger Collins.' They shook hands. 'I'm the new manager of Tegwins' office. Apologies if we appear a little disorganised; I only got here yesterday myself, but don't worry, I know boats better than most things so if you've got any questions, I'll hopefully be able to answer them. If not we'll contact the builder later tonight when they're up.' He gushed. 'I'm guessing it's an eight hour time difference?'

'Seven, actually,' Han Sen said. 'You were close enough though. I'm glad I made the trip; I like the look of it already.'

'Well, I'm certainly glad you did too, and yes it is a super boat,' Roger said. 'I'll show you around and then we'll take her for a spin. There's a bit of fog around but they tell me it's lifting. We've got radar and stuff so it shouldn't be a problem. We'll start from the bottom up, in the engine room, and when we're doing that, Nicole can rustle up some coffee and maybe some lunch for when we get back?' The young French girl nodded with a smile for their potential purchaser. 'Great, let's go then,' the enthusiastic Roger said, rubbing his hands together, smiling broadly at Han Sen.

Roger was surprised how easily he fell into the salesman's role. The fact that this boat should have been his didn't especially bother him. He was delighted with the quality of the boat, knowing he had made the perfect choice. He was also relieved to be away from Lichtenstein

Re and all the depressing and tedious administrative things to be done there. This was living for the day, something he should have done years ago. He was happy, he would be even happier when Hilary and the kids arrived, hopefully in a few weeks' time.

He made a particular point of showing his customer the engine room in great detail, having been told that he was an engineer. Even Roger thought it was impressive, the machinery sparkling in its gloss-white, the polished-aluminium checkerplate floor, spotless and gleaming under the bright fluorescent light. The bewildering array of valves were each labelled with a brass nameplate, the pipework running perfectly parallel, colour-coded for content and marked with flow direction arrows. It definitely hit the spot with this guy, Roger thought with a nod and a smile towards him. He was looking around in absolute awe. If engine-rooms sold boats, then this was the best engine-room for a salesman to have.

'The engines are MTU, same with the generators. German quality; best in the world,' Roger said authoritatively. 'All of the other kit is American, the watermakers, the air-conditioning, the water pumps and the hydraulics. The Americans do have the best support around the world if you ever get stuck,' he said. 'Seen enough?'

Han Sen nodded. 'It's a work of art,' he said, still looking and touching.

'I'll show you the rest of it,' Roger said, gesturing politely for his guest to climb the stairs before him.

They emerged onto the aft deck, kicked their shoes off, and went into the large saloon area. 'It's largely open plan. I...' Roger coughed. 'Excuse me, the guy who had this built was not a great lover of built-in furniture, I think his idea was to buy off the shelf stuff and have it installed.'

'It's just perfect,' Han Sen said, 'Kha was right, this is a great boat, perfect for what I want it for.'

'Kha Shung the boatbuilder, you know him?' Roger said, hoping he had made the right connection.

'Yes. He and I go to the same temple. He recommended this boat to me,' Han Sen said.

'Ah I see, and do you mind if I ask what your plans for it are?' he asked, hoping he didn't sound too nosy.

'Not at all. It will be a kind of waterborne temple, for the under-privileged kids and the old people in the area and anyone from the community who is interested, really,' Han Sen said with a slight hesitation. 'Like a floating temple,' he confirmed, nodding his head.

'Oh, I see,' Roger lied, he was a weirdo after all. 'Let's go for a spin.' They both went up to the flying bridge and Roger started the engines, 'Thanks Nicole,' he called out as the young girl slipped the ropes. Han Sen went down to haul them in.

'Been driving boats for long?' Han Sen asked politely as he came back up to the flying bridge. The boat by now was just clearing the harbour breakwater, the fog rolling towards the shore across the calm sea.

'Yes. I spent a long time in the Caribbean skippering charter boats. 'Driving a boat is second nature to me.' He tapped the radar screen. 'Have to keep an eye on this baby today,' he said. 'Hopefully the sun will burn through the fog before too long. We'll go out for a few miles into the Tyrennian Sea and we'll see what she can do, if you want to spend some time below, I don't mind,' he added, looking at the shirt-sleeved Han Sen. The fog was making it decidedly chilly. 'Or there's some foul weather gear down below, it's up to you,' he said, one eye on the gloom in front of them, the other on the radar screen.

'I'll let you concentrate and have a look around downstairs,' Han Sen said discreetly and went back down the ladder. He heard the engine tone increase and felt the boat accelerate forward, he guessed to something like twenty-five miles per hour, or knots, he wasn't sure. He made a mental note to brush up on his nautical terminology as he walked into the saloon. He remembered the gaudy gin-palace they had been on in Kaohsiung two years ago. Or was it three? This boat's simple functionality was in total contrast - plain teak, simple lines, sparse décor throughout. There were two large cabins and three small ones, plus one further crew cabin. He went down the steps to the lower deck and into what he guessed they called the master stateroom. He smiled to himself, this was way too big. Just like the large sports-car adage, there was probably a direct link between the size of a man's state room and the reputed size of his reproductive organ. He sat down on the sumptuous king-sized bed. Actually, he thought, I might invite Raya on board before any modifications are carried out. Just the two of us. She would love it. Wow he thought, we all deserve a bit of luxury in our lives every now and again, don't we?

He felt the engines race. It was at this moment that Han Sen's world very suddenly turned sideways. He was thrown from the berth and slammed into the port side bulkhead that had become the floor. A deafening explosion of splintering timber and breaking glass assaulted his eardrums, followed by the combined noises of deathly powerful scraping and rapidly churning water. Some huge unworldly force had picked the boat up and was pushing it through the water on its side at a crazy rate. He was hurting, his face was bleeding from the impact of smashing against the hard wooden bulkhead. He slowly picked himself up, but all he could see and hear was dark water rushing past the porthole that was now in the floor, the other porthole now in the ceiling and the whole boat vibrating terribly from the force of being pushed along on its side. Not for the first time in his life he was terrified. After a short while, the floor began to tip to one side, he fell towards the back of the cabin as the boat tipped at an even more frightening angle. He couldn't tell what was happening any longer, nothing was making sense.

Then all of a sudden it was deathly quiet. The boat must have been thrown off whatever had been propelling it. An overwhelming chomp, chomp, chomp, chomp noise grew very loud, very quickly and then gradually receded to nothing.

Han Sen lay pinned on what was the aft-bulkhead of the master stateroom looking upwards towards the bow that was now the ceiling. The boat seemed to bob gently for a while as if in a gentle swell, the cabin becoming darker as the deep blue water rose above the level of the portholes. We're sinking, he thought, panic rising. He could swim but not very strongly, would he be able to hold his breath for long enough to get out of here?

Gingerly he stood up. The boat seemed to be going back to its original sideways attitude. He crouched and slid towards the port bulkhead, this time looking for a way out. He saw water seeping under the main door to the stateroom. He tried the handle, it was tight, and so he gradually applied more force. Suddenly the door gave way and Han Sen was washed away in a torrent of water that rushed into the room. The water level in the cabin rose rapidly, bringing him up with it. He felt the bed with his feet for a short while before the swirling water took him. He gasped for breath, knowing it could be his last. Realising it was his only chance, he began to fight against the flow of water and somehow get through the cabin door. Then he was being bounced between the sides of the narrow corridor leading upwards and away from the stateroom, he paddled with his feet and swung his arms inexpertly in an attempt to make progress upwards towards the galley and hopefully the saloon. His eyes were open, but all he could see was a swirling mass of water and unrecognisable objects. He imagined it was like being in a washing machine.

After what seemed like a lifetime of struggling against the water and thoughts of certain death, he was in the saloon, the water almost at the level of the patio door. He gasped for breath; he'd seen enough old film footage to know that the boat was going down, this was probably its final death throe, soon there would be nothing, just him and the sea. The cruel sea.

He briefly hung on to the patio door-frame as it slid below the waves, the aft deck with its beautiful teak deck was rapidly approaching, all he could do was strike out at what he hoped would be the correct moment. He cleared the aft bulwark by inches as it rushed past him, almost taking him with it towards the sea bed. He had a brief moment of exaltation as he realised he had made it, he was clear. Then the vacuum caused by the boat's downward momentum took him. He felt large pockets of air rushing up past him and an incredibly powerful force dragged him down and down.

He hadn't had time to take a breath, and now his lungs were burning. He was angry, angry at the sea, angry with the boat, angry with himself. He thrust himself sideways with as much force as he could, it was his only hope of getting out of this downward current. He pushed and pushed. With his eyes still open, he could see the daylight above him, the top surface of the sea a milky tumescence, an impossible distance away. Keep going, keep going, he urged himself, think about that first breath of sweet air. He tried hard to ignore the exhaustion and the despair that was threatening to overwhelm him.

Roger felt the huge bulk of the container ship before he saw or heard it, a barely perceptible stirring of the breeze made him look to starboard. Emerging from the foggy gloom was an enormous dark-blue ship, probably 150 feet high, and 100 feet wide. The bulbous-bow was just visible beneath the bow wave that it rent apart with a ghostly, silent ease. He looked up and saw the white lettering standing out against the blue steel plating, even picking out the slight imperfections in the welding. He sat at the fly-bridge controls of the insignificant yet perfectly and lovingly formed little boat, transfixed, wondering idly where in the world Kitchener Bay was, and why this fateful ship named after it was about to destroy his life. Whoever was driving the thing was in a real hurry.

He frantically pushed both engine controllers forward as far as they would go. With his free hand he wrenched the steering wheel to port, managing to turn the boat perhaps one degree from the perpendicular before the ship was on him. The towering hull seemed to hang over the boat for a long time before the leading edge of the ship came into crunching contact with the gleaming white fibreglass of the flying bridge. He looked on, horrified as the steel sliced through the fibrous plastic not five feet from where he was sitting. He knew he was going to die, imagining being crushed between the ship's hull and various parts of *Tania too*. His thoughts flickered to Hilary. Sorry, my darling, he thought, I love you so much. Sorry Sam, sorry Jules, sorry I never got to know you. I was never much good as a dad. Always thinking about myself. And money, of course. Money, money, money.

The boat flipped onto its port side and Roger clung to the small steering wheel, his legs dangling in mid-air. He watched in stomach-churning bemusement as the boat wedged itself between the ship's hull, now fully embedded almost to the centreline of the boat, and what could only be the bulbous-bow below them. *Tania too* was being propelled sideways at what he guessed was about twenty-five knots. He thought of letting go and taking his chances, deciding against it when he thought of the propellers, probably the size of houses, knowing he wouldn't stand a chance of avoiding getting dragged into those.

Roger heard the sickening crunch as the forward end of the boat began to break up. He could feel it start to slip backwards off the bulbous bow. His instinct was telling him to hold on to the steering wheel for as long as he could.

Suddenly, the boat toppled away from the ship, the force of the landing ripping Roger's hands away from the steering wheel and he dropped into the swirling grey water below. He entered the water feet first, fully expecting *Tania too* to fall on top of him. In a mad panic to get away he flipped himself over and swam down and away as fast as his leg and arm muscles would take him.

Still swimming down with furious strokes, he was deafened by the sound of the ships engine and thrashing propeller as the massive ship passed over him. He was grateful for the suction force from the propeller that was helping to drag him back up towards the surface. This force diminished as the blackness of the ship pounded away from him. He opened his eyes to the cold, watery greyness. He had to breathe, he had to breathe and quick. He righted his body and pushed upwards towards the milky surface, his lungs suddenly burning. The only thought in his mind was the need for oxygen. I must get oxygen.

He broke the surface in a fluster of rage, confusion, helplessness and exhaustion. He trod water, coughing up seawater and vomiting. Remembering swimming lessons from school, he floated on his back for a while as soon as his lungs were clear enough, resting his aching muscles and getting his breathing under control. Eventually, he righted himself and looked around him. The *Kitchener Bay* had disappeared into the foggy gloom, completely oblivious to the carnage in its wake. *Tania too* was bow-down in the water and in her final death throes. The stern rising high as the water all rushed into the badly damaged forward end. She was sinking slowly but surely into the calm water. Roger looked around for something to hang onto, a piece of wreckage, anything. He was not a strong swimmer and wondered how long he could survive treading water.

Too bad about the Chinese guy.

35. The Raft of Change

Han Sen broke the surface that he had been looking up to for so long in the deep watery gloom. Air had never tasted so sweet. For the first two minutes he breathed half air, half seawater. He coughed and wretched and coughed again and thrashed around with his arms and legs in an attempt to keep his face clear of the water.

'Mr. Sen,' came a voice. Was he imagining it? He looked around frantically. Through the fog he could just about see a head and a waving arm, he guessed about fifty yards away.

'Mr. Sen, are you out there?' the voice sounded again.

'Over here!' he shouted, waving an arm. 'Over here!' he called again, his voice echoing in the fog.

'Stay there, I'll swim over,' the voice rang out again.

'Hurry, please.' Han Sen said weakly, hoping the yacht-broker hadn't heard him. He felt so tired, the water was trying to drag him down again. He promised himself he would learn to swim properly when this was all over.

As he watched the broker swim towards him, a large white capsule noisily broke the surface just in front of him. There was a muffled explosion followed by a tortured groaning and loud inflation noises as the sponson of orange rubber pressurised and expanded itself into a five man liferaft. Han Sen blinked; he couldn't believe his eyes.

He looked across to see the yacht-broker had stopped swimming and was half laughing, half shouting, 'Yes! Thank you God! I told those bastards I wanted a liferaft fitted. Yes!' He punched the water and resumed swimming, this time towards the raft. He grasped the side of the raft and shouted to Han Sen, 'Stay there and I'll come across to get you.' He hauled himself into the boat head-first, his head emerging from one of the side flaps. He paddled the craft over to where Han Sen was still desperately treading water.

The broker reached out towards him from the open side of the liferaft with the paddle.

Han Sen grasped the end of the paddle. 'Am I pleased to see you,' he said, wanting to cry tears of relief.

Roger pulled him to the side of the liferaft with the paddle, then hauled the limp Han Sen on board. 'Bloody hell, mate, it nearly got you, didn't it?' he said as he laid him down gently on the floor and wrapped a space blanket around him.

Han Sen nodded breathlessly.

'I guess we lost that sale then,' he said.

Han Sen laughed, the pain in his lungs making him cough. 'What happened?' he eventually spluttered.

'Container ship. Bloody enormous thing. Going way too fast. It was partly my fault, the radar was set to the wrong scale. It showed up on the screen almost as it was on top of us. The thing was fully laden, quite low in the water. Hit us plumb amidships, we rode for a while on the bulbous bow before the engine room filled with water, that's when we fell off and sunk. He wrecked our boat and didn't even notice. Just kept on going at the same speed. I never thought you'd make it. You were downstairs, right?'

'Yes, I was in the biggest cabin. It was scary, I'm not a very good swimmer either. I am very lucky. Buddha must be watching over me today.'

'Yeah, and me. Here, have some water.' Roger lifted Han Sen's head and slowly tipped some water into his mouth. 'You're going to have a nasty scar there,' he said looking at Han Sen's ragged lip.

'I smashed my head into the bulkhead when it first hit,' Han Sen said, fingering his lips. 'It's nothing compared to being alive though.'

'No, you're right. Someone should be along shortly, hopefully not another bloody great container ship,' Roger said, poking his head out of the canopy door and looking around.

'Not twice in one day, surely,' Han Sen said. They both laughed.

'Luckily this liferaft is fairly high-spec. I wanted to make sure my family were safe. It's got some provisions and space blankets, it's even got a distress beacon which is probably signalling to the rescue people as we speak,' Roger said.

Han Sen was slightly confused. 'Your family?'

'Yes. My Father had a boat once called *Tania*. That's why I called this one *Tania too*. But my company went bust. I took the job with the broker to get away from it all, I had a need to get back to something that I really love doing. I'm hoping the wife and kids will be out here soon, too.'

'I hope you still have a job when you get back,' said Han Sen.

'Oh yes, it's all insured,' Roger said. 'Besides, I reckon the container ship's insurer will be paying the bill. The bloody idiot must have been doing twenty-five knots, probably trying to make supper in Genoa or somewhere.' He raised his eyes to the heavens. 'Want some more water?'

'No thank you, Mr Collins,' Han Sen said. 'You're very kind. It sounds like you know a bit about insurance.'

334

'Well, I inherited an insurance company from my father when I was twenty-eight. It was a large company, 500 employees, in the centre of London. I had the big house in the country, fast car, loads of money, but it was never enough, I always wanted more.'

'You were a very lucky young man, luckier than most by the sound of it,' Han Sen said.

'Yes, but I never realised it at the time. I think that's the problem with money, the more you have the more you want. But wait a minute, you're rich, aren't you? You were going to be spending at least a million quid on that boat. The boat that's now a submarine,' he laughed, looking at Han Sen. 'Are you warm enough?' he asked, pulling the space blanket so it covered his whole body.

'Yes thank you. You're right, I am rich but in my country being rich is not about having money. The Buddha teaches us that wealth is something to strive for, but it is measured in happiness and joy. Being able to appreciate things around us; nature, our family, our work colleagues, our whole world. We are only here for a short period and we are only the temporary keeper of material possessions. OK they may make life more comfortable, and sometimes they generate a feeling of wellbeing but it is all transient. They don't really matter. What matters is the world we all have to live in. Sorry, I don't mean to preach,' he smiled at Roger.

Roger had a look of astonishment on his face. 'No no, that's amazing. So you said before that you wanted to buy the boat for the temple?'

'Yes, for the poor kids and the older people, they deserve a better life and I thought if I can buy this to give them some pleasure, then their world will improve. My world will improve too; I will be happy that they are happy. That is how we live. Most of the profits from my company go to the temple and the local community, that's why we have no homeless people or problems with drug addiction unlike most Western economies. When we do well as an economy, everybody benefits.'

'Wow,' Roger said. 'Is everybody religious then? In Taiwan, I mean.'

'No not really, most people don't think of Buddhism as a religion. It's more a way of life. If you really want to know, I can tell you what the Buddha said about it.'

Roger shook his head, looking on with a half-smile. 'Go on then, now is as good a time as any.'

Han Sen coughed slightly, before beginning,

'Do not believe in what you have heard;
do not believe in traditions because they have
been handed down for many generations;
do not believe anything because it is rumoured
and spoken of by many;
do not believe merely because the written
statement of some old sage is produced;
do not believe in conjectures;
do not believe merely in the authority of your
teachers and elders.
After observation and analysis, when it agrees
with reason and is conducive to the good and
benefit of one and all,
then accept it and live up to it.

Roger looked at Han Sen, 'The Buddha said that?'

'Yes. He was born about 500 years before Christ, into a royal family. He had everything in his young life. It was only when he grew up that he recognised that people got sick, got old and died. This shocked him. He left his royal household and went on to define the middle-way between complete self-denial and a luxury lifestyle, the middle way that banishes suffering. This later became known as Buddhism. It's really quite simple.'

'Suffering? Who suffers?' Roger was looking intently at the Cambodian.

'Almost everybody without the help of the Enlightened One. According to him, desire and attachment are the principle causes of suffering. His words capture it better than anything:'

'On life's journey faith is nourishment,
virtuous deeds are a shelter,
wisdom is the light by day,
and right-mindedness is the protection by night.
If a man lives a pure life nothing can destroy him;
if he has conquered greed,
nothing can limit his freedom.'

Mesmerised, Roger said, 'My father, who founded Liechtenstein Re, always used to say that money was only a means of exchange. Perhaps I should have listened to him a bit more.'

'Liechtenstein Re?' Han Sen said.

'Yes, that was his company, my company.'

'You are, or were, my insurer. My company is called Han Choy Inc. I think you also insured a company from Hong Kong called VSS?'

'VSS, the company that brought Liechtenstein Re to its knees. Mr. Vernon Saunders, if I'm not mistaken.'

'Yes, Vernon,' Han Sen smiled. 'He was the one who persuaded me to build the MassageOmatic.'

They looked at one another, both sets of brains rapidly processing their thoughts. Roger was the first one to break the silence. With a short expellation of air, he looked down at the liferaft floor and massaged his neck with his free hand. 'Jesus,' he said, looking back at Han Sen. 'A few months ago I might have wanted to kill you. It sounds ridiculous but I actually feel like thanking you, Mr. Sen.' He looked again at the short oriental man wrapped in the space blanket. 'You remind me of a friend of mine in England called Charlie, he's Australian. He fell off the mast of a sailing ship, broke his back, and is now in a wheelchair. He's the most positive man I've ever met, got me my first job sailing boats. I still owe him for that. You have the same look in your eyes. You know things, Mr. Sen. Things that other people don't.'

'I was a monk when I was seven years old, the same as all Cambodian boys were in the 1960s. I had a teacher called Hem Suvorn, he taught me the teachings of Buddha and the ways of the world. He was my hero then, and still is.'

'We both had our heroes then, when we were young. You should go see him, show your respects if he's still around.'

'Yes, I will. I've never been back to Cambodia, the Khmer Rouge killed my parents, brothers and sisters and my wife's family too. The thought of going back was too painful.' Han Sen paused. 'You're the first person I've ever said that to.'

'Pol Pot! My God.' Roger said, looking at Han Sen. 'The Khmer Rouge killed millions. I am sorry to have reminded you of your experiences, truly I am.' Roger glanced down at the floor of the raft as if in contemplation.

'No need to apologise. I always made sure that whatever I did, I did to the very best of my ability, and kept listening to the Buddha. It means I am living lives for the lost ones I loved, safeguarding their memory and their good works on earth. Making sure nobody died in vain – that's what drives me, I think.'

'It was my greed that bought my father's company down,' Roger said, still looking at the floor of the raft. 'I just wanted more material things to fill my life with. To give me the supposed comfort that says to others – I'm more successful than you. But it's all bullshit, isn't it, Mr. Sen?'

'Yes, if you measure wealth by what you're able to buy. This is the cause of suffering. Buddhists don't do suffering if we can possibly help it. We measure wealth by how happy someone is because it means more to us. That is the measure of success for my company - we make products that make people happy, by and large. When we make money from selling the products, we give the money to the community. This makes even more people happy.'

Roger laughed. 'It all sounds too good to be true, Mr. Sen. It's like some big hippy ideal to most Westerners.'

'Yes. We like ideals. But you know, meeting you like this, in these circumstances, has something pre-destined about it,' Han Sen said.

'You think so?' Roger asked.

'Well, I wouldn't mind betting that that container ship was loaded with quite a lot of my products. It nearly killed the pair of us and then you rescue me from certain death.'

Roger smiled, 'Do you think someone is trying to tell us something?'

'Maybe. I feel also that I am partly responsible for putting your company out of business, and you are showing every sign of coming through the whole experience a better man for it. We should both come out of this as better people,' he looked at Roger. 'Or there is no Buddha in the temple.'

The bright orange liferaft continued to drift lazily in no particular direction on the flat-calm Mediterranean Sea, the thinning fog continuing to swirl around it. The two men inside were laughing. They were both laughing like they had never laughed before.

Also by Lindsay Ross (www.lindsayross.co.uk):

Hugo is a selectively mute teenage boxing sensation from the Isle of Skye. He finds himself at the centre of a murderous signing-on dispute between a partly reformed Isle of Dogs gangster and a bear-baiting oligarch from Vladivostok.

Totally besotted with Charlene the gay boxing promoter, and swayed in more ways than one by his unsubtle boxing compatriot Eva, will Hugo find his destiny? Will the Metropolitan Police find their man?

Find out in this rip-roaring crime comedy from the author of Perfect Roger.

Printed in Great Britain
by Amazon

42922652R00188